Pyramid of Khafre, Giza, Egypt

In the grav-lamp light of a sealed vault, Kaffer refocused his electromagnetic sensors on the minutely dissected human brain spread before him and cursed the limitations of his confinement. Here, almost within his grasp, was the secret of true time travel—photogravitic transference at will in four full dimensions, unfettered by the necessity for mechanical stimulation of analogs as the Pacificans did with their temporal effect focalizer.

The existence of individuals with the natural ability to manipulate dimensions was something Kaffer could deal with. He suspected their evolution was connected with gravitational variations in the Earth itself. And he had only to pinpoint that evolutionary change to duplicate their abilities.

He concerned himself with studying them and eliminating them. But he was impeded by the arrival of the Whispers and Edwin Limmer. Still, he had set in motion the plan that would eliminate the World History Investigative Society and its friends . . .

By Dan Parkinson
Published by Ballantine Books:

The Gates of Time
THE WHISPERS
FACES OF INFINITY
PARADOX GATE*

Timecop
VIPER'S SPAWN
THE SCAVENGER
BLOOD TIES

*forthcoming

FACES OF INFINITY

Book Two
of
The Gates of Time

Dan Parkinson

A Del Rey® Book
THE BALLANTINE PUBLISHING GROUP • NEW YORK

A Del Rey® Book
Published by The Ballantine Publishing Group
Copyright © 1999 by Siegel & Siegel Ltd.

All rights reserved under International and Pan-American Copyright Conventions. Published in the United States by The Ballantine Publishing Group, a division of Random House, Inc., New York, and simultaneously in Canada by Random House of Canada Limited, Toronto.

Del Rey and colophon are registered trademarks of Random House, Inc.

This book is a creation of Siegel & Siegel Ltd.

www.randomhouse.com/delrey/

Library of Congress Catalog Card Number: 98-92822

ISBN 0-345-41381-4

Manufactured in the United States of America

First Edition: April 1999

10 9 8 7 6 5 4 3 2 1

For:
Randy Scott, Jennifer Scott, and Carolyn Hope Parkinson

And for:
Kelsi Orsak; Cory, Taylor, and Ashby Spaulding; Danielle Jordan; and Desiré Hendricks

Grandchildren are the seeds of eternity.
—DP

Author's Note

In an infinite universe, there are only two truly significant places: here and yonder.

Likewise, in all of eternity, there are only two truly significant times: now and then.

Here and *now* are precise locations. *Yonder* and *then* are all that lies beyond, in any direction. Both east and west are yonder, both past and future are then. All the limits that exist are here and now. Beyond these lies infinity.

We are bounded by our perceptions. We see the universe through peepholes. We distinguish between large and small, between a lot and a little. But rarely, constrained as we are, can we compare absolutes like *everything* and *nothing*. And except for those inspirations that come at the rarest of moments, it is virtually impossible to perceive that these seemingly ultimate extremes—everything and nothing—are precisely and irreversibly the same thing.

To experience such revelation is to glimpse infinity. To see infinity is to perceive the perfect simplicity of a universe in which a point, a figure eight, and a polyhedron are identical in all respects but one: the matrix of the prime dimensions. These are the parameters of existence: height, width, depth, and duration. Of these, the most elusive is the temporal dimension, duration—the dimension of time.

Awareness may be defined as "I think, therefore I am."

Sentience begins with the product of awareness: "I am, therefore I was and will be."

The eye perceives up and down, left and right, near and far. But without time—without duration—these concepts have no meaning. It is the mind itself that perceives past and future. And the mind, once *all* of the dimensions are mastered, has no limits but its own. Unconstrained, its capability is infinite. It alone applies, to those puzzles presented by the physical senses, the element of time.

Given time, all things become clear.

—Dan Parkinson

Preface

Gleanings from *The Quest for When*, an overview of the implications and historical roots of bichronic time travel, compiled by Teal Fordeen (elscan 0-991-06ht. sm 103.11, trilev archives):

Glossary of Selected Terminology

Time   A dimension of existence. One of the four prime dimensions of physical reality. Directions within this dimension are past and future. The primary measurements are duration, velocity, and sequence.

Bichronism   In Actualist physics, the view that time is two separate phenomena: Time1, or T1, is experienced duration; and Time2, or T2, is elapsed sequential duration, "real" or "historic" time.

Velocitation   Alteration of elapsed T1 as an effect of relative velocity, on mass. While T2 is a dimensional constant, T1 is subject to shift within the continuum. Such shift results in direct correlation with the velocity loop represented by the photogravitational spectrum.

Temporal effect focalizer   Instrument designed by George Wilson, a specialist in temporal displacement with the Institute for Temporal Research. Perfected between 2035 and 2039, the T-effect focalizer, or TEF, is essentially an energy

1

exchange device. It reverses polarity within the photo-gravitational spectrum, and projects the sequence of reversal—light to slow light to pure gravity to free-fall gravity to new light—into a specified three-dimensional zone. The transition is virtually instantaneous relative to measurable time, and the resultant temporal effect is a T1 shift experienced by any physical body within the projection zone.

World History Investigative Society (WHIS) Authorized by the Universal Experience Bank of Pacifica in the year 2744, WHIS received the support of Sundome Central for an expedition to the beginning of time. Subsequent findings of dimensional gates and bridges in the precontinuum resulted in continuation and expansion of the WHIS enterprise.

Participants in the WHIS experiments became known as Whispers.

∞

The Lord God is subtle, but malicious he is not.
—ALBERT EINSTEIN

∞

The drill site was bright under low, freezing clouds—even brighter than full daylight would be in such weather. The glow of gravlumes made it an island of brilliance, even in the middle of wind-flurry night. Bright light, Spangler thought, but colder than a well-digger's ass. Right now his own—and everything else about him—was cold to the bone.

Throughout the day a strong, ice-fanged north wind had whined across the wide plains. The sullen, dry snowfall that came with darkness only made it worse. Hard little flakes rattled against his parka hood like birdshot as he made the rounds of his meter route for the third time this shift. The only windbreak between Deep Hole and the North Pole, some of the crew had decided, was the chain-link fence by the motor pool.

Usually, the field meters were read once per shift, but something was going on in the hole. Whatever their sensors were telling them upstairs, they wanted data confirmation. Pressures, temperatures, mudflow, and soundings—it was getting hot and heavy in the hole, and the drillers were excited. The drill stem was doing strange things, and all the shifts were on alert. Just in the past hour, three copters had landed at the HQ pad.

On the platform high above him, horns blared again and signals flashed, like myriad little lightnings in the bright snow mist overhead. He thought of blowout warnings he had seen in other times, on ordinary bores. But this was no ordinary bore.

This was geodetic-tectonic exploration on a grand scale. This was Deep Hole, and it was the fifth time tonight that the alarms had gone off. Through the fitful, gusting snowfall, he saw people hurrying here and there—off-shift floormen and derrick-men mingling with geologists, tectonists, theoretic physicists, and others whose functions he had heard but never understood.

As he approached the bank of thump recorders near the main lift someone jostled him and he stepped aside. For a moment, big blue eyes flashed at him from the fleece-lined hood of an oversize parka. "Excuse me," she said, and hurried on. Delilah, Spangler thought. Dr. Delilah Creighton. Another hustling figure in a nylon parka, one of the day people. He had seen her often in the past few months, coming on shift as he went off, but she didn't always wear the parka. More often, she wore faded sweats or a T-shirt and jeans.

He read the seismometers mechanically, feeding their data into his electronic clipboard while he logged in his readings by compact phone. Then he headed for the next bank. Passing a rank of field floods he glanced sourly at the brilliant globes on their little mushroom-shaped pedestals. How many times, during these past three winters, had he paused instinctively before one of these ubiquitous gravlume globes as though to warm himself in its rays?

But the damn things didn't make enough heat to thaw a snowflake. Just light. "The wonders of modern science," Spangler muttered. "Whatever became of incandescence and vapor arcs and radiant heat?" Still, the little lamps were the perfect light. They were everywhere, and they could be anywhere, without cords or circuit plugs, without the sky web of power lines that so many electric lights would have required.

In just the past few years, Frank gravlumes had virtually replaced both electrical and fuel-fed illumination devices across large portions of the world. Simple, efficient, and self-activating, the Frank Inertial Reaction Energy light was a technological paradigm, as revolutionary in its way as the wheel, the internal combustion engine, and the microchip. The device had been compared to both safety pins and sliced bread in the simplicity of its function. It utilized inertia to generate compaction-illumination, literally converting the force of gravity into light. And it maintained itself by simultaneously reversing the process.

Not perpetual energy, but perpetual regeneration—just like the universe itself.

A decade earlier, nobody had ever heard of gravlumes. Now they were everywhere. And here, on the open plains where Project Deep Hole was under way, the globes shone like thousands of bright stars lighting a square mile of short-grass prairie and everything upon it.

Now in its third year of exploratory drilling, Deep Hole had spawned a sprawling, self-contained community of nearly a thousand people. Around the periphery, barracks buildings huddled along paved streets separated by jogging paths, exercise areas, and fences from the libraries, office buildings, maintenance barns, electronic display centers, and auditoriums of USGS Seward base.

Scattered among these were the laboratories, shops, and stages of a dozen scientific disciplines. There were cafeterias, base stores, a school, even a dispensary hospital. Inward of these amenities were clusters of warehouses, supply depots, a motor pool, and finally, the 160-acre inner compound that was Deep Hole's drill site.

Ranks and rows of giant steel tanks formed the two-hundred-thousand-barrel reserve and working pits for the drilling fluid system, each diminishing string of long, free-flow tanks flanked by the earthen pits where little mountains of drill cuttings grew higher each day. Huge stacks of drill pipe sat on pads nearby, the thirty-foot lengths numbered and placed to be lowered in triple strings as Deep Hole penetrated further and further into the bowels of the earth.

At the center stood the drilling rig itself, a rearing colossus dwarfing everything around it, its base platform seventy feet above the surface to allow for the maze of sensors, miles of intertwined pipe, and blowout preventers beneath it. The control "doghouse," a solid, three-level structure the size of a county courthouse, appeared tiny in comparison with the massive structural-steel assemblies around and towering above it.

For nearly three years now, the drilling had gone on nonstop around the clock as progressively smaller and harder drill bits bored further into depths never before drilled—in search of something no one could identify but everyone knew was down there, somewhere.

The drill's target was extensively but vaguely documented as a *gravitational anomaly*. Somewhere beneath the earth's surface, something was moving contrary to every accepted theory of gravitation. It was why they were all here. The mission of Deep Hole was to find it and identify it.

To date, the huge drill had sunk a shaft more than seventy thousand feet straight down—nearly fourteen miles! Three times the depth of the deepest wells on this continent, and half again the depth achieved by those Siberian drillers in the Tunguska uplands before the breakup of the USSR.

Nobody was really sure what the Russians had been looking for. Some thought they were out to prove Kropek's theory of terrestrial electromagnetism, but what they had encountered was something else again. That, along with the gravitational anomalies of 1998 and some old theories about Tunguska, had led to the Deep Hole project.

Three years of tedious drilling, and now—just in the past two days—there was an almost palpable excitement among the tight-lipped scientists who monitored every foot of depth. Something was happening in the hole. Something more was about to happen.

Spangler was approaching the flow meters when a flicker occurred—an abrupt, general shifting of the scene around him. It was instantaneous, like a flash of bright light too quick for the eye to register. Spangler blinked, momentarily confused. He recalled having a sense of brightness about this place, as though thousands of brilliant lights had been here, making night into day. But there was no such thing. It was the same old drill site, all dark shadows and dim glows from snow-muffled lamps. He shrugged, wondering how long he had been this tired. He felt heavy, dragged down, as though he were carrying a great weight on his shoulders. At a row of steaming arc lights he stopped, letting the heat of the big lamps seep through his parka, relieving the chill. Almost at his feet, the pavement groaned and cracked, opening a jagged rift that ran for several yards. He felt so tired, he barely noticed it.

Up on the platform the drill engines also sounded sluggish, and Spangler noticed vaguely that the people moving here and there around him were plodding about like old people, almost in slow motion.

He moved on, to the meters, and raised his clipboard, squinting in the murk. The spitting snow obscured the little incandescent bulbs strung around the platform like Christmas tree strings, and there was barely enough light to see the graphs. He pulled out his flashlight. Odd, he thought vaguely—that fading impression he'd had, as though the lights should somehow be much brighter. But of course, they weren't. They were just like always.

As he approached the rank of seismograph recorders near the main platform, someone bumped him. He staggered, wondering vaguely why he felt so damned heavy and awkward. Blue eyes in the shadow of a parka hood glanced at him. "Excuse me," she said. She turned away and paused as the sound of the engines above ground down to a struggling rasp.

"There's something wrong—" she began, then pitched back against Spangler as the earth beneath them shrugged violently, seeming to rise up and up like flotsam on a tidal wave. A cacophony of sound erupted around them. Up on the platform people were shouting and things were falling. Spangler tried for balance, but his legs felt like rubber. The person clinging to him screamed and sagged. They fell, rolled, and a sheared-off brace from somewhere high overhead thudded into the cracking pavement just inches from them. The light strands swung and danced crazily under the weight of their lamps, then parted like sparking shots, their echoes drowned in a burgeoning roar that seemed to fill the world, driving awareness ahead of it.

Spangler was pinned to the heaving ground by the sheer force of the rising earth as miles of prairie headed skyward, bursting and shattering as it flew, dissolving into an enormous cloud of tumbling debris that shot upward and outward.

Spangler felt his ribs breaking like frozen straws. An intolerable weight atop him writhed desperately, and blue eyes bulged as her face was crushed against his.

There wasn't even time for a scream as Deep Hole's penetrating drill, fourteen miles down, found the thing it sought and cataclysm erupted.

The Headhunter

Trenton, New Jersey
December 31, 1959

The party had been a modest affair—just a gathering of a few friends at Luigi's bar to say farewell to a remarkable decade and ring in a new year. For all of them it was a time of hope and great dreams. But for Neal and Rose Lipscomb it was a most special evening.

Neal had kept the news until the evening, when they were together, then had quietly shown her the letter in the comparative privacy of the alcove at the end of the bar. Her eyes had shone with excitement. It was his appointment to the research staff at the Institute in Princeton. It was the life's work he had labored so long to prepare for—his endowment, to pursue his work in cosmological gravitation. At the age of thirty-three, Neal had his license to follow in the footsteps of his mentor, Albert Einstein.

There was no need for words between Neal and Rose now. They both knew what the letter meant. It was their future, theirs and the baby's, due within the month. Together they read it again, and their eyes turned to the little framed photograph of Dr. Einstein that hung on the wall behind the bar.

"Thank you, Albert," Neal whispered, recalling the years of mind-stretching discussions that were his association with the quiet little giant, the great privilege of simply having known the man. Einstein was gone now, dead almost five years, but his legacy lived on in Neal Lipscomb and others like him.

"He would have been proud of you, Neal," Rose said now. "He would have told you so."

With a smile, he gently patted her firm, protruding belly. "And of him," he said. "His little namesake, Albert."

They rejoined the party then and quietly toasted the passing of 1959 and the impending arrival of 1960. Then they went home, early, so that Rose could rest. On the car radio a commentator was counting down the end of a decade and summing up the score of the year just past—Fidel Castro's expropriation of U.S. sugar mills in Cuba, President Eisenhower's visits to ten nations, the induction of Hawaii as a state, the deaths of John Foster Dulles, Cecil B. DeMille, and George C. Marshall, the USSR's *Lunik* reaching the moon, Ingemar Johansson's victory over Floyd Patterson for the heavyweight title, Philip J. Noel-Baker's Nobel Peace Prize . . . Neal smiled ruefully. There would be no mention of something so academic as the physics award to Chamberlain and Segre for discovery of the antiproton. But no matter. It was that discovery, and its significance to relativity, that had finally opened the door to Neal's grant.

"For every action," he murmured, "there is an opposite and equal reaction. Matter and antimatter, synthesis and dispersion . . . gravity and light . . ."

Beside him Rose caught her breath and shifted in her seat. The baby was being pugnacious again. "Our little Albert is an impatient sort," she said. "He wants to get on with his life."

"Maybe he'll do big things when he's grown." Neal grinned. "He has an adventurous spirit."

"He's doing big things to me, right now," she said.

Past Steuben Boulevard the streets were empty and silent, post-lit tunnels through a dark zone of warehouses and shipping docks. Neal glanced at his watch. The year 1959 had an hour and twelve minutes remaining in it.

He turned on Waldheim and stopped. The street was deserted, but a barricade stretched entirely across it—some sort of yellow tape hung with little flashing lights. "We'll have to take the next street," he said. He shifted to reverse, backed half around to make his turn, and started as a loud knock sounded against his closed window. A man with a flashlight stood beside the car, peering in. Neal had the impression of rain gear—slick vinyl coat, floppy hat, gloves, and high boots.

Neal opened the window and blinked as the light hit his eyes.

"Are you Neal Lipscomb?" the shadow behind the light demanded. "Dr. Neal Lipscomb?"

"Yes, I am," he said. "What's the—"

The thing that came out of darkness past the light was a blade. Neal barely felt it as it sliced across beneath his chin, opening his throat in a gaping cut from ear to ear.

The world dimmed, a confusion of surprise, shock, and horror dimming to nothingness. The last sound he heard was Rose's scream.

In a deserted warehouse, the man in the vinyl rain gear stopped the car, killed the ignition, and got out. Blood dripped from his raincoat and pooled in the seat where he had been—blood that was no longer flowing from the gaping wound in the throat of the dead man still propped inside.

The man walked around to the passenger side and opened that door. The dead woman lay slumped forward in the seat, and slid partly out as the door opened. With a sigh of disgust, the man dragged her out of the car and laid her on her back on the cold, stained concrete beside it. Her death wound was similar to her husband's, but not so neat. She had reacted, tried to fight back. Her left arm and right cheek were open to the bone, and the mortal wound in her throat was jagged— diverted cuts, repeated several times.

Kneeling, spattered and soaked with the gore of his kills, the man used his knife to cut away the abdominal sections of her clothing, then set the razor-sharp blade against her breast bone and sliced downward, deep and sure as a butcher slices through the skin and membrane of a fresh-slaughtered animal.

Beneath his hands, her belly opened up and writhed spasmodically as the unborn child in her womb flailed and twisted.

Again he cut, and again, and the movement ceased. Leaning closer, he reached into the abdominal cavity and found the fetus—an almost full-term boy, dying even as he tore it out.

Again he went to work with his knife, this time carefully, meticulously . . . dissecting.

When it was done he stood, holding two pounds of soft tissue in one hand. This he placed into a polystyrene container, and sealed it. Removing his vinyl wraps he stripped naked, washed himself down briefly with water from a hose, washed the plastic container, then walked to a doorless alcove and dressed himself in nondescript clothing of khaki and flannel. He pulled on rubber-soled shoes and a shabby duck-cloth coat. From a wooden shelf he retrieved a can of gasoline, and walked around the bloody car and its grisly contents, splashing the fuel here and there. With a second gasoline can he soaked a section of the warehouse wall and the piles of broken pallets and sacking beside it.

Retreating then, he pulled from his pocket a small, gray plastic wafer with tiny lights on its surface. With the polystyrene container in one hand and the wafer in the other, he activated a signal with his thumb. In his palm the little lights began a countdown sequence. Thrusting the wafer back into his pocket he removed a Zippo lighter and struck a flame. He counted to three, flung the lighter into the gasoline-soaked rubbish, and watched as the fumes ignited, then the fuel itself.

Like a wild thing, the fire grew and spread. The man counted quietly to himself. Abruptly he felt heavy, and the movements of the flames slowed, dimmed, then erupted into a blinding flash of unbelievably intense white light. Within the light, everything visible faded away.

The transition was not instantaneous, but its duration was too tiny to be detected by human senses. The light faded as quickly as it had blossomed, and he was standing in a place of stone— stone walls, stone floor, stone ceiling. It was a vault of a room, cold and dry, heavy with the scents of formaldehyde and antiquity. The millions of tons of unseen stone above and around it were a palpable force—enormous weight in suspension.

There were no doors, no windows, no openings of any kind except the dark rectangles of little air shafts high in the four walls. The chamber was a sealed vault, without entrances.

The primary feature in the room was a long stone shelf along one side, where large glass jars stood in line, all filled with fluids. In some of them, shadowy shapes were submerged like big, soft oysters in murky juices. In others was only fluid. The shadows at the far end of the room held a dark, huddled shape like a large engulfing chair with someone small sitting in it. The light in the chamber, from little globes set here and there on the shelf and the floor, seemed to stop short of reaching the seated shape.

The man faced the chair shape and raised the polystyrene container. "Kaffer, I've brought you Albert Lipscomb," he said. "This is his brain, extracted before his birth. It is as you directed." He set the polystyrene container on the shelf next to one of the jars. "Now keep your promise. Pay me."

"You will have what you desire," a voice in the shadows of the chair said. "But I have more work for you."

"No more like this," the man growled. "This . . . this does nothing for me. It isn't satisfying."

"You will do whatever I ask," the dry voice said. "Remember, I have others. You could as easily never have been born as Albert Lipscomb there . . . or the rest. But no, I will not ask you to kill again, this time. There is other work to do. Work for a rich man."

"Rich and powerful," the man prompted.

"Rich and powerful." Kaffer's dry voice was almost a chuckle. "You are those now, in your time. With all the . . . the *satisfaction* you want. You will find it so. I have arranged it. Power and fortune, and the history to account for it."

"You play with history as a child plays with toys," the man said.

"More than you know," the voice murmured. "The history you know is not the history I found when I began. Each of these—" A shadowy hand moved, indicating the row of pickled brains. "—each was a threat to me because of a skill they shared. But there are others, who must be dealt with differently. You will do that. Through you, I will eliminate the means by which they came from the future to the past. Only I will remain. Time is mine. I will not share it."

"Time," the man said. "It is always about time."

"These organs are the brains of time-benders," the voice said. "Somewhere in each brain is a . . . a difference. They would have moved through time, by sheer force of will. These others now are different. With them it is no skill, merely technology. You will attend to that for me. See the lights, around you. These lights feed on inertia. They hold the clue to that technology. You will see that it does not develop."

"And how will I do that?"

"Ideas can die unborn, just as people can," Kaffer said. "Power can smother innovation. Good-bye, Carter."

"Wait!" The man glanced around, at the stone chamber. "I want to know . . . where we are. Where and when. And who are you, Kaffer? That isn't your name, is it?"

"Of course not," the voice said. "My name is not of your time. It would mean nothing to you. Just letters and numbers. Kaffer will do. And that name should give you a hint as to where we are, if you knew your history as you claim. This place once belonged to a man called that—Khafre. Or Khefren or Chefren. This is—was—his tomb."

"Khafre . . . you mean we're in a—"

"Egypt." Kaffer chuckled. "The pyramid of Khafre. This vault contained the remains of the architect who designed this monument, and the workers who sealed the king's chamber. Khafre didn't want his immortality interrupted by treasure seekers."

"But the pyramid has been opened," Carter protested. "I read about that. They found the burial vault."

"They found a facsimile," Kaffer said. "The real king's chamber and its anterooms, including this vault, were never found. They have no entrances. Now, good-bye, Carter. Your destiny awaits you in your own time."

Carter would learn nothing more and returned to the center of the chamber, where a gleaming metal pad covered the stone floor. Above it, suspended from the ceiling, was a little cone of some material that might have been metal, crystal, or both. It rested in a nest of coiled copper wire. Without looking back, he stepped onto the pad and stood there. For a moment, nothing happened. Then the light around him faded to a dense, slow darkness, which burgeoned to sudden radiance.

He opened his eyes. He stood in a large, ornate room—a penthouse room with windows opening upon walled gardens that looked out over a great city.

His logical memory told him he had not been here before, yet he knew the place and knew that it was his. History had been altered, and the personal details of his part of this new history flooded into his mind. He was Carter Vaughn, and this was his world.

∞

To have resolved all stresses is to be past tense.
—AMON GIBBS, *Insights*

∞

I
Gravity
1998

The cattle had not slept. Long after darkness descended they wandered the pasturelands by waning moonlight, cropping now and then at the short grass, raising their heads sometimes to low—the dull, mindless calling of brutes not driven by thirst or hunger, but simply by a lingering uneasiness that impinged upon their dim consciousness.

At first they remained bunched, but there was no comfort now in herd behavior. There was no disturbance, no hint of any threat, only that persistent feeling of wrongness that each animal felt. By threes and fives they wandered off, scattering across the ten sections of grassland that was their world.

It was past midnight when a dozen of them came together again, at a fence corner on a hillside. They came from two directions, diverted by barbed wire as they wandered downward, and when they met, the uneasiness among them increased. They bawled, milled there, and the wire sang as a line post went down—then another.

Suddenly there was no more fence to contain them, and they moved on, down the hillside, toward the dark highway below and the darker valley beyond.

A Boeing 727, with normal fuel and payload, weighs approximately 150,000 pounds—seventy-five tons of sleek mass as tough and durable as aviation engineering can design, as delicate and sensitive as the thin air of configurational semi-vacuum that suspends it aloft in flight. To an experienced commercial pilot, the message of the airframe is as clear as the readings of the instruments arrayed before him.

At twenty-two hundred hours, a blue-striped white 727 rode the starry sky thirty-three thousand feet above western Kansas—winking lights in darkness far above a dark, sleeping land. Captain Jim Shreve, at the controls of Intercon Flight 162, felt the sluggishness through the yoke even before his eyes registered the anomaly on the airspeed indicator. Flight 162 was slowing, its lift diminishing. Moments ago, the airspeed had been 280 knots. Now it was slipping toward 250.

"Check engines," he ordered.

Macklin had noticed it, too. He scanned the instruments, just as Shreve was doing. "One . . . two . . . three . . . check. All engines normal," he verified. "We haven't lost any."

"Well, we've lost *something*." Shreve eased the throttles forward to the stop. The airspeed indicator wobbled, but remained at just above 250. With a glance at his copilot, he eased the yoke slightly and tripped his mike. "Air control," he said. "Kansas City Center, this is Intercon one-six-two. Unable to maintain altitude three-three-zero. Request clearance to descend to a lower flight path."

There was only the briefest pause, then air control responded, "Intercon one-six-two, we show you west-southwest, three hundred and sixty miles, bearing zero-four-two degrees. Verify?"

"Affirmative," Shreve said. "Heading zero-four-two, altitude thirty-three thousand feet."

"You are clear of traffic, Intercon one-six-two. You are cleared to descend to two-niner-thousand feet."

"Thank you, air control," Shreve said. "Beginning descent." He eased the yoke forward, watching the airspeed indicator. Lazily the reading drifted upward. At thirty thousand feet it hovered around 280. Shreve continued the long descent, leveling at twenty-nine thousand. Again he checked his instrument banks. All engines were running smoothly. The airspeed was beginning to edge upward again.

Macklin verified the readings, then glanced around. "What the shit was that all about?" he wondered.

"I don't know." Shreve shook his head. "If I didn't know better, I'd say we got about eight percent heavier for a few minutes there."

Five miles below, tiny specks of light approached each other on the dark surface of the earth—two vehicles half a mile apart, moving southward along a lonely highway, and a third one going north. They were all approaching the bridge over a wide, dry river bed.

On a clear night in the central plains, you can see forever, Eddie Ridge told himself as he topped out on caprock above the Cimarron Valley. Southbound from Colby, pulling a forty-foot reefer with forty-five thousand pounds of cheese, he was just two hours out on the run down to Houston. He figured to make Abilene by morning.

From the crest above the valley he could see the lights of little towns in several directions—Sublette far back on his left, Hugoton ten or twelve miles away on the right, Progress ahead, maybe fifteen miles across the valley. U.S. 83 dipped easily downward, toward the Cimarron sands, curving away to the right as it went. Beyond the curve was a long bridge, then a reverse curve up the other side—maybe eight miles from crest to crest, he estimated.

It was after midnight when he had left Colby, and he had seen few other vehicles. In the past hour there had been only the Hastings tool rig that passed him five miles back and was now just taillights half a mile ahead. Nobody else—just the yard lights of farmsteads and stock pens and gas wells, widely scattered, and the distant little towns. Anybody with a lick of sense was sound asleep at this hour, he reminded himself.

Starting down the long curve toward the bridge, he was almost glad to see distant headlights coming his way from the other slope. Even miles away, he knew it was a car. At least truckers weren't the only fools out on the road tonight.

The Kenworth's big Cummins engine changed its pitch slightly as he entered the curve, and he glanced at his dash. The rig felt and sounded tail-tucked on the incline, almost like it was running ahead of an overload. But he had checked the load himself and knew exactly what he carried.

With a sigh, he stretched his shoulders and turned up the radio. An old Reba tune. Listening to Reba always made Eddie think of Rosie. He glanced at his speedometer, eased back to seventy, and relaxed. "That's the night that the lights went out in Georgia . . ." Reba sang, the lyrics drowning the deep thrum of the KW's big engine, the whisper of its eighteen wheels on the asphalt. Who put that out the first time, he asked himself. Maybe Carol Lawrence?

On the flats approaching the bridge, the Kenworth drifted left, and Eddie countered its tug. The bridge was ahead now, coming up fast . . . too fast, it seemed. He glanced at his dash. Ninety miles an hour! "What the hell," he muttered, gripping the big wheel. The tach read a smooth 2,000. The Hastings tool rig that had been far away was just ahead now, too close. Beyond the bridge, the other vehicle—the car—was approaching now. Eddie touched his air brakes, felt the sickening float of beginning skid, and backed off. He was crowding the Hastings rig, but there was still space. Better just to get past the bridge, then slow down on the upgrade. There would be more room there to gentle down a speeding semi.

In the instant the KW cleared the approach, guardrails whisking past, the beams of the tool rig up ahead picked up a milling darkness just beyond. Eddie's breath whistled through his teeth.

Cattle! There were cattle on the bridge! Just ahead of the Kenworth, too near, the tool rig's brake lights lit up like a Christmas tree.

There was no time to think. Eddie crowded the right rail, knowing what would happen even as it did. The car coming from the south saw the cattle too late and swerved, the only direction it could go. Its headlights flashed in his eyes. He hauled to the right and heard metal grinding against concrete. He saw the tool rig swerve and rebound, skidding sideways, quartering into the bridge rail. The oncoming car went under its fender, spun, and followed. Steel tangled with steel in a blaze of showering sparks.

". . . 'cause the judge in the town's got bloodstains on his hands . . . ," Reba sang.

The KW bore down on the spinning, sparking wreckage, and Eddie felt a scream rise in his throat. Felt it, but never heard it. A blaze of pure, white light—so intense that it seemed solid—enveloped him. In its unbelievable glare everything ahead stood out in stark relief, frozen and motionless—the toppling tool rig, the deformed Buick rising from the road, welded to the tool rig's caved-in cab, a whole cow in midair, upside down, the exploding bridge rail . . . sound and radiance gone dark and still in the instant of its own echo . . .

And the dark sand of the dry Cimarron, coming up to meet the falling wreckage.

Jill Hammond yawned, gave a final brush to her short-cropped, gray-streaked hair, and set her starched RN cap in place, scowling at the mirror. Even with the stimulus of a hot shower and fresh makeup, she still looked sleepy in the uncompromising glass. Worse, she *felt* sleepy—a sluggish, lethargic sleepiness that defied her efforts to shake it off. The very air in the quiet room seemed dense and heavy. She turned, startled, as an abrupt, insistent tapping sounded at her bedroom window. The sound stopped, then started again—a sharp, erratic ticking sound like a little hammer striking glass.

She glanced around, knowing that she was alone in the little duplex apartment. The doors were still locked, as she had locked them seven hours earlier.

Again the sharp, insistent sound came, loud and near in the stillness, and a tingle of instinctive fear touched her. She fought it down. "Don't be an ass," she told herself. "It's just a noise."

With a shrug of annoyance she crossed to the window and opened the blinds. The sound ceased instantly. It was still dark night outside. Dawn was an hour away, and at first she saw nothing except the dark shrubbery outside the window. Then the rapping came again, loud and abrupt. She flinched and looked down. A crow stood on the sill, staring up at her through the glass. It flicked an angry yellow eye at her, as though judging her and finding her wanting. Then it pecked again at the window, loudly and impatiently.

"A bird," she muttered. "Nothing but a bird." Abrupt movement in the darkness beyond caught her attention, and she caught her breath. In the shrubs were more birds—crows, sparrows, finches—dozens of bird heads flicking this way and that to look into the light. They seemed to be everywhere.

She leaned close to the glass, looking upward, shading her eyes against the reflected light from her dresser and toilet lamps, noticing again how heavy the air seemed—as though a storm was imminent. But the sky was clear, a high plains sky full of bright stars.

"Weird weather," she muttered, glancing again at the birds, then at her clock. It was twenty minutes to sign-in. With a final quick appraisal in the mirror—everything in place, uniform spotless, just a touch of lipstick and eyeshadow—she gathered her gear, turned off the lights, and stepped out into the stillness of predawn. The air was heavy and still, but there wasn't a trace of clouds anywhere above.

"Weird," she said again, locking her door and heading for her car.

At the staff entrance to Paxton Memorial she noticed Tombo Hawthorn's panel truck sitting with its cargo doors open. She smiled slightly as she walked past. Of all the sixtyish people in the world, she thought, only Thomas Bowman Hawthorn would drive a twenty-year-old fleet van with Mickey Mouse decals and a racing bike rack on its roof.

In the main hall she saw Tombo himself, carrying an armload of blueprints, a clipboard, and two sawhorses with black and orange stripes. She smiled and he grinned, adding his usual wink. Despite his sun-etched features and his unruly shock of white hair, he still had that boyish look that Jill remembered from long years past . . . a lot of years. "Did you notice the birds?" he asked. "They aren't flying."

"I noticed that." Jill paused. "Maybe we're in for a spring storm."

"Not likely," he said. "Probably just a bunch of lazy birds."

He transferred his load to a waiting cart. "You look mighty fetchin' this morning, young lady."

"Why, thank you, sir." She mimicked a curtsy. "And what is our town's most sought-after recluse doing here this time of day?"

"Trustees decided the OB corridor needs nice paneling." He shrugged, glancing at his clipboard. "Thought I'd get some presheet up before the crowd comes in."

He would probably do the entire paneling job himself, Jill knew. In the past few years Paxton Memorial had become, in some ways, Tombo Hawthorn's pet project. The primary reason could be seen on the Memorial Wall in the main lobby—three names among the dozens inscribed there: NICHOLAS HAWTHORN (1957–1971), JOSHUA HAWTHORN (1959–1971), and BETTY HAWTHORN (1936–1992). Since the death of his wife, Tombo had "adopted" Paxton Memorial. As a volunteer, he served it and tended it. In some ways, it had become the defining feature in his life.

"You look a little tired this morning, Jilly," he said now. "Atmospherics are acting up. Makes everything seem draggy. You wanta try out a new bike this afternoon? I just finished it. All alloys, with Royce gears. You might even be able to keep up with me."

"You'll never see the day I can't run circles around you, Tombo Hawthorn," she snapped, then grinned. "I get off at three."

"Good!" he said. "Tell Molly I left a hall traffic plan at Receiving. And by the way, they'll need you in ER. A tool hauler and a car ran off the 83 bridge. Two ambulances rolling, ETA here maybe ten minutes. The call just came in."

"Thanks. See you this afternoon, then."

From her locker in the staff lounge, Jill cut through the empty Diagnostics wing, enjoying a final moment of serenity. Here they kept regular hours, and there was nobody around yet. Just beyond was the clock room, then the ER, where there would be no serenity—not with wreck victims on the way.

Outside the staff elevator she stopped and stepped onto the scale, as usual. She adjusted the weights and slid the counter, then slid it again. "A hundred and *forty*?" she whispered. "What's wrong with this thing?"

She started over, checking the weights this time, peering at the calibrator. Again the scale balanced at 140. "That's crazy!" she muttered. "Nobody gains eleven pounds overnight!"

With full morning, the heaviness of the wee hours lifted. That general feeling of lethargy that so many early risers had noticed seemed to melt away with the rising sun of a bright day. And the birds were flying again. At IHOP and the Blue Goose, there was some speculation over coffee and doughnuts, but no one seemed to have anything to elucidate on the night's "weird weather."

At Paxton Memorial, though, the morning remained unusual. Extra staff had been called in, including several area doctors and a dozen of the hospital's ward nurses, to handle the rush in the ER. It had started with the wreck on 83—two passengers in the northbound Oklahoma vehicle were DOA and two more were critical, treated for immediate trauma and transferred to intensive care. The driver of the drilling-tool rig, a Texan, had multiple fractures but was stable.

Then, by the time these victims were in treatment process, others began to arrive. Three broken hips, an arm and a wrist fracture, all from falls at home. Two more fall victims were brought in from a local nursing home, and a man with a bleeding head wound—a framed painting had broken its hook and had fallen on his head while he slept. These were lined up behind four coronary arrests, a cranial embolism, and a spontaneous spinal compaction.

Tombo Hawthorn got his OB corridor marked and measured for paneling, taped up a couple of rolls of presheet, and placed an order for materials, then put away his barricades. The job would keep for a day or two, when the traffic might be less.

Home, to Tombo, was a house, garage, and shop on North Sheridan. The house he used only for its spare bedroom, where he slept, and for its plumbing. He hardly ever set foot in the rest of it, and hadn't really looked at it for years. Memories lived there—memories that were best avoided.

Mrs. Lindquist was there when he arrived, doing the weekly cleaning. He showered, shaved, and looked at the morning mail, then went out to the shop to check his on-line messages. There was a fax from the Limmer Trust, reporting his earnings, and there was E-mail on the computer—another vaguely urgent-sounding message from Lucas, suggesting that he "get his ass over to Eastwood."

This message he put aside, though he was a bit puzzled at the urgent tone of it. It was vague, as E-mail on open Internet tends to be, but it hinted at something extraordinary.

In recent years, Tombo had avoided his little brother—not out of any alienation, but because he felt like a fifth wheel around Lucas and Maude. They had a life to live and they were living it. They didn't need a worn-out old man around dragging them down with his occasional bouts of dark moodiness.

Then, lately, there was this new thing they were doing. Tombo had heard a little about Lucas's latest venture. He and Maude were involved in some wild scientific thing with the Limmer Foundation. Time travel, Lucas said. They had talked about it by phone. Tombo hadn't listened much. He saw no real future in time travel, even if such a thing were possible, and coming from anybody else, Tombo would have rejected the whole conversation as lunacy. But this was Lucas, and it involved Ed Limmer.

Mostly, though he kept quiet about it, Tombo believed what his brother told him. It was weird, it was incredible, but he felt it was true. If Lucas had expected excitement, though, he was mistaken. Tombo had listened, then he had stopped listening. "Don't tell me any more, please," he said quietly. "I don't want to know about it."

"You don't . . . but *why*, Tombo? Time travel! Just think about it!"

"I am thinking about it," Tombo had said. "I'm thinking that time travel is a thing of the past."

They hadn't talked much since then. To Tombo Hawthorn, the past was not a pleasant subject. The very idea that a man could go back—go back and see again what he had lost—was more than he could stand.

Still, looking again at Lucas's message now, Tombo shrugged. I've come to terms with it, he thought. Maybe it's time I faced the issue squarely. What harm can it do?

Maybe Jill Hammond would like to go along, for an outing.

From the house, he went to IHOP for breakfast, then drove out to the airport to visit for a time with Curtis Welles at his shop. Tombo and Curtis were both widowers. For a while they had shared an obsession with bicycles, but now Curtis was off on something else. He was trying to design the ultimate ultralight—a rotary-wing personal aircraft that could be stowed in the bed of a pickup, and could be set up and flown by one person with minimum time and effort, and with a safety system based on positive airfoil control.

The thing Curtis was testing this morning, doing low-level loops and turns over the wheat fields west of the airport, looked more like a collapsible kite than an ultralight. But the grin on his homely face when he brought it down was pure glee. "I'm close, Tombo," he said. "Real close. If *Sparrow* there isn't a true prototype, she's just a step away from it. Come on, I got two seats. I'll show you!"

For two hours or more the pair wheeled and soared above the town and the surrounding countryside. The little engine purred contentedly. Stubby, nylon-fabric foils rode the air while wide, freeable rotors—cloth over rigid frames—swooped and feathered with every current of morning breeze.

Sparrow wasn't quite perfect. They had to sit very still and lean into the turns, using their bodies as ballast. Tombo noted this instability, but Curtis merely shrugged. "I'm working on it," he said.

Still, unpredictable or not, *Sparrow* did fly. The contraption flew very well, indeed. It took to the sky as a fish takes to water, and seemed to revel in its element. Every few minutes, Curtis would find a thermal and kill the engine—a two-cycle lawn-mower motor—and they would spiral aloft in great circles, riding the morning air.

"Funny thing," Curtis remarked as they looked down at miniature houses hundreds of feet below, "last night when I tried to take the bird up for a night spin, I could hardly get it off the ground."

"You fly this thing at night?"

"Sure. To document its lift in nonthermal conditions. Next thing I need to do is a day cross-country. I could use some help with that. Anyhow, last night I had a hell of a time getting it up. Felt like I was flying a brick. But about sixty feet up, it changed. Light as a feather. Then I swear it didn't want to go down. Like hitting ground effect thick as syrup. I'd get to about thirty feet and honest to God, it bounced!"

"Probably an inversion layer," Tombo said. "Weather was real funny early this morning."

"I wish you'd come in on this with me," Curtis urged. "I don't have the specialties to develop this alone. I need a partner. With your knowledge of atmospherics and alloys, we could build us a real bird."

It wasn't the first time he had invited Tombo in. Curtis knew Tombo had a comfortable endowment from the Limmer Foundation, but it wasn't really the money that prompted him. It was a caring thing, a thing a friend would do. Curtis was as alone in his world as Tombo was. He found solace in his enthusiasms and sought to share them. Tombo found that this time he was tempted. Maybe it was just the exhilaration of the morning flight over sun-slanted fields, but he thought about it.

"I'm putting off the hospital job for a few days," he said. "And I'm thinking about running over to Eastwood for a while, to see my brother. Would that be far enough for your cross-country?"

At two o'clock, Tombo was back at the hospital, with two sleek titanium-alloy bikes on the roof of his van. "How'd you like to get our exercise where the wind doesn't blow so hard?" he asked when Jill Hammond came out, carrying her nurse's cap in her hand.

"I suppose so," she said distractedly. "Where do you have in mind?"

"Eastwood. Since you're off tomorrow, we could see some flint hills scenery for a change this evening, then stay over. I've been wanting to show you off to my brother and his wife. How about it?"

She didn't even hesitate. "Of course, I'll go with you, Tombo. I've been wondering when you'd let me meet your family."

As she packed a small bag at her apartment, Jill said, "You know, this has been the strangest day! I never saw Paxton so busy. Like an epidemic of unrelated traumas."

"I noticed." He nodded.

"And now, to top it off, somebody stole a scale."

"A what?"

"A *scale*. The calibrated scale from the staff corridor. It always sits right there by the elevator. Everybody uses it. But now it's gone, and nobody seems to know where it went."

∞

Everything that ever was still is, in that same when where it has always been.

—ANYA BRESKIN, *The Yesterdays of Now*

∞

He stood at the very lip of the maintenance sconce, seven feet beyond the observation deck railing and more than three hundred feet above the tiny strip of halogen-lit pavement that was a city street at night.

Defeated, destitute, and sick at heart, he was beyond desperation. He had reached the end of his rope. A man bereft of hope, he had come here to make an end of humiliation, an end of the disappointments of a world where only cynicism could thrive.

Cold, erratic wind shoved at him, this way and that. It pasted his stained, torn tuxedo pants around his trembling legs and toyed with his thinning gray hair. He had lost his glasses, but he didn't need them. He knew where he was going, and he wouldn't be reading again. Nothingness . . . perpetual sleep . . . was a simple step ahead. Not even a step. All he had to do was lean into the wind.

They said I'd be a smash on Wall Street, he thought with bitter irony. My formulas. My theories. My wonderful, simple little discovery . . . God! What an innocent I've been! Let my guard down. Hell, I never even had it up. Everybody's looking for a new idea, they said. Originality sells! Invention is the magic wand that makes it rain money. Sure, it rains money! But only for the swindlers and the cheats. Invention? Innovation? That isn't what business is about nowadays. It's about packaging and marketing and delayed option clauses. Used to

be about building a better mousetrap . . . didn't it? Now it's
the bottom line and nothing else. Sharks in a feeding frenzy,
scavengers feasting on the scraps.

Who the hell are these people? he asked himself, as aston-
ished as when he had first asked it. I don't know these creatures. If this is their world, then *where is my world*?

Management will love this, they said. A lamp that lights
itself! Dynamism from gravity! How wonderful! Who'd have
thought of using inertia as a sling instead of an anchor? Perpetual energy. A breakthrough. The classic better mousetrap!
Commerce will beat a path to your door. Just wait till management sees this!

What management? There's nobody out there but accoun-
tants and lawyers and beady-eyed MBAs. There aren't any
managers anymore! Just the terrible triad. Don't buy it, just
take it . . . Just sell it, don't make it . . . If it isn't broke, break it!

They beat a path, all right, he thought. But it wasn't commerce at the door. It was slicksters and thieves. Sharks.

In the uncaring wind, his face contorted with the pain of lost
ideals. Tears of frustration and defeat glistened in his eyes. There
was nothing left. They had it all now. Well, not quite all. They
had left him his IRS audits . . . and his mounting debts.

Slowly he rocked back and forth, feeling the shift of his own
inertia each time he teetered toward the distant street below.
Inertia as a sling, gravity producing energy. He didn't look
down now, at the almost-deserted depths. Instead he raised his
anguished eyes heavenward, where low clouds hung dull and
somber, pierced by the taller buildings beneath them.

Somewhere below, within secure walls, deals had been
closed like doors slammed in his face. The dealers favored the
players with the chips. Innocent and enthusiastic, he had come
to the party, only to find his life's work already dissected and
parceled out, with no share left for him.

"Sorry, David," Bill King had said through his plastic smile.
"Sorry, but that's business."

"You sold me out!" he had accused, incredulous.

King hadn't even argued it. "You came to us, remember? I

only agreed to present your idea, and I did. Carter Vaughn pays my rent, David. Not you."

"This is what it comes to, Irene," he muttered now, his voice thin against the cold, playful wind. "A whole life's work, a life spent believing that if you do the right thing, everything will come out right. Well, at least you don't have to be here to see this.

"I'll be a smash on Wall Street, they said. I'll bet not one of those bean counters would know how to calculate the exact impact down there. But then, why should they care about the force generated by 160 pounds of spun-off profit potential falling 323 feet? Inertia reversal doesn't matter to anybody. Hopes and dreams and ideas don't matter. Only money matters."

Direct conversion of gravity to photoelectric energy—a simple reversal of the direction of kinetic flow. This was his life's work. But did they want to see its results? No, only to control the investment potential it would generate. Three hundred and twenty-three feet of free fall, and he wouldn't even light up when he lit.

"Good night, Irene," he breathed.

He closed his eyes tightly and rocked forward, giving himself to gravity and the wind. Just for a moment, he told himself bleakly, he could lose himself again in pretense. This time he would pretend he was flying.

He leaned, felt his weight shift to his toes at the edge of the glass-and-steel precipice, and his dinner jacket snugged sharply around his shoulders.

"Very messy," a high, reedy voice said, behind him. He almost lost his footing, swiveling around to look.

The person holding his coattail was tiny—not much more than four feet tall. She—somehow he knew it was a she, though her head was as hairless as a fresh, pink egg—had both feet braced against the little wall of the sconce and was gripping his coat with both hands. The little garment that covered her from neck to feet, like a pilot's jumpsuit, revealed no particular contours. But it was her eyes that held his attention. They were the biggest, darkest eyes he had ever seen.

"You might want to reconsider this," she urged, struggling to hold him against his own inertia. "You'll almost certainly change your mind on the way down, and just imagine how you'll feel. At that point it will be too late."

"It's already too late!" he shouted, angry at the interruption. "It's all over! Everything! Let go!"

"I can't," she piped. "My hands are cramped. I'm stuck. Do you want to kill me, too?"

A gust of wind staggered him and he reeled, his arms windmilling for balance. "Will you turn me loose?" he demanded.

"I'd like to," she assured him. "Just give me a minute. You might not mind splattering yourself all over that paving down there, but I'd just as soon not. Have you ever actually seen what surface impact does to a human body? It's disgusting!"

"It's your own fault! You grabbed me!" He wrenched at his buttoned lapel, trying to free himself of the restraining jacket, and felt her tug falter.

"My feet are slipping!" she shrilled. "Help me!"

The wind and the height caressed him, inviting him to peaceful oblivion. But if he went, she would go, too. With a thin cry of frustration he threw himself back and down. His right knee collided painfully with a scaffold anchor. His hand skidded on wet metal, and his face scraped against rough, tar-bedded pea gravel. He lay stunned for a moment, then groaned as protesting pain coursed down him—first his bleeding face, then the deeper, throbbing bruises in his wrist and his knee.

Beneath his bulk, something small squirmed and protested, then pulled itself free. Little feet scuffed on the pea gravel, and a little face not like most faces leaned close to study him.

"You're a mess," she decided. "But you'll live."

"Get away from me!" he whimpered, abruptly aware of his pathetic position. He lay bruised and bleeding on a cold, damp rooftop, with all the grim determination of moments before—the agonizing resolve to just once, just one last time, take his fate into his own hands and do something right—fading away. He had been ready. Now he was uncertain.

"I can't even jump off a stupid building!" he moaned to himself. "Simple thing like that, and I can't get it done!"

"You're a pretty sorry specimen, all right," the little person agreed. "I think you should reconsider your whole life, if you're that unhappy with it."

"That's what I've been doing!" he grated. "What right did you have, to interfere?"

"None, I suppose." She shrugged. "But after traveling further than you can imagine just to see you, then chasing you all the way up here, I didn't want to lose you before I at least gave you my card."

"Your . . . your card?"

"Yes." She produced a little white business card from somewhere and handed it to him. Unbelieving, he squinted at it in the light of a rooftop sign, and she held out a pair of glasses to him—his own glasses.

"You dropped these in the elevator," she said.

With his glasses in place, he peered at her. "Who . . . who or *what* are you?"

"I'm KT-Pi," she said casually. "I'm a Whisper. But you don't know about Whispers, of course. We haven't happened yet. Just read the card."

Beneath an odd little logo—like two parentheses joined by an elongated X—were the words:

ANYWHEN, INC.
—Excursions, Tours, Sightseeing—
Adventures in Extratemporization
—HAVE A NICE TIME—

Sitting on the cold, damp roof, thirty floors above city streets, blood dripping from his cheek, his violated knee aching, his bruises throbbing fiercely, he stared at the innocuous little card.

"What?" he said finally.

"It's another option." The strange little person beside him shrugged. "You might want to look into it. Have you ever been to Kansas?"

Peaks of Otter, Virginia

It was the kind of evening God made mountains for, Jessica thought, marveling at the fragile rose tint in the funnel of sky that dipped down between the pines ahead. In the past few minutes, as the afterglow of sweet sunset darkened toward night, a stillness had settled across Amber Gap. Somewhere a whippoorwill, maybe as enthralled by the evening as she was, tried to put it to music.

Jessica put her back into the rhythmic thrusts of her arms, increasing her pace slightly to match her rhythm to the bird's song. The soft crunch of gravel beneath the wheelchair's tires was an earthy counterpoint to the medley.

It was four miles around the circuit—from her front porch ramp to little County 33, then left along Plum Hollow to the old bridge, and back by way of the footpath below old U.S. 11. For more than ten years now, hot or cold, rain or shine, Jessica had traveled this little circuit almost every evening. It had been her running path at first, before the accident. Now it was a wheel path. Four miles, and every foot of it held memories.

Just across the old bridge, up the slope from the path, was where Ranger had died, under the wheels of a gravel truck, on their last run together. Ranger had been chasing squirrels. The truck was hauling rock for the interstate. Jessica hesitated there now, just for a moment, then went on. It wasn't how she wanted to remember Ranger. Memories elsewhere were better—Ranger bounding around and beyond her, scouting the path, his tail a flag of frolic to match the toothy canine grin he turned toward her every few steps.

Up on Swayback's slope, half a mile away, endless headlights crawled among the distant forest like bright beads. The interstate wasn't part of the early memories, but it was there now, and she avoided looking that way. It was up there on the curve, just three years ago, that her little VW had gone off the road, leaving her without use of her legs.

Deep inside her still was that smoldering, boxed-in rage that she kept hidden because its existence was an ugly discord and she didn't like herself very much when she felt it.

There had been a person behind those blaring headlights that came at her in the wrong lane—a faceless person nobody ever found. Having no one to blame left a void in her sense of rightness. The void, like a vacuum, had filled itself. She hated the interstate. It had come to Amber Gap and brought its raucous debris—a gaudy strand of otherness running through pristine seclusion, leaving in its wake each day a widening cesspool of change—bulldozed clearings, gaudy little structures, and flashing signs. And always the outpourings of cities—raucous, intrusive people whose manners didn't fit the simple, timeless rhythms of these mountains—and who just didn't care.

People like the person behind the wheel of that red Ferrari. People who could devastate other people's worlds and never look back.

Still, it was rare to see strangers this far off the interstate, and Jessica was startled when the three young men stepped onto the path ahead of her. They must be lost, she thought, wheeling toward them. Then the nearest one grinned a feral grin, and the others spread slightly to flank him.

"Looky what we got here," one of them said. "It's the welcome wagon."

"You ever did it with a cripple, Mario?" another leered. "Me, I never did, yet."

"Nobody else around," the first one said. "She must be all ours." There was a faint click, and a knife blade glittered in the fading light. "How 'bout it, sweetbread," he taunted. "You wanna have some fun?"

Jessica heaved at her wheels, pivoting the chair, but it was too late. One of them grasped the head bar and flipped her over backward. She rolled from the chair, helpless without the use of her legs.

They gathered over her, pinching and pummeling, tearing at her clothing. She tried to scream, but a foul-smelling hand muffled her voice.

Then something whisked past her frantic eyes, and there was a sodden thud, like a ripe watermelon bursting. One of the attackers lurched back, out of sight, and in that instant a second one wheezed and doubled over as a large foot sank itself into his midriff.

The third assailant, the one with the knife, glanced up and gasped a curse. Loosing his hold on Jessica he straightened, started to back away, and something slim and swift lanced out, catching him in the face. Dark blood sprayed, and he toppled backward. Then in the dusk a large man stood over Jessica—a man right out of the history books; coonskin cap, fringed buckskin shirt over wide shoulders, thick, short whiskers, and eyes like thunderclouds.

He paused only to glance at her, then stepped past and raised a sleek long rifle, thudding it downward, butt first, like a man driving survey stakes with a post. Once, twice, and again the butt descended, and each time there was that ripe, liquid thud—skulls being smashed.

Then he knelt beside her. "Be ye sound, missy?" he asked in a deep, concerned voice.

Big hands like gentle iron set her chair on its wheels, then picked her up and sat her in it. This done, he stood back, pulling off his coonskin cap to bow slightly.

"Beggin' yer pardon," he said. "I might have saved ye that ruckus had I reckoned aforehand what them heathen was about. But they shore won't be troublin' ye again, I vow."

She tore her gaze from him and stared around, dumbfounded. The three outlanders lay sprawled and still, blood pooling beneath their smashed heads. "They're all ... all dead." She shuddered. "You *killed* them."

"Well, yes'm, I reckon I did," he admitted. "Only thing to do with varmints."

"Who ... who are you?" Jessica breathed, staring up at him. The odd, wild figure now was a silhouetted shape against a dimming sky, and she became aware of the faint scent of him—like woodland leaves and campfire smoke. His costume, she realized, was no costume at all. It was just his clothing, as natural to him as the catlike grace of his stance.

"Pardon, missy." He bowed again. "Didn't think to introduce myself. I'm Higgins. Jack Higgins, late of Butler's

Rangers. I've been sent to find ye, for them that would have words with ye."

"Them that . . . ah, where are they?"

Gently he leaned and took her hand. "I'm not right sure, missy, but don't fret yourself about it. We be there directly."

"Where?"

"Place called Kansas," he said.

∞

Heads and tails are the same coin. Left and right hands are sides of the same person. North and south meet at the poles. Darkness is diminished light and light is diminished darkness. Difference is often similar and opposites sometimes identical.

Still, there *are* irreconcilable things—life and death, joy and grief, right and wrong. In a world of confusing similarities, we distinguish between such absolutes, and knowing the difference is what raises us from bestiality to humanity.

These are mileposts on the upward road—the road to infinity.

—LAWRENCE ALAN JONES

∞

III

Instability Adrift

East Central Kansas
Present Time

The happy roar of a John Deere garden tractor without a muffler rattled the windows on the sunny east side of Lucas Hawthorn's house as Maude Hawthorn picked up the telephone. Clamping the receiver to one ear, covering the other ear with her free hand, she said, "Hello?"

Faintly, she heard a voice on the line, but could not distinguish the words. "Just a minute, please," she said. Carrying the handset, she went to the sunporch door, through to the outside door, and opened it wide. "Beejum!" she shouted. The mower was just rounding the tulip bed, heading back. She stepped out and waved. "Beejum!"

The tractor veered slightly as its driver looked up. A black face hung with little ropes of black hair grinned at her through bristling whiskers as Beejum returned the wave.

"Shut that thing off!" Maude shouted, gesturing.

Beejum looked puzzled, then grinned again. Braking the tractor, he cut the ignition. In the abrupt silence his grin widened. "Aye, aye, mistress!" he called. "I've shut th' bloody thing off!"

"Thank you." Maude nodded. "Now let's have a little quiet, if you please!"

"Aye!" Beejum winked. "Shore leave, then?"

"Right," she agreed. Passing through the sunporch, she returned to the interrupted telephone call. "Sorry about that," she said. "Hello."

"Lucas Hawthorn, please." A woman's voice, with a touch of either anxiety or impatience.

Closing the kitchen door behind her, Maude glanced at the oak doors across just ahead. Once, recently, there had been a seldom-used formal dining room beyond those doors. Now there was something else entirely. And the doors were closed. "Lucas isn't available right now," Maude said. "May I take a message?"

"Is this Mrs. Hawthorn?"

"Speaking." Maude sighed. The next words, she was certain, would be a cheerful, "How are you today, Mrs. Hawthorn?" Lucas was right. Every telephone scam and boiler-room operation in the country operated from the same training manual, with the same tired script.

She shrugged, preparing to hang up. But the voice said, "Mrs. Hawthorn, my name is Daisy Blake. I'm in Wichita, on assignment from WHP New York. I wonder if I could visit with you. I have a few questions—"

"If it's about that Chad Ryan thing," Maude interrupted, "we've already commented on that. We are not in the special effects business in any way. Mr. Ryan is simply mistaken. That's all."

"I don't know any Chad Ryan," the caller assured her. "This is about . . . well, I'm not sure what it's about, but it has to do with the Fabergés and . . . look, I really need to talk to Mr. Hawthorn about it. Could I come out?"

Maude glanced around the empty kitchen, frowning. There never seemed to be any Whispers around when a person needed them. She glanced again at the oak doors, tempted to interrupt Lucas, but just then a tiny bell sounded and a faint, pulsing hum came from the closed doors. The TEF was in use.

"I'm sorry," she told the telephone. "We really have nothing to say to the news media, about anything. Now, if you'll excuse me, I'm trying to get ready for company."

"Mrs. Hawthorn, please! It's not news media. It's about Anywhen, Inc., and the Romanovs—"

"Sorry," Maude repeated, and clicked off. With a sigh she

crossed to the sink to fill the percolator. Outside, Beejum stood under an elm tree, watching the kitchen window. At the sight of Maude there he waved cheerfully, plopped a curl-brimmed western-style straw hat onto his shaggy ebon head, and shouted, to nobody but himself, "Look alive, y'bloody swabs! All hands a'deck to make sail. Tops aloft, lively, now! Lord luv a duck, yon's frigates on th' tide!"

With a grin of pure, primitive glee, he climbed aboard the John Deere tractor and started its engine. The roar was ear-splitting. With a clash of gears, the machine lurched, swerved, and bore northward on the tide, leaving a fresh wake of new-mown Bermuda grass behind it.

"If Lucas doesn't put a muffler on that thing this week, I'll do it myself," Maude muttered, measuring ground coffee into the basket.

The racket outside softened a bit as Beejum's erratic path headed off toward the north lawn. Maude shuddered, remembering the neat little spirea hedge bordering the driveway around there, and the nurtured beds of daisies and sunflowers she had perfected just a year ago.

Still, the world had changed for the Hawthorns since the coming of the Whispers. Nothing, including old priorities, would ever be the same again. The fact that a nautically minded Australian bushman direct from the early 1800s was at this moment running happily amok with a garden tractor among her pet posies was far from being the strangest thing Maude Hawthorn had encountered lately.

The little bell sounded again, and Maude hastily cleared the kitchen table. She set out a tray of strawberry tarts and petits fours, and turned as the oak doors slid open. Beyond, what had once been a dining room now was a gray vault of a room with shuttered windows and treated-canvas draperies. The floor was neat rectangles of shiny steel, brazed at the joints. By the far wall stood a short, spidery derrick of steel beams with a sleeve of interwoven copper coils at its apex. Within the coils rested a small conical device that might have been metal, or clear plastic, or a shiny melding of both—the temporal effect focalizer. The TEF, which with its suspended electromagnetic system and its cables connected to the lenses and receptors that captured both sunlight and the raw gravity of a phenomenon called the Nordstrom Singularity, was the heart of the Whispers' temporal booster station.

Here, in the interior of the secluded Hawthorn house on a quiet street in the incorporated development named Eastwood, in what had once been Maude Hawthorn's dining room, was the place—or the phenomenon—referred to by the Whispers as Waystop I. An accelerator for people migrating from the far future. Migrating through time.

Within the steel-floored room now were five people—three men, a little bald Whisper, and a pretty, auburn-haired young woman in a wheelchair. Lucas Hawthorn stepped into the kitchen first. He slipped an arm around Maude's shoulders and winked at her. "Hi, babe," he whispered. Then, "This is my wife, Maude. Maude, I'd like you to meet Dr. David Frank, Ph.D., and Miss Jessica Tinsley. You already know . . . no, you don't, do you? They just came through yesterday, while you were in Wichita. Well, the frontiersman there is Jack Higgins, and that's KT-Pi. She's part of that scouting team L-383 picked up. Jack's doing odd jobs for her."

"Come in, please," Maude invited. "I have coffee almost ready." She focused a sympathetic gaze first on Jessica Tinsley— whose knuckles were white on her chair wheels and whose eyes were as big as walnuts—then on David Frank, who wore the remains of a tattered tuxedo and stared back at her with dazed eyes. Both of them bore scratches and bruises. Both, in fact, looked as though they were in shock. Maude turned to frown up at her husband. "Hasn't anybody had the courtesy to explain to them how they got here?" she demanded.

"I thought Teal Fordeen would fill them in." Lucas shrugged. "This is a Whisper project, assembling these people. All I know is Anywhen, Inc., might get some paying clients out of it. Where is Teal?"

"I don't know. I haven't seen any of them at all, till now. Even Peedy hasn't been here this morning. This one—" She indicated KT-Pi. "—is the first Whisper I've seen today. By the way, do you know anything about any Faberjays or Romanoffs?"

"Where are we?" The woman in the wheelchair strained this way and that, looking around. "I don't understand."

KT-Pi tilted her head, frowning. On her little face—a face whose diminutive features and huge, dark eyes appeared fragile and incredibly childlike until one looked deeply into those molten eyes and realized that this was no child—the frown seemed out of place. From a pocket somewhere she produced a little gray device and tapped a code onto its winking surface. She held it to her ear for a moment, then put it away. "Odd," she said. "L-383 should respond, but there is only a preempt. The closed loop is refusing contact."

"What does that mean?" Lucas asked.

"It means that Teal Fordeen and the others at L-383 are too busy to respond," the Whisper said. "I don't know why."

Dr. David Frank was gazing around at the neat house he found himself in. One moment, it seemed, he had been sprawled on the roof of a New York City office building with this little bald person holding his hand. The next moment he had been getting to his feet in a room with steel-plate flooring, and there had been two other people there—the buckskin-clad frontiersman and the girl in the wheelchair. Then this Lucas person had entered the room, welcomed them to wherever they were, and now they were all in somebody's sunny kitchen.

"What is this place?" he managed. "Where are we?"

"*When* and where . . . that's the appropriate question." Lucas Hawthorn smiled. "Today is tomorrow . . . or at least it was, yesterday, which is when you were. Miss Tinsley was several months back until now. And this place is Waystop I. You're in Kansas."

"Maybe I should try to explain," KT-Pi suggested.

"Help yourselves to the coffee," Maude Hawthorn invited. "I expect you'll need it."

Closed Loop L-383

Loop L-383 had a precise location in three-dimensional space, but it wasn't precisely *in* that location at any given moment. Neither was it, at any time, in any precise time, though on the average it was usually exactly when it was.

L-383 was a closed loop. In the conduit opened by the Whispers through historic times—a phenomenon of velocitational shift of T1—L-383 was for practical purposes a self-correcting anachronism. In T2 it had never actually existed and by its very nature never would. But it did exist, physically as well as temporally, constantly renewing itself by the same principle in which it constantly eliminated itself. By nullifying its own existence from moment to moment, it perpetuated the fact that there was an existence there to nullify.

Even to most of the Whispers, such rarefied temporal theory was beyond conscious cognition, but L-383—and other closed loops like it—served a necessary purpose in their project. L-383 was, for this sector of the continuum, Whisper Central. It was headquarters for the technical support team headed by Teal Fordeen.

The command center, where Teal Fordeen and a dozen other Pacificans gathered now, had the appearance of an enclosure, surrounded as it was—in all six physical directions—by virtual reality displays of galactic intervals, blended with intermittent, scrolling columns of symbols and formulas. The appearance of enclosure was necessary. The human mind is capable of grasping—or at least ignoring—almost any combination of sensory input that human senses can perceive. But no mortal mind, not even the trained minds of thirtieth-century specialists in temporal theory, is prepared for the experience of an infinite nothingness. Psyches simply cannot cope. In this sense, the virtual displays were as much screens as data displays.

But for the small, bald people gathered in front of one of the virtual walls now, the data was unmistakable. The wall might have been a topographic map, turned inside out. Its contours were ranging curves of bright color, curves and flows and concentric rings of neon red deepening to blues and purples as they progressed outward.

"Could this be the Deep Hole nodule?" Deem Eleveno suggested. "It's obviously a gravitational singularity of some kind, drifting upward toward the earth's surface. But it's too early for Deep Hole, and this thing is erratic. It seems to be drifting. There are convection distortions all up and down the spectrum."

"No question of effect," Toocie Toonine added. "We have significant gravitational anomalies. The hospital scale's readings are correct."

"Crustal shift?" Deem pointed to another display zone, where columns of figures reeled across a pattern of arrowhead designs. "The tectonic flux is twenty-six percent of arc. Meridian prime ten to M-prime sixteen . . . and widening."

At the topographic screen Toocie murmured, "I don't see crustal shift. Gravitational acceleration, conical, Illinois to Arizona, intensifying toward center. But there's no related tectonic activity, and no stratum focus. Besides, we know this isn't volcanic. Peedy Cue is on-site with a gravitic analyzer. We're getting direct read."

"Projected shock, then," Teal Fordeen speculated. "It's transglobal."

"Source? The South Pacific?"

"Asia," Teal said. "The folkloric Seven Days of Silence is in the range just a few years downstream. That occurrence *could* have been a massive crustal rift."

"There's no evidence that the Asian cataclysm affected the Kansas plains," Deem objected. "Didn't we determine that the Deep Hole phenomenon was probably a latent effect from the Tunguska event in Siberia, in 1908?"

"We've only surmised that," Teal said. "We don't know for certain. For all we know, these could be sequential gravitic shocks. Our tectonics don't read past core basalt."

"Peedy's analyzer is grounded in the Tunguska event," Toocie noted. "If there's a connection, it will show it."

"Well, that particle singularity under Kansas is drifting

upward." Deem shrugged. "Whatever is happening, it's happening now, in both T1 and T2."

"Correction." Deem peered at a virtual shield. "Degree of arc effect decreasing. Now nineteen degrees, decreasing."

"It's bobbing," Teal realized. "It has broken free within the planet. Now it's just wobbling around at random. Receding now, but it will move toward the surface again. Interesting. It must shield itself—possibly a light-conversion process at its surface. Otherwise it would annihilate everything it touched."

"It *must* be Deep Hole." Toocie shuddered. "When the drill hit that thing, it created a time storm that made the Arthurian Anachronism look like a child's whimsy."

"But we know when Deep Hole happens," Oel Six reminded them. "Besides, this behaves more like a bubble than a rising singularity."

"Do we really know about Deep Hole?" Toocie gazed at Teal. "We've already found little anachronisms coming upstream from the explorer teams. We can't be certain that anything will occur as it did. Suppose Deep Hole implodes early and encounters the conduit and these loops. What will it do with us in it?"

"We need Frank's conversion principle," Teal stated. "Without it, we have no probability. If we aren't *then* when it happens, we will never have been then at all."

"Well, you're late," Deem noted. "Dr. Frank is already at Waystop I. Do you want to retrosync, to be there ahead of him?"

"I'm unstable. My atomic matrix is thinning. I've absorbed too much potential duration already." Teal shook his head. "For some reason I seem to be accumulating absorbed duration. I could ricochet. KT-Pi is there with him. We'll trust her to—"

"She's just a scout!" Deem protested. "She isn't trained for rechronism."

Toocie moved closer to Teal. For a moment she scanned him with a handheld device that registered its findings— accumulated absolute duration—on a console screen. Teal's reading was very high, his physical mass quite low. As leader of L-383, Teal jumped around in T2, or elapsed time, far more than any of the others. A long series of intermittent jumps in short-range T2 had just been completed, arranging for a second booster waystop upstream in the 1800s. For some reason, the jumps had affected him, and he was literally—and abruptly—growing old. Even with the ability to travel through fixed time, Whispers still bore the weight of T1—experienced duration. It occurred and had to go somewhere. In practice, repeated exposure to unstable probabilities—a condition of all downstream, or forward, transmission—tended to cancel out this overload. But now it seemed to be failing. Teal was on the verge of backwash.

"I agree with Teal," Toocie said. "And Peedy has already entered T2 at the singularity site. We will have to rely on KT-Pi."

With another concerned glance at Teal Fordeen, she went to a UEB console and tapped in codes for a scan of the conduit, loop diagnostics, and a review of Teal's T1 accumulation. Even before the virtual screens began their scans, she felt a deepening dread. They knew and had known what was happening, but none had anticipated how abrupt the effects of decreasing eventuality might be.

Waystop I

"We, my associates and myself, are from what you consider the future," KT-Pi explained over coffee and pastries. "I entered—or will enter, if you prefer—retrosync in 3009 as a volunteer observer. I was assigned to a research team scouting upstream placements for sequential booster relays. That is how I happened to meet Mr. Higgins. He is indigenous to a likely interval in the 1780s range, in what is now called Kentucky."

"I'm not any such a thing," Jack Higgins interrupted. "I was born in the year of Our Lord 1751, in Williamsburg. I just happened to be in the Shawnee lands with Cap'n Butler when—"

"Indigenous only means you were there when we met," KT-Pi said gently.

"We thought these little bald-heads was Injuns," Higgins growled. "Then one of 'em shot me with my own rifle. Been a goner for certain, if it hadn't been for Katie here. She mended me at a Quaker gentleman's house in Philadelphia. That was 1703, they claim."

Dr. David Frank and Jessica Tinsley looked at each other as though searching for sanity in an insane world. "Time travelers," David breathed. "How is such a thing possible?"

"They do it all the time." Lucas Hawthorn shrugged. "You get used to it, after a while."

"One of the principles is your own discovery, Dr. Frank," KT-Pi said. "You were, after all, the first to prove the relationship between gravity and light."

David stared at her. "Gravity and . . . and *light*? All I ever did was invent an inertia-powered generator."

"Exactly." The Whisper nodded. "You reversed the static polarity of inertia through stabilized mass. You closed the ends of the photogravitic spectrum. It was because of your findings that later theorists compared gravity to light and found that each is the extreme extension of the other. Stars and black holes, Doctor. Yin and yang. The fundamental engine that powers the universe."

Outside, the muted roar of the garden tractor ceased, leaving a blessed stillness in its wake.

"I wish you'd put another muffler on that thing," Maude muttered, casting an accusing glance at her husband.

He shrugged indifferently. "Beejum'd just take it off again. He likes the noise it makes. Guess it reminds him of didgeridoos or something."

"Why don't you show him how to remove the whole engine?"

"At the rate he's going, he'll be redesigning the engine soon enough. For a primitive, that man's a mechanical genius!"

Maude turned to Jessica, explaining, "Beejum's Australian. An aborigine on walkabout. We sort of snagged him off a sailing ship just before Krakatoa blew up. That was 1803, I think."

Jessica blinked, looking dazed. Here in this sunny kitchen,

in this pleasant house, everything seemed so *normal* . . . sunflower wallpaper, family pictures here and there. Through a doorway she could see a piano and parts of two walls, one hung with an eclectic display of pictures and knickknacks, the other with various antique firearms—everything from a bell-muzzled musket to an ornate eighteenth-century fowling piece. There was even a whaler's harpoon gun among the displays. A normal house, reflecting normally atypical people. Normal—until she glanced through the archway at the steel-floored chamber where an odd, wire-sleeved cone was suspended atop a tower of structural steel beams. She had found herself in that chamber less than an hour ago, with the tiny, huge-eyed person who called herself KT-Pi.

"Light?" David Frank muttered to himself. "And *gravity*?"

"The TEF mirrors the absolutes, with electromagnetic waves and photoelectric impulse," KT-Pi clarified for him. "There are people—they call themselves timers—who apparently accomplish the same thing without devices. Teal believes they somehow tap the primal energies, but we don't know much about them." She glanced at Maude, reluctant to say more. Maude's younger sister was one of those unique adepts.

The outside door opened, then the door from the sunporch, and Beejum stepped into the kitchen. His bewhiskered black face split in a friendly grin, and he swept off his rakish Stetson hat.

"G'day, mates." He beamed.

"This is Beejum," Lucas introduced.

Dr. David Frank put down his coffee and shook his head, like someone trying to awaken from a confusing dream. "Why did you bring me here?" he asked KT-Pi. "What do you want?"

"I'd rather have Teal Fordeen explain it, David," the little Whisper said. "It's his project, really."

"What project? Please explain. Please tell me something that makes some kind of sense!"

"It's about your invention," KT-Pi said reluctantly. "You see, it was never produced in the . . . the present reality. The people you sold it to—"

"They didn't *buy* it!" he snapped. "They *stole* it. Bill King sold me out to Carter Vaughn."

"Yes. Well, they don't want the technology. Only to control the rights. So they buried it. It was never released, and without it, a lot of the technology we use—a big piece of what we know—will never have been learned. Your device is a pivotal discovery in the development of temporal transit."

He stared at her. "It never happened? But you're here . . . and I'm here. *Aren't I?*"

"Well, yes, but only because the probability change hasn't peaked yet. But it will, unless the situation is corrected. By you and Miss Tinsley, among others. We need your assistance to make that happen."

"But if it . . . if it happens, then it will already have happened! Either it did or it didn't!"

"If it didn't," KT-Pi said quietly, her big, dark eyes unreadable, "then both you and Miss Tinsley died recently."

In the stunned silence, Beejum poured himself a cup of coffee and helped himself to pastries. "Me, I come swap-out wi' a water cask aboard *Skibberoo*." He grinned. "Likely as wombats in th' wet-wash, but 'ere we be."

"Welcome to the wonderful world of anachronism." Lucas shrugged. "For every after there must be a before."

"Could somebody explain to me what *I'm* doing here?" Jessica Tinsley demanded. "I never invented anything, and I wouldn't know a probability curve if one bit me. But now you're saying I'm part of all this . . . this . . ."

"It really can be confusing, dear," Maude sympathized. "Believe me, I know. This time thing is—"

"Yeah, but why me?"

"Because of Carter Vaughn," KT-Pi said. "You're his weakness, temporally speaking."

"I don't even know the man!"

"He doesn't know you, either. But he has some bad habits, and one of them put you in that chair."

"That's who it was?" Jessica was silent for a moment, letting it soak in. "I sort of follow you . . . about the probability thing, I mean. In a really weird way, I think I understand. You're looking at historic sequence, but from outside."

"It's about time," Maude explained helpfully.

∞

Be very careful what you wish for in this life.
Wishes have been known to come true.

—LAURENCE ALAN JONES

∞

IV

Spontaneous Velocitation

Tunguska Rivers Region
North Central Siberia, 1908

"Jesus H. Christ!" Eddie Ridge hauled hard on his wheel, his feet stabbing wildly at clutch and brakes. Clinging to the whip-sawing wheel with one hand, he mauled the big rig's gears with the other. The Kenworth exploded through a snowdrift, shot past a solid wall of upthrust gray stone, showered ice and gravel over the vertiginous edge of a deep chasm, and whined down a tumbled twenty-degree incline to bounce, howling and crashing, across an ice-rimmed stream and onto a climbing slope deep in pristine snow.

In an instant the eighteen-wheeler skidded, began a jack-knife, righted itself, and buried its snout in white drift to come to a shuddering halt while exploded snow fell around it—a blizzard of its own making.

Shaken and white-lipped, Eddie unwrapped himself from his steering wheel and peered around. He felt as though half the bones in his body were severely bent, if not actually broken. And he had a nosebleed.

Muted daylight flooded the big cab, but he could see nothing beyond. Every window in the cab was plastered with snow.

He took a shuddering breath—the first one lately, it seemed— and icy air flooded into his lungs.

"What th' hell's goin' on here?" he muttered. Somehow, in the chaotic descent down the snowfield, he had shifted out of gear. Now the truck rested, purring contentedly, its big diesel engine throbbing quietly in the silence.

Long moments passed, then Eddie eased the driver-side door open. Fine powder snow cascaded down on him from the roof and foils as he stepped down to the footboard and peered around.

Where spring had been, now there was gray-white winter. Where rolling plains had been, now there was a jumbled landscape of jagged and stony breaks with windswept snow drifted in all directions and white-capped mountains in the distance.

It had been night. Now it was full daylight, with a bright, cold sun standing above the distant mountains.

The KW's nose was almost buried in deep, packed snow, and high, plowed furrows of the stuff formed a long, erratic wake behind it.

Eddie's breath drifted around him like little frosty clouds. The sullen, drifting breeze was ice-cold on his face, his hands, and his T-shirted torso. "What in God's name? . . ."

With a shudder of amazement, he swung around, climbed from seat to door top to snowpacked roof, and stretched tall to look in all directions. The landscape, as far as he could see, was a vast, empty silence. To his right were rising, forlorn vistas of stone and snowfields. To the left, far off, was a misty gray endlessness that might be winter forest. But nowhere was there anything that looked remotely like where he had been just moments—it seemed—earlier.

Nothing he could see, for that matter, looked like anyplace he had ever actually seen in his life. Nowhere was there any sign of roads, transmitter towers, bridges—*nothing!* The only movement anywhere was a distant hawk, soaring in the cloudless azure sky.

He climbed down again, plopped himself into the driver's seat, and huddled there—confused, frightened, and lonely. He hadn't the slightest hint of where he was or how he got here.

In the cab, a beeper demanded attention. The temperature gauges were creeping upward, the oil pressure downward. The rig's radiator was packed in snow, and it was beginning to protest. Mechanically, Eddie shut off the engine, then wished he hadn't. The silence was cold and lonely. He keyed his radio from FM to AM and back, searching wavelengths. There was nothing. Not even real static. Only the thin, lonely hiss of empty air. Both of his CBs were silent, as well. He ran the squelch to zero and found only empty air.

The mercury thermometer behind the cab read forty-one degrees Fahrenheit.

After a time, he dug his sheepskin coat, wool cap, and gloves out of the duffel and put them on. Then, for lack of any better ideas, he got out a shovel and broom and began clearing icy debris away from the rig's big grill. Maybe with the snow removed, he'd be able to see how much damage he had. If he could see it, maybe he could fix it. And maybe if he could get it running, he could get from wherever he was to . . . well, to someplace else.

All the time he worked, his eyes were scouting the terrain. There had to be a road *somewhere*. But until he found it, he would have to seek out natural paths that the truck could handle.

At least he wouldn't starve, he assured himself. In addition to whatever was in his duffel, he also had a few tons of refrigerated cheddar cheese.

When he had the grill and radiator cleared, he started around the rig's off side, shoveling snow, checking tires, stooping and peering as he inspected the undercarriage, connections, and running gear. The right side of the reefer was a mess—gouged and dented by the bridge railing he had scraped. But the damage was cosmetic. The trailer's hull was sound, and the running gear unharmed. He was nearing the rear of the trailer when he heard a repetitive scraping sound nearby. Tools in hand, he peered around the tail in time to see a little cascade of snow rise and fall atop the far drift. In the same instant he saw the trail of prints—small footprints, clear in the scored, level wake made by the trailer's axles.

The footprints came from somewhere behind, up on the opposite slope, and wound erratically down across the gully to the rear of the trailer, where they circled this way and that.

Again a little puff of snow appeared beyond the trailer, and Eddie hurried around to get a better look. At first he thought it was a child, busily clearing the drift around the rear wheels.

But when the figure straightened, scooping a load of snow with his spare shovel, he saw that it was no child. He didn't know exactly what it was, though. It looked like a little man—very small, almost dainty-looking, and clad in a one-piece blue garment from neck to feet.

His eyes were twice the size of ordinary eyes, and he was as bald as a billiard ball.

"Oh, hello," the little person said as Eddie slid to a halt. "Where are we?"

Eddie stared at him. "Damned if I know. Aren't you about to freeze?"

"Not really." The creature shrugged. "My batteries are fresh, and my thermostat is functioning quite well." He indicated a sort of pouch at his side. "More than I can say for my comlink."

Eddie peered at him again, with renewed interest. "You run on batteries?"

"Of course not! But my garment has capacitor-generated heating. My name is Peedy. Peedy Cue. What's yours?"

"E. J. Ridge. Eddie."

"Well, Eejay Ridgeddy, your operation of this vehicle is rather bumptious." Peedy pointed past him, indicating the long, erratic track of the Kenworth. "You threw me off way back there."

"You were hitchin' on my rig?"

"I was just observing," Peedy said.

"Well, what the hell happened? I thought I was in one hell of a wreck, then this light flashed and I was . . . here. Wherever *here* is."

"Probably both *wherever* and *whenever*," Peedy corrected him. "That light was a spontaneous photogravitational exchange, I think. I've never seen one before, but I'm sure that's what it was. Given that premise, it stands to reason that we have experienced temporal transfer. And since nothing around us seems at all problematical, this must be somewhen upstream. *Upstream* in T1 is the past. Downstream—at least without the assistance of a retrosynchronized observer—is nothing but shifting potentials."

Eddie stared at him. "What the hell does all that mean?"

"Simply that we have gone back in time."

"You're crazy."

"That is unsubstantiated. But my credentials relative to the subject of time are not. My original discipline is loop-base dimensionation, you know. With a subemphasis on T1's geographic relativity."

"Huh?"

"If I knew *when* we are," the little person explained, "I would know *where* we are. It's one of my specialties."

Eddie backed away a step, tilting his head as he studied the little person. "What are you, some kind of alien?"

"Of course not. I'm a Whisper."

"Yeah . . . right," Eddie muttered. "Whatever you say. And you came along on my rig to observe. Observe what? A bad wreck?"

"A gravitic anomaly," Peedy explained. From his pouch he pulled a little blue thing that looked vaguely like a glued-together deck of cards. "I was correlating relative masses, with this inertialog. A device of my own design, I might add."

"Gravitic . . . you mean, as in *gravity*? Like Isaac Newton?"

"Forget it." Peedy shrugged. "Gravity is a weighty subject. We have things to do. First we should get off this hill. I suggest we go that way. There's smoke out there." He pointed toward the distant forest.

Eddie squinted. Now that the weird little person mentioned it, there did seem to be a hazy, smoky look to the air a way off in the distance. "That's either east or west of here," he announced. "I know that, because it's the opposite direction from the sun. So it's . . . ah, is this morning or evening, do you suppose?"

"It is approximately midday." The Whisper's tone was of studied patience with a lesser being. "And that smoke is north. We're in a high latitude, obviously. Subarctic. The season is early spring, from the lack of color in those hardwood forests lower down. The sun is south of us, and its transit in the past three hours has not exceeded twenty degrees above the apparent horizon."

Eddie glared at the odd, diminutive person. "Nobody likes a smart-ass," he advised.

"I can determine simple directions," Peedy sniffed. "Can you?"

"So what?" Eddie snapped. "I can drive this truck. Can you?"

The Whisper turned away abruptly, facing northward. His big eyes were narrowed. "Did you hear that?"

Eddie heard it. It sounded like gunfire in the distance.

They were nine days east of Petropavlovsk when the unseen enemy opened fire again, and Captain Aleksandr Sergeievich Novik halted his march. With the precision of long practice the column of horsemen and carts shifted, becoming a defensive unit—a little self-contained stronghold in the wilderness with upturned carts and fallen logs as its walls, and a ring of ready rifles as its teeth.

Even as the dull echoes receded into murky distance, the company braced itself for attack, as it had done so often—a dozen times it seemed—in the past few days. From the barricades, Cossack horsemen streaked out to seek the source of the firing.

"Again a delay," Captain Novik cursed, his eyes scanning the mute forests along the trail. "Again the sniping. They want us to bear left again. They drive us toward the forest."

In his mind he traced the scant maps he had studied of this godforsaken region. From Petropavlovsk he had intended to make straight for the Yenisey crossing at Krasnoyarsk. But that route was far behind them now. Each day, it seemed, they had missed the opportunities to bear southeastward, heading instead up into the steppes of Angara, toward the barely charted wilderness beyond. Each day of the past five, unseen snipers had harassed the column, each time forcing a judgment to move further east—or northeast—into the godforsaken Tunguskas.

"They herd us like sheep," Novik muttered. "And we never even see them." Just this morning he had sent out Cossacks to reconnoiter the passes remaining to them. The options were becoming very few. To the south now, easily a week's forced march away in the best of conditions, lay the Trans-Siberian Railway and civilization. Not much real civilization, of course, but a semblance of it. But here, in the sprawling ice-forests along the rivers Nizhnyaya Tunguska and Podkamennaya Tunguska, was only wilderness.

"Those are not wandering Irkutsk out there," Novik had told his lieutenants. "Not stinking Evenki. Those are determined rebels. They certainly intend to drive us into a trap. Do not underestimate them."

Since entering the wilderness, Novik's company had been flanked and taunted repeatedly by wandering Irkutsk bands—primitive nomads roving the land, looking for whatever they could find. First there had been Yakutski tribes, then the Evenki, now the Tungus. The Irkutsk were a nuisance, but hardly a threat. Each time they were seen, a few mounted Cossacks were sufficient to disperse them.

But then had begun this intermittent sniping. The casualty list so far was two good horses and a Magyar porter. And in the past two days there had been evidence of Chukchi raiders along the trail. This put a new complexion on the situation. Novik and his lieutenants were nervous about what lay ahead. The Chukchi were no sullen, Mandarin-like Irkutsk. They were of the Tatar race—determined, well organized and fiercely independent. They had never recognized—or even tolerated—Russian sovereignty. Their slash-and-run raiders were often well armed, with German and Austrian repeating rifles. Further, they were known to trade among the Irkutsk, and Novik had no doubt that his party's location and strength had been thoroughly scouted.

The enemy had no way of knowing what thing of value this column escorted, of course. Even Aleksandr Sergeievich didn't know what lay within the iron-bound box that the bearded monks guarded. But to a Chukchi warrior, just the presence of Imperial Russian troops—especially Cossack horsemen—was reason enough to stage an ambush.

A dozen fires blazed and smoked within the company's tight little encampment as the long sun of northern dusk settled

lower into the distant Tian Shan mountains. The fires were a
necessary comfort in these climes. Their blaze held the biting
cold of forest breezes at bay, and their smoke discouraged the
hordes of mosquitoes and midges that arose like clouds from
the icy steppes to torment the company.

The insects of Siberia were like the people of Siberia, Novik
thought—always a nuisance and always there. The stinging
gnats were as endless as the forests of Tunguska, as maddening
as the constant turmoil of the imperial court in St. Petersburg
with the Duma on one side, the peasant-prophet Rasputin and
the Tsarina Alexandra on the other, and Tsar Nicholas II floun-
dering in the middle.

Militants, mystics, and mosquitoes, Novik thought ironically. A wonderful combination—a triad that could surely
drive men, women, and horses insane.

Mother Russia, discomfort be thy name.

Two by two, the Cossack riders reappeared, coming out of
the wintry gloom of the surrounding forest—fur-clad men with
ready guns in their hands, hard eyes under thick-furred caps
searching this way and that as they came. The snipers had
faded away again, like ghosts in the forest.

Bear to the left, the attackers seemed to demand—further
north, into the wilderness. The arrogance of it made Novik
seethe. Such arrogance implied a threat of superior force.

Just ahead, trails forked, and Aleksandr Sergeievich Novik
made a decision. Not this time, he decided. This time we turn
southward, toward Angara Pass . . . toward Nizhneudinsk and
the rails. In the center of the little encampment, bearded monks
guarded their iron-bound box.

"Stinking fanatics," Novik muttered to himself, glaring in
their direction. "Do not be concerned about your precious box.
I myself shall see it delivered at Vladivostok, as ordered."

The box was a solid little vault the size of a cartouche crate,
sitting on the floor of a horse-drawn cart. It was securely
locked and bore no sign of either origin or destination. Sixty
pounds of laquered container, it offered no hint of what was
inside. Captain Aleksandr Sergeievich Novik had his suspi-

cions, though. He had heard the rumors that Rasputin was using his mesmeric gifts for more than just debauchery. The Mad Monk, some said, was systematically looting St. Petersburg. And with the Tsarina Alexandra under his hypnotic influence, he had the might of Imperial Russia to assist him in his theft.

The imperial power in this case, Novik surmised, was the Prussian-born mercenary, General Erich von Stelm. As commander of the Fifth Cossack Cavalry, von Stelm was Captain Novik's direct superior. Novik was, therefore, an accomplice in the transport of stolen treasures to Vladivostok for shipment abroad. There was nothing he could do about it. Orders were orders.

"Damnation to the rebels," he told his lieutenants. "We go no further into their wilderness. At the fork, we turn south."

He did not know until several hours later, as the cold sun touched the Angara highlands westward, that the Chukchi had anticipated his decision. In a pass where the climbing trail wound among brooding cliffs, the Tatars were waiting. German-manufactured rifles thundered and echoed as they opened fire on the Cossack column.

The big Kenworth came down the draw at forty miles an hour, and Eddie Ridge concentrated on keeping its wheels under it. He had been tempted to leave the refrigerated trailer behind, but just couldn't bring himself to abandon payload. A long look at the draw from the plateau above showed no particular pitfalls—just a winding, cliff-walled crevasse leading to lower elevations. So now the rig barreled downward, winding and pitching, and Eddie used his compound gears as a halter and his brakes only to keep the rpms below three thousand.

Beside him in the big cab, Peedy Cue clung frantically to the seat belt engulfing his small middle, and gawked at the truck-high rock walls speeding past on both sides. "Slow down," he breathed, over and over, but Eddie ignored him. He knew his rig, and he knew that the threat of bottoming out on the uneven surface of the shale-and-gravel bed was greater than the threat of breaking an axle or skidding into a jackknife turn.

Somewhere ahead were dry, icy gravel flats, and beyond was a wide track leading into a forest. All this had been visible from above. At least, that was what Eddie hoped he had been seeing from that distance. The flats were a mile or so ahead now, he estimated, though the rock walls of the gorge hid everything from view.

Roaring and rattling, the KW barreled around a right-hand bend. Abruptly the tops of the walls on both sides sprouted people—fur-clad, furtive figures leaping and ducking. Eddie glimpsed surprised dark faces among the furs, then a rifle bullet whanged off the KW's hood and through the windshield, high and left.

"Shit!" Eddie swore through clenched teeth.

There were people everywhere now—up on the banks, swinging to point guns at the big truck, and in the draw itself, darting and scuttling to get out of the way. Eddie hit the horn, and the Kenworth howled with a bone-chilling shrill.

Dents and gouges appeared in the once-polished body of the tractor. Another bullet hole blossomed in the right side screen, and driven lead ricocheted inside the cab. In his rearview, Eddie saw the on-side gate of the trailer swinging free on its hinges, slamming against stone as the Kenworth swept the left margin, showering ice and gravel behind it.

There were horses running ahead of the truck now, terrified animals with flapping stirrups on blanketed saddles. Some of the horses had fur-clad men atop them, clinging frantically as they ran. Heads turned, and beardless, raven-haired faces gawked back at the charging monster.

"Indians!" Eddie muttered.

"Tatars," Peedy corrected. "Tatar horsemen. Raiders. We're in Siberia!"

The draw widened, and the frantic horses scattered on both sides. Like a juggernaut from hell, the KW blared through, still thundering downward.

Horn wailing, tires screaming, the big rig hauled sharp left around a bend, and ahead were more people—ranks of mounted men on prancing horses. Fur hats, fur coats, gleaming high boots, and strap-hung rifles raised, the ranked horsemen held their ground for a moment, taking aim.

"And Cossack regulars!" Peedy Cue chortled. "Oh, this is wonderful!"

"Shit," Eddie Ridge muttered, stabbing at useless brakes.

The raised rifles barked, echoing above the blare of the diesel's big horns, and bullets whanged and whined around them. Then as the truck bore down on them the Cossacks wheeled and scattered, opening a path. Here and there among their flaring furs were flashes of color—the blues and crimsons of the Imperial Russian brigade uniform.

Just behind the second rank of horsemen a group of dark-robed, bearded men scrambled left and right as a horse-drawn cart skidded sideways in the draw, its panicked dray-beast trying to turn and flee. The Kenworth smashed into the side of the cart, grinding it into the gravel. Bits and pieces of debris flew, and there was a heavy thump atop the cab as something solid impacted there. A gawdy-uniformed soldier with brass-trimmed cuffs peeking from the sleeves of his fur coat waved frantic arms, screamed something, and dodged aside as the juggernaut thundered past. In his rearview, Eddie saw the swinging tailgate come around at the man, then both soldier and tailgate disappeared from his view.

In the high cab, fragments of tempered glass flew from shattered windows. Then the men and horses were behind them, and ahead the gulch widened toward tapering flats.

Eddie Ridge spat out a mouthful of pebbled glass and threaded the bouncing eighteen-wheeler expertly along a weave of ruts and gullies. The gravel deepened here and became smoother.

"Thank God," he breathed, realizing that whatever had happened back there, he was still alive. Ahead lay a fan of gravel flats, and beyond it a wide, funnel-like opening into murky gray forest.

"I made it," he sighed. "God bless Texas, I made it!"

"Not quite yet, I'm afraid," an irritating, high voice beside him said. "You had better take a look behind us."

Eddie glanced at his rearview, just as the big mirror exploded into knife-blade shards surrounding a bullet hole. The whines of ricochets echoed from receding rock walls. Fragments of mirror clinging in their frame multiplied the image there. A hundred yards back, a solid mass of mounted men with thundering guns flew down the draw, in pursuit. Coppery-skinned Tatars and bearded Cossacks, they seemed to have put their differences aside for the moment. Now they rode together, heels drumming their lathering mounts, rifles barking—all chasing the Kenworth.

"Jesus H. Christ!" Eddie snapped.

Beside him, Peedy Cue snugged into his harness and gripped his braces. "Shut up and drive!" the Whisper ordered.

With bullets whining and clanging around it, the Kenworth careened across the sloping gravel fan and bounded like a charging beast across a shallow, ice-bound stream. Spray and bright shards whirled in the little tornadoes of its backwash. Climbing the far slope, Eddie Ridge double-clutched like a madman, riding his gears while he wrestled with the wheel. On the brushy flats beyond, the big rig mowed down spindly vegetation and headed for deep forest. Clouds of mosquitoes swept past its hurtling flanks.

"Got ourselves a problem," Eddie gritted, fighting the gears. "This thing feels like it's hauling rock. Gears don't mesh with the revs."

"Marvelous!" Peedy's little fingers danced on the clustered dots of his card-deck analyzer. "We're gaining mass . . . very rapidly. We've almost doubled our relative weight, just in the past minute or so."

In the shattered wing mirror, Eddie saw their pursuers diminishing behind them. Some of the horses had fallen. Others were struggling and fighting their bits. In the gray forest closing in on both sides, branches were falling from the trees. The Kenworth lurched and labored, sagging into its springs.

Then, around them, trees began to fall. Just ahead, beyond the nearest forestation, the earth rose like a monstrous, rising bubble—like a mountain being born. And everywhere, tall trees crumbled and toppled away from the rising crest. As slowly and relentlessly as flowing syrup, the cloudy sky above the "dome" dipped downward to meet it. The sky seemed to be inverting itself, and just above it was a lowering darkness as black as the void.

"Tunguska!" Peedy's voice was as deep as a well, as slow as the passing of eons. "The Tunguska event! It *is* gravita-tio-nal. A sur-fa-cing sing-u-lar-i-ty! Ma-a-r-v-e-l—"

Abruptly, the little analyzer in his hand glowed, then shone with a light so bright it seemed to penetrate his dainty fingers. With a prolonged gasp, the Whisper threw the thing from him. It tumbled in slow motion, clattered against the dash, and drifted to the floor with a hollow, echoing thud that went on and on.

Eddie felt himself sinking into the driver's seat and felt the truck's wheels settling into soft soil as it struggled to maintain momentum. His head throbbed, his vision blurred, and he felt his heart pounding as he tried to breathe. Tremendous, slow pressure seemed to be crushing against him from all sides. He clung desperately to the big wheel with whitening fingers, then lost his grip. He couldn't breathe, and his hands felt like they weighed a ton.

Around them, the world darkened. It was as though some-one had turned off all the lights. Dark gray, vague silhouettes, then a darkness so intense that it seemed to fill the cab of the truck. And nothing moved. The world was a frozen place, deep and buried, enclosed by crushing darkness.

Sound and sensation diminished ... seemed to stop entirely ... and the flash of brilliant light that flared then was a solid, brutal thing that picked them up, flung them around, and whirled them into a spiraling vortex of violent, dazzling motion and calamitous sound.

"Holy sh—!" Eddie's scream was a record played back-ward, slowly and under water. *T-i-hs-i-loh!*

There was no up or down, no directions at all. There was nothing, anywhere. There was no anywhere. The Kenworth hung suspended—nowhere, hanging on nothing, twisting in a wind that was no wind. All around it, or maybe behind it or below it, forces beyond imagining collided in a brutal, elemental impact that absorbed itself within itself even as it occurred.

Eastwood, Kansas
Present Time

Daylight came from somewhere, and Eddie opened dazed eyes. The Kenworth lay on its side among squashed flowers on a lawn of freshly cut Bermuda grass. Beyond was a paved driveway leading to a modest brick house, where people were emerging. Ignoring the piteous moans of Peedy Cue, who was head down in the sleeper behind the driver's seat, Eddie tried to collect the tail ends of stray and rampant thoughts.

"I'm alive," he breathed. "I'm . . . am I alive?"

He unwrapped himself from his steering wheel and turned for a better inspection of the little man excavating himself from the debris of the sleeper. Peedy Cue was stark naked. Intuitively, Eddie surmised that the Whisper's battery pack had shorted out, and his clothing with it.

He noticed, too, distantly, that every part of Peedy was as devoid of hair as his head was. With a groan, Eddie found footing in the wreckage and struggled upward through a gaping, open side window.

Fresh, warm air wafted around him as he emerged, blinking at the incredible sight of his fine machine. Pitted and bent, it lay like a dead thing among sun-drenched shrubs and flowers. Its tanks were ruptured, its fenders crumpled, its trailer a skeleton with body metal torn away in great, gaping strips. Every visible tire was blown out.

He peered over the crumpled, bullet-scarred roof at the twisted wreckage of his beautiful, eagle-emblem deflector, now bent almost in half and tossed aside as though torn from the cab frame by its roots. Bits of wreckage were strewn here and there, among them a solid-looking wooden box with iron straps. Somewhere aft, someone was pounding on metal and yelling in words he could not understand. It sounded like Russian.

And directly below the crumpled roof, a barefoot black man in short pants and a cowboy hat stood on a green garden tractor and grinned up at Eddie.

"G'day, mate," the apparition said cheerfully. "Cobber in yer aft 'old says 'e wants out."

∞

Pragmatism The shortest distance between two points is a straight line.

Conversism The intersection of two straight lines is a point.

Perspectivism In the universal sense, there is no such thing as a straight line.

Cynicism So what's the point?

∞

Afternoon sunlight slanted through the lace curtains of Maude Hawthorn's kitchen, highlighting the puzzled features of the motley group assembled there.

"The Tunguska event," Peedy Cue repeated, peering out from the folds of one of Maude Hawthorn's best quilts. "It happened in the year 1908 in central Siberia. It has been one of the world's great mysteries. No one ever knew what happened there. Some have argued that an extraterrestrial body—a giant meteor or a comet—impacted there. Others have suggested a nuclear device, or even a spontaneous hydrogen fusion event. But whatever it was, it literally obliterated four hundred square miles of terrain. It leveled forests for thirty miles around, it sheared off the tops of hills, and its blast was heard—and felt— over a quarter of the globe."

"I read something about that, years ago," Lucas Hawthorn nodded. "Meteorite or something."

"It wasn't a meteorite," David Frank corrected him. "The site was thoroughly explored in 1919. There was no crater. That was the puzzle." He peered at the little, bald creature in the quilt, then at one of the other two newcomers—the truck driver, Eddie Ridge. The third recent arrival was an Imperial Russian Army officer, who now sat on an iron-bound wooden box out in the fenced lawn. He seemed to be in a trance. Beejum and the woodsman, Jack Higgins, were wandering

71

around the capsized truck, nibbling on cold cheddar cheese and inspecting the wreckage.

The Russian's name, according to Beejum, was Aleksandr. *Captain* Aleksandr Sergeievich Novik of the Tsar's Fifth Cossack Cavalry. How the aborigine knew that seemed as much a mystery to Beejum as to anyone else. "Th' bloke tol' me" was his only explanation.

It was a tableau almost beyond imagination: a battle-scarred eighteen-wheeler lying on its side between daisy patches on the manicured lawn of a quiet suburban house, its wreckage forming the background for an eighteenth-century backwoodsman, a nineteenth-century seagoing Australian bushman, and a prerevolution Russian Cossack officer. But then, David Frank had become numb to the unexpected in the past few hours.

Somewhere in the back of his mind he wondered if he would ever again be surprised by anything.

"Are you people saying you were actually *there*?" he insisted now. "You—and your truck—were in Siberia in 1908, when that event occurred?"

"And it just happened?" Jessica Tinsley added, leaning forward in her wheelchair. "Just now?"

"Damned if I know." Eddie Ridge shrugged and shook his head. "I don't know where in hell I was or how I got there. I don't even know where I am now. And look at my rig! Who's gonna pay for my rig?"

"A rising singularity," Peedy Cue muttered. "I think that's what happened there. A fragment of black hole, drifting upward through the earth's crust. Antimatter emerging from its electromagnetic cocoon and meeting matter. Fascinating! And it obviously triggered a spontaneous temporal effect."

"I doubt it," the other Whisper beside him said. "Tunguska may have been spontaneous, but the temporal transfer wasn't. Your analyzer triggered that, just like it triggered the first one that sent you back there."

"How could it have done that?"

"Who knows? You admitted you constructed the device yourself. Possibly you reversed the polarity in its receptors and somehow made transmitters of them. Photogravitic principle isn't your specialty, Peedy."

"Should have stuck to tape measures," Maude suggested.

"Absurd," Peedy snapped. "Even if I had . . . 'triggered,' as you say . . . a temporal transference from the Tunguskan singularity, such a thing could have flung us anywhen in time. The possibilities would be infinite. So how did we get here and now?"

"Your analyzer was on T1 comlink," KT-Pi surmised, spreading tiny, eloquent hands. "Did you have it set for relay to L-383, through the TEF unit in Waystop I? This is Waystop I."

Peedy Cue looked embarrassed. "Oh," he muttered. "Yes, of course, it is."

"The singularity you encountered in western Kansas was just a gravitic bobble," the feminine Whisper elaborated. "L-383 confirms that. It may have been a precursor, but it obviously wasn't Deep Hole. Still, there *was* a gravitational anomaly, and your analyzer dominoed it into a temporal transference— directly from one photogravitic event to another. Pretty good evidence that Tunguska and Deep Hole were related phenomena."

"Deep Hole?" Jessica Tinsley peered at her. "What's Deep Hole?"

"Tempus rampant!" KT-Pi shuddered. "Deep Hole was a . . ." she hesitated. "Never mind. It hasn't happened yet."

"Well, *Tunguska* happened!" David Frank asserted. "Close to ninety years ago. Are you telling me that . . . that *cataclysm* was nothing but light and gravity?"

"Just like your inertia lamp discovery, David." KT-Pi nodded. "But a lot bigger. Four-dimensional energies on a planetary scale, contained in three dimensions. Tunguska was devastating. Like Deep Hole was . . . will be . . . if your lamp hadn't been present to maintain a field of aperture."

Outside, an imperious siren blared, and Lucas went to look out the window. "Well, by God, it's the high sheriff himself this time," he said. "What did you say when you called the law, Maude?"

"I just told them there was a truck in my daisies."

* * *

"I don't believe it," Sheriff Clay Connors said for about the tenth time. Big, solid, and usually laconic, Connors had been awed from the moment of his arrival by the sheer unlikelihood of the panorama on the grounds of Lucas Hawthorn's little fenced acreage in Eastwood. Now, it seemed, the more he heard and saw, the more fantastic the story became.

The sheriff had been meaning to pay a quiet visit to Lucas and Maude Hawthorn. Ever since that weird day when three prominent missing men and two missing investigators had walked into his office, everybody trying to blame everybody else for something and most of them claiming that the Hawthorns had somehow sent them back in time, he had meant to look into this Anywhen, Inc., business. Lucas Hawthorn had even invited him to come for a visit, and offered him a sample time tour.

He had meant to, but more pressing issues kept interfering. Now, though, he wished fervently that he had looked into all this earlier. Turning full circle, slowly, he looked at the wrecked truck, the bizarre collection of people around him, the Hawthorn house, the new-mown lawn, and finally at his own feet. "I don't believe any of this. Somebody better start explaining things to me, so they make sense."

"Righto, mate." The black man with the fuzzy pigtail and the cowboy hat stepped forward, a big, helpful grin on his whiskered face. "It's like was this capsized whoozis a schooner—a three-master, say—as got caught up in a black squall an' drove inland on rising tides. Now the tide's out an' 'ere she lays beached, wi' not a mark around 'er to say 'ow she got here. It's like—"

"Shut up, Beejum," the sheriff snapped.

"Eh?"

"He means belay that," Lucas Hawthorn explained to Beejum. "That isn't what he wants to know."

There was some commotion at the front gate, where a small crowd of rubberneckers was impeding traffic on the sedate residential street, and Connors looked that way. Whatever it was, the uniforms there seemed to have quelled it.

Scowling, Connors turned to his investigators. Myers and

Soames were not his deputies, technically. They were on loan from the Sedgewick County Sheriff. But they were veterans in dealing with "Hawthorn incidents." Both swore that they, along with some big shots from Wichita and a well-known—in his own opinion—television personality, had been sent back in time by Lucas and Maude Hawthorn, who had a time machine set up in their dining room.

The big shots maintained—and Connors had no doubt they truly believed—that they had visited the island of Krakatoa before it blew up, and had been passengers on a nineteenth-century Australian sailing ship. The deputies even verified that part of it.

Further, their weird story had been corroborated by no fewer than six seemingly reliable witnesses, including the Hawthorns themselves. One of the witnesses was this same black bushman, Beejum, who supposedly had been a sailor on that antique ship, the *Skibberoo*.

"What's happening here?" Connors asked his deputies now. "What's this all about?"

"Well, sir, it's another time-travel thing," Soames recited, thumbing his notepad. "Seems like this Eddie Bridge was—"

"Ridge," Myers corrected. "His name is Ridge."

"Right." Soames nodded. "Ridge. Well, sir, it seems he was just driving along U.S. 83, minding his own business, when—"

"Two hundred and twenty miles west of here!" Connors rasped.

"Yes, sir. North of Progress. Anyhow, there was cows on a bridge, and a bad accident, and Ridge couldn't stop his rig in time to avoid it. Then the next thing he knew he was stuck in a snowdrift on a mountain with a Whisper, and when they got the rig to moving again—him and the Whisper—they got caught up in a war between the Caustics and the Traitors."

"Tatars," Lucas Hawthorn said helpfully. "They were *Cossacks* and *Tatars*. They were in north central Siberia in 1908— at the time of the Tunguska event, which wiped out a thousand square miles of whatever was in the way. We were just talking about that when you got here."

Connors groaned and closed his eyes as tightly as he could. When he opened them again, everybody was still there.

"Shit," he muttered. Then, "All right, this truck is layin' here in these flowers, and it looks like it's been through hell, but there isn't so much as a tire mark leading to it. How did it get here?"

"Time travel?" Soames volunteered. "That's what they do here."

Connors gritted his teeth. "Time travel," he growled. Clay Connors couldn't imagine any circumstance but one, that would prompt him to requisition investigators from another county and take them—not send them but *take* them—all the way to Eastwood to look into an unverified traffic report. That one special circumstance was the reported location of the overturned eighteen-wheeler on the residential lawn of Lucas and Maude Hawthorn. Now he was here, and he wished he hadn't come.

The more he encountered the Hawthorns, the weirder things became. Déjà vu all over again!

"The Russian over there," Myers offered, "the one sitting on the box, he was one of the Cossacks involved. Somehow he got inside the vehicle and came back with them when they came back to now."

"And the other passenger?" Connors demanded. "Where is he?"

"His name is Peedy Cue," Maude Hawthorn volunteered. "He's in the house, with KT-Pi. She's a Whisper, too. Peedy's embarrassed to come out."

"He's embarrassed," Connors repeated. "Why?"

"He doesn't have any clothes," Maude explained. "His suit evaporated when his batteries burned out. KT-Pi's tuning the TEF to take him back to L-383 for some clothes. They may already have gone."

"L-383 again! And just where *is* this . . . this L-383?"

"It isn't really anywhere," she said. "L-383 is a closed loop. It's a sort of Whisper Central. It's out of place and out of time. It's a repeating wave of temporal resonance, so it's not actually anyplace."

"That's one way to put it." Lucas chuckled. "Like Mandy said, time travel is always feast or phantom."

"You should talk to my sister," Maude told the sheriff seriously. "She knows about these things . . . wherever she is."

Connors stared at them one by one, then closed his eyes and shook his head like a man besieged by gnats.

"The Russian gentleman over there," Soames continued, "is Alec . . . Alex . . ."

"Aleksandr," Myers said. "Aleksandr Novik. He's an officer in the tsar's Imperial Army."

"Right." Soames nodded. "And that's Dr. David Frank. He invented a gravity lamp and tried to jump off a building in New York City. The lady in the chair is Jessica Tinsley. She was assaulted by hoodlums in Virginia, but Jack Higgins—that's the gentleman over there with the dead animal on his head—he interfered on her behalf."

"Intervened," Myers corrected him. "Took 'em out with his rifle butt."

Connors sighed. "Exactly what laws have been broken here?"

"Not many, that we can exactly pin down." Myers shrugged. "Miss Tinsley says Higgins killed those perps—her alleged attackers—but that was another time, and not in this state. The eighteen-wheeler has at least twenty-six bullet holes in it, that we can find, but it seems like all those shots were fired in 1908, and on another continent entirely. We've verified the traffic accident on U.S. 83, but Mr. Ridge couldn't have been involved in it, not and be here now. About the only citations that might stick are an uncorroborated speeding charge against Mr. Ridge—he said his truck got heavy and went ninety-plus in a fifty-five zone—and maybe a public nuisance charge against Mr. Beejum for operating a mower without a muffler."

Visions of an earlier inquiry, full of the same bizarre elements and involving some of the same people, flooded through Clay Connors's mind. "I don't see Ed Limmer," he growled. "Last time we had a time-travel mess Ed Limmer was right in the middle of it. Where is he?"

"Somewhere in 1887, last we heard," Lucas Hawthorn said.

"He's installing an accelerator on the next upstream skip, about then."

"Jesus." Connors shook his head again. His roving eyes lit on the morose Russian. "What's in that box he's sitting on?" he asked.

"Don't know, Sheriff." Myers shrugged. "He won't let anybody near it. I guess we'd need a search warrant to find out. Or at least an interpreter. The Russian doesn't speak English."

" 'E doesn' know w'at's in th' tucker, either," Beejum said helpfully. "All 'e knows is, some cobber called Rasputin stole it, an' 'e's bound to take it to Vladivostok."

"You speak Russian?" Connors asked.

"No' a bleedin' word of it, mate. It jus' comes."

"And that's stolen property in that box?"

"Cap'n thinks so."

"I'd call that probable cause," Connors pronounced. "Let's open that thing up and see what's in it."

Myers and Soames glanced warily at the fur-clad Russian. Novik was watching them with the same uneasiness, his hand on the hilt of his saber. "After the fight, we will," Soames decided.

"You heard me," Connors growled.

So, after the fight, they did. When the deputies approached Aleksandr Sergeievich, he brandished his sword and they reached for their guns.

"Here, now!" Lucas roared. "None of that!"

Jack Higgins easily disarmed the protesting Russian, and Beejum sat on him while Soames and Myers carried the heavy box around to the patio and used Lucas's hacksaw to open its locks.

Despite its drab, iron-bound exterior, the box was an exquisite piece of crafting. Its components were the finest of rock maple, hand-fitted to perfect tolerance at every joint and bound with iron straps. The lid and sides were one continuous tongue-and-groove joint, so fitted that, when closed, the container was practically airtight. The twin locks were cast-iron-cased padlocks with steel clasps. It took Soames nearly five minutes to open them.

Inside was a compartmentalized nest of polished walnut and vermilion velvet. Brilliances danced as they opened the lid.

They gathered around, gawking at the contents. Cut, matched diamonds, emeralds, and rubies by the hundreds adorned myriad shapes and figures of rose gold, bright silver, and pure, hand-wrought yellow gold.

"My God," Connors breathed.

"Mercy!" Maude whispered.

Gradually, dazzled eyes began to sort out various components of the trove.

"What's that big thing there?" Soames pointed a hesitant finger, afraid to touch anything in the fabulous assortment.

"The crown of St. Peter," a woman's voice said, deep with awe. "One of the most famous lost artifacts in history. And those are . . . my God, are those real Fabergé Eggs? They are . . . Alexandra's lost dozen! *Hristovim Yiktnitsa!* The Fabergé nativity set!"

As one, they turned. Hair the color of sunset framed a pixie face with wide-set, startlingly green eyes. She wore blue jeans and a rumpled, too-big sweatshirt the way some women wear Dior. Suddenly aware of all the curious eyes upon her, she tore her gaze from the treasures and smiled a dazzling smile.

"Hi," she said.

Quick eyes scanned the faces around her, paused speculatively at Lucas, then fixed on Maude. She produced a manila envelope from her strap purse.

"You must be Mrs. Hawthorn," she said. "I'm Daisy Blake, WHP New York. I called you, remember? I apologize for climbing your fence, but I really need to talk to Mr. Hawthorn . . . about this."

She handed the envelope to Maude. It contained a half-inch-thick bundle of papers—photocopies of newspaper articles, letters, pictures. Maude leafed curiously through the first three items and caught her breath.

Two were copies of articles from old newspapers—the Kansas City *Star* and *The Topeka Daily Capital*. Both were dated in August 1887, and both were accounts of a warehouse fire in Topeka, in which various official state records and public archives were destroyed. The *Star* article displayed rotogravures of a building fire, crowd scenes, and people coming from a smoking building. The third item was an enhanced, enlarged black-and-white print of the same old tin-type photo, showing just a portion of the scene. Three men and a woman were clearly visible. Two of the men were emerging from smoke and chaos while the third, seen from behind, waved away people just beyond the cropped image. With the first two men was a small, attractive woman of middle years, clinging to the arm of the older man. Plainly visible in the enhanced reproduction, tears glistened in her dark eyes and streaked her smoke-smudged cheeks.

Stunned, Maude stared at the portrayed faces. One of the emerging men was her husband, Lucas Hawthorn.

He wore a smudged, scorched-looking T-shirt with an imprint clearly visible on its breast: a logo like two parentheses and an elongated X, the words *ANYWHEN, INC.*, in three-inch block letters, and the slogan *Have a Nice Time*. That very same T-shirt—and several more just like it—rested now in a drawer in the bedroom. They were brand-new, and they were the only ones of their kind.

"That's you in the picture, isn't it?" Daisy Blake asked Lucas, who was looking over Maude's shoulder. "More than a century ago, in Topeka, you escaped from a burning building."

Lucas stared at the picture. "This never happened . . . not that I remember. Not yet, anyway. Where did you get these things?"

"From WHP, I suppose," Daisy said. "The articles and the picture were slipped under my door, with a business card. 'Anywhen, Inc.' I did some preliminary research, then caught a Wichita flight. I just had to find out what these pictures were all about." She turned to look at the treasure box again, wide-eyed. "My God! Is it possible those are real? The Alexandra collection disappeared from Russia more than a century ago!"

They gathered around her, staring at her. Clay Connors snapped, "You're a reporter?"

"Researcher." Daisy shook her head. "I freelance mostly. Patent and documentary work, family crests, old land titles, you name it. My main client is the World History Project. It's part of the Carter Vaughn financial conglomerate. Tax write-off stuff, you know—cultural research interests. They hire me to track peculiarities, for museums and universities mostly."

"I thought you were just another reporter," Maude said.

"And you don't know who delivered these pictures and things?" Connors pressed.

"A courier, I suppose. From the WHP coordinator, or maybe from ACN directly. Mr. Vaughn sometimes initiates research jobs himself. He's fascinated with history, they tell me."

Lucas glanced around. "Take a close look at this picture, Sheriff."

"It's true, isn't it?" Daisy Blake looked from one to another of them, then again at the glittering treasure box. "That really is the crown of St. Peter, and . . . and those are the real Fabergés?" Excitement smoldered in her green eyes. Then she turned and gazed again at the splendors in the open box. "I feel like I've just popped in on a treasure hunt.

"It *is* real, isn't it! Those *are* the lost Romanov eggs! *Anywhen*, Inc.! You people . . . what do you do, travel in time?"

Connors shut out the woman's chatter and squinted at the pictures. "It's you, all right," he assured Lucas. "And that's . . . that's Tombo with you!"

"It sure is."

"Who's the woman?" Maude peered at the picture.

"I don't know," Lucas said. "But I know this other man, the one who's turned away."

Heads together, they studied the picture, and Sheriff Clay Connors caught his breath. "My God," he whispered. "I . . . I think it's me!"

Beyond the lawn, beyond the gate, the noise level was increasing. There were a lot of people out there now, crowding for a peek at the big Kenworth and trailer capsized in the flower bed.

Connors scowled. "We're drawing a crowd," he muttered. "Myers! Soames! Close that box and get it inside the house. Then call for more uniform backup, for crowd and traffic control."

"Yes, sir." Soames nodded. "Ah, do we call in the Highway Patrol on this?"

"Highway Patrol? Why?"

"Well, there's an overturned truck here—"

"And the nearest state highway is three miles away. Just call our own people, Soames. We'll keep this cozy until we find out what the hell it's all about."

As they closed the treasure chest, Dr. David Frank edged close to Daisy Blake. "You said Carter Vaughn," he said quietly. "You mean the investor? That Carter Vaughn?"

She nodded. "He owns ACN ... American Consolidated. Do you know him?"

"I know him," David said bleakly.

∞

Anything that can happen will happen, sooner or later. In the natural course of sequences, sooner usually occurs before later. In straight-line T2, the past always determines the future. But in T1 terms, duration is not limited to the flow of sequential T2. Thus the experience of a later event may well preceed the experience of an earlier one, and each occurrence, happening simultaneously in T1 and T2, may be generated or altered by reaction to the other.

Immediacy, therefore, is a multiple measurement in dimensionality, and *sooner* and *later* are relative and interchangeable terms.

Paradoxical semantics thus becomes critical to practitioners of temporal displacement. If concentration on when something happened confuses what it was that happened, sequential perception becomes unreliable and runaway anachronisms can result.

—*The Waystop Users' Manual*

∞

VI

Eventuality

Tombo saw the crowd from two blocks away—a congestion of vehicles and people, startling in the slanting sunlight of early evening. He slowed his van, leaning forward at the wheel as he peered ahead.

"Somebody have a wreck?" he muttered. "Those are police cars. And that's Lucas's gate, where they are."

"I don't see any ambulances," Jill Hammond noticed. "Just cars and trucks and people, and some heavy machinery. Winch trucks and a crane thing. What's everybody looking at?"

"At Lucas and Maude's place? Lord only knows." He slowed again, edging around knots of people in the street. Just ahead, a uniformed Sheriff's Department deputy had traffic halted while a mobile crane with a lowered boom maneuvered itself into Lucas's driveway and through the gate. Other uniformed officers closed the gate after it. Up the street, an armada of rolling stock stood waiting—light trucks, delivery trucks, and cargo vans, with their owners' names displayed on their sides. There were trucks from DelMar Packing Company, Sunflower Dairies, Sedgewick Grocers' Supply, Mid-America Refrigeration . . . even a pair of Rainbow Bread trucks.

The deputy in the street raised his arm, waving traffic by. Tombo lowered his driver's-side window.

"Keep moving!" the deputy signaled. "Let's keep the street clear!"

Tombo pulled to a stop beside the man. "What's going on?" he asked.

"Just keep moving, sir," the deputy ordered. "I've got winch trucks waiting to get in here."

"But that's my brother's house. That's where I'm heading."

"Sheriff's orders, sir." The deputy glared. "No admittance. Now move on!"

Tombo returned the glare. "Are you telling me that Clay Connors won't let me visit my brother?"

The deputy blinked. "You know Sheriff Connors, sir?"

"Dang right I do. Where is he? I want to talk to him."

"The sheriff is inside there, sir. But he said no admittance."

Tombo made a show of noticing the younger man's name-plate and badge. "Are you refusing to let me see the sheriff, Deputy Smith?"

"Well, I . . . ah . . . just hold it a minute, sir." The man tapped at his handset, listened to it, then said, "Emma, this is Jake. Can you raise the sheriff for me? Yeah, direct, please. Tell him I got a situation at the front gate here."

Along the elm-shaded walk, small crowds of onlookers shifted, and Jill glimpsed activity beyond the fence-shrouding hedge. There was something in there that was big, white, and rectangular. It looked like the tail of a semitrailer, lying on its side. "What *is* that?" she asked.

"It's an overturned eighteen-wheeler, ma'am," the deputy said. "Kenworth with a big reefer. Kind of an unusual sight in this neighborhood."

Tombo strained against his wheel, trying for a better view. "A truck? How did it get there?"

"Don't know, sir. Maybe the sheriff can tell you."

"Maybe so. What's in it?"

"Well, it's a refrigerated unit. Its cargo is about twenty tons of cheese. That's what the grocery trucks are for, I guess, is to move all that cheese. The semi went off the road and wound up here."

"Off the road? What road?"

"Highway 83, sir. Just north of Progress."

Tombo stared at him. "That's a five-hour drive! We just came from there."

"Yes, sir." The deputy shrugged, then held his radio to his ear again. He spoke to it, and then listened. "Is your name Hawthorn, sir? Thomas Hawthorn?"

"Yes, it is."

"Then you can go on in, sir." He waved at another deputy standing at the gate. "Jim there will direct you."

As the van crept around a TV crew and into the drive, a man appeared at Tombo's window. He wore a loud coat and looked as though he got his haircuts at a beauty shop. In the wing mirror Tombo saw another man right behind him, carrying a video camera. Tombo stopped. "Who are you?" he asked.

"I'm Charles Bronson," the nearer one said. "KVNU News. I'll just walk along with you here."

"The hell you will," Tombo said. "That's private property in there. Are you invited?"

"I'm a reporter," Bronson assured him. "This is a police investigation scene. Now if we can move along, I might make the six o'clock local segment."

"Go walk with somebody else," Tombo said. He hit the horn, and the gate deputies peered at him.

"I thought I told you people to clear this drive!" Jake the deputy shouted menacingly.

With a sour expression, Bronson backed off. Tombo drove on through the gate, and the deputies closed it behind them.

"His name's Charles Bronson," Jill noted.

"Yeah. Last week it was probably Mel Gibson." Tombo picked up the little citizens band transceiver lying on the seat and thumbed its key. "Rover to Sparrow," he said. "Hey, Curtis! You got your ears on?"

"Sparrow *One*!" Curtis Welles's voice was distant, but clear. "You forgot the *one*, Rover! This thing is now a full-scale proto-type, remember?"

"Yeah, copy that." Tombo sighed. "*Sparrow One,* what's your twenty?"

"I got Wichita on my port beam," Curtis responded. "Maybe fifteen miles back. I'm over . . . ah . . . either Derby or maybe

Colfax, I guess. I'm about south of the double cloverleaf, where the turnpike curves off northeast. Got a tailwind here, and I bet I'm doin' seventy or eighty."

"I'm in Eastwood," Tombo said. "Just got to my brother's place. Can you see Eastwood yet?"

"I think so. Big spread of landscaped places dead ahead. Suburbia at its sprawliest. Fresh paint on the water towers. I'm maybe fifteen-twenty minutes out."

"Good. You got that street map I gave you?"

"Got it right here."

"Okay. Just find Bradley Mall and follow Fairmeadow from there. It's the long street leading east from the north lot. Lucas has several acres. You can land out back on the sod. You won't have any trouble spotting the place. There's an overturned eighteen-wheeler in the front yard."

"Well, that's original," Curtis allowed. "Beats hell out of pink plastic flamingos. See you in a little bit, Rover. Sparrow One out."

"Rover out." Tombo guided the van around the front lawn turmoil of overturned eighteen-wheeler, winch rigs backing into position, workmen putting down skids on a boom crane, and various cargo trucks preparing to salvage cheese from the wrecked reefer, and swung back into the curved gravel drive just in front of the house.

As he stepped out, holding the door for Jill, a burly, buckskin-clad eighteenth-century woodsman, an Australian aborigine in a cowboy hat, and a bearded Imperial Russian Cossack wandered past, arguing loudly in various languages. The bushman paused, grinned, and tipped his Stetson.

"G'day, mates," he said, then scampered to catch up to his companions.

The front door opened and a very small, hairless person with huge eyes peered out at them and waved.

"Good heavens!" Jill breathed. "What kind of place is this?"

"It's just Lucas and Maude's house," Tombo assured her. "They tend to live in interesting times."

As they approached the front door it opened, and Lucas Hawthorn stepped out followed by the small bald person.

"Tombo!" Lucas grinned, clasping his brother's hand. "I'm glad you got here. Wait'll you see what we're doing!"

"I can hardly wait," Tombo said. "This is Jill Hammond. Friend of mine. Jill, this is my crazy brother, Lucas."

Lucas ignored Jill's hand and swept her up in a bearlike hug, then stepped back, looking her up and down. He nodded with real approval. "So you're the reason Tombo's quit being a recluse," he said. "I'm not surprised. You're even cuter than your picture."

"My . . ." Jill glanced up at Tombo. "What picture?"

"Oh, the one in the Kansas City *Star*, back in 1887. But I guess you don't know about that. It hasn't happened yet. I just saw it myself. Well, anyhow, come in. Come in! Maude's inside, and a lot of other people. Been a busy day. Way too much time covered and not enough time yet to sort it out. Did you know about the Romanov jewels? We've got 'em here. And Clay Connors is here, and the fellow with that wrecked truck. I guess you noticed the truck . . ."

"Kind of hard to miss," Tombo drawled. "Lucas, there'll be an ultralight putting down in your backyard in a little bit. Friend of mine, Curtis Welles. It's a test flight. He might be a little confused."

"No more than I am," Jill Hammond muttered.

The little bald person stepped to her side and took her hand in small fingers, gazing upward at her chest. "Hi," it said. "I'm Peedy. Do you mind if I—"

"Peedy, behave yourself," Lucas snapped. Then, to Jill, "Just ignore him. Peedy's a Whisper. He has a mammary obsession. Come on in. Make yourselves at home. Maude will show you around."

Lucas headed for the door and they followed. "I tried to warn you about all this," Tombo muttered to Jill.

"I wish I'd taken you more seriously," she said. "I just thought you were being weird. Are you telling me there *really is* time travel? People really can do that?"

"I'll have Beejum meet your friend when he lands," Lucas said, over his shoulder. "Beejum's never seen a flying machine, but nothing much surprises him. He's on walkabout."

Reaching the door, he turned and shouted, "Pete, see if you can get the rest of those trucks in here, and get that cheese transferred! I'll be inside if you need me!"

Near the overturned eighteen-wheeler a workman turned and waved. "Good as done, boss!" he shouted.

"That's what I've been telling you," Tombo answered Jill. "There really is time travel, and my brother is right in the middle of it. Ed Limmer started it. He's from the future. He always said he was, but nobody believed him back when he was old. The Whispers are from the future, too. A long way in the future. Limmer works with them. He got Lucas to set up a sort of booster station here for their migration to the far past. Now they're all up to their ears in anachronisms, naturally. But don't worry. You'll get the hang of it. Given time, it all makes sense."

"Didn't you tell me there's no future in what your brother's doing?"

"That's my own opinion." Tombo shrugged. "I said time travel is a thing of the past, because it amused me to say it that way. But truly, it is. The past, barring anachronism, is accomplished fact. The future, though, is nothing more than a mess of unsorted potentials. Maybe for the Whispers the future is concrete, but that's only because it's their past. For us, the moment we are experiencing right now is all we can be certain about. The future is nothing more than eventuality."

They stepped through Lucas's open door, and Tombo almost tripped over a Whisper—not the one they had met called Peedy, but another one. This one was even smaller, more delicate-seeming, and somehow—despite an absence of distinctive contours—very feminine.

"You know, then?" she asked, looking up at him with large piercing eyes. "About eventuality?"

"I . . ."

"Well, maybe not." She shrugged. "But I think you understand. Hello. I'm KT-Pi." Turning away, she scampered after Lucas.

"Adorable," Jill breathed. "Like a child . . . but she's no child."

The little Whisper caught up to Lucas and tugged at his hand, then engaged him in quick, earnest conversation. Lucas nodded and glanced around at the newcomers.

"Tombo, you and Jill want to see the TEF in action? A taste of time out of time? Something's going on at L-383. Teal Fordeen can't come here, but he wants to talk to some of us. You can come along if you want to. Maybe you can help."

In many ways, the closed loop was the ultimate accomplishment of postcataclysmic temporal technology. Creation of a fourth-dimensional conduit through the spatial matrix of the universe, though profound, was only a logical extension of theory that had existed at the beginning of the twentieth century. Even the ability to calibrate such a conduit's spatial placement and thus provide accurate access and egress within three flowing dimensions was—though a formidable task for the evolutionary survivors of Pacifica—still only the perfection of a craft.

But to effectively remove a segment of temporal reality and close it upon itself, forming a self-sustaining and life-supporting environment removed from spatial dimensions as well as from temporal continuity, was quite another matter. One of the originators of the process was a brilliant temporal engineer named 1TL-0014. A technologist with the Universal Experience Bank of Sundome 2991, Teal Fordeen joined the World History Investigative Society as a downstream transferee in 2744 to assist with creation of the WHIS conduit, and accepted permanent appointment when the Arthurian Anachronism was discovered at 2050.

Development of the closed loop as a staging device was a painstaking and sometimes heartbreaking project. Early attempts often resulted in disasters. Project teams were flung into intergalactic space by calibration errors, fossilized within mountains, subjected to primordial forces on accidental over-leaps, or simply dissolved when unforeseen dimensional anomalies encroached upon the exquisitely delicate balance of force and stasis that was the "fabric" of the loops.

One closed loop was simply lost, without a trace. L-270, a

team of historians and temporal technologists headed by the brilliant—if unpredictable—historical geneticist 1KHAF4, had disappeared into the past beyond Arthur's time storm after reporting evidence of temporal gates and bridges in the early quadrants of the universe. L-270 had never been accounted for.

But the Whispers persisted, and by Time2 date 3006 the closed loop was dependable technology.

When L-383 was created, to serve as the staging base for Arthurian bypass and for the placement of TEF boosters along the conduit, Teal Fordeen volunteered to head the project.

Anyone experiencing a Whisper closed loop sheds all pre-conceptions regarding time travel. The reality of a closed loop is beyond comprehension, but also beyond question. The arrayed displays and controls hint at the enormous energies held in fine balance to create spatial dimensionality within shifting constants. The screens of virtual reality enclosing a wide, circular spatial environment are brilliant but intangible—the eyes of the loop as well as psychic shields for those within.

To look beyond the virtual screens is to see a reality too profound for human senses to grasp—gravity and light in exquisite counterpoint, endlessly spewing, gathering, and ingesting all of those elements that are not elements at all, but simply the by-product of an infinite photogravitic cycle.

To look beyond apparent reality is to see the motive force of the universe at work.

It was here, in the indescribable reality of L-383, that Teal Fordeen welcomed his abruptly assembled collection of visitors from Lucas Hawthorn's house.

"Let me tell you a story," he said, when he had their full, glassy-eyed attention. "It is about eventuality."

∞

A rolling disk presents a single surface, a continuum repeating itself infinitely as it goes. But with each turn it covers new ground. This is the principle behind the closed loop in quadridimensional engineering. It is also the paradox of progressive infinity. It remains changeless, but is ever changing.

—TEAL FORDEEN, *Basics of Temporality*

∞

VII

Delta

Closed Loop L-383

"Eventuality," Teal Fordeen said, emphasizing the word. "We face a crisis of eventuality. History is being altered. Your natural future—and our very existence—is being erased. We summoned you here—some of you—because the root of the problem is in your era. It is your future that is in danger, and you have the right to assist in solving the problem—if it can be solved."

"This is . . . is just amazing," Jill Hammond whispered, clinging to Tombo's arm as she turned this way and that, trying to see everything at once and trying to understand at least some fraction of what she saw. The place they found themselves in was like a great, round theater, she thought.

On all sides were shimmering, flowing patterns of light and color—virtual displays dancing in holographic detail: galaxies swimming in infinite space, swirls of coalescing brightness here and there, and everywhere scrolling columns of symbols like numerical sequences and mathematical equations. Lesser curtains of shimmering, iridescent light patterns intruded into the field, dividing the peripheries of the visible space into pathways, cubicles, and unseen corridors. Among these the small, bald, big-eyed people came and went, busily doing things that she did not understand.

Around her, the others who had gathered in the steel-floored room at the Hawthorn house, then suddenly found themselves here, seemed as mesmerized as she was. They had been introduced briefly to L-383 by various Whispers, with Lucas and Maude Hawthorn adding their comments, which confused as much as they clarified. There had been no hesitancy in the explanations, but the impact of this "place," the sheer, unimaginable strangeness and beauty of it, was beyond their grasp. They had been introduced to a dozen of the little people called Whispers, and particularly to Teal Fordeen, but no quick introduction could smooth the shock of actually meeting so alien-seeming a people in such mind-numbing surroundings.

"Are they . . . are they really *human*?" Jill murmured.

"As human as we are, dear," Maude Hawthorn assured her. "They just come from a very long way in the future."

Pacificans, the little people called themselves and their kind. These particular Pacificans were associated with a scientific, investigative order called WHIS. They were Whispers.

For Tombo, it was a little easier. Over the years he had heard the odd stories about Ed Limmer, the benefactor of the Hawthorns. Tombo himself, with some friends, had found the old man in a wheat field in western Kansas, back in the early fifties.

Limmer claimed to have lived a life in retrosync before starting back to the time of his birth. Limmer had traveled with the people of the World History Investigative Society—the Whispers. They had aided him in his search for a perfect justice somewhere in the future.

The Limmer Foundation was built on remarkably successful investments in commodity futures. The Limmer Trust had provided financial security for both Lucas and Tombo.

Limmer had disappeared, many years ago, and they presumed he was dead. But then, recently, he had returned. Lucas was convinced it was him, though he was much younger now. Limmer and the Whispers had chosen his brother's house as a waystop on their journey to the beginning of time. Had anyone but Lucas told him that, Tombo wouldn't have believed it. Yet he did believe it. Time travel! It was true! In a way, Tombo had known all his life that it was, but it wasn't a thing he wanted to think about. Time was the measure of mortality, and mortality hurt. The past was where Betty still lived, and the kids. Some-when, back then, they were as they had been. But they were gone now. The idea that he might actually go back—go back and see them again, knowing what must follow—was more than he could bear.

He steadied his racing mind and focused on Teal Fordeen. "Eventuality?" he asked. "What do you mean by that?"

Teal Fordeen nodded. "I will explain," he said. "Please hear me out."

He indicated the odd-looking chairs that had been provided for them in the large central area of the loop. The chairs seemed almost insubstantial, extrusions of some filmy substance that looked like spider silk. But they were comfortable enough—as though they had been hastily designed for people larger than those who created them.

"Eventuality," he said, "is the convergence of probabilities to create fact. I understand that you yourself, Mr. ... ah, Tombo, have said that temporal displacement—time travel—is a thing of the past . . . that there is in fact no future until a future occurs, when it also becomes past.

"Hypothetically—and from some basic perspectives—this is true. But it is misleading. It implies that the past is thereby unalterable and the future does not exist. Neither implication is correct. Your future—" He looked from one to another of them. "—is our past. So what seems conjecture from your viewpoint is, to us, accomplished fact. The future does, in fact, exist—the future that you, in your time, are building. It is our past, but your future. Day by day, you create it, and you have the power to alter it."

Jessica Tinsley had been watching with fascination as a group of Whispers nearby made delicate adjustments on a control board. With each touch of their busy little fingers, a virtual display behind them shifted slightly, and she felt she could discern a pattern there if only she could concentrate enough.

But now she tore her gaze from the tableau to frown at Teal Fordeen. "How about our own past?" she demanded, spreading her hands to indicate her useless legs and the wheelchair that was her prison. "If we can correct the past for you people, how about making some corrections for ourselves while we're at it?"

The leader of the Whispers gazed at her, his big eyes aglow with sympathy. "A fair question," he said. "The answer is, maybe you can. By your actions, you can correct your own past to some extent. In helping us, you may also help yourselves. We would not have approached you, otherwise.

"This is something you must understand. We do not wish to create historical change. On the contrary, we propose to correct changes that have been made by someone else. In mainline probability, Miss Tinsley, the accident that injured you never happened." He turned his gaze to David Frank. "And you, Dr. Frank . . . in the natural course of history your invention was not stifled. It was produced and marketed. The inertial energy conversion device you designed became a technical paradigm. You were the Edison of your age. Gravity lamps and other devices using your system became as universal and omnipresent as automobiles and plastic bags. The gravity light was the safety pin of your era. They were everywhere. Virtually everybody in the world had and used at least one. And because of gravity lamps, the science from which temporal transference evolved was discovered. Your kinetic dynamism—the energy-inertia equation—is the Rosetta stone of Actualist physics.

"Without the worldwide kinetomagnetic field generated by the common use of gravity lamps, the Deep Hole incident in 2009 is simply another Tunguska event—only many times as devastating. A three-dimensional megaplosion resulting from the surfacing of a fragment singularity within Earth's mantel. A physical disaster of enormous proportion, from which the world can never fully recover. A disaster from which no good is derived.

"By present course of events, this is how it will be. But it wasn't that way, before history was altered. Deep Hole occurred, but its spatial devastation was limited, and it gave us the answers to many dimensional riddles. Without Deep Hole and the kinetomagnetic field that channeled most of its force into the fourth dimension, time travel could never have developed.

"We have discovered that we have enemies. There are those who do not want time travel to develop naturally. They have already tampered with the normal sequence of events, to prevent Dr. Frank's discovery from being utilized. They—these enemies of ours—do not want WHIS to ever exist. They want Deep Hole to be simply a geographic cataclysm, throwing the world back into the dark ages.

"Should that occur, it is unlikely that time-travel technology ever will be perfected. Even now, because of their interference with natural history, the probabilities of our very existence—here and now—are decreasing rapidly. WHIS and everything we have done are a diminishing eventuality. An entire future is dying, being smothered by anachronism, and we need your help."

A female Whisper standing just behind Teal edged closer to him and rested her hand on his shoulder. Her name was Toocie Toonine and she was an exquisite, doll-like creature with the largest, darkest eyes any of them had ever seen.

Those eyes now held a desperate plea as she said, "Teal Fordeen speaks only of posterity, but he himself is dying. See the deterioration in his posture . . . on his features."

Instinctively, Jill Hammond moved toward the Whispers, ready to test for pulse and temperature. Then she realized that she didn't know what to observe. Who were these people? How could they be at once so human and so . . . different? Certainly more than random evolution had played a role here.

"What's causing it?" she asked.

Toocie Toonine shrugged. "Age," she said. "He has accumulated too much duration, in missions beyond the loop. Within a closed loop like this, effective duration is minimal. But outside, in ordinary Time2, it occurs. We use a form of retrosynchronic therapy during sleep to counteract its effects. But with the downstream alterations in history, we have lost our continuity link to Sundome. Without linear continuity there is no retrosync. Each exposure to T2 ages us and we cannot reverse it. You must help us! We have no other recourse, except for you."

Each in his own way, the Waystop visitors struggled with it, trying to grasp the enormity of what the Whispers said. In Teal Fordeen they saw the future beginning to unravel.

"You talk about *enemies*," Clay Connors ventured. "Who are these enemies, exactly?"

"Delta," Teal Fordeen said, spreading small expressive hands. "We call them Delta, because those two we have identified are so marked. They carry a sign, like a little tattoo or brand. A small, roughly equilateral triangle. We believe there are at least four of them, and because of their actions and their brands we assume that they are under the control of a fifth entity—some intelligence, whether a single person or a group, that we cannot identify."

"These people travel in time?" David Frank pressed.

"They move in time. They are not timers, but they—or those directing them—have access to transtemporal technology. We believe they use the TEF, just as we do."

Clay Connors's bulldog frown deepened. "If you've only identified two of those people, why do you think there are four?"

Another Whisper, one called Zeem Sixten, stepped forward now to stand beside the Whisper leader. "The things they have done have a pattern," this one said. "The long-range results of their manipulation of history seem to focus on a kind of historical stasis, a changeless future shaped by a private intelligence for its own purposes. The . . . the *pattern* of that stasis is a kind of static infinity, without cultural or evolutionary progress of any kind, possibly forever. Such stasis is—forgive the poetic license here, but the analogy is quite descriptive—a sentence of living death for all future generations of humanity. There will be no hope of anything ever getting better with time, if Delta succeeds.

"The intelligence directing this alteration even signals its intentions. The delta symbol is not only a triangle, it is also one side of a pyramid. And the pyramid is one of the symbols of infinity. It symbolizes stasis—infinity without change."

"Then this *pattern*—" David Frank frowned. "—this is the reason you believe there is a fifth, ah . . . *enemy* controlling the other four?"

"The projections so indicate," Zeem Sixten agreed. "That, and the symbolism itself. An equilateral pyramid—a four-sided pyramid—actually has five sides, you know. The fifth side is the base."

There was silence among them. Then the trucker, Eddie Ridge, raised his hand. He hadn't been specifically invited to this party, but he had tagged along anyway. "So who are these two guys you know about?" he asked. "I mean the triangle ones. You said you know who two of them are."

"We've sent one of our own people to deal with one of them," Teal Fordeen said. "Deejay requested the assignment, and the T2 location is a bit early for any of you now. But the Delta most immediately concerning us—call him Delta One—is a man of your own time, a man most of you know about. In mainstream sequence he was a common psychopath, eventually locked away, but that has been changed. He is quite famous in the 1990s, in the present altered history. At least two of you know him. He is the man who manipulated the acquisition of your gravity lamp, Dr. Frank. As it happens, he is the same man who caused Miss Tinsley's injuries. And you, Miss Blake—" The Whisper's big, sad eyes singled out Daisy Blake, the reporter from WHP New York. "—I believe you know him personally, since you work for him. His name is Carter Vaughn."

"*Carter Vaughn?* But wasn't it Carter Vaughn who sent me here? He—"

"We brought you here," Zeem Sixten corrected. "*We* sent you that message, not Carter Vaughn."

"Carter Vaughn is a Delta," Teal Fordeen said softly. "He has specialized in the elimination of temporal adepts. Now he is eliminating temporal technology."

Behind him a virtual display went dark, then an image appeared there, huge and three-dimensional. A shadowy, deserted warehouse interior, an old automobile with 1959 New Jersey plates, a blood-spattered man in rain gear kneeling beside the corpse of a young woman. The knife in the man's blood-drenched, gloved hand was a filleting blade, as sharp as a razor.

They watched in horror as systematic butchery occurred.

"My God," Tombo whispered.

Beside him Jill Hammond's face went pale as she realized what they were seeing.

"Jesus H. Christ," Eddie Ridge muttered.

Jessica Tinsley covered her eyes with her hands, shaking her head.

The man in rain gear had a face, and the face was one they had all seen many times, on television and in tabloids. But now he wore no concealing makeup, and a little mark was clearly visible just above the bridge of his nose. A quarter-inch tattoo, a simple triangle. For agonizing moments the gruesome scene proceeded, then the virtual screen went dark again and swirling galaxies reappeared.

"What you have witnessed didn't happen in original history," Teal Fordeen said tiredly. "But in history as it stands now, it *did* happen—December 31, 1959, New Year's Eve. The infant's name was Albert Lipscomb. In natural history he was born in February 1960 and was the man who validated Riemann's theories of set point topology. We suspect he also developed autotemporal skills. There are some indications that he might have actually met Archimedes and possibly Euclid.

"Albert Lipscomb was one of dozens of probable timers who now have ceased to exist—to have ever existed—in just this manner. They never entered the altered T2 continuum. They literally were never born. As we may never be, unless this thing is stopped. We have tried to alert timers to the danger, but now the most immediate danger is to us."

"Help us, please," Toocie Toonine murmured.

Daisy Blake's eyes were huge, her face as pale as cold winter. "Why am I here?" she asked, her voice ragged. "I have nothing to do with any of this."

"You have a child," Zeem Sixten said gently. "A little girl, age eight years—"

"How do you know that?"

"We know," the Whisper said. "Just as we know that she is exceptional. Really quite an extraordinary child."

"Yes." Daisy nodded. "She is unusual. She . . . does things. I mean to have her tested . . ."

"Your child is a timer," Teal Fordeen said. "She is just beginning to find her talent. When she does, she will use it, and Delta will know."

"Oh, God," Daisy whispered. "Lucy . . ."

Again there was a silence, then Dr. David Frank straightened his shoulders and pushed his eyeglasses up on his nose. "Timers," he muttered. "*Time travelers*. It's hard to believe. Still, it makes sense. You *timers*—"

"Time explorers," Teal corrected. "We use technology to move among the dimensions. Timers, as we call them, use only their minds."

"Carter Vaughn is no older than I am," Frank pressed. "But that . . . that scene was forty years ago. Is he a timer then?"

"No, he is not a timer. None of the Deltas are, as I said. But they—or someone—has the technology to manipulate dimensions, as we do."

"Then what about these *timers*?" Clay Connors pressed. "Are they helping you in this hunt?"

"We have very little contact with timers." Zeem Sixten shrugged. "We broadcast an alert, which we hope some of them will heed to protect themselves, but what each temporal adept does or does not do is a private decision. Timers rarely find it necessary to associate with us."

"Let me explain," Teal offered. "The timers are not a group, not an organization as we are. They are simply a variety of random individuals who, for some reason, have developed a temporal ability. Some of us theorize that it might have to do with where and when they were born, and with the emergence of gravitational singularities within the Earth's crust. Those components of the brain having to do with balance, home instinct, sense of direction . . . these people may in fact be an evolutionary step. But they aren't a group or a movement. Most of them probably don't even know one another."

"And they are a problem or a threat to *someone*," Zeem added. "Someone—someone with technology like ours—is hunting them down and killing them before they happen. Carter Vaughn is part of it."

"Carter Vaughn ruined me," David Frank said. "What do you want me to do?"

Jill Hammond had drifted away from the group, her stunned attention drawn by the incredible beauty of three-dimensional light patterns within one of the virtual reality displays. She stood apart now, feeling at once dazzled and overwhelmed. Never in her life had she dreamed of anything like . . . like all this. At a tentative tug on her sleeve she started and glanced around. The little Whisper, Toocie Toonine, stood beside her, looking up at her with huge, amused dark eyes.

"The patterns are crustal tectonics." The Whisper pointed. "Pretty, aren't they? We've been plotting the movements of a gravitational anomaly beneath Earth's surface. That's it, there where the reds converge."

"What is it?" Jill asked.

"You might call it a black hole. It's a particle of pure gravity drifting upward from the core. It's what caused . . . will cause . . . Deep Hole in 2003." Toocie smiled. "You were wondering about us, weren't you?"

"Well, yes." She looked at the diminutive size, the bald head, the enormous eyes of the little person. "I understand about you being from the future, but why are you . . . all of you . . . so? . . ."

"Why so different from you? We don't know, exactly. The fact is, we really aren't sure who we are. There is a dark time in our past, when a great deal of what we knew was lost. But we *are* human, Jill. We're as human as you."

"I'm sorry." Jill grimaced, embarrassed. "I was transparent, wasn't I ?"

"Quite understandable." Toocie shrugged. "We must seem very strange to you. The differences are more cosmetic than profound, though. We think we may have been an experiment. Genetically altered morphology. A created race, if you will. Designer people! Somebody made us like we are. Then the earth shook and lands were sundered and we developed in isolation, on a subcontinent that doesn't even exist in your time. Pacifica. Our records—our heritage—were gone. We have theories about our origin, but we really don't know."

"But . . . you have *time*! Can't you just go back and look?"

"No." Toocie's huge eyes went sad. "We can't. There is a wall."

"So you . . . you travel back. Why?"

"We want to see how it all began," Toocie said simply. "We of WHIS have set ourselves a purpose. Somewhere in the beginnings, theoretically, the history of it all was not so defined. We believe there may be more to existence than what elapsed time and human observation have shown. By the way, there is something here that might interest you." Beyond the verge of a screen she pointed and grinned. Jill's eyes widened. It was the missing scale from Paxton Memorial Hospital.

"Here's real technology for you," Toocie Toonine said. "This instrument gave us our first accurate reading of the gravitational anomaly we are tracking."

Waystop I

It was quiet in the Hawthorn house after the transfer to L-383. Outside was turmoil—cranes and winches hooking up to set Eddie Ridge's Kenworth-and-reefer rig back on its eighteen wheels; pallet handlers shuttling refrigerated cheese from the big trailer to an armada of light trucks and cargo vans for transfer to storage in Wichita; uniformed deputies unsnarling traffic in the street beyond the gate; and Pete Swain running here and there, supervising the whole operation.

But inside was comparative serenity. Aleksandr Novik stood guard over the Romanov treasure, deputies Soames and Myers stood guard over Novik, KT-Pi and Peedy Cue stood guard over the TEF chamber, and Jack Higgins with his ever-present long rifle stood guard in the main hall. Beejum was in the backyard, happily dismantling Lucas Hawthorn's John Deere garden tractor while he waited for Curtis Welles to land his ultralight. Everyone was, for the moment, present and accounted for.

Thus it was a bit startling when the patio door opened and two men entered, one of them carrying a large video camera.

Soames and Higgins arrived in the kitchen at the same moment, to head off the intruders.

"No unauthorized visitors," Soames rumbled. "Sheriff's orders."

"Who the devil be you pair?" Higgins demanded. He blinked and half raised his rifle when the second man's battery flood came on and the camera started rolling.

"News media," the first intruder said importantly, speaking distinctly for the lapel mike attached to his coat. "Charles Bronson, KVNU News. I'd like a statement about the situation here . . . get the hillbilly, Buddy. Slow pan from the coonskin to those moccasins, then zoom in on the musket. Great costume. What's this, a party?" He aimed a hand mike at Soames. "Can you tell us what's going on here, officer?" At the sound of oiled steel sliding free, he glanced to his left, at the open doors of the sunporch. Aleksandr Sergeievich Novik had drawn his saber and was moving to block the entry against intruders. "Buddy, swing left! Get Napoleon there. Holy shit! This is wonderful!"

Soames glared at the men. "Get the hell . . . I mean, please turn off that camera and leave these premises! No press coverage! This is a restricted area!"

"Sure, sure . . . we're just . . . Buddy! Zoom on that door there! The kid with the *Star Trek* suit! What's in there, behind him?" Crowding past Soames, Bronson scampered across the kitchen and peered into the TEF chamber. "Hey! An iron floor! Get this, Buddy!"

"Get out of here!" Soames roared.

Peedy Cue skittered back, out of the way, as the cameraman pushed past him, following Bronson. "Is this a problem?" he asked Soames.

"I'm trying to get them out of here!" Soames said. "Sheriff's orders."

"Oh. Well, that's no problem." Peedy turned. "KT-Pi! Preset observation coordinates, random mode! Activate!"

In the TEF control booth beyond the steel-floored former dining room, KT-Pi fingered a control, and the temporal effect focalizer cone on its little derrick glowed slightly. In the chamber, a sudden, slow darkness emerged, followed by a flash of light. Somewhere a little bell rang.

Soames stared into the empty chamber. "Where did they go?" he wondered.

"Some preset observation itinerary." Peedy shrugged. "A tour of historical events. Something the Hawthorns have been refining for their Anywhen, Inc., clients—when they have clients. I'm sure your friends will find it interesting. Coordinates, KT-Pi?"

From the booth, KT's high voice said, "Upstream 137, bilateral topology, previous historic observation ABS-94. That's July 3, 1863, by T2 register. Location, Adams County, Pennsylvania. On the Anywhen, Inc., itinerary it is listed as Pickett's Charge."

Adams County
Pennsylvania, 1863

Charles Bronson was barely aware of the sudden darkening and slowing of the odd room around him. It was abrupt, and even more abrupt was the sudden, blinding flash of light that grew around him and seemed to literally kick him into space. It all happened too fast to think about, even if he had wanted to think about it, which he didn't. His attention was completely occupied by the horde of running, leaping, shouting men all around him—men with big bayonets mounted on big muskets. They swept past him on both sides, close enough to jostle him rudely, and when he glanced around there were more of them—hundreds, thousands, a *sea* of armed men, all coming at him with bayonets.

"Holy shit!" Charles Bronson screamed. "Hit the dirt!"

He dived for the ground, and booted feet thundered around and over him. Someone kicked him, and he shrieked and rolled. He was kicked again, stumbled over, and pummeled, then the ground erupted nearby with the sound of thunder. Dust and debris flew, a burgeoning cloud full of flailing, tumbling men. Bronson rolled again and thudded into the shallow shelter of a rainwater gully half-hidden by tall grass.

The thunder went on and on, deafening explosions that filled the air with dust and acrid smoke. A man without legs fell half-across him, bright blood spraying in the hazed sunlight. Bronson gagged, whimpered, and threw up.

Somewhere nearby, almost drowned in the din of war, Buddy's querulous voice demanded, "What in the name of living hell is going on?"

All around them, men ran, shouted, screamed, and died in great rolls of exploding thunder. Charles Bronson, KVNU Wichita, buried his face in the blood-soaked earth of a Pennsylvania wheat field, covered his ears, and prayed. Six feet away, hidden in the brush of a fallen fence row, Buddy Cline did the thing he did best. His viewfinder glued to his eye, he rolled tape.

∞

Can't think of but one way to defend yourself against an unknown assailant who can hit you yesterday. That's to find him and stop him before he figures out where you were then.

—CLAY CONNORS, Sheriff of Butler County

∞

VIII
Alternate Eternity

Waystop I
Present Time

Curtis Welles's contraption was a study in mixed lineage. Mingled within its design were elements of the box kite, the hang glider, the ubiquitous Frisbee, and the autogyro. It was not yet perfect—not in Curtis's estimation—but one thing was for certain. It flew.

Legally, *Sparrow* was not even an aircraft. As an ultralight, it was considered a toy. It was forbidden by law to fly more than five hundred feet above the ground, though in the wide sky of western Kansas, where nobody was much inclined to meddle, Curtis had assured himself that his bird could climb considerably higher than that. It was capable of a sustained air speed of fifty to sixty miles per hour, and its free rotary airfoils gave it some remarkable attributes: The faster it went, the higher it wanted to be. Against a strong headwind, *Sparrow* headed for the sky. With a tailwind, it hugged the terrain and went—as Curtis said—like a bat out of hell.

And its total weight fully fueled was barely two hundred pounds—a fourth of its takeoff lift capacity.

Only a few minor design problems remained. The worst of them was a fluttering instability that resulted from sudden weight shifts. Curtis had learned to balance the craft with his own body, leaning this way and that to counteract slight variations in *Sparrow*'s equilibrium. But he knew this peculiarity would have to be corrected before others used her.

He had notions of graduating "Death Wish," as his children

108

called his latest toy, into the realm of experimental aircraft with an eye to marketing it. He had already been approached by some people interested in funding the development for a piece of the action. But he hesitated. He shared Tombo Hawthorn's distrust of those busy, covert financial megacorps that seemed to be buying up the world these days, and that ACN outfit seemed to be the worst of them. Curtis had a feeling that ideas as cute and innovative as *Sparrow* might just disappear into the gaping maw of mindless commerce if a man wasn't careful.

He wasn't ready to cast his baby into the shark-infested waters of speculative finance just yet.

Sparrow's little two-cycle engine purred happily as Curtis flew over the spreading Flint Hills and into the airspace of sprawling Eastwood. Rangeland gave way to subdivisions, then to the developed acreages of the comfortably disaffected, and he picked out landmarks and followed avenues.

The lazy sun lay upon the high plains westward when he spotted his destination—a dozen fenced acres facing on an elm-lined residential street, where little clogs of curious traffic crept past wrought-iron gates manned by sheriff's personnel. Beyond the gates were flower beds in a landscaped lawn, and heavy equipment working to right an overturned tractor-trailer rig.

"Gotta be the place," he decided. He circled once, just for the hell of it, then vectored in from the south, aiming at the tree-lined pasture that was Lucas Hawthorn's back lot. *Sparrow* took the crosswind in her wings and fluttered her rotors, then abruptly shuddered and dived as sudden extra weight was added to her frame. Veils of maroon chiffon whipped across Curtis's goggles, blinding him, then were quickly withdrawn. *Sparrow* did a diving figure eight and sideslipped, flaunting her precarious equilibrium.

As Curtis swore and fought to regain control of his craft, a dark-haired young woman settled into the right-hand seat beside him.

"I'm sorry about that," she said. "You must think I'm very rude, just dropping in like this."

He gawked at her. Big, greenish eyes in a pretty face, gauzy evening dress of maroon and black, with pearls at her throat. "Who are you?" he demanded. "How did you? . . ."

"I'm Mandy." She smiled. "Amanda Santee. I'm Maude's sister. And you're Curtis Welles, of course. So this is the famous *Sparrow*!"

"Where the hell did you come from?"

"I was in Argentina," she explained. "Fiesta del Sol, for Juan Perón. Evita was there. But you mean, how did I get here? I'm a timer, Curtis. I'd just as soon you didn't tell everybody that, but it's true. I transferred to *Sparrow* from the roof of the Buenos Aires Sheraton. It's something Lucas and Adam figured out. Time shifts in midair don't leave photogravitic tracks for TEF sensors—or other timers—to pick up."

Curtis got *Sparrow*'s nose up and adjusted her tail foils. "Is that a fact," he growled. "What do you mean, *famous Sparrow*?"

"Well, she will be," Mandy assured him. She pointed. "Someone's waiting for us."

In Lucas Hawthorn's back lot, a scrawny, bearded black man was hopping about, waving a cowboy hat at them. Even from final approach they could see his big toothy grin.

Sparrow bounced happily a couple of times and settled to a stop on newly mown grass. Even before her rotors stopped, the black man was there, studying the craft with shrewd eyes.

"G'day, mates," he said. "Dinkum fine piece o' riggin', this. Yer 'rang wants a proper bow, though. Skips about a bit, wi' out that." He prowled around the ultralight, bright dark eyes tracing its components. Then he stopped, and his grin was one of pure joy. "Lord luv a duck!" he said. "It's got a muffler!"

Pyramid of Khafre
Giza, Egypt

In the grav-lamp light of a sealed vault deep within the massive, ancient stone of Khafre's Horizon, Kaffer refocused his electromagnetic sensors on the minutely dissected human brain spread before him and cursed the limitations of his confinement. He almost had the answers he sought, but all the tools and technology at his command could not take him further.

Here, almost within his grasp, was the secret of true time travel—photogravitic transference at will in four full dimensions, unfettered by the necessity for mechanical stimulation of analogs as the Pacificans did with their gravity-light generator and their temporal effect focalizer.

Here, in the brain of a natural timer, lay the means by which some few extraordinary human minds managed to control the counterpoint flows of light and gravity and reverse the two, creating slow light followed by a wave of new light, driven by gravity unleashed, and thus kick themselves anywhen they wanted to go.

The sensors tantalized him with glimpses of the mystery of timers. The brain of the dimensionally adept differed from the ordinary human brain not in one variation, but in four—in each hemisphere, a slight deepening of the cortical lamina with its associative fibers; a puzzling complexity of the occipital lobe, as though a redundancy of ganglia had developed here; and in the highest frontal lobes, a singularity: the fibrous sheath of the efferent conduits seemed more complex, with some of the neuron paths seeming to go nowhere.

It was a dead brain, like the others he studied. It had no synapses, and thus no certain way to determine their paths.

The variations were tiny, submicroscopic. But they were real, and Kaffer was certain they held the secret of this brain's ability—had it lived—to perceive and manipulate the full range of dimensions. The brain of a *timer*.

He almost had it, but not quite, and the tools to complete the study were beyond his reach.

Damn the Whispers, he fumed. They should never had gotten past the Arthurian Anachronism. They should be safely confined to the far future, where he could deal with them freely. Their very presence in pre-Arthurian times had upset everything.

The existence of timers, in these upstream reaches—of individuals with a natural ability to manipulate dimensions—was something Kaffer could deal with. He suspected their evolution was connected with gravitational variations in the Earth itself. They had no common cause or purpose. They just existed, and he had only to pinpoint that evolutionary change to duplicate their abilities.

He concerned himself with studying them and eliminating them. But they would have been easier to deal with had the Whispers and their stray protomorph, Edwin Limmer, not come along. The very presence in these earlier times of a technological base had given direction to the timers—direction and an understanding of their own powers. And because of it, Kaffer had to work from hiding.

The only defense against a time traveler is secrecy. If a timer can find you, he can kill you—maybe not now, but yesterday. Or last year.

Fortunately for Kaffer, the natural timers occurred randomly and unpredictably. They seemed ordinary children leading ordinary lives until their abilities developed. When they did become timers, he knew them. And knowing them, he could trace their origins. Were it not for the Whispers, he might have systematically exterminated these natural nuisances, ending all threat to himself. Then he would not have been forced to hide in this hole.

He had no doubt that the Whispers were aware of him. They would have discovered him by now, but for this hiding place he had found.

There are places a time traveler cannot go. Specifically, he cannot go where no one has ever been or ever will be. Events in T1 must have a spatial link to events in T2. No loop or conduit penetrates the unreachable. Presence in a physical place where no one can be is a paradox too strong to counteract. The secret vault in the pyramid of the Pharaoh Khafre came close to meeting this specification. It had no entrance. For millennia it had not had one, nor for millennia to come. Unlike the secret places within its larger neighbor, the Pyramid of Khufu, Khafre's vaults would not be found by Weimar-Long's archaeologists in 2014.

Kaffer's trick had been simple. He had *made* an entrance,

for himself. In the sealed vault was a slave TEF and photo-gravitic generator planted while human slaves—Semites, Nubians, and Goths—still labored at the outer casing of the pyramid. The TEF was tuned to L-270's signals and pro-grammed for its resonance. The generator was focused on Sol and the Nordstrom Singularity, with Polaris as point of refer-ence. The analog capacitors were fully charged. There was even a spare TEF from L-270's inventory, hidden in a niche on the stone. When Khafre's escort vault was sealed, Kaffer's means of access was already inside it.

No one now alive except Kaffer himself and those he had recruited—his Deltas—had been inside. So for them there was no paradox. He was here, and could bring them here at will, using the electromagnetic inference of his own TEF. This place existed in their attainable environment. They had been here when there *was* an entrance. For Kaffer, through his slave focalizer, the inaccessible was an open gate.

Within Khafre's Horizon, as its builders had called it, Kaffer was secure from temporal discovery. Secure—and trapped.

Still, he had set in motion the plan that would eliminate the Whispers. It had taken the combined efforts of three of his Deltas to block the proliferation of gravity-transfer devices, and now he was about to lose one of those Deltas. But it was of no consequence. The plan was in effect.

An alarm from his TEF sensor told him the time was now. Delta Two was coming in. Kaffer set his screens and moved to the control console. A shadow among shadows, he waited.

The man who appeared before him was tall, gray-haired, and physically commanding. He was also, obviously, under severe stress.

"I'm discovered," he said thinly. "A . . . a *creature* con-fronted me in an elevator at Roanoke. A little . . . *person* with big eyes. It told me . . . told me it knows what I've done. All those times! It knew about Saigon. The tankers . . . Oswald . . . Greenpeace . . . it knew! It wanted information. Then when I pulled a gun, it disappeared. You have to hide me, Kaffer. I've been loyal to you. Now it's your turn! Put me in another time, or something."

In the shadows, Kaffer's eyes narrowed with contempt. "You poor fool," he said. "You think you can just disappear? *You?* You are an idiot."

"I didn't tell that creature anything! What could I tell it? I don't know who you are. You know that. What do I know to tell?" With awkward hands the man swept his coat back and drew a large gun. "You can't just turn me out!" he shouted. "Not *me*! Consider who I am!"

"You are who I made you," Kaffer toned, his voice as old and dry as the stones around them. With a delicate finger he touched a control, and the man jerked upright, spasms wracking him. On his forehead the tiny triangle glowed slightly, then disappeared. Still jerking and flailing, the man fell. For a long moment he writhed on the metal floor, then he lay still. The gun he had drawn was halfway across the chamber, thrown there by a hand in intense spasm.

"Fool," Kaffer muttered.

Resetting the controls of his TEF, he activated its generator. The little focalizer cone glowed faintly, and beneath it there was an abrupt, slow darkness, followed by instant light, instantly gone.

Kaffer scanned his readings, triggered a photoelectric impulse screen to eradicate the traces of transference from his guest's arrival, then went back to his studies. He did not need to review any events. Those reviews had come a long time ago, in sequential time.

Roland Hedrin, the "Wizard of Pennsylvania Avenue" and trusted confidant to two presidents of the United States, had been found dead in a public elevator in Roanoke, Virginia. The cause of death appeared to be a massive cerebral hemorrhage.

Now there were only three Deltas. But he could recruit replacements easily enough, just as he had recruited Carter Vaughn to replace the mad timer Quark. He would have no more natural timers in his service. He had learned from Quark that they were far too dangerous. There were always ordinary people ready to sell their souls to be extraordinary.

There was no hurry, though. Three Deltas now might be enough. Without David Frank's inertial conversion device, the future events curve was already shifting. Eventualities were changing as the probability of TEF, of the Pacifican findings, even of WHIS itself dipped into a diminishing curve.

Soon—in terms of duration—there would be no future time-travel devices, none in all eternity except for the technology shielded within Kaffer's closed loop. Without technological time travel—without the Whispers—the natural timers would be easy, unsuspecting prey.

By then, he was sure, Kaffer would have the genetic principles behind the timers' talent. And when he had it, he would make it his own talent. No one on earth—past, present, or future—had the genetic-engineering knowledge that Kaffer had collected. The genetic sciences had made vast leaps following the era of fragmentation. In less than four hundred years—from sometime after the Arthurian Anachronism of 2050 to about 2410—genetics had progressed from primitive tampering with DNA formations to a practical art.

Survival alteration—sometimes called enhanced evolution—had been carried to its fullest in the so-called Pacific Age. Then most of the technology had been lost during the vast disruptions that followed the transpolar schism.

Or so it was thought. One extensive set of records remained, hidden away. And Kaffer had those records. Alone and covert, he had carried on the development of genetic science from its frontier of stable mutation to his own discoveries in auto-alteration. Many unsuspecting lives, animal and human, had gone into his experiments. But the end justified the means. He had learned that while corpal autogeneration is inefficient, cranial modification had almost no limitations.

Several hundred innocent people died under his instruments before he was satisfied that he could modify himself. He considered the cost negligible, in view of the results. Any mental capability within human range, he could instill within himself, if he had the proper chromosomal codes. And that, he knew now, included mastery of the four dimensions of existence.

It was during that period of his life that Kaffer decided, privately, that he could be God. He could grant himself the power to shape the world to his own liking.

The technology of those around him gave him the means to control history. His own technology would give him the means to control time.

The codes he needed rested within the brains of a few aberrant individuals gifted with dimensional aptitude. He had collected and studied a variety of these brains. He was very near to finding the genetic key, yet still it eluded him. So, systematically as was his way, he began a new approach.

He had noted that the known timers occurred during a very narrow chronological period. Every one he had found had been born—or at least conceived—between A.D. 1940 and A.D. 1972. There was something in that period of time that had caused these mutations.

Had there been other such periods? On impulse, Kaffer scanned again his records of the Deep Hole incident, the only known gravitemporal occurrence in the history of its time. Every mature timer's origin—among those he had tracked down—was from sixty-three to thirty-one years prior to that event. A significant percentage of them had been born in the great plains of North America. Were there other, later, timers? He didn't know. But possibly there were earlier ones. There had been speculation among the Pacificans that Deep Hole was somehow related to the Tunguska event ninety-one years earlier, in 1908.

Kaffer plotted a time frame prior to 1908. Sixty-three years earlier was 1845. Thirty-one years earlier was 1877. Given fifteen to twenty years for maturity of their skills, then, there might have been timers in central Asia during the period A.D. 1860–1897.

He would scan the histories of that time, and if he found traces of temporal activity, he would send Delta Three to collect some brains.

He was so close now. So very close. He could feel the proximity of success.

The world would be his then, and he would shape it to suit himself. And when it was as he wanted it, he would keep it that way forever. He would choose another name for himself, as he had chosen names before. This time the name he chose would be the name of God.

For eternity. For all infinity.

Kansas
Present Time

Through the sunporch window in Lucas Hawthorn's house, Captain Aleksandr Sergeievich Novik watched the long sunset across the back acres and came to terms with all the strangenesses that had occurred in this almost endless day.

By his reckoning, it was nearly three days since he had watched the dawn break over snow-capped peaks at the cold little bivouac in the Tunguska wilderness. He had never heard of a day lasting so long. *Ahdeen bolshoi dneh!* And so much had occurred since it began—so much that was unexplainable!

It seemed to have begun with his decision to turn southward, toward the rails. The fierce attack by Tatar rebels, as he reviewed it now, should have been no great surprise. Of course, they had been there. They knew that there were limits beyond which an officer of the tsar could not be pushed, and had accounted for that in their strategy. The snipers harassing him had not been simple Irkutsk. They had been Chukchi Tatars, and the trap they laid had been predictable.

That much he might have expected. But the rest of it—no sane man could have imagined anything so bizarre. The great hurtling machine roaring down from the Barzan slopes, as much a surprise to the Tatars as to his own Cossacks. The swinging gate that had caught him, hurled him into the interior of the thing, and then closed itself. The thundering, rattling ride in darkness, clinging to strapped crates of cold cheese, and his final emergence into a land so unlike the place he had been that it boggled the mind—a place where bizarre, unintelligible beings gathered and then disappeared in a room with a steel floor. These things were not natural, he decided.

In his mind's eye he saw again the bearded, fanatic face of Rasputin, and he knew what had transpired. The mad monk with the hypnotic eyes had cast a spell upon him. Even as he looted the tsar's treasures in St. Petersburg, even as he seduced both the empress and her daughter, Rasputin had paused to work his evil magic on his own unwilling courier. Nothing was as it seemed. It was all illusion, the dark magic of the mad monk of St. Petersburg.

But among the mind-clouding weave of sorceries were a few things Aleksandr Sergeievich understood—things like the animals he could see in the distance, beyond the wire-weave fence past the cropped acres. Aleksandr Sergeievich knew horses, and those he could see in that far pasture were fine animals. There were buildings over there, too, and among them must be a tack barn. For such horses, somewhere there were saddles and headstalls.

If he had a good horse under him, a man might ride beyond the sorcerer's images—might emerge again into a wilderness he could understand, and from there make his way to the Trans-Siberian Railway, which led to Vladivostok.

As he gazed out across the distance, thoughtful in the sunset, a thing came out of the sky—a thing like a fluttering, purring mechanical bird. Aleksandr Sergeievich had seen flying machines before—clattering assemblages of struts and guy wires with wide wings stacked like lateral sails—but this was the first he had seen with wings that spun like a windmill.

"Shtoh?" he muttered, curious. *"Ah, da! Mahksin leetyet . . . autochiro,"* he decided, classifying the thing.

It lit in the grassy acres not far away, and the odd black man he had seen before scampered out to meet it. Two people climbed out of the *mahksin leetyet*—a white-haired old man with carriage goggles and a beautiful young woman dressed in fabrics of maroon and black.

They came toward the house, and Aleksandr Sergeievich tried to ignore them, to concentrate on escaping from this mad dream. Yet as they came near, his gaze was drawn again to the woman. She was beautiful. But more than that, she reminded him of someone he had once known.

"Anya," he breathed, suddenly remembering a pretty child first seen long ago. "Anya Karasova Breskin."

A furious part of Aleksandr Sergeievich's mind heaped new curses upon Rasputin for his magics—magics that so tampered with reason that a man imagined things that were not there. The woman in the maroon robes was not Anya Karasova. Beyond her striking eyes, heart-shaped face, and lustrous dark hair, she did not even look like Anya Karasova. Anya Karasova had been hardly more than a child—twelve or thirteen at most—when Aleksandr Sergeievich saw her. She had been among the personal retinue of General Boris Miruslav at the siege of Tsaritsyn in Volgograd Krai.

As a young officer attached to the expeditionary force thrown against *Naradnaya Volska* rebels there, Aleksandr had marveled at the methodical efficiency of the field artillery conducting the siege. He had heard that General Miruslav was a master at force deployment, and at Tsaritsyn he had seen it with his own eyes. The siege had lasted only four days, and the shelling had been a pleasant outing for many aristocratic families. They journeyed from St. Petersburg and Moscow to enjoy the diversion.

A veritable city of gaudy pavilions, markets, and gaming booths had sprung up on a hilltop overlooking the fortified town, and everything from shaded watchtowers to milled-lumber bleachers had been erected there for the comfort of the spectators as they watched the pageantry of crushing military exercise. A Viennese orchestra had performed in the central pavilion each evening, and it was there that he first saw Anya Karasova. She had been one of the brightly gowned young gentlewomen who performed a dance during the entertainment.

Even then, there had been something about her that was not easy to forget. She had danced her ballet segment perfectly, but somewhat mechanically. She had seemed somehow distracted, and in her dark eyes had been a strange look, as though she had just come from some extraordinary experience. The expression had made her seem older than her childish years.

He had seen her a few times more, in St. Petersburg, first with a group accompanying her uncle on an inspection tour, and later in the company of the young Grand Duchess Helena. They were the closest of comrades, it seemed. The two of them, lovely children just entering womanhood, had been like two buds on the same rose stem, just coming to flower. But of the two, it was Anya who remained vividly in his memory. This woman somehow reminded him of her.

Anya Karasova had vanished a long time ago, when Aleksandr Sergeievich Novik was still a lieutenant, stationed in Moscow. He had never quite forgotten her, though. A beautiful girl, certainly, but always in his mind she was a puzzle. From the very first, there had been that mysterious quality about her, as though she knew marvelous and troubling secrets. In her eyes was an odd impression of wisdom—a look of *knowing* that was beyond description. It was almost as though this girl had seen both yesterday and tomorrow.

But on an autumn day in 1899 it was whispered that Anya Karasova Breskin had disappeared. Some said the girl died in a Bolshevik riot in Kiev, but that was only speculation. No one knew—or said—what had become of Anya Karasova.

She was never found. But Aleksandr Sergeievich never forgot her.

The woman from the flying machine had that knowing look, too.

"Kto et-tah?" Aleksandr Sergeievich demanded, not looking around.

Detective Soames didn't understand the words, but the question was clear. "That's Amanda Santee," he said. "She's Mrs. Hawthorn's baby sister."

∞

A little plain logic would be useful now and then. But in a world of conditioned reflexes, a little logic can be damned hard to find.

—TOMBO HAWTHORN

∞

IX

Pursuance

Benedictions had sounded in the cathedrals of St. Sophia and St. Vladimir an hour before. Now evening twilight hung over the Dnieper as the last of the riverside cart-merchants made their way up the steep switchback paths leading to the old streets above the river, while boatmen tended their nets in the shallows flanking the abutments of Petrov Bridge. Over on the low east bank, the lights of the village of Poznyaki cast twinkling reflections across the chill water.

In the city atop the high west bank, squadrons of brightly uniformed Imperial Guards patrolled the old streets around the Lavra while gilded carriages rolled along the lighted avenues leading to Kiev Tsenteh, the new theater and arts district. The Feast of St. Andrew this year featured the opening of a touring company production of Tchaikovsky's *Swan Lake*. After four years of performance at St. Petersburg, as well as in several European capitals and even in America, the acclaimed ballet had come at last to the Russian provinces. It had been performed at Moscow and Odessa, and now was opening in the "Mother of Towns," Kiev.

The occasion was virtually an event of state, corresponding as it did with a visit to Kiev by the Grand Duke Vladimir and his daughter, Helena. Thus a grand entourage of notables from the court of Tsar Nicholas II was in Kiev for the formalities.

At seventeen, the Duchess Helena was a comely, vivacious creature full of the capricious zests of her age and station.

Though surrounded by hawk-eyed matrons of the court, she craved adventure. And in this quest she had a loyal ally. Anya Karasova Breskin, the niece and ward of General Boris Miruslav, was Helena's age, and the formidable pair had made a high art of escapades. It was the profound wish of many in the House of Romanov to get both of them safely married off before they did irreparable damage to the Russian Empire. There was even talk of a union of Helena with the Prussian prince, Ferdinand, or possibly with Nicholas of Greece. But these were no more than rumors.

Attempts had been made to separate the terrible twosome of St. Petersburg for their own good, but it seemed there was no keeping them apart. Thus on this expedition to Kiev, it was no surprise that the Grand Duke's party had, as its military escort, General Miruslav's own crack Cossack Dragoons, with the general himself appointed as liaison.

"Gdyeh Helena, tahm Anya," the matrons said, shaking their heads. Where Helena is, there, too, is Anya.

Glittering pavilions lined Thoroughfare Constantin where it approached Kiev Tsenteh. Here *ahtdyelak* merchants displayed their wares amidst a torchlit montage of balalaika performers, jugglers, Pecheneg dancers, acrobats, and trained bears.

Imperial Cossack horsemen pushed their haughty way through the crowds, clearing the way for the coaches of the nobility, while hard-eyed soldiers of the tsar formed a human barricade against the surging proletariat. The gaudy uniforms of the soldiers in line only emphasized the contrast between the glittering elegance of the nobility and the ragged garb and pinched faces of those they ruled.

In a great coach midway back in the parade, Helena Vladimiyevna's bright eyes gleamed with excitement. "See the dancing men, Anyitsa!" She pointed. "Such strong legs! Such shoulders! Oh, I want to stop here!"

"It is not safe, Imperial Highness," a matron cautioned. "These are troubled times."

Anya Karasova had been as excited as her friend at the lights and the music. But now, abruptly, she felt troubled. An urgency prodded at her mind, a dread that seemed to come from those dreamscape realms that were her private puzzle, and to crawl along her spine like rivulets of ice water. She peered left and right at the pressing crowds, then lowered her head. Abruptly, in and around the coach, there seemed a darkening—a slowing of all movement as though one had narrowed one's eyes for a moment and held in view what had just been seen. The flash of light that followed was so brief, so intense, that it barely registered on the senses of even the most alert and intuitive of those around them.

An instant only, then it was gone, but in that instant Anya Karasova had changed her position in the carriage. She had been sitting sedately beside Helena on the coach's high seat, directly in front of the armed bootmen on the rear pedestal. But now she was half-turned, not sitting but crouching, and she grabbed Helena by the arm. "Get down!" she snapped, literally pulling the grand duchess from her seat to the floor of the coach.

A bullet from somewhere ahead slapped the cushions where Helena's shoulders had rested and slashed through the wood panel behind. A bootman screamed, folded over, and pitched headlong from the coach. Then the night was alive with the barking of guns and the shouts of people. To the left and ahead, the festive crowds evaporated as though by magic, and wild-eyed men with blazing guns stormed through—directly into the path of the Cossack Dragoons.

The soldiers reacted instantly. As though of one mind they spread in a wedge-shaped line and charged. Ahead of them, men in the drab wrappings of laborers held fast for a moment, brandishing rifles, axes, and scythes, then fell like wheat in the harvest field as the Cossacks swept through them—through and back, their horses wheeling as on a parade ground, guns roaring, flashing sabers red with gore.

Behind them along the avenue, Imperial Guards pushed into the scattering crowds, firing their repeating rifles almost at random. From the rear, dragoons and lancers thundered forward to clear the fray. Again there was that odd instant of slowing, of darkening, followed by a flicker of intense light too quick for the senses to register. This time, no one noticed at all.

The din and fury of battle cloaked the instant occurrence in confusion.

It was all over in less than a minute. The crowds had disappeared into smoky darkness, leaving scores of dead and injured on the cold ground behind them. Some of the casualties obviously were proletarian assassins. Many more were only bystanders, caught unaware by the sudden fury of a terrorist attack.

The Imperial troops reformed around the cluster of carriages to assess the damages. The attack had centered on the grand duke's coach at the head of the line, though other vehicles had taken fire. Four carriage occupants and seven liveries were dead, a dozen others slightly injured. Splintered railings and gouges in fine lacquer showed where bullets had scored the coaches. Several horses lay dead in their traces. But incredibly, not a single member of the nobility had been touched—though for a few minutes some of them, including the Grand Duchess Helena, were unaccounted for.

Helena Vladimiyevna was unhurt, though. She was found almost buried under a pile of quaking servants and matrons on the floorboard of her coach.

In the confusion, it was twenty minutes before Helena noticed the absence of her best friend. "Anya?" she called, looking around at the littered, trampled thoroughfare. "Anya Karasova? Anyitsa? *Gdyeh Anya?*"

The search, organized by General Miruslav himself, was thorough and exhaustive. But eventually they gave up. Anya Karasova was gone, not to be seen again.

He didn't know exactly where he was. He was wherever and whenever Kaffer sent him, as usual. But he knew who he was and what he was to do. In the shadows beneath Petrov Bridge he waited, watching as the last stragglers of evening made their way up the steep paths to the high streets above the river. At his belt, hidden by the heavy coat he wore, was a long, thin knife as sharp as a surgeon's scalpel. But this time he would not require the knife. This time he would use the charged hypodermic needle in his sleeve, and the large sack folded over his shoulder—a drawstring sack like those the fishermen carried sometimes, to bring their catch up from the river.

Kaffer wanted this one alive.

Atop the high west bank the man blended with the traffic on darkening old streets and headed for the lighted avenues not far away, where torches danced and gay music swelled above the din of crowds. On the outskirts of the crowd he noticed furtive movements here and there, men with covered weapons converging on the lit way. Carefully, with his free hand, he drew out a little gray object smaller than a playing card and concealed it in his palm. Tiny lights danced upon its face, doing a countdown.

He was almost at the main thoroughfare—part of a waving, gesturing crowd held back by soldiers—when the thing in his hand tingled and made a tiny blip. His trained senses noted the strange slowing and darkening, followed by the instantaneous flash of brilliant light, and he took advantage of the blinking eyes before him to sidle through the line of guards. The carriage he sought was only yards away—a high-booted coach with footmen, where a brightly clad girl sat on the high rear seat while another dazzlingly clad nymph crouched beside her, reaching for her arm. The girl on the high seat was pulled down, into the floor cavity, and several other women fell on her there as gunfire erupted all around.

In an instant, all was chaos, and he used the confusion to leap to the coach. Drawing his hypodermic he flung open a panel, then blinked as the dark, knowing eyes of the second girl faced him squarely and again there was that instant of dark slowness followed by brilliant light. He heard a distinct pop just beyond his reaching fingers, and they closed . . . on nothing at all. The girl was gone.

A rifle shot whined past his ear, and he ducked barely in time to avoid a thrusting bayonet from the side. With one more puzzled glance at the interior of the coach, he threw his tow sack into the face of an approaching soldier, turned, and ran. As he ran he thumbed a spot on the little gray wafer in his pocket. Agonizing seconds passed as he ducked this way and that, past screaming knots of people, heading for the darker streets beyond. He rounded a corner, slid to a halt as a squadron of mounted dragoons thundered toward him, then the odd slowing sensation came again, and this time it seemed to carry him with it. The scene around him faded and blinding light engulfed him—light that picked him up and flung him ahead of its tide.

"I was right!" Kaffer muttered. "A fully functional timer in 1899 . . . a decade before Tunguska." From the ancient shadows, his voice was thin and angry as he addressed the big man standing thirty feet away on the steel slab in the center of the rock vault. "How did she escape you?" he demanded. "You should have been there the instant her transfer was reversed."

"I was there," the man said. "But she was too quick. She saw me and she did it again. She jumped to somewhen else."

"Then she must have known why you were there," Kaffer rasped. "She must have seen it all, in that first occurrence."

"So she got away." The man frowned. "You said yourself, if there's one, there will be others. Find another one."

In the shadows, Kaffer hissed. "Protomorph idiot!" he shrilled. "That girl is a timer, and she saw you! What makes you think she didn't also see where you went? She might even trace you here! I don't know what these rogue talents can do. We have to find her now, and you have to kill her! I have . . . ah! I have a trace! Name of the numbers, what power she has! Find her now, Cantrell! Find her and kill her!"

Kaffer set his controls, touched his panel, and the TEF above the steel slab glowed. Cantrell disappeared in a darkening and a light.

She didn't know what this thing was that she did. She had never known, except that since childhood the feeling had been there, that there was far more in this world—even the parts of it that were her daily life—than her eyes could see or her ears could hear. It was as though she had become gradually aware of a superficiality in everything, the way drawings on paper are superficial, the way a painting—though it may fool the eye— lacks the depth that a sculpture has. In just this way, Anya

Karasova had come to feel that everything was more than it seemed. Everything had hidden depths, extensions in secret directions, if only one could see them.

Eventually, she had realized that she *could* see beyond what was displayed. It was all in how one looked at things.

There *was* more to the world than the untrained senses discerned. And realizing this, she realized also that she could . . . could *move* herself in directions that others could not even see.

It was a skill, she decided. She had practiced it, gradually becoming more adept. She had even tried to share the skill with Helena Vladimiyevna, but the grand duchess was unable to grasp it. Discussing it with her tutors had been pointless. Fra Dominik had simply gone glassy-eyed and changed the subject. Madrika Jeshua had muttered incantations and ordered Anya to double her prayers and study the catechisms.

Sometimes Anya felt like a mink among ferrets. Was she different, or was everyone else different?

Still, cautiously, she practiced the shifting thing, fascinated by it. She could see what happened before it happened. All she had to do was go there and look. But then they had journeyed to Kiev and set out for the ballet. En route something had told Anya that she should look ahead. She did, and she saw Helena die. More than that, there was a big man with a needle and a sack . . .

She knew she had saved the life of Helena Vladimiyevna by pulling her from the path of a bullet. And she knew she had saved herself, as well, by flinging herself blindly into the maelstrom of incredible, driving light that her talent called forth. The power of it—fully unleashed by terror—had been stunning. She had never felt such a surge.

Now she found herself in a place that was like no place she had ever seen, and she didn't know where she was.

The land around the terraced hilltop where she stood, for all its grandeur—forested rises sloped in all directions, and a pretty waterfall nearby caught the high sunlight like exploding diamonds—looked compact. It had a neat, tidy appearance, like a miniature landscape on a dollhouse stage. A self-contained little world, as though nothing in the world was either unaccounted for or very far away.

In neat, contoured fields along the lower slopes and in the little valleys, tiny people worked. And on the crest of a hill beyond the nearest valley stood a castle like no castle Anya had ever seen. It was ornamented in brilliant, delicate colors, and its sloping roofs flared outward at the eaves like the skirts of ballet dancers.

She was alone on the hill where she stood, and had just started to make her way down the slope to where the people were when something familiar registered in her mind. It was a sensation like the dark-to-light sensation that always accompanied her visits to yesterday or tomorrow, but somehow different. It had a cold, mechanical feeling about it . . . and it was not hers.

Anya Karasova turned, and there was a man where she had been. With a gasp, she recognized the big man from the Kiev boulevard, the one with the sack and the needle. The one who—in her first view of him—had done something bad to her. This time he carried no sack, no needle, but at sight of her he drew a long, slim knife and started toward her. Cold dread sprang alive in Anya's heart, and she turned to run—and tripped. She rolled, saw the man bearing down on her, raising his knife, and once again she willed herself away. Sudden slowness, darkness, and driving light, and again she found herself in another place.

It was nighttime—a murky, sodden night with its low-cast sky full of fire and thunder. Great shafts of light swayed and danced in the clouds above, where winged monsters flew.

Anya picked herself up from the wet, sooty pavement, staring around with eyes gone huge. Distant explosions rolled across the night like devil drums, and everywhere the sky was alight with piercing beams and exploding shells. A barrage like nothing she had ever experienced, even during the shelling of Smolensk by her uncle's troops. She was in a deserted street, surrounded by the looming silhouettes of empty-looking buildings. The damp, cold air was ripe with smells of acrid smoke and sewage. All around, sirens and Klaxons wailed hollowly, and through their chorus she could hear the constant, throaty growl of the dark, winged things sweeping overhead.

Suddenly someone had her by the hand. Strong fingers on her small fingers in a firm, gentle grip. She screamed and tried to do the shifting thing again, but it was countered, overridden somehow by a stronger will.

The man holding her was tall, dark-haired, and seemed to exude a gentle strength. "Not like that, Anya Karasova," he said, and even though his words were in some language other than hers, she understood him.

"Like this," he said. Abruptly the slowing, darkening sensation came, much stronger than she had ever known before, and the cresting wave of blinding light that followed it was not a random push but a pure, directed force.

The exploding, reeking city was gone. They stood together in a cold, bouncing cylinder lined with shadowy metal beams and curved girders. It was a dark, cramped space, full of looming shapes. The only light came from little clusters of winking lamps where shadowy people lurked, and from flares of light coming through little windows, accompanied by deafening explosions. Anya leaned to peek out of one of these windows, then reeled back. The view she saw was hell, seen from above. She was inside a broad-winged flying machine, looking down at devastation below. A city burned and blazed there, alive with great, exploding fires.

At a console, one of the shadowy people turned and gawked at them—a young man in uniform, with earphones on his head. "*Was ist los?*" he demanded. "*Ist verboten! . . .*"

The tall man smiled reassuringly, put a hand on the young German's shoulder, and deftly coldcocked him with a short punch to the temple. "Sorry, Hans," he said as the uniformed one slumped in his seat, out cold. The man loosened a buckle and lifted off a belt with a holstered pistol on it. "Luftwaffen Luger," he said. "Good, functional, ugly piece of hardware." His hand tightened on Anya's, and again there was the slow-dark-fast-light shifting sensation.

Anya opened her eyes. They were in a pleasant room in a little house on a tree-lined street. A lazy afternoon breeze stirred lace curtains at a window. There seemed to be no one else there but them, yet the man beside her seemed to fit the place, as though he had always known it.

Still gripping her hand, he said, "You've been lucky, Anya Karasova. Cantrell tried to chase you, but now he can't find you, so he'll backtrack. He has time. But then, so do I. You just stay put while I see what I can do."

Even in her confusion, she noted again that his words meant nothing to her. They were not *pa-Russkyi*. They were in a foreign language. Yet as he gripped her hand, she understood their meaning. She was to remain here, to wait for him.

"Shtoh? . . ." She turned, gazing up into knowing dark eyes. *"Kahk vas zahvut?"*

For a moment longer he held her hand. "I'm Adam," he said. "I'm a timer, like you." Then he released her and stepped away. An instant of darkening and light, barely perceptible, and he was gone.

Anya looked around the house, no longer surprised at anything she might find. It was not a large house, but it was tidy and comfortable, and it had conveniences she barely recognized—basins with running water faucets, *elektryik* filament lamps, a commode with a water closet. Such things were known to her, but existed only in the more elegant buildings where . . . or when . . . she was from.

Sitting beside a curtained window she watched wonderful *mahksins* roll along the paved street beyond. Anya Karasova had seen automobiles before, but only two of them—puttering, bizarre little contraptions displayed as toys on Grovnik Square in St. Petersburg. Here, though, there seemed to be dozens of them—gleaming, efficient-looking vehicles operated casually by common people.

She noticed that each *mahksin* wore numbered metal plates front and rear, apparently to identify it. Idly, she noted the inscription on one of these as it rolled past: sw-898. And in smaller characters, in the Roman alphabet commonly used in the western nations: KANSAS, 1954.

∞

The human brain is a data process device so far superior to any computer ever conceived by mankind that comparing the one to the other is like comparing the universe to a stick. It is believed that approximately 12 percent of the brain's functioning capacity is utilized in conscious thought, and another 17 percent in maintenance and direction of all the body's functions from basic metabolism to walking, talking, and using tools. Thus we account for 29 percent of the brain's activities. The remaining 71 percent of what this remarkable organ is doing at any moment is a mystery to us.

And within the physical functioning of the brain exists yet another, infinitely more complex phenomenon: the mind. We know almost nothing about what a mind is, let alone how it works.

—J. WILLIAM NAGENT, PH.D.

Institute of the Humanities

∞

X
Encounters

Hansford County, Texas
May 3, 1947

"I'd give a dollar for an honest drink of well water right now," Clyde growled. "I swear I swallered a tadpole just then."

Beside him, squatting on the mud bank of Hackberry Creek, Hank muttered something unkind about his flashlight and slapped it with a hard hand, then played its faltering little glow on the muddy water. The flashlight was genuine U.S. Army surplus, but so were the old batteries in it. It emitted barely enough light for a man to fart by.

"Wasn't likely a tadpole," he pointed out. "Too early in the year for tadpoles. You prob'ly just swallered a minnow."

"I believe I know a tadpole when I taste one," Clyde said. "Take off your shirt an' I'll strain some water through it."

"Use your own damn shirt," Hank grumped. "Mine's all I got between me and th' chills." He selected a patch of muddy water, put his flashlight away, cupped his hands, and drank. "Gawd," he admitted. "That's awful. Tastes like cow manure."

"Wouldn't be surprised," Clyde agreed. "That's about all there is around here, is cows."

The last glow of twilight was fading across the western hills, and a cool night breeze whispered across endless miles of sagebrush and short grass. Henry Ford stood dark and lifeless atop the low cutbank behind the men. The battered old car hadn't set wheels on a real road in years, but Hank swore it knew every section of the Lazy K by heart. It had left a fender wedged between rocks down on Cow Creek, lost its muffler on top of Indian Hat, and dribbled various small parts over half of the Panhandle. It had survived storms, sideswipes, and gullies, had herded cattle and hauled fenceposts. Henry Ford was a proud, scarred veteran of many a rough-and-tumble season on the Lazy K. Yet now it sat dejected, brought down by a cracked distributor cap.

The tall, misshapen silhouette it presented now against a vast and starry sky was only partly automobile. The rest of it was a huge stack of porcelain toilet fixtures on their way to Lazy K headquarters.

" 'Nother goddamn beautiful evening," Hank allowed, scanning the sky from beneath a floppy old hat. "Not a cloud in sight, an' just look at them stars!"

"Dry as a bone," Clyde agreed. "I swear this whole country's gonna just dry up an' blow away. Guess Willie won't be back before mornin'. Prob'ly had to hitch all the way to Amarillo to find a distributor cap."

"More likely headed for Dumas." Hank shrugged. "But I reckon he'd have to stop off at Sunray to say howdy to Miss Polly Baker. I got dibs on the backseat, Clyde. You sleep on the floor. Land, I don't know when I seen such stars! There's the Big Dipper, an' the Seven Sisters, an' just look at that Milky Way! It's bright as a calèche road!"

"I seen stars," Clyde grumped. He walked around Henry Ford, checking the ropes on the load of plumbing fixtures. He loosened a few knots and removed a pair of threadbare old quilts used for packing. "Three commodes!" he growled. "You know anything about installin' commodes, Hank? What do they run on?"

"Water." Hank shrugged. "Just water, is all."

"Water." Clyde shook his head. "I'd give a dollar for a drink of clean water right now." After a moment of silence, he turned to his friend. "Hank? I got us quilts here. I . . ."

Hank stood like a man frozen, staring into the northern sky. Clyde squinted at him, then followed his gaze. The thing he saw there, coming out of the north and moving faster than anything he had ever seen before, was no star. It was bright and it was big, and it kept getting bigger as it approached.

"What the hell is that?" he hissed.

Closed Loop L-270

Closed Loop L-270 entered the maelstrom of time storm in the solstice of 2999. It was the fourth and largest expedition of its kind—a direct assault on the violent perpetual paradox known as the Arthurian Anachronism, centered at Time2 coordinates ES: 37° 2'N, 101° 0' W, 3,533' sel., T2 04-14-2050, 1200 LT.

L-270's approach to Arthur's Infinity was conceived and developed by the eminent temporal theorist 3RB4ST, known as Arby Forrest, under a grant from the World History Investigative Society. Forrest's idea was, simply, to attempt penetration of the anachronism by static navigation of a single dimension—time. Thus L-270, while fully empowered and equipped for quadrilocal displacement, began its journey at the exact physical site where the time storm existed, but 499 years later in T2.

The massive closed loop was founded geographically on the site of Deep Hole, where the twin temporal effect focalizers (TEFs) of Arthur Rex and Edwin Limmer had counterresonated to create the Arthurian Anachronism in 2050. It was the site of King Arthur's Camelot, the seat of the old Panhandle Federated Free Zone, headquarters of the Institute for Temporal Research and site of the ITR takeover from which Arthur arose in 2029 to become Arthur Rex in 2033.

Here, at this place, was the essence of dimensional volatility. Here had been Deep Hole, where the raw universal force of dimensionality was first captured on Earth. Here, too, was the epicenter of the perpetual time storm that was Arthur.

Here L-270 was created, by reversing the photogravitic polarity of a dedicated T1 conduit until it met itself tomorrow. The resulting temporal loop was self-regenerating and equipped with all the life supports and shields Whisper technology could provide. Its mission was upstream penetration of the anachronism, to serve as an anchor for creation of an open conduit from the future to the past.

3RB4ST—Arby Forrest himself—took charge of L-270 with 1LMPV9 as chief chronologic navigator, 14IVXM as resident quantum theorist, and 610LBE as field tactician. The crew of forty-seven was expanded to include several WHIS liaison personnel and an observer from the Universal Experience Bank, a brilliant historian and genetic theorist named 1KHAF4. As UEB's designate, a defined portion of L-270 was set aside as quarters and laboratory for Khaf Four and his assistants, shielded from the rest of the loop by virtual reality fields.

Arby Forrest did not like the arrangement, and he didn't like Khaf Four. The historian was a remote, uncommunicative individual, and Arby suspected he had no interest in any proceedings but his own. Still, it was the will of UEB, and Arby kept his peace.

On the twenty-first day of the sixth month of the year 2999, Loop-270 closed itself, becoming a temporal blur with a three-hour light-speed resonance. It locked its locii on three physical dimensions and activated its TEF field. Enormous, exquisitely balanced forces—raw gravity and undiluted light converted to their electromagnetic analogies of pure magnetism and whole-spectrum illumination—saturated the loop with equal and opposite fields, and the TEF synchronized their reversal. Time quite literally stopped in L-270 as the forces changed places, becoming in the instant a black hole, a matrix of slow light, and a tidal wave of pure, inconceivable radiance that swept the entire singularity ahead of it—back into time past at light speed times nine.

L-270 hit the anachronism head-on, braced by three-dimensional stasis. The event was too violent and too brief for human synapses to register, though in that instant L-270's sensors noted, and its banks stored, more data on broad-range eventuality than the entire archive system of UEB had in its collective banks.

The moment L-270 hit the time storm—potentiality colliding with improbability—its occupants knew they had succeeded. L-270 was upstream from the anachronism, free of its swirling paradoxes, a fully functional T1 phenomenon adrift in pre-Arthurian history. They also knew, within moments, that they were in temporal lock and their tangible-dimension anchors were gone. Instead of resonating securely on Arthur's castle, or in the commons of ITR's complex, they were drifting southward over a star-lit, treeless landscape at a ground speed in excess of six hundred miles per hour and an altitude of about eighty feet.

Whispers scrambled to their virtual screens and readouts. In T2 locus, L-270 had materialized in the spring of the year 1947, above the rolling plains of the upper Texas Panhandle. Remarkably, for a temporal loop, the phenomenon was tracking exactly this section of Time2 while it drifted just above earth's surface.

"The anachronism chewed us up and spat us out," Arby Forrest decided. "And it left us with an anomaly—a temporal loop fixed in time. We are *somewhen*."

"Somewhen in pre-Arthurian time," Elem Peevy noted. "Mission accomplished."

"Only the first part of it," Sixten Elby corrected him. "Without T2 variation, our matrix will collapse. We'll be nothing but castaways in this time if we lose our loop. Can we maintain?"

Virtual screens blanked, the Whispers peered out at a sight never before seen from a closed temporal loop—observable scenery. In a night filled with stars, wide prairies rolled past just below. Here and there in the distance were little clusters of lights—small towns, ranches, creeping brightnesses where lonely vehicles moved along a narrow, paved road.

"Indigenees," Khaf Four muttered, to no one in particular. "Pre-Arthurian protomorphs. An opportunity for hands-on study. First samples."

"We're drifting in the second dimension," Ivy pointed out. "We're that close to paradox! Only this motion keeps us from stasis!"

"There's only one thing to do," Arby pronounced. "If we can't regain our temporal variance, we'll have to stop and regenerate."

"There are no records of a closed loop shutting down," a UEB observer noted. "We have no precedent."

"But we have the tools," Arby decided. "Given a fixed base in three dimensions, we'll try to regenerate L-270."

"I hope we can," Sixten Elby muttered fervently.

"I'd like to gather some samples of indigenous intelligence while we're here," Khaf Four said.

"No sampling!" Arby ordered. "Remember the prime directive. We are to traverse history, not alter it! Slow to a stop and put us on the ground, Elem. Everyone! Stand by to generate closed loop!"

Hansford County, Texas

Speechless with wonder, Hank and Clyde crouched beside Henry Ford on the bank of Hackberry Creek and watched the thing's approach. Desperately, they tried to place it in some semantic context that they could understand. Lights, shapes, colors, proportions—their eyes saw all of these, but nothing in their experience equipped them to explain what they saw, even to themselves.

The thing was *big*! Big as a thundercloud. Bigger than any . . . thing they could imagine floating in the sky. And it was *bright*— yet with a dizzying brightness that seemed to shift, to change from instant to instant. It was as though the thing was made of light and darkness, a huge bubble of swirling patterns that kept changing too quickly to see. Whatever it was, it was coming right at them. But not so fast now. It was slowing. For a moment it seemed to hover, almost directly overhead. Then with huge solemnity it drifted downward. It settled on the ground a hundred yards away, just beyond Hackberry Creek. It settled, seeming to flatten itself into the very ground. Then it disappeared.

Clyde and Hank blinked, looked at each other, then turned their attention again to the expanse across the creek. Where the . . . the *thing* had been, now there were clusters and piles of dark shapes in the starlight, and little people scurrying around, some of them carrying lights. They heard voices—chattering, clipped-sounding voices like a lot of children talking all at once, and talking very fast.

Stray beams of light illuminated individuals here and there, and Hank gawked at what he saw. The little people even *looked* like children . . . but not exactly. There was nothing random or playful in the pattern of their movements. They seemed to know exactly what they were doing.

They were all dressed alike, in some kind of jumpsuit garment, and they had the biggest eyes the men had ever seen. And they were bald as cue balls.

"Jesus Christ!" Clyde muttered.

A beam of light shot out, played over the two men and their old car, and one of the creatures broke off from the rest, trotting toward them. It had almost reached the creek bank when a high voice was raised behind it, and it stopped and turned. The voice came again, sharp and commanding. The creature across the creek hesitated, played its light over them again, then turned away and went back to its companions.

Long, breathless moments passed, then the crowd of creatures tightened, coalesced around their stacks of whatever, and a glow grew around them—a glow like the ghost of the great, brilliant bubble that had brought them here.

The glow faltered, dimmed, then grew brighter. Suddenly it was again a huge, swirling radiance of shifting patterns—a great, bright saucer quivering and shining with vitality. Within it, radiances grew, then everything about it seemed to dim and ponder . . . like light slowing toward darkness.

The process accelerated in a heartbeat. From brilliance to black void, an instant in transition, then light so bright it was beyond perception flared across the miles, and with a crash like sudden thunder the whole thing was gone. Except for an odd, singed circle in the grass prairie where it had sat, it was as though the phenomenon had never been there at all.

Long moments passed. Finally Hank drew cool prairie air into his aching lungs. He didn't recall having taken a breath anytime lately. His throat felt as dry as dust, and his eyes were moist. "Did you see that, Clyde?" he rasped, hardly more than a whisper.

For a long time, Clyde didn't respond. Then he shifted his frozen gaze, shuffled his feet, and turned away to lean against Henry Ford.

"No," he said. "No, I don't believe I did."

L-270

L-270 lived again, and the crossing of the anachronism had given them new knowledge. For a time they tested the loop, shifting into stasis in one dimension and then another, pressing the theories to see how they stood up in the field. By releasing linkage with one or another of the spatial dimensions, they found that a temporal loop can endure normal T2, if only for a limited duration.

Spatially, they centered their tests around the geographic area of Deep Hole, flitting here and there in short-range time for repeated durational experiments. To startled indigenees who witnessed these tests, L-270 was an almost indescribable phenomenon that would appear in the sky at random times and places, sometimes momentarily stationary, sometimes moving at erratic speeds and in unlikely directions. These UFO sightings were reported and described in various ways, with one analogy repeating itself—*saucer*.

To the unprepared observer, outside the loop, L-270 often had the appearance of a big, whirling, radiating saucer. And sometimes it left tracks where it had been—marks on the ground, artifacts, bits of debris. These things only added to the mystery.

The most baffling of these findings was a crash site. What was found there was the shattered remains of what might conceivably have been an aircraft of some kind, and four dead creatures—creatures like small, bald people with big eyes. Paranoid officialdom landed on this finding as a hawk lands on a hare, closing doors, hushing the matter. Just as a number of other peculiar discoveries had been hidden, so was this. Little

was generally known about the incident, beyond the specula-
tions of a few creative souls whose words could be dismissed
as the result of overactive imaginations.

L-270 had learned truths about anachronism—specifically the
revelation that dimensions are interchangeable and mutually
dependent. But L-270 could not communicate these findings
downstream without a conduit. Without allowance for the new
principles by those downstream, L-270 could not anchor a
transanachronistic conduit.

Arby Forrest, Sixten Elby, and Elem Peevy worked constantly to find answers, while Ivy and others of the team put
L-270 through its tests. With each new finding, the loop itself
became stronger and more self-reliant, a little world of its own
existing just beyond known dimensions, regenerating itself
moment by moment.

On the most far-flung of the tests, L-270 emerged into spa-
tiality in a period so far ahead of history that the only living
things registering on the nightmare landscape of the virtual
screens were microscopic single-celled organisms swimming
in soups of mineral brine, smoke haze, and methane. Here the
sensors revealed temporal anomalies.

"Gates and bridges," Sixten called them. "It's as though
eventuality runs rampant at this stage. Anything can happen,
and usually does. The probabilities for downstream are limit-
less. It's evolution time."

"Gates and bridges." Arby nodded. "We may be seeing the
reality of parallel timelines here, but what becomes of them
downstream?"

"Some disappear," Sixten said. "Some just fade out as their
probability declines. It could be that some of them weave
together again in the future, and that fits our theories. We
know that T2 isn't a single strand, but a woven bundle of
probabilities . . . like a rope."

"And if even one of those probable strands passes 2050
independently, before weaving back into mainstream, then we
have a link to the future." Elem grinned. "Maybe there's a
timeline out there that doesn't have an Arthur in it."

"It's worth trying," Arby decided. "I want a comlink message implanted in every T2 eventuality we can identify. Tell WHIS what we have found here. Give readings, and submit our equations on the transanachronism problem. If we're right, the link will go through. It's just a matter of time."

There was another matter, though, that still required attention. It was a matter of housekeeping, basically, but it was annoying. Ever since L-270's first materialization in pre-Arthurian time, their maintenance sensors had been detecting unexplained periodic changes in onboard mass. Now with time on their hands, the crew conducted a search and analysis of the entire closed link.

"We've found nothing," Ivy reported at a command assembly. "We've searched everything except the sealed quarters of our UEB personnel."

"Then we must investigate there, too." Elem shrugged. "*Something* is altering our contained mass. We have to know what it is."

Khaf Four glared at the other Whispers around him. "You will leave my space alone," he said. "That is UEB territory."

"Which reminds me." Arby's big eyes narrowed in speculation. "Where are your assistants, Khaf Four? They have not registered on signal-roll since we left the middle twentieth century."

"They are not your concern," Khaf Four snapped. "They were assigned to me."

"Everything about L-270 is my concern," Arby pointed out. "I have never inquired about your private sector, 1KHAF4. Or about the doings of your assistants or what takes place in your laboratory. I respect your seclusion, 1KHAF4. But the welfare of the loop takes precedence. I must satisfy myself on the matter of mass alteration. We will investigate your quarters. I hereby authorize it."

"I object!" Khaf Four shouted, then realized his objection was too late. Crew teams had entered his private sector the moment the authorization was declared. "So be it, then." He shrugged. "You might as well all see what is there. After you, Commander."

At the entry to the historian's sector, ashen-faced Whispers were waiting for them. "You had better see this for yourself, 3RB4ST," one of them said.

The space was a chamber bounded by virtual screens, all displaying data on various world history scenarios—a vast array of alternate probabilities, all being processed by extensive data systems. In the area bounded by the screens were dissecting tables with shrouded shapes upon them. Two of the shrouds had been pulled back, revealing the mutilated bodies of two protomorphic humans—an old man with facial whiskers and a young girl.

"Samples," Khaf Four said casually. "I require them for my work. They are products of their times, you see . . . products of their histories."

Arby stared at the historian, feeling sick. "Where are your assistants, 1KHAF4?"

"They were useful for ballast." The historian shrugged. "They and one of the excess hydroponic locks approximately equalled the weight of these four. It wasn't a very good deception, I admit, but it was adequate for a time. Now it no longer matters. I have what I need."

"What you *need*?" Sixten hissed, as one in shock. "What . . . what is it you think you need?"

"L-270," Khaf Four said. "The loop is all I require for my purposes."

He turned to an alcove, reached into it, and brought out a thing that fairly reeked of age and lethal purpose. Not since the end of the twenty-third century had such items been common. Not one of those staring at him now had ever seen one, except in a museum. But they knew what it was—a fully operational zen-gun.

Without hesitation, Khaf Four pressed the stud and watched Whispers fall around him. He killed Arby first, then two of the searchers who were nearby, then Ivy and Sixten Elby. Only when all those around him were dead did 1KHAF4 stop firing, and then it was only to count the bodies. That done, he set out to tour the entirety of L-270, killing as he went. In T1 duration, it took him almost nine hours to hunt down and eliminate the entire expedition. But when it was finished, he was alone in the closed loop L-270 and the loop was his.

He jettisoned the bodies over a steaming Cenozoic sea, then made some modifications in the dimensional controls and adjusted the settings. His next task was to find a secure place to stay, while he rearranged future history to suit himself.

∞

If ever there was a bastard project, it was Deep Hole. Its mother was the United States Coast and Geodetic Survey, its father a smuggled laser disk, and its midwife the National Science Foundation. The data disk disappeared in the breakup of the Union of Soviet Socialist Republics. It reappeared at Langley, Virginia, in 1995. It contained secret records of an uncompleted exploratory drilling project in Siberia, abandoned at a depth of more than fifty thousand feet—at the time, the deepest hole ever drilled by man.

What intrigued NSF, even more than the core data, was the series of bizarre stem behaviors and directional anomalies encountered by the Siberian drillers. Six-inch, diamond-bit, three-comb drills in solid, hot granite do not meander unless something pulls them with great force. Lodestone attraction—magnetism of an unprecedented power—was suspected, but ruled out. The only remaining explanation was gravity. The area had a history of bizarre gravity occurrences. The force acting on *Grigov I*'s drill stem seemed to be intense gravity, far beyond anything previously encountered. And the direction of it changed radically past thirty-two thousand feet. "Down" became almost due eastward, and the shaft stress from the weight of the drill head seemed to approximately double every 1.866 meters.

The location of Deep Hole in western Kansas—approximately 37 degrees 2 minutes north latitude, 101 degrees 0 minutes west longitude—was based on a history of surface gravitic anomaly similar to that of the Siberian site.

The Deep Hole project began in 1999 and ended abruptly in 2003.

—from *The Hellhole*

∞

XI
Testaments

Eastwood
Present Time

In the evening Tombo and Jill rode their bicycles along the Walnut, circling around to the park atop Shepherd's Bluff. They hadn't talked very much since their abrupt return to Lucas and Maude's house from L-383. There was just too much to think about, to shape all the revelations and new concepts into the narrow confines of ordinary words.

Even to Tombo, who had known for most of his sixty-odd years that there was a lot more out there than the senses perceived, the vivid actuality of time travel experienced was mind-boggling. He could only guess how it had affected Jilly.

For her part, Jill Hammond felt stunned and disoriented. The whole thing—the Whispers, the visit to their fantastic loop, the staggering beauty of the "place that wasn't exactly anyplace," and the heartbreaking tragedy of what she had heard and seen—was almost too much to comprehend. Added to these almost unbelievable revelations was another, overriding enormity. These people had shown her *time*, in a way she had never understood time—a way she couldn't possibly have seen it, until now.

Again and again she was buffeted by the feeling of having suddenly awakened from a tight, gray little world of narrow dreams into bright, mind-filling reality. She would never again see her universe in quite the same way, now that she had glimpsed it through Whisper eyes.

Through it all, another realization pushed forward, demanding center stage. For the first time she understood a thing about Tombo Hawthorn—a thing that explained many things. This thoughtful, gentle man, with his laughing eyes and his piercing intellect—this man she had secretly adored since she was a child and he not much more—was *afraid* of other times. The ghosts that haunted him were ghosts of love, but they were all the more painful for that.

Tombo Hawthorn had outlived the ordinary fears a long time ago. He was the most fearless sane person Jill knew. He wasn't afraid of today, and certainly not of tomorrow. But he was afraid of yesterday.

There had been no promises made, no pact pledged, in that strange interlude of their visit to L-383. Teal Fordeen and the other Whispers had told their story and answered all the questions any of them could think to ask. If there was a plan, as Maude Hawthorn had said, it was as vague and shifting as history itself, and all of them in their own ways understood that nothing more definite could be designed. The threat posed to world history by Delta, and the reactions of those involved, was like a mighty chess game—a four-dimensional chess game—in play on a universal board. The situation and its components changed with each move.

David Frank and Jessica Tinsley had been chosen by the Whispers, because there were specific tasks that they could do, if it suited them to do so. Daisy Blake had likewise been chosen, because one she loved was at risk and she was in a position of opportunity. Lucas and Maude had the TEF capabilities of Waystop I. Tombo had been chosen, too, Jill thought, though no reason was obvious. The truck driver, Eddie Ridge, had been an innocent bystander caught up in the game, but he had quickly volunteered to help.

The rest of them, the county sheriff and his two deputies and herself, just happened to be there as far as she could see. But like Eddie Ridge, Jill Hammond had been outraged at the story they heard.

There was no doubt in her mind that every present-day

person in that L-383 meeting would do anything possible to assist the Whispers, given the chance.

There had been no ceremony of parting, no promises made. Teal Fordeen had talked quietly with a few of them—Tombo included—while other Whispers demonstrated the virtual reality screens and some of the analytic equipment. Toocie Toonine had seemed to be watching Jill closely, speculatively, but had not approached her again. Then the Whispers had wished them all well and indicated that they might be contacted.

Moments later they were all back in the transfer chamber next to Maude's kitchen, and the wall clock indicated that no more than a few minutes had passed since their departure. For some of them, that silent, unarguable clock had hammered home what all the theories and explanations—even their fantastic visit to L-383—had not quite achieved. Hours had passed, but only minutes were gone. In the moments of their return, they saw and understood the enormous implications of double time—Time1 as duration, pliant and variable, weaving its random way around and through the solid reality of relentless Time2, controlling the events of history as a rider controls his steed.

At the crest of the bluff Jill swung down from her bike and set it against an elm bole, then removed her riding helmet and shook out her cropped hair. It was a perfect Flint Hills evening, cool breeze soothing the sunburned edges of a warm day while the vastness of sky overhead deepened in hue beyond wisps of pink cloud—graceful streamers executing pretty curtsies for the setting sun.

It was so peaceful! Jill wished it could remain so, forever. But in Tombo's gaunt profile—looking out across the Walnut—she saw grim determination. He had decided, she knew. This thing his brother was involved in, had become a cause for Tombo. And the reasons went beyond the story they had heard. They went to this man's heart, with all the old hurts and scars that were in it.

"Past and future," she said quietly. "Time . . . as accessible as the directions of a road. It's what you've been hiding from, isn't it, Tombo?"

He nodded, not turning. "They're back there," he said.

"Betty and the kids . . . in that past these people treat as though it were just another present, they're all still there. Still . . . alive, back then, just as they always were. I'm not sure I'm ready to face that kind of reality, Jilly. Even to see other people's pasts, in other places. It's still the past, and maybe I just want to keep it that way."

"Everybody has a past," she pointed out. "Grief is part of memories. You're not alone in this, Tombo. You never were."

"Everybody *is* a past." He frowned. "We just don't think about it much." He shook his head sadly. "Maybe it's easier for some people than for others. Maybe there's a special knack to going on. I don't know how strong I am, Jilly. It must take a special sort of equanimity to . . . to even think about becoming involved in the lives of dead people."

"Maybe it *is* a knack," she said. "I guess I do it every day, in a way. It's part of being a nurse. You always know that nobody lives forever. I just try not to think about the things I can't change."

"How do you do that, Jilly? What *do* you think about, down deep, when inevitability stares you in the face?"

"I just concentrate on how I can help." She shrugged. "I think about what I can do to make the moment—*this moment right now*—better for somebody."

He looked at her for a long silence then, peering deep into her dark eyes, looking for elusive answers to old questions. Finally he said, "There'll be work for me in this. I have to do what I can. For Lucas, of course, but also for all those other people. I have to, because there's something terribly wrong— somebody doing something awful—and I know about it now, and I can't just do nothing."

"I know," she murmured.

"Time travel!" Tombo squared his shoulders, turning toward the last rays of sunset. "I was right. There's no future in it. Even Teal Fordeen doesn't know how any of this will come out. The future is the product of a shifting past. Infinite variations in infinite combinations. Nothing is certain at all . . . except that it's dangerous, Jilly. Any involvement might bring retaliation. What we heard, what we saw . . . there's an intelligence at work behind all that, and it's malignant. You don't have to be involved in any of this, you know."

"I know," she said again, but now in a different way. Standing beside him, in the twilight, her compact stature barely reached his shoulder. But her determined posture was a match for his own. "I know I don't have to. But I am. You're not the only one who can't abide untreated trauma, Tombo Hawthorn. So count me in. I've already called the hospital. I'm on back leave."

Curtis Welles told Beejum to leave *Sparrow* alone. He told him a dozen times, but it didn't do any good. So he kept watch from the sunporch, under the suspicious eyes of an antique Russian with a nasty-looking saber. When the aborigine appeared from the garage with a heavy cart loaded with mechanic's tools, Curtis gave up and went out to join him. By the time he got there, Beejum was happily removing *Sparrow*'s muffler.

With a sigh, Curtis went around front and got Tombo's van. He pulled it alongside *Sparrow* and got out, waving his arms. "Get away from here, you . . . you heathen!" he barked. "This is *mine*! Let it alone!"

When Beejum backed off, Curtis got his own wrench and uncoupled the bird's rotor housing. He set the apparatus aside and pulled the bolts on the stubby airfoils, placing each elevator carefully into the van. These done, he removed the tail-fan chain and uncoupled the tail assembly. This went into the van, followed by the motor—now minus one muffler—and its tanks and mountings.

Hovering nearby, Beejum removed his hat, profoundly impressed. "Lord luv a duck," he muttered, impressed. "Fair dinkum knockable, 'at is!"

What remained was an alloy cage with twin seats and wire-spoke wheels. These separated into four components and joined the other sections in the van.

With everything else stowed away, Curtis looked around for his rotor assembly, and went pale. One of the blades had been removed, and Beejum was busily stripping the fabric from its frame.

" 'Ere's yer want," the bushman explained. "Needs a bit o' dip, don't ye see. A proper 'rang cuts air twice, not once."

"Leave that alone!" Curtis demanded, grabbing the half-skinned airfoil. "It took me two days to sleeve that frame."

With a growl he loaded the remainder of *Sparrow* into Tombo's old van and slammed the door. When he turned back, Beejum shrugged elaborately, stooped, and selected a blade of grass.

"It's like this," the Australian said. He held the blade of grass high and dropped it. In the still evening air it fell a few inches, looped, and began a fluttering rotation, swaying randomly this way and that as it descended.

" 'At's how ye looked comin' down," Beejum explained. "Now 'ave a look at this." He picked another grass blade, pinched it between strong, dark fingers, and bent it laterally, then held it up. It was angled a few degrees now, arced in the center, between straight ends. He held it high and dropped it.

This time, the fall was not random. The bit of grass dropped, found the air, and whirled, a flattening arc that carried it several feet away before it settled to the ground.

Beejum grinned and spread his hands in an expressive shrug. That's just how it is, his gesture said.

"Well, I'll be damned," Curtis muttered. "A boomerang."

Lucas Hawthorn and Eddie Ridge were halfway back to Eastwood, from Wichita, when the reality of his own situation finally hit Eddie. Lucas had taken the truck driver to the city to arrange for repair of his Kenworth. The reefer and its contents were somebody else's concern now, but the tractor was his. It belonged to him and the bank.

They had found a diesel shop and arranged for a pickup and tow, and were eastbound on 54 Parkway when Eddie snorted, sat up straight, and went wide-eyed. "My God," he said abruptly. "I'm dead!"

At the wheel of the Explorer, Lucas turned to frown at the trucker. "You're what?"

"Dead," Eddie repeated. "I'm dead. I died in that crash on the 83 bridge."

"No, you didn't," Lucas assured him. "You probably would have, but you weren't there. You jumped back in time before it happened. So you weren't there when you died . . . I mean, you weren't there to die. You can't be in two places—much less two times—both at once. At least, I don't think you can."

"Well, I *would* be dead, but for that. My God, it feels strange."

"Welcome aboard," Lucas sneered. "You and the rest of the world. Everybody dies, sooner or later."

"That's not what I mean. You heard that crippled girl. And that Dr. Frank. They'd both be dead now, except that some-body interfered. And that Russian, and Higgins . . . they'd have been dead several lifetimes ago. But they weren't there to die. That's how I was. My number was up, for sure. I saw it coming. But then I wasn't there anymore, and now I'm here. I died, but I'm not dead! That dang Whisper with his whatzit . . . he saved my life."

Lucas shook his head and turned on his lights. It was getting dark. "The Whispers have saved a lot of lives." He shrugged. "I'm not sure they mean to. Saving lives isn't their business, and they don't like to meddle. But they're people, like us, and when people get involved with other people, sometimes they save their lives. The Whispers have time technology. Time's tricky, but it doesn't change anything, by itself. People do that."

"I'm still alive because of them," Eddie Ridge said stub-bornly. "I owe them."

"If you say so," Lucas conceded. "Everybody lives as long as they're going to live. And everybody dies when they die . . . but only if they're present for the occasion."

Once it had been the dining room of the Hawthorn house. Now it was a transfer chamber for the elusive dimension of time. Where multipaned windows had stood behind sheer lace cur-tains framed by fine drapery, now there were only walls hung with builder's cloth. Where Kasimir rugs had rested on oaken floor, now the floor was sheets of gleaming steel, brazed at the seams. The only furnishing was a tower of metal beams supporting a maze of copper wiring resting within elaborate pivots and gimbals. Nested within the copper coils was a cone of metallic translucence—the TEF. Things like glass cables led upward through the ceiling. A framed slot in the wall behind the tower indicated the control booth, located in what had once been a utility closet.

Through open double doors with a rope barricade, Maude Hawthorn, Daisy Blake, and Jessica Tinsley watched as a colony of Whispers was shunted through the chamber—migrants from a distant future to some unimaginable past.

"They're boosting," Maude explained. "That's why they needed a waystop here. It's a booster, to accelerate them back through time to the Leapfrog booster in the 1880s. From there they go on back. They're looking for gates and bridges . . . whatever that is."

Beyond the open doors a little signal bell sounded. The TEF, in its nest of wires, glowed faintly, and in the empty room something shifted. To those watching intently, it seemed as though everything in the room darkened and somehow slowed; even though nothing had been moving, the sense of slowing was distinct. Then the space seemed to flare with a brilliant light. It was all so quick—so mind-numbingly abrupt—that it seemed more like something imagined than something real. For an instant the room was full of shadows—living shadows as in a crowded elevator glimpsed too quickly to be truly seen—and in that same instant the darkening, slowing, and flare of light occurred again.

In far less than the blink of an eye, a group of people— dozens of them—had been there and gone, propelled through unseen dimensions by energies too elemental and too enormous to be perceptible to human synapses.

Somewhere the little bell sounded again. The boost was complete.

"They still travel," Maude muttered, mostly to herself. "Even with their very existence on the verge of annihilation, they still go back, looking for what it all means."

"My God," Daisy Blake breathed. "I see it, but I can't grasp it. It makes me dizzy, just to watch."

"Amazing!" Jessica Tinsley said. "Absolutely amazing."

Amanda Santee came in from the hall. She had monitored the boost in the control booth.

"Not really amazing," she said. "Remarkable technology, but it's simple enough in practice. Light and gravity are identical extremes . . . opposite sames. Reverse aspects of a commonality, like heads and tails on a coin. They're the two ends of the photogravitic spectrum, and the spectrum is a closed circle. It's the same principle that drives Dr. Frank's inertial energy lamp. Reverse either aspect of the photogravitic phenomenon, and you reverse both. Light becomes gravity and gravity becomes light. Each requires the other and each generates the other. It's black holes and stars. The fulcrum of the universe. It's what fuels creation . . . what the three spatial dimensions and everything in them are made of, and its motive force is duration, the fourth dimension.

"The Whispers use the energy of that reversal to traverse time. They literally travel faster than light, by placing themselves in the matrix of slow light that occurs in the instant of reversal, then letting the new light push them ahead of it. You did the same thing when you shunted to L-383 and back."

"But they go to other *places* as well as to other times," Daisy pointed out.

"Three-dimensional location doesn't mean much from the perspective of four dimensions." Amanda nodded, helping herself to coffee. "It's just a matter of navigation. When you look at a map, you're in three dimensions looking at two. You can focus on one place, then on another, just by shifting your eyes. Looking at three dimensions from four is like that."

Jessica Tinsley wheeled her chair around, cocking her head as she gazed intensely at this remarkable person—this *timer*—who was Maude Hawthorn's younger sister. "Is that what you do?" she asked. "You and the other timers?"

"In principle, yes." Mandy nodded. "But not the same way. The TEF is technology. It's science, a craft based on analogs—magnetism for gravity, electron transfer—electricity, if you will—for light. They're good analogs. Magnetism and electricity always coexist, at right angles to each other, and they're close cousins to the prime elements. Magnetism is to gravity as electricity is to light. The TEF manipulates these analogs to trigger photogravitic reversal. We—those of us who have this timing thing—apparently bypass the middleman.

"I can't explain how. It isn't a craft, it's an art. We have the talent and develop the skill. We have a sort of feel for the prime dimensions. We are *aware* of them. All four of them. And we learn to manipulate ourselves within them. When we do, the light-gravity thing happens."

Daisy Blake nodded. "Lucy thinks that way," she said. "She says that if something doesn't last, it doesn't happen. Sometimes she gets conversation confused by answering questions before they're asked. She gets so frustrated sometimes, because I can't keep up with her reasoning. She says I only see parts of things."

Amanda sipped her coffee and leaned against the counter, her eyes becoming sad and distant. "It *is* frustrating sometimes," she reflected. "When I look at a sculpture or a mountain range or a hummingbird or a child, I can only *see* its physical presence. But at the same time I sense—I visualize— its *entire* presence. I see it with everything but my eyes, and I want to see it that way, too. I want to paint it, to carve it, to . . . who knows? The fourth dimension makes all the difference in the world. It's beautiful. Incredibly beautiful! But it's just so damned hard to see!"

There was a long silence. Maude found cups and filled them.

"Is that how my little girl will be?" Daisy asked.

Mandy shrugged. "Probably. Maybe even more. Maybe she'll be the one who learns to depict it, so everybody can see."

"If she lives long enough," Jessica said bluntly. "Those Delta people . . ." She shivered.

"Well, we've got to do something about that," Maude rasped. Then she turned to gaze at her sister. "How about you, Mandy? Do you think those monsters know about you?"

"They probably do." Mandy shrugged. "I never knew to keep it secret . . . to hide my past, day to day, the way Adam did. Somehow he always knew. I guess his parents must have known, too. There is nothing, anywhere, to connect him to his past. I have learned to cover my tracks, but not my history. Most of us didn't have that foresight. So we're vulnerable to yesterday."

"You haven't said why you came." Maude moved closer, raising a hand to touch her sister's cheek with concerned fingers. "You're doing something dangerous, aren't you . . . you and Adam?"

Mandy started to smile reassuringly, started to give an easy answer, then hesitated and lowered her eyes. "Something, yes," she said quietly. "It would be much more dangerous not to, you know. I just wanted to see you again first. I don't know when I can come back."

In the converted dining room the bell sounded. A moment later the little Whisper KT-Pi appeared at the doorway. "Teal Fordeen has suggested an approach to our problem," she said. "The various coordinates have been calculated. Where are the others?"

Maude tore her worried gaze from Mandy and glanced around, counting noses. "Well, Dr. Frank is asleep in the TV room. He was exhausted. Mr. Higgins is outside someplace, as usual. Tombo and his lady friend went out on their bicycles, and Lucas took Mr. Ridge to find a repair shop for his truck. The sheriff and his men went back to El Dorado, so that only leaves Alex . . . ah, Captain Novik. He's right in there, in the . . . now where did he go?"

They moved to the sunroom door. Outside, in the evening light, they could see Beejum and Curtis Welles taking Curtis's airplane apart. But the sunroom was empty. Novik was gone, and so was the box containing the tsar's treasure.

By the time he was missed, Captain Aleksandr Sergeievich Novik was miles away. He had a good horse, finely saddled, and he had the Romanov jewels strapped on behind him, hidden by his fine Russian bear greatcoat.

He had a general idea where he was, though he had no idea how he got here. He was in Kansas, and Kansas was—as he recalled—in the middle steppes of the United States of North

America. The Grand Duke Vladimir had toured this country in the 1870s, and his accounts of it were well known.

The idea that a great deal of time had passed since his encounter in the Tunguska wilderness mystified him, but it stood to reason that—no matter what else changed—the shape of the world remained the same.

The distances involved were daunting, but Aleksandr Sergeievich reminded himself of that old Russian truism: Every journey begins with the first step. West of here would be highlands, and beyond them mountains. The passes through those mountains pointed toward the great sea. Across that sea, on its northern lanes, was Vladivostok.

He had his rifle, his saber, and his gear. He had his wits, and a good horse to ride. Men had made great journeys with less.

With the setting sun as his guide, Captain Aleksandr Sergeievich Novik set a course westward . . . toward Mother Russia.

∞

Past involvement is not for everyone. You just can't help being aware that some of those around you are dead.

—EDWIN LIMMER, *The Stowaway Journal*

∞

XII

Ampere's Song

Tsaritsyn, Volgograd Krai
July 1888

Hot *Sukhovei* winds swept across the Volga beneath a coppery sky—winds that could suck the stamina from a man unshielded by shady windbreaks, but that cleared the air and tempered the blazing sun, giving sharp detail to the bleached horizons. While fanatic rebels stifled in their barricaded quarter of the old city, for those outside, it was a pleasant, lazy day. A perfect day for reducing a stronghold.

Drifting smoke from two days of artillery bombardments had cleared away during the subsequent lull, and the view of the town was excellent. Those gathered on high ground around the military perimeter could see people coming and going on the streets below, the patrols of gaudy soldiers around the marketplaces, even glimpses of movement in the battered old quarter itself, where people scurried through the ruins, taking advantage of the momentary quiet. From the hillsides, one could almost feel the thirst and taste the hopelessness of those trapped there.

The *Naradnaya Volska* was only the latest of the little bands of fanatics that always plagued Russia. Political *menyesvics*, outcast from the Bolshevik majority in the Duma, they had pre-empted a shipment of Mannlicher rifles and attempted a stupid raid on the summer villa of Baron Grigori Kratsky. Routed and retreating to Volgograd, the rebels fled as far as old Tsaritsyn and went to ground. They occupied four blocks of buildings there, but with their rifles they effectively controlled the entire old quarter, holding hostage some three thousand people and most of the region's fabrication industry. It was a minor rebellion, simply a nuisance, but it *was* an affront, and General Boris Miruslav's artillery took the field to punish the offenders.

There was no hurry, though. The Imperial Army had a cordon around the entire city and guard units patrolling all sections but the old quarter. General Erich von Stelm's Cossack Cavalry was bivouacked in the field, awaiting the final assault on the rebel zone.

The enemy was going nowhere, and both the season and the event lent themselves to grand spectacle. The most diverting festive event of a lackluster social season had been the inaugural presentation of Rimsky-Korsakov's *Scheherazade* in St. Petersburg. Despite the genius of the composer, the performance had been poorly received. Yet the occasion had implanted in the patrician bourgeoisie an appetite for further entertainments, which in recent weeks had been fed by the success of Tchaikovsky's new Fifth Symphony.

Enterprising capitalists out of Moscow recognized a market for spectacle broader than a theater stage, and *Naradnaya Volska*'s little rebellion in Volgograd provided the opportunity. Now nobility and notables flocked to witness the extermination of the rebels, and commanders of the military used the delay to parade and exercise their troops.

While entrepreneurs erected spectator accommodations and sold tickets for the shelling, wagers were made as to whether it would be artillery, cavalry, or infantry that brought the final silence to the unfortunate town. It was welcome entertainment in a boring time, and those who had the means came from all around to watch the show.

Observation towers had been erected for the comfort of the elite among them, and plank bleachers lined the hilltop in front of the pavilions and tents that were their accommodations. As crowds gathered, acrobats and Gypsy dancers performed for thrown coins. Liveried porters and personal servants by the hundreds swarmed here and there, attending the needs of their superiors. Among these proletariat were more than a few whose hearts and kinships lay with the besieged rebels trapped in the old quarter below, but what was happening here was the way of the world. One does not ponder circumstances one has no power to change.

A few cooks and porters working the kitchen tents may have noticed the man with the stitched belt, but only in passing. He was a stranger to them, of course, but in this place most of those they saw were strangers. He was a large, intense man whose language was obviously not theirs. Though he spoke to no one, any man who cared to notice would know that his speech, like his origin, was not *pa-Russkyi*.

But then, there were many languages spoken here. Frenchmen, Germans, Poles, and Slavs were everywhere in such a gathering, mingling with Serbs, Austrians, and even occasional Mandarin expatriates. But no one questioned where the silent stranger was from. He was just there.

The man's clothing was not quite of common cut, his boots were finer than most, and he had a barbered look about him that was unusual outside the pavilions of the bourgeoisie. But the oddity that remained in mind was the wide belt of his sweeping greatcoat. The belt was tooled leather, with minute stitching in its design, unlike anything anyone had seen.

He strolled here and there along the hillside, looking at everything. For a time he stopped to watch the stringing of copper wires around a large, low platform where evening performances would be conducted. Workmen had set up a steam-driven electric generator and were wiring the area for illumination, using the new American Ediswan lamps.

It was obvious that the stranger had purposes of his own, though, and none felt obliged to interfere—especially when *Sukhovei* whipped his coattails as he loitered near the clustered private pavilions of the *syemyani*, the families of notables. Some with sharp eyes glimpsed then the weapons that he carried.

"An ice hunter," a wrinkled old Serbian stock-tender told his comrades. "His eyes are never still." But each among them knew it must be someone else the hunter sought, and so it was none of their concern.

*   *   *

"Pli bona pano sen butero, ol kuko sen libero!" the Grand Duchess Helena snapped. With an angry gesture she swept to her little feet, scattering pages of elaborate text across the carpeted floor of the high tent. *"Malbonega kaj ... ka ... oh,* bother! This Esperanto is nothing but silly chatter. I want to dance!" Twirling grandly, high on slippered young toes, she spun toward the laced flap and pulled it open to peer out. Gusting *Sukhovei* wind, not yet calmed by evening, stung her cheeks and ruffled her hair.

"Highness, please!" Olga Malenina protested. "You know we must complete our studies each day!" As usual, about twice a week, the instructress found herself almost at wit's end. How could any ordinary tutor be expected to teach patience and restraint to an eight-year-old grand duchess of the House of Romanov? In desperation she turned to her other pupil. "Anya, dear, please reason with her. We *must* learn the Esperanto this season. We must all learn it. It is the emperor's express wish!"

"Da, Damskinitsa." Anya Karasova Breskin shrugged, gathering up fallen papers. "The tsar believes that Esperanto will be *Lingvo Internacia,* just as Dr. Zamenhof proclaimed when he devised it. But Helena is right, it *is* extremely boring."

At the tent entrance Helena turned, taunting the teacher with an impish grin. "You see? Even 'Anya second-sight' is bored with syllables and inflections. Besides, Dr. Zamenhof is a Jew! What do Jews know of languages?"

"Who would know more?" Olga asked. "Who but the Jews have prospered in every civilized tongue and invented a few more of their own?" She raised one eyebrow, matching the child's victorious grin. "Would you prefer to study Yiddish, Highness?"

"I would rather dance!" Helena frisked and twirled again, her long gown billowing outward like the rim of a spinning top. "Will evening never come?"

"In an hour," Olga promised. "The sun is setting now. Soon there will be lights and banners and music all around . . . and a cooler breeze. Then we will put on your ball gowns and dancing slippers, and you may both cavort on stage to your heart's content. For now, though, let us recite. *En la komenco Dio kreis . . .*"

With a flip of her braids, Helena subsided. *"En la komenco Dio kreis la ĉielon kaj la teron. Kaj la tero estis sen forma kaj dezerta, kaj . . ."*

"In the beginning," Anya Karasova whispered, keeping up with her friend, "God created the heaven and the earth. And the earth was without form, and void, and . . ."

The words droned on, in Russian and Esperanto, sounds and meanings weaving in and out like vines on a trellis. Anya let her mind wander, toying with the reality of passing, plodding time. She wished it would change. She wished . . . and it seemed, suddenly, to concede to her desire. A turn of mind—the merest hint of thought command applied in a certain way—and everything about her seemed to slow itself abruptly, slowing and somehow darkening. It was a strange sensation, sudden and dreamlike, a sense of foreboding power as though she could control—and *was controlling*—the very passage of the seconds.

She repeated the tiny mind-nudge, and there was brilliant, blinding light. Only it was too quick to be light, too quick even to be a perception. But she was no longer in the stifling big tent. She was standing in a crowd of people under a starry sky. Cool breeze bathed her cheeks, and as the crowd parted she saw bright little lights illuminating a bannered stage where young girls danced to the music of a string quartet. There was Helena, and Karin Gudenova and the Prokov twins and . . . she gasped and turned away, backing further into the pressing crowd of proletarian spectators. Someone jostled her, and she turned again, then froze. Beyond the crowd was a steam engine set on pilings, and a large thing like a split kettle with wires, and there were two men.

They faced each other, crouching, like feral animals circling for attack. What happened then was so abrupt, so livid that her mind recoiled from it, and again there was that instant's slowing, darkness, and sudden light.

The wind had subsided, abruptly as it usually did with sundown, and the big tent was still and cozy. *"Kaj Dio diris: estu lumo,"* Helena Vladimiyevna recited, *"kaj fariĝis lumo."*

"Let there be light," Anya Karasova finished with her, "and there was light." She heard the words as she said them, but as though through a fog, and her voice sounded odd to her. Vaguely she realized that she was no longer seated on the ottoman couch, but standing.

They both glanced at her—Helena and Olga—with sudden concern. "Are you ill, child?" Olga asked.

"What is it, Anyitsa?" Helena peered at her. "Did you see another vision?"

"I . . . I saw myself dancing." She nodded. Her eyes were large and frightened as she gazed at them. "And a man. There was a man . . . a screaming man with no voice. He had fire . . . blue fire . . . on his head and on his feet."

As twilight crept up the valley beyond Tsaritsyn, Adam strode the busy hillside above, searching. He made no attempt to hide his presence or camouflage his appearance. An outsider among outsiders, he was aware of the startled, curious glances turned toward him as he searched. With 1940s American attire and a holstered Luftwaffen Luger picked up aboard a Heinkel 111 bomber over London, he was as obviously out of place as he was literally out of time. Yet his very presence, on that hill in 1888 Volgograd, seemed to say that he belonged there, and those before him scurried aside to let him pass.

Only once did Cossack guards challenge him. But in an instant of slowed light and brilliance—too quick to register as more than the blink of an eye—he was gone, seemingly into the crowd. Puzzled soldiers pressed into the crowd, but the man they thought they had seen was not there.

Adam was pressed for time in "real" time. Evening had come and already the grandstand and bleacher benches were filling. Lanterns moved here and there, and the hundred brilliances of the platform's electric lights just below illuminated gaudy banners, streamers, and drawn curtains where the performances were about to begin. In a little gazebo beside the stage, a string quartet was tuning up.

Beyond the platform, little girls in brightly colored dancing gowns were being shepherded by matrons toward the stage . . . little girls only moments away from their deaths.

The best account of the incident he had found was in the London *Times*, dated four weeks from now, a detailed translation of the reports of four witnesses—two Russian junior officers, an Armenian journalist, and a visiting diplomat in the service of the Regent Luitpold of Bavaria.

It was only a few measures into the overture from Rimsky-Korsakov's *Snow Maiden*, the account said, when a band of unknown assassins opened fire, killing fourteen people in a "fantastic barrage" of small-arms fire. None of the assassins, thought to be partisans in the *Naradnaya Volska* rebellion, were ever found. But among the dead were six little girls, three of them connected with the House of Romanov. One was the daughter of a grand duke.

The reprisal that followed would be noted in history as a particularly brutal act of civil suppression, the writer predicted. The shelling of Tsaritsyn was not limited to the old quarter, as planned, but became instead a general assault. While thousands of shocked spectators watched, the entire town of Tsaritsyn was methodically blasted to rubble and its fleeing populace run down by the avenging Cossack Cavalry of General Erich von Stelm. It was that *Times* account that gave von Stelm the appellation "Butcher of Volgograd."

The incident at Tsaritsyn would alter the course of history.

If it happened.

But there was no band of assassins here, Adam knew. There was only one assassin—a time traveler with a Delta tattoo and a twentieth-century Uzi. The man had missed Anya Karasova Breskin a decade from now, and lost her in a second attempt four hundred years ago, thanks to her elusive skill. So he had back-traced her to childhood—here, in 1888. He meant to make sure the girl never grew up to be a timer.

The strings went silent, pulleyed velvet curtains drew back, and on the lit stage were six statuettes in silken gowns, motionless in six basic dance postures. Then the quartet lowered resined bows onto taut strings, and the first sweet, prolonged note of Rimsky-Korsakov's overture drifted out on the evening air. The exquisite statuettes stood motionless through that long, single note, as though frozen by the music, then began to move in response to tone and tune . . . six pretty little girls, slim and graceful, creating the artistry of dance that was the very soul of Mother Russia.

Adam saw him then, lurking in the shadows of the steam engine's housing—a big man in a long, full coat drawn at the waist by a wide, stitch-tooled belt. Even as Adam spotted him, the Delta agent pulled open the lapel of his greatcoat and withdrew a boxy, short-barreled thing that no one of this time would have recognized as a weapon.

The spatial distance between the two of them was at least fifty yards—too far to run in the moments remaining, but an easy shot for a nine-millimeter Luger. Adam's hand went instinctively to the weapon at his side, but even as he did, his mind was calculating vectors in another dimension. He needed more than to stop the assassin. He needed to know his origin.

An instant's shifting of photogravitational values, and he was directly behind the man, a second earlier. Rimsky-Korsakov's ringing, melancholy E minor still echoed, pierced now by lyric ripples, and twenty yards away six exquisite statuettes thawed and moved on a lit stage. As the Delta agent opened his lapel, Adam growled, "Drop that or you're dead."

The Delta froze as the Luger's muzzle pressed against his spine.

"That's good," Adam said. "Open the belt and let the Uzi fall."

Carefully, the man did as he was told. "You speak English," he rasped. "Who are you?"

"I'm the one who'll kill you if you don't answer my questions." The Luger prodded brutally, and the Delta stepped forward, away from his fallen weapon. "Your name?" Adam demanded.

"I'm Cantrell," the man said. "You're a timer, aren't you!" With sudden resolve, he turned his head, glancing back.

"I am," Adam said. "But you're not. Whose TEF sent you here?"

"I wouldn't tell you that even if I could," the Delta said. "You don't know the power you're dealing with here."

"Then you tell me what I'm dealing with!" Again he prodded with the Luger, and Cantrell lurched forward, toward the tall, split kettle with its coils, insulators, and protruding wires. They were between the engine and the generator now, blocked from the view of most of the hillside crowd.

Cantrell took another step, then lunged to the side and turned, his hand whipping to a pocket. Adam almost shot him then, but the hand came out with no weapon, only a small gray rectangle with tiny lights on its surface. Like a sparkling credit card. A TEF comlink. Adam had seen such a thing before.

Crouching, Cantrell braced himself for the bullet he expected, then sneered. "You'd have shot then, if you wanted to shoot. But you don't. So . . ."

Use it! Adam willed, silently. *Use the comlink!*

Cantrell's thumb was on the card's face, but he hesitated, his eyes going suddenly shrewd. "Oh, no," he growled. "That's what you want, isn't it! He said you timers can track a shift. You want me to lead you to him! So you don't want me dead."

Beyond the muted thumping of the engine, the faint whine of the generator, loud applause erupted as the quartet launched into the "Snow Maiden's Theme." Like a striking snake, Cantrell launched himself at Adam, ignoring the Luger. Adam back-stepped instinctively, crouching and turning to take the man with a shoulder. But the impact didn't come. The leap was a feint, and Cantrell folded, diving for the fallen Uzi.

For a big man, he was surprisingly quick. Adam barely managed to sweep the gun away with a booted foot, and took a numbing fist to his kneecap as he did. He stumbled, recovered, whirled, and lashed out, his boot going for the man's chin. But Cantrell had straightened, reaching for another weapon, and Adam's kick thudded squarely into his chest.

Cantrell staggered backward, trying to recover his balance. His hands flew wide and he backed again. Suddenly then, blue fires erupted from him, hissing halos at his head and his feet. As the generator's exposed copper leads crackled and thrummed, Cantrell stood stiff-limbed as a dancing marionette, 440 untransformed volts of high-amperage direct current—ten thousand watts of raw, killing power—coursing through him.

The thing that fell away from the generator was a charred, smoking corpse.

Adam crouched in shadows, scanning the area. There were people everywhere, but almost all of them had their attention riveted on the lit stage where pretty little girls whirled on tiptoe, a bright garden of spinning tops. The filament lights had dimmed momentarily, but now they shone brightly again. Only one face in the crowd was turned toward him, a child's face with wide, frightened eyes . . . the exact same face as one of those on the stage just below. For a moment the girl stared, horrified, then dark-slow-bright twinkled and she was gone.

Quickly, in the gloom, Adam gathered up the things Cantrell had dropped. Uzis didn't belong in 1888, nor did stitched belts. He almost missed the little comlink, lying facedown on the scuffed earth. Then he was tempted to activate it, to see where and when it would take him. "He," the Delta had said. "He" was the control. Where "he" was, the comlink might go.

And "he," whoever he was, almost certainly would be prepared to receive the comlink's holder.

A name tugged at his memory, syllables uttered in another time and place by a renegade timer with a Delta mark. The name was Kaffer.

Adam dropped the card into a pocket, snared the Uzi's magazine and action with the belt, and slung it across his shoulder. There was nothing else to recover. Any other anachronisms Cantrell might have had on him would be ashes or molten blobs now, unrecognizable and meaningless.

The body would be found in a few minutes. There would be an inquiry, producing no real answers. An unidentified man had fallen against the generator's main feed, electrocuting himself.

The shelling of Tsaritsyn's old quarter would proceed, and *Naradnaya Volska* would be history—humanity enacting its natural course of events, sometimes messy and often cruel, but unaltered by temporal interference.

Adam glanced where the little girl had been, gaping from the crowd of spectators. Then he paused for a moment, watching the little dancers on the stage. Bright flowers twirling among bright lights. "Dance, little Anya," he whispered. "You'll dance the dimensions soon enough."

He was profoundly impressed. Eight years old, and already her velocitation was quick and clean. And she most certainly didn't even know she was doing it. Who was there to explain to her that she had such a power? Her abilities, like his, were purest art, unique and individual.

The comlink in his pocket was not art, though. It was craft—technology from a far future time. Maybe those who lived by such technology could decipher it.

∞

Like passengers in a public conveyance, we are all in motion, all together, all the time. In fixed sequential time, or T2, our spatial lives are committed and confined. We are in transit, heading into the future minute by minute, one day at a time. Perceived duration, or T1, is the means by which we can, if we choose, get out and walk.

Time travel is thus a relative accomplishment. It is not fourth-dimensional motion that one achieves in manipulating T1, but *independent* motion—the freedom to initiate independent alterations of velocity and direction within the fixed dimension of time.

As with any independent course of action, there are special hazards inherent in the decision to depart from normal T2. One must always bear in mind, for instance, that uncertainty is the very substance of the future, while nostalgia is a thing of the past.

—*The Waystop Users' Manual*

∞

XIII

Tangents

Denver, Colorado
Present Time

Eddie Ridge might have sworn that the Kenworth tractor was his own, restored. It was practically identical in every respect but one: This KW was brand-new—*factory* new—a beautiful, custom T-800 with its black paint gleaming, its chrome scratchless as a mirror, and its odometer displaying less than two thousand miles.

He had already been in and out of the cab three times in the past five minutes. He had fired it up, tested everything that could be tested on a lot, and crawled over it, under it, and through it. Now, with eyes as big as walnuts, he walked around it, whistling between his teeth. A 104-inch standup sleeper, twin 150-gallon side tanks to fuel the spotless Cummins 444 diesel engine, chrome everywhere from its thirteen-foot standing pipes down to its fender farings, polished aluminum rims with ten-hole budds . . . it even had an eagle-emblem deflector, just like the one he had helped scrape up out of Maude Hawthorn's flower bed.

"Jesus H. Christ," he muttered. "It's her, all over again."

The tractor stood ready under a bright, mountain-country sun, purring contentedly and waiting for someone to put highways behind it.

"Thought you might be pleased." Lucas Hawthorn grinned. "When Whispers set out to replace something, they're meticulous about it."

"Sure like to know how you folks managed this," the dealer

172

rep said. "This unit's brand-new, but it was built twelve years ago. Where's it been, in a factory museum or something?"

"Something like that." Lucas shrugged. "You got the papers on it?"

"Right here." The rep handed the bundle over to Eddie Ridge. "I guess it's yours," he said. "Everything's prepaid. Even the Texas registry, as ordered. Uh, what are you going to do with it?"

A grin of purest delight spread across Eddie's face. "Drive it," he said. "I'm gonna drive the hell out of it."

The rep winced. "I don't suppose you want to sell it? I might get together maybe a hundred fifty—"

"Nope," Eddie said. He strolled around the softly thrumming KW again, then climbed up and slid into the driver's seat.

"Two hundred thousand, then? Listen, that truck's a mint classic. I hate to see it just go on the road."

"She's *meant* for the road!" Eddie peered down at him, then at Lucas. "Come around and get in," he said. "I'll take you back to the airport."

Before getting aboard, Lucas shook hands with the rep, thanked him for his help, and handed him a business card. "You seem to like old things new," he said. "Why don't you look into this? I guarantee you'll find it interesting. Just give us a call."

The rep looked sadly at the beautiful classic getting ready to roll. "What's he gonna do, haul for that big well over in Kansas?"

"Something like that." Lucas shrugged.

The gleaming KW negotiated the show lot and turned right, into the thoroughfare traffic on Butte. The rep winced as a slick Camaro ducked past a lumbering cement truck and narrowly missed wrapping itself around the KW's front bumper. The big rig's horns blared majestically, and the KW made a path for itself and headed south.

"Christ!" the rep muttered, shaking his head. Then he looked at the business card in his hand. It carried an odd little logo, like a wide X between parentheses, and the inscription,

ANYWHEN, INC. He read the descriptive lines and read them again, frowning. "What is this?" he muttered. "A joke?" At the bottom was the cheery slogan: HAVE A NICE TIME.

On the way out to Centennial on I-25, Eddie put the big diesel through its paces, gear by gear. "I love it!" he chortled, over and over as they rolled high and proud along the freeway. "God, I just love it! You said y'all would see about fixing my truck, but you never said I'd get a new one!"

"It was Peedy's idea," Lucas said. "I think he felt responsible for what happened to your old one."

"I swear." Eddie shook his head. "Peedy, huh? But who paid for all this? Do Whispers have money?"

"When they need it," Lucas explained. "It's just currency. This probably came from the same place as the rest of the financing for this project. Four oil drums full of twenties, fifties, and hundreds, lifted off a pier at New Orleans. It was bound for a bank in Bogotá."

"*Drug money?* Jesus, man, those people play rough!"

"Yeah, they did. Right after those drums disappeared, one whole faction of the Colombian cartel was wiped out. But it's all over now. That was in 1991."

"I thought Whispers didn't mess with people."

"Those weren't people. Those were cocaine dealers."

"Oh." Double-clutching deftly, Eddie switched lanes to put a dozen lesser vehicles behind them.

"Watch yourself," Lucas warned. "Texas plates are about as popular in Colorado as June bugs at a bean supper. You got your route planned?"

"I'll cut east at Colorado Springs," Eddie said. "Pick up I-70 and head for St. Louis. Then 64 to Charleston and 77 south. 'Bout four days, I figure."

"Fine. How about a stopover at Lenexa?"

"I guess so. Why?"

"There's a big, new truck stop there, just on the left at the Overland Park underpass. It's the jump point."

"I can find it." Eddie nodded. "What do you mean, jump point?"

"You can't very well meet a 1996 deadline without being in

1996, and we don't want an outbound transit the size of a truck originating from Waystop I right now. Teal thinks the Deltas might be tracing temporal wakes."

Lucas took a glittering card from his pocket, glanced around the big cab, then slid the card under a vinyl panel on the dash. He pushed it down out of sight.

"This is a TEF link," he said. "It's something Zeem Sixten came up with. I gather he got the idea from you and Peedy. Anyhow, when you get to Lenexa, look for that truck stop. Pull in there and stop in the north lot, facing out toward the highway. Make it about eleven tomorrow night. Check your cellular phone ahead of time. You got the Waystop number?"

"I've got it. What's going to happen?"

"Simple. You change your registration plates at Lenexa. Put on the '96 plates. They're here under the seat. Then call when the traffic is clear around the station, nobody going in or out. The TEF is already coordinated for that station. The TEF link will trigger it. You'll have maybe two minutes to drive out and head on east, like we've planned. It just won't be this year anymore. It will be 1996. You take it from there. By the way, Jack Higgins will be waiting for you. He wants to go along."

"Why?"

"For Jessica's sake, I guess. Miss Tinsley."

Eddie thought it over. "Okay," he decided. "But make him take a bath first and put on some decent clothes. I don't want him stinkin' up my new truck with his damn rawhide suit."

"It isn't rawhide, Eddie. It's buckskin. They're different things."

"Whatever," Eddie snapped. "He still smells like piss-elum smoke. An' if he scratches my cab with that old flintlock, I'm gonna jump all over him."

Lucas glanced at the truck driver and stifled a grin. You would, too, wouldn't you, he thought. Like a banty rooster on a timber wolf.

"Lordy me," Eddie crooned happily, setting his speedometer on a precise seventy to glide majestically past a Denver Police radar cruiser. "I do just flat-out love this truck!"

Springfield, Missouri

"I heard you'd licensed your gravity light, Dr. Frank." Leon Jessup crossed his arms on his desktop and gazed at the man across from him. "Heard you'd got a sweetheart deal with one of Carter Vaughn's companies."

David Frank nodded wryly. "I did. But it was a mistake. I thought my best bet for marketing the gravlume was through a megacorporation. That's what everybody told me."

"Yeah." Jessup shrugged. "Common knowledge nowadays. Can't hit the market with an innovative product unless you hit it big. Triple-level administrative infrastructure, push-button endorsements, rubber-stamp OSHA and EPA approvals prefiled, coast-to-coast mass outlets on shelf-space shares, packaging with psychologically manipulated eyeball appeal, synchronized media blitzes, and a zillion-dollar advertising budget so everybody's Aunt Tizzy can't live another day without one. Hallelujah, Corporate America! Sometimes I think that whole scam is what keeps little outfits like ours alive. All the MBAs have their heads stuck so far up each others' asses that they don't see us coming."

Frank grinned sheepishly at the entrepreneur. "Had I but known then what I know now," he said. "Anyhow, it all went sour. So I'm looking for somebody to build and market my gravlume."

"Gravlume? Why do you call it that?"

"Actually, it's patented as the Frank Inertial Reaction Energy System, with some subsidiary patents on application. But I like gravlume. Gravity-induced illumination. That's what it is."

Jessup drummed his fingers thoughtfully, then leaned back in his chair. "It's a wonderful invention, David. It's a real first! And of course, I'd be interested. We're already tooled up to make shape-critical, lightweight pressure vessels, and we're experienced in solid-liquid technology. It isn't that far from there to your inversion pedestal.

"But honestly, the way I heard it, it isn't yours to sell. Word is, you assigned all rights to Vaughn Enterprises, with no performance provisos and no backout option. That means it doesn't belong to you anymore. It belongs to Carter Vaughn. Ironclad contract, lock, stock, and barrel. At best, all you have is your name on a patent record. We can't touch a patented process without assigned rights. I'm truly sorry, but that's the way it is."

"What if I were to tell you that my patent is unencumbered? That there is no contract with Vaughn Enterprises?"

"Then that would be a whole new ball game." Jessup leaned forward again, his shrewd eyes probing. "Are you telling me that, David?"

"If I did, I'm sure you'd want to verify it for yourself. I imagine there are discrete ways to do that? Some central record system regarding contractual rights?"

"There are ways, of course."

"Then why don't you look into it, Mr. Jessup? You might find that we *do* have something to talk about." He fidgeted for a moment, then pushed back his chair. "I'll leave a number where you can reach me for the next twenty-four hours. If I don't hear from you by then, there are other people I can talk to."

Jessup stared at the mild, self-effacing man before him, seeing something he had missed before—the stubborn determination of a shy, quiet thinker pushed too far. The man was challenging him! "Do you know what it will cost me to have the U.S. patent records searched on this kind of notice? What assurance are you offering, Dr. Frank?"

"None at all." Frank's grin had iron in it now. "I'm dangling a bait for you. What you do about it is up to you. I liked what you said about small companies like yours, Mr. Jessup. It made sense. Now I'm curious to see if you'll put your money where your mouth is."

"I'll be damned," Jessup muttered. Then he relaxed, returning the man's grin as he stood and extended his hand. "It's a pleasure to meet you, Dr. Frank, no matter what comes of it. Leave that number with me, where I can reach you." They clasped hands, and the visitor turned to leave. "Oh, and, David . . . ," Jessup said.

Frank turned.

"About that name, *gravlume*. It really stinks. Sounds like a weaving process, or some kind of a toy. The Frank Inertial Reaction Energy lamp should be called by its given name, don't you think? F-I-R-E! It's FIRElight, David. Give it some thought."

New York City, New York

Flagging a cab at Newark, Daisy Blake felt as though she were stepping out of a dream. A part of her wondered, literally, whether the past few days had really happened at all. Across the Queensboro Bridge, in Manhattan, the feeling of awakening was even more pronounced. There was something about the noise and stench of the city, the thronging mobs crawling around the bases of great, decaying monoliths, the constant rising of edifices from the rubble of past wonders, the mingling reek of food preparation and stench of primitive urbania that brought her up short as the scarred cab fought its way onto First Avenue, seemingly powered as much by the combative proclivities of its driver as by the fuel in its tank.

She was home again, and suddenly everything in recent experience seemed far away and unreal. Time travel, Kansas, the Romanov jewels, Whispers, *everything*—even the mind-numbing beauty of that "place" they called L-383—might have been nothing more than the imaginings of a wild sojourn into fantasy.

"Welcome to reality, Daisy," she muttered as the cab slowed and stopped still, besieged by blaring horns and pugnacious shouts. They were engulfed in a traffic jam. Daisy withdrew from her reverie and looked around. There were people everywhere, huge crowds of them jostling this way and that, and the street was lined four deep with stalled vehicles. The flow of motion indicated some kind of mass demonstration spilling over from the west toward Hammarskjöld Plaza. Like waves of frightened humanity flowing across First.

Here and there she saw clusters of determined people carrying posters and banners, gawdy slogans like "Asian Accords Now!" and "Intervene In Beijing!" One particularly colorful display hurried by, carried by two men and a woman: PEACE OR REST IN PEACE! THERE IS NO SUCH THING AS REGIONAL NUCLEAR WAR!

" 'Nother demonstration," the cabbie said apologetically. "Looks like the worst one this week. What do they think, the U.N. reads picket signs?"

"So what's this about?" Daisy asked. "I've been out of town."

"The Asian Panic, what else?" The cabbie shrugged, turning to look back at her. "Everything's fallin' apart over there, and they're throwing some nasty stuff around. CNN says there are fifty-sixty thousand warheads along the Mongolian Plateau, all with their fuses lit. Me, I don't know. I just wish old Dung and the Soviet bunch hadn't left all that stuff lyin' around for the loonies to play with." He turned again, looking around them with tired, cynical eyes. "We're gonna be stuck here a while, sorry."

"I can take the subway, I guess," she decided. She scribbled a note and handed it across with a fifty. "Will you bring my luggage to this address?"

"Sure thing, lady. Be another fifty when I get there."

"Fine." She noted his name and ID from the registration over the dashboard, and added the cab number. "Just ring up. Apartment 4-C. I'll be there when you get there."

On the street she made her way along East Forty-fifth, westbound, pushing through crowds of people—the usual crowds, redoubled now by hordes of "Intervene in Asia" demonstrators flocking eastward. Hundreds of voices made a constant, chaotic chorus as she passed, and she barely listened. But then she heard words that brought her to a halt. She turned, her eyebrows raised, looking at the dozen or so people in the little cluster between stoops. Out-of-towners, obviously. They all carried cameras and Bloomingdale's bags. They clung together out of the main flow, trying to see everything all at once.

"What did you say?" Daisy demanded.

The nearest man blinked at her, touched a tentative hand to his clean straw hat. "Ma'am?"

"About Anywhen," she pressed. "I heard somebody say something about Anywhen."

"Oh, that was Helen." He indicated the woman next to him. "She just got her wires crossed. She thought we were here to see the World Trade Center bombing. But this is the wrong year for that. This is the U.N. Siege."

She stared at them, first one and then another. "You're tourists? *Time* tourists?"

"Yes, ma'am. I'm Bob Walch, from Emporia. We're from 2000, on an Anywhen tour. The Abyss Premonitions package. The U.N. Siege is our third premonition. What tour are you on?"

"A different one," Daisy said, feeling dazed. "Have a nice time."

"Yes, ma'am. You, too."

Heading for the subway, Daisy felt light-headed and disoriented. The feeling of distance from recent events was gone, replaced by a new realization. All of that, back there in Kansas, had been real. This was home, but that was the *real* world, out there.

If there had been any lingering doubts in her mind, Dennis put them to rest. Dennis was short, dirty, distracted, and maybe twenty years old going on a hundred. He was sitting cross-legged outside her apartment building, eating raisins and waiting for her.

"I don't know, man," he answered vaguely when she asked what he wanted. "They just told me to be here. So here I am."

"Who told you to be here?"

"Them." He shrugged. "The bug-eyes. Man, did you dig that quantum mainframe they got? Must be a jillion megs ROM! Three-D virtuals a hundred at a time . . . RAM up the kazoo . . . what a motherboard that system must have! I—"

"Bug-eyes? You mean the Whispers? *They* sent you?"

"Yeah, man, like I said. They let me surf their menus and tap two-three of their dedicated source trees. Crazy! Then they said come here, an' zapped me to Central Park West. So I'm here."

"Here to do what?"

He shrugged dreamily. "Dunno. Hack, I guess. What I do best."

"Hack. As in access to data banks?"

"Piece'a cake."

She led him in and upstairs, wrinkling her nose at the odor of him. At her apartment door she pointed at the hallway floor and said, "Sit."

He sat.

"You stay out here," she told him. "Do you want something to eat? Or a glass of water?"

"Root beer, man." He nodded. "An' where's the john?"

"End of the hall. And there's soap there. Why don't you use it!"

Secure in her apartment, Daisy paid off and dismissed Mrs. Lostracco, hugged her surprised daughter as though there were no tomorrow, then headed for the telephone.

"Charlie?" she said when he answered. "When you said you'd do anything for me, did you mean it? . . . Yes, I mean for money! . . . Yes, *good* money! But I need you to start right now. And we'll need some help. This is a lot more than a research job. This time we're going to the files after hours . . . Yeah, I mean like when it's locked . . . The stock exchange . . . No, we're not robbing the World Financial Center! It's more like just breaking and entering . . . The whole building, yes. And the record files. Look, I'll tell you more about it when you get here, but make it quick! And bring your tools. I've got things to do, and boy! Do I have a job for you!"

Waystop I

It was Maude Hawthorn who found the extraneous blip on the TEF log scan. Word had begun to get around about Anywhen, Inc., and there was a fairly steady trickle of business these days as customers showed up, curious to sample excursions into the past. Anywhen, Inc., had done no advertising except for its rather vague business cards, but word of mouth is a powerful marketing tool.

Pete Swain and his family had visited a now-deceased aunt. That had led to at least three other local groups chartering brief time-trips to events of interest. The Fosters had visited the sacking of Lawrence, John Barton and his son had witnessed the shootout at the O.K. Corral, and the Heatherly sisters had gone to nineteenth-century Wichita to meet Carry Nation.

Despite everything else that had been going on lately— Amanda's brief visit, the truck in the daisies, the trip to L-383, the furor over the Whispers' request for assistance in dealing with a malignant temporal force, the stir caused by Beejum and Tombo's friend Curtis Welles setting up shop in the tractor barn to modify Curtis's flying machine, and the search for a missing Russian—Maude hadn't slacked off on booking tours. After all, business was business.

She kept the excursions brief and harmless, but they added up and she had started keeping a travel log to keep track of them. Tying the TEF in to its own computer had made this simpler when Mandy modified a ledger program for her and linked it directly to the TEF's coordinator boards. Now the computer pretty well kept track of who was when and for how long.

Whisper transits were coded not to register. After all, they were just passing through. But every other "send" put a numbered blip on the scan that corresponded to a ledger entry listing particulars of that tour.

What with one thing and another, though, it had been several days since Maude balanced the ledger, checking the scan against entered logged-on time tours. When finally she did, she blinked, frowned, and went back through the whole process again. There was no doubt about it. After all the ledger accounts were identified, there was still an extra blip.

Maude was alone at home when she found the discrepancy. Lucas had gone off to Denver to get Eddie Ridge a new truck, Mandy had left again on "timer business," Tombo and his girlfriend were gone off somewhere, and all the other houseguests of the past few days were away helping the Whispers. Maude stared at the strange blip, could not account for it, and decided there was only one sure way to find out what it meant. She fed retrieval codes into the TEF control program in the converted closet that was now a control booth, and activated the cone.

Through the observation slot just outside the TEF field she saw the transit chamber go dark—that slow-seeming instant of darkening that she had seen so many times now—and sensed rather than saw the flicker of unbearable brilliance that was a wave of faster-than-light transference culminating in the chamber.

Where an empty, steel-floored room had been, there were now two men—two dirty, bedraggled, desperate-looking men who gazed around with wonder. Not leaving her closed booth, Maude keyed the mike beside the viewing slot. "Gentlemen, identify yourselves, please," she said.

They both jerked at the sound, as though they had been shot. Then the taller one swallowed, squared his shoulders, and said, "What is this? Are we back where we started?"

"I suspect so," Maude admitted. "This is Anywhen, Inc. But I can't seem to find your booking or your itinerary. Please tell me who you are, just for our records. It will only take a moment to verify, then I'll send you right back to whenever you were."

"In God's name, please don't!" The second man dropped to his knees, clasping his hands. "Just . . . just let us get out of here and go home. They'll kill us back there. Execute us for espionage, they said. They think we're Confederates out of uniform. They already took Buddy's camera out and shot it, and we're next!"

Maude shook her head, at a loss as to what that was all about. "Please just give me your names," she asked again.

"I'm Milton Skinner," he confessed. "I used to be Charles Bronson, but I've had enough! This is Buddy Cline. We've . . ." His desperate eyes lit then on the open doorway into the kitchen and the open patio door beyond. With a shriek he scrambled to his feet and bolted, his friend right behind him.

By the time Maude reached the kitchen window the two were climbing the north fence, heading for places unknown.

She went back to the booth, activated the main search-files program, and began the task of reviewing hundreds of unsorted entries on the scrolling screen. Eventually she found what she was looking for—an unlogged transit activation. Two unpronounceable, multicharacter Whisper names came up on the margin. She recognized them both.

KT-Pi had made the send, authorized by Peedy Cue.

"I'll have to remember to ask Peedy who those people were, when I see him," she told herself.

∞

Mind is a victim of its self, it seems.
Grand understandings stand just out of sight,
awaiting but the willingness to see.
Elusive truths occur to us in dreams,
then disappear from wakeful scrutiny.

We're tantalized. We analyze, define
hard evidence. By logic's stubborn light
we quantify, ignoring symmetry.
We struggle so! Yet just a turn of mind
might show the faces of infinity.

—Perceptions

∞

XIV

The Multilateral Continuum

Giza, Egypt

The encasement of L-270 in the Pyramid of Khafre was as precise as water in a jug. As a temporal phenomenon, the closed loop had no fixed shape or physical dimension. Chronologically static, in a vacuum it would have appeared a globe. In free air, subject to the forces of planetary attraction and spin, it assumed the shape of a thick saucer. The loop contained three-dimensionally stable matter, but it was not limited to three dimensions. Like the temporal conduit from which it was derived, the loop was a section of temporal transience—a self-regenerating vortex of fundamental energies, an island of T1 duration feeding back and back upon itself.

It had no shape and—except for the matter enclosed within it—no physical mass. But it did have three-dimensional volume. That volume—approximately 2.2 million cubic yards—fit handily into the 2.6 million cubic yards of the Pyramid of Khafre, Khafre's Horizon, the second of the great pyramids at ancient Giza. In a sense, L-270 *became* the pyramid—a 180-minute temporal resonance within a fixed three-dimensional structure five thousand years old. Only the outer skin of Khafre's monument remained untemporized, a shell of red granite and Tura limestone encasing a hole in time.

And within the hole, alone and malignant, the creature called Kaffer dreamed of vengeance while he plotted his version of infinity.

He felt thwarted, and each frustration added to his anger. It should all have been so simple, once L-270 breached the Arthurian Anachronism and emerged in pre-Arthurian time. By eliminating everyone else within the closed loop, he had assumed total control of the phenomenon. From there it was— or should have been—only a matter of modifying history so that his realm was not just of this sector of time, but of all time. Kaffer's desire was to be a god, and he had the means to do so within his grasp . . . almost.

Somehow Arby Forrest had managed to get a message downstream before his death. Other closed loops had followed L-270 through the maelstrom. The first had been L-316, which sacrificed itself to establish a pre-Arthurian "anchor" in the year 1953, opening a conduit upstream from 2050. The second had been the expeditionary loop L-383, exploring the era and creating accelerator ports for what was becoming a migration of Pacificans back through time.

It was an insufferable setback for Kaffer, and his response was cataclysmic. By altering the roots of history from which time-travel technology had sprung, he set out to eliminate time travel itself—all except his own.

In the Deep Hole incident of 2003 he found the taproot of temporal technology. The first contact of an exploratory drill with a fragment of pure gravity—a piece of black hole rising from the earth's tiny neural core—was by all probability calculations a global disaster of enormous proportion. That drill bit, breaching the surface tension of a ten-million-cubic-meter globule of pure negative force—pure antimatter—set off an implosion that pulverized a quarter of the world's surface and triggered a new global ice age. Probability indicated centuries of chaos, leading to a neo-Paleolithic world in which the only advances would be those it suited Kaffer to allow.

By all probability, that was the result, but eventuality had intervened. Because of a late-twentieth-century discovery— that light could be derived directly from gravitation—the world by 2003 was effectively shielded by a field of kinetic reversal. Every instant of every day, billions of tiny facsimiles of the universe's conception were occurring—primal gravity becoming primal light through photogravitational flux.

Deep Hole still occurred, but the result was that of eventuality, not probability. Most of the instant's enormous primal energy was shunted directly into the fourth dimension. As a global disaster, Deep Hole was about on a par with a significant meteor strike. Its primary effects were temporal, rather than physical. It scattered bits of anachronism as far upstream as the 1930s and downstream into the Arthurian time storm itself.

And from its rubble, temporal technology was born.

To the megalomaniac mind of Kaffer, global chaos was a reasonable price for his objective. If he couldn't start with a malleable twentieth-century world to achieve his personal infinity, he would start with a Paleolithic world crawling out of global devastation.

So the Frank Inertial Reaction Energy principle was consigned to obscurity—a set of unpublished patents buried in the data banks of the United States Patent Office, sealed by a license contract in the custody of his tame psychopath, Carter Vaughn . . . Delta One.

The alteration had been made. Incident by incident now, probabilities should drift toward the cataclysm of 2003. Kaffer knew it must occur, but he yearned to observe its progress. Simple observations—routine scrutiny of circumstances and events as drilling began at Deep Hole—would have assured him that his plan was proceeding. But he could not observe personally. Emergence from L-270 was to risk discovery by L-383, or by one or another of those natural timers—gifted individuals whose fetal development had coincided with a gravitic anomaly, resulting in minds that could velocitate at will. The existence of such freaks was a matter of record. His first Delta agent, recruited from the indigenous population, had been one of them. But Quark was dead now, the victim of powers like his own.

Subsequent Deltas were not timers. They were carefully selected nontemporals. Until the emergence of the Whispers, Kaffer had used them—among other purposes—to track down timers for his study.

He had discovered the physiological basis of timers' abilities, and needed only a finer analysis of their genetic makeup to duplicate it in himself. But like the desire to watch his historical changes progress, the means to decode a strand of DNA was beyond the shelter of his pyramid and thus beyond his reach. The genetic laboratories he needed did not exist in the pre-Arthurian era. They were concentrated in the period 2388–2410, and the only access to that future was the Whispers' conduit.

Angry and frustrated, Kaffer prowled T2 within the pyramid shell. Without moving from the precise three-dimensional coordinates of Khafre's Horizon, the enclosed reality that was L-270 still could range across nearly five millennia of historic time, from the first sealing of the Pyramid of Khafre on the equinox of the Year of the God Kings 334 to the verge of the Arthurian Anachronism. But beyond the instant of its own pre-Arthurian emergence half a world away, in A.D. 1947, it was blind.

It was the classical "probability paradox." Upstream time—earlier time—was fixed and viewable. Downstream time could be observed only at the point of occurrence. Scanning sensors focused on the 1990s produced only one image on the loop's internal holograph displays—a view of cleanly jointed stone blocks, the encasing shell of Khafre's monument and thus of the loop it contained.

Kaffer had relied upon his Deltas, especially Cantrell, to provide input on occurrences in the immediate pre–Deep Hole era.

And now Cantrell had disappeared. He had gone to nineteenth-century Russia to eliminate a timer, and had not returned.

After Quark, Kaffer had elected to employ four Deltas. He liked the symmetry of the pattern—the triangle "delta" representing changelessness, the four deltas conjoined on a rectangular base to form a perfect pyramid. *His* pyramid. The symbol of a changeless world order lasting forever with himself as its apex—its God. Eternal stasis. Infinity.

He had chosen his Deltas methodically, for their strengths and their weaknesses. He had observed them as adults, then gone back to recruit them as children. In each head he had planted his destruct device, and in each psyche his demand for total allegiance.

Delta One was the perfect psychopath: remorseless and intelligent, totally unreliable except in one respect. Carter Vaughn would always do what benefited himself, and to benefit himself he must serve Kaffer.

Delta Two was the egoist: the complete politician, power-mad and readily corruptible—not a great intellect, but a clever, convincing man whose charisma gained the respect of others like himself. Roland Hedrin had been very useful, until he let himself be discovered by Whispers.

Delta Three was the ideal soldier: once recruited and indoctrinated, he followed instructions without question. A living robot of a man, not especially smart but totally reliable, he seemed immune to fear and did not hesitate to do anything—anything at all—that Kaffer ordered him to do. Of them all, Cantrell was the one Kaffer trusted for reports on the world outside L-270.

Delta Four was the fanatic: devoid of any human emotions, any normal desires, Delta Four lived for one thing only—to see the merciless hand of vengeance fall upon all those who were "evil." For Delta Four, Kaffer had made himself the judge of wickedness. Elusive and covert, Delta Four was a perfect social saboteur. Asian probability projections verified as recently as Carter Vaughn's latest report read like a chronicle of Delta Four's agenda: the amassing of nuclear forces in central Asia, Soviet and Chinese warheads aligned along a three-thousand-mile front while tolerances deteriorated daily. Hell was about to break loose in Asia, thanks largely to the dedicated meddling of Delta Four. From the beginning, it had been Kaffer's plan to reduce half the world and focus his attentions on the other half. The impending Asian conflicts—Delta Four's assignment—would accomplish that.

Even for Kaffer, though, personal dealings with Delta Four were upsetting. It was like dealing with a spider. He rarely called on her now for interviews, and even less often for specific tasks. But when he did, the results were lethal and final.

There had been these four. Now, apparently, there were only two. Hedrin was dead, and he could only assume that Cantrell was dead, too.

In the King's Chamber of the Pyramid of Khafre, on the stone bier that had held the sarcophagus of Pharaoh Khafre, Kaffer had generated a small virtual display—a schematic model of the world order that was his dream. Fantastically and minutely complex, a holographic polyhedron consisting of hundreds of megabytes of sociological, physical, and sequential data, the display was a pyramid within a pyramid. The perfect social order, Platonic utopia with no tolerance for variation. A self-sustaining global stasis with every sentient creature accounted for—breeders, tenders, producers, assemblers, distributors, supervisors, controllers, and wardens, and at the vertex of it all himself, directing everything. Suitable work for a god.

At the display's flanks, calendar chronometers scrolled busily, keeping track of L-270's temporal placement second by second, registering the corresponding T2 times outside the shell of Khafre's tomb, and recording the loop's precise condition and resonance—180-minute-long waves of T1 duration at a frequency of three to the negative 666th power impulses per millisecond, the velocity of pure gravitational pull, exceeding eleven times the speed of light.

The one-time historian of UEB and observer on L-270's mission into the time storm, the scholar 1KHAF4—Kaffer—glanced at the chronological readings. Smug lids drooped over large, dark eyes, and he rubbed dainty fingers against the sides of his bald head, massaging the temples. At this moment, beyond the blind limestone and granite of the Pyramid of Khafre, the year was 1998. Many things were happening out there in concurrent time, but few of them mattered. What did matter was that, at this moment, the secret of Dr. David Frank's inertial energy device was locked safely away—its fate sealed by a license agreement secure in Carter Vaughn's private vault.

That contract was a guarantee that there would be no gravity lights to interfere with cataclysm when Deep Hole's drill bit touched the Oglalla Singularity five years from now.

On a waiting console Kaffer touched keys, and a readout scrolled across a virtual screen. Covertly, he analyzed the pulse rate, breath rate, perspiration count, metabolism counts, and synapse patterns of Delta One, a third of a world away. Carter Vaughn was either copulating or tormenting someone. Vaughn was a man with broad sensual appetites and not the slightest trace of conscience. Murder and mutilation had appealed to him for a time. He had enjoyed his work for Kaffer until he became bored with it. More recently he had become a sexual sadist, and his power in the American corporate world gave him virtually free rein to satisfy his desires. Sex and torture—the taking of pleasure and the giving of pain. His biological readings said he was doing one or the other—or both—right now.

Either way, Delta One was in good health and was enjoying himself. The synapses indicated no dread or concern—only pleasure. Therefore nothing was going wrong. Carter Vaughn might lie. He was, in fact, a pathological liar. But his fundamental chemistry did not lie. Certainly the man known as Delta One would have been considered a monster in any age—a Jack the Ripper, a Marquis de Sade, a Caligula, a Vlad the Impaler—but his brain patterns were reliable. He knew of no cause for concern.

1KHAF4 relaxed a bit. Everything was as it should be.

West Central Kansas
Present Time

Twenty-five miles southeast of Dodge City, on Highway 54, a Cossack on a Farmall pulled into the town of Bucklin.

Aleksandr Sergeievich Novik had come a long way in three days and learned much about this strange world. Two of those days had been spent just getting past the sprawling city of Wichita without being stopped. There had been instances of confrontation—once when he killed a pig at Haysville, then had to pay its owner in silver rubles from his purse, and again outside of Cheney where he traded his requisitioned horse for a ride to Pratt aboard a farm truck.

It had been a nervous hundred miles, but in the process he had learned to barter in this new land and had picked up a smattering of the *Angliske Lingva* spoken here. He knew he had left a trail of puzzled people behind him, but mostly the reactions he had met were friendly curiosity. In this land and this time, Aleksandr Sergeievich understood that he was a peculiarity. His stained, dusty uniform, his high boots and voluminous britches, his lapel insignia and cross-strap leather belts, his slung saber, his fur hat, the great bearhide cloak he carried like a rolled pack on his back, his rifle protruding from it, even the heavy box he carried on his shoulder—all of these were objects of fascinated scrutiny wherever he went.

The language barrier had been a minor inconvenience. He discovered that most people understood basic hand signs if not the words that went with them. But he was lonely. It would be nice, he thought, just to have someone to talk to.

At Bucklin he stepped down from the Farmall and waved a friendly salute to the young man who had provided the past five miles of his transportation. Then he stood on a wide, sand-sifted thoroughfare and looked around. The main road passed straight through town, east to west, and he could see the distances where it went. The land here was like the high Siberian steppes—immense and monotonous, flowing smoothly away toward impossibly distant horizons.

He had some idea of where and when he was. This was the central plains of North America, most of a century beyond his time. In geographic distance he was thousands of miles from home—at least five thousand miles, and maybe as much as ten. For the other part of it, the distance in lost years, he simply tried not to think about it. It was more than a lifetime.

I do not belong here, he thought. I should sit down right here, on this box, and close my eyes, and maybe in a heartbeat I would die and wither away and become dust. And who would care? Who would even know? By all that is right, I died a long time ago—long before most of these people were born.

And yet, there was the problem of honor. I am Aleksandr Sergeievich Novik, he reminded himself. I am Russian by birth, aristocrat by some fraction of my blood, an officer by decree, and a Cossack by design. I do not sit down and die. I strive. I go on, and if the journey is impossible, I simply try harder.

Across the sandy blacktop of the highway, a little restaurant presided over a gravel parking lot. He was hungry, thirsty, and in need of rest. These would be available there. When the highway was empty of *mahksins* he hoisted his box and crossed.

There were a few vehicles in front of the place, and people inside. At a table near the entrance a gray-haired, middle-aged couple sat, watching him with fascinated eyes as he entered. The man half rose from his chair, seemed about to say something, and the woman placed a cautious hand on his sleeve. She whispered something. The man hesitated, sat, and opened a small leather case. They peered into it, looked up at Aleksandr again, and then back into the case.

He strode past them. At the nearest counter a wide-eyed girl stared at him.

"Gdyeh twalyet?" he asked politely.

She cocked her head. "What?"

Behind him the man at the front table spoke up. "He's looking for the men's room, miss."

"Oh," she said. She turned and pointed.

"Spacebo." He nodded.

The toilets were at the back of the room, two doors in a short hall. Little stick figures marked the doors. He chose the one without the skirt. Inside, he relieved himself, washed his face and hands at the sink, and rearranged his burdens.

The gray-haired man from the front table was waiting for him when he came out. With wary excitement, he asked, *"Russkyi, da?"*

"Da," Aleksandr admitted. *"Ya Russkyi."*

The wariness faded. "Ah, Alek . . . Aleksandr Sergeievich?"

Aleksandr was mystified. *"Da."*

Suddenly the man was smiling broadly, pumping his free hand. In rough but intelligible Russian he said, "Welcome! I'm Michael. Michael Constantine. We've been waiting for you. Mama said you'd be here, and here you are!"

"Waiting . . . ," Aleksandr tried, then tried again. "You are waiting for me?"

"Of course. We . . . oh, but I can't tell you that. Just come! Sit and have some food. Something to drink. Then we'll go. Our car's just outside."

He ate with Michael and Beatrice Constantine. They were friendly people, full to bursting with some secret thing that they were determined not to tell, not even by hint. Still they talked, and though Michael spoke the mother tongue poorly and Beatrice hardly at all, still it was pleasant to exchange words that Aleksandr could understand.

Their "car" was a long, quiet white machine that went like the very wind, it seemed. "Only going about sixty," Michael told him, indicating a dial on the dash. "Cruise control—I use it all the time."

The road rolled out ahead, westward, and eventually Aleksandr Sergeievich eased his white-knuckled grip on the upholstery and leaned back to enjoy the ride.

The sun was low in the sky ahead when they rolled into a town larger than the dozen or so they had passed, and Michael turned his wheel right, then left for several blocks, then right and left again. They pulled up in the driveway of a pleasant-looking little house, and Michael opened his door.

"Come in, come in," he said, a grin of anticipation creasing his aging face. "Mama's waiting for you."

The front door opened into a cool, shaded room with upholstered furniture here and there among a myriad of other things. Framed pictures were everywhere, ornaments and whatnots filled glass-fronted cabinets, and . . . Aleksandr's eyes widened. On one wall, dominating the painted plaster surface, a very old bearskin cloak was hung, spread for display. Just above it, crossed on pegs, were an old rifle and a saber—*his own* rifle and saber, except for the patina of age.

Beyond an open door he glimpsed a high bed. An old woman lay there, half-upright on white pillows. A very old woman, with hair like a halo of spun silver around an alabaster face.

"Come in, Aleksandr Sergeievich," Michael urged. "Leave

your belongings there on the couch, if you want to. They'll be safe. No? Well, bring them along then." He turned toward the bedroom door. "Mama? He was there, like you said. We brought him."

With Beatrice right behind him, Michael crossed the living room and went into the bedroom. Aleksandr hesitated, thoroughly confused, looking around with wonder, then started to follow them. But there was someone else there, standing in his way. He gasped. "Anya? Anya Karasova? Are you . . ."

She said nothing, but she smiled a radiant smile, came toward him, and clasped his hand.

Something happened then—something just beyond perception. Aleksandr shifted his amazed glance, and the room was different. The bearskin, rifle, and saber were gone from the wall. The furniture was different furniture, and the room was simply decorated, not cluttered as it had been. Even the colors were different. And the street beyond the open window was less noisy than it had been . . . more serene.

Beyond the open bedroom door was an empty room. The bed there might have been the same bed, but its covers were different and there was no one in it. There seemed to be no one else here at all . . . just himself and the lovely young woman holding his hand and gazing up at him.

"Ah, I know," she said softly in perfect Russian. "It is much to digest, is it not? Did you recognize our child? But of course, you couldn't, yet. But never mind, Aleksandr Sergeievich. It will all be clear, in time."

"But what . . . are you really you? Really Anya? I mean . . . why am I here? What is it about?"

"I am really me." She smiled. "Just as I was the day I saw you at parade in St. Petersburg. I watched from the balcony. You rode a fine black horse with white stockings, and the thirty men in your troop all rode matching sorrels. Do you remember? You looked up and saluted me, and made all your Cossacks salute, as well. I thought you were the most handsome soldier I had ever seen, and I made my matron tell me who you were because I had seen you other times. Even when

I was just a little girl, I always saw you. And now you are here."

He gazed into lustrous dark eyes and felt that he might drown there. "Here . . . yes, I am here, but? . . ."

"You will understand," Anya told him. "As much as anyone can understand. The year now is 1938, and there is time here for us—a little time before and a little time to come. For now it is enough that you are my husband and you have come home."

∞

Annotated Concepts:

1. Space and time always occur together. Everything that exists or occurs has the dimensional coordinates *x, y, z,* and *t*. (*Nobody is anybody without four references.*)

2.
$$F = G\,\frac{M_1 M_2}{d^2}$$

   (*The lower you are, the harder you fall.*)

3. Inertia cannot exist in a gravitational field, except as a volatile stasis. Either gravity or light, superimposed on such "conditional" inertia, results in a spontaneous and apparently instantaneous generation of the other. The circuit of flux in such a reaction can be represented schematically as a circle with gravity and light at 0 and 180 degrees on the circumference, slow light at 90 degrees, and free fall at 270 degrees. (*Enlightenment can be heavy stuff.*)

4. Each dimensional coordinate has two directions, each intersecting all other dimensions simultaneously at any point. (*The most coincidental thing about coincidence is that there's so much of it.*)

DERIVATIONS: A. EINSTEIN, I. NEWTON,
EUCLID, G.F.B. RIEMANN, N. TOLAFSSON

∞

XV
Counterforce
L-383

"It *was* a TEF link," Teal Fordeen confirmed. "But now it isn't anything. Just a dead solid-state matrix."

"It wasn't dead when I found it," Adam mused, gazing at the virtual reality field behind the Whisper leader's console. In the display a delineated terrain rotated slowly, little specks of light in sparse patterns on an undulating surface of greenish grid lines. "It glowed. One face of it had little dancing lights. I guess I should have traced it then."

"You couldn't have." Teal shrugged. "It would have cost you a hand if you'd tried. It was a dedicated link, code-sealed and destruct-programmed. Only its holder could use it."

"The question is," Amanda Santee said, coming from behind a star screen where a portion of the Milky Way flowed like bright beads in deep velvet, "where did it come from? A TEF link is Whisper hardware."

"It isn't ours," Zeem Sixten said defensively. "We don't use detonating plastics. And our device is autoinventory. Everything we have is accounted for."

Teal had started to speak, but now he lowered his big eyes. "That is correct." He nodded. "The TEF link you found isn't L-383 equipment."

"But it *is* your technology," Adam noted. He pointed at the moving holograph behind Teal. "What's that? Road maps?"

"In a way." Teal nodded. "We're reading the link's spatial coordinates. It won't tell us when it was set for. The temporal vectors were soft-mode. They died with the card's electronics. But maybe it will tell us where."

"Those are visual perception coordinates, aren't they? Geographic views?"

"Geotopography," Teal explained. "We learned the hard way that simple cartography doesn't work for time travel. Planet Earth is an irregular globe with an uneven surface, and the globe is in motion—rotating on a shifting axis, orbiting elliptically around a star that is following a weaving path through a spiraling galaxy in a swirling universe. There are no fixed points of observation, except on the planet's exposed land mass itself. So we construct visual images of actual terrain and navigate from there."

Mandy moved around to stand beside Adam. Nearby, KT-Pi stifled a smile, noticing how the hands of the two protomorph timers touched, lingeringly, as always when they were together. They're just as human as we are, the little Whisper thought. Maybe more so, because each of them is unique. These two timers are as comfortable with us as we with them. But other timers might not be.

"And the TEF link contains such an image?" Mandy asked.

Teal nodded. "Exactly. All TEF links do, as a fail-safe. We believe we can match it to a location in our banks. So far we have several possibilities. There is a fair terrain match in Greenland, for instance, and two in Africa—one in South Africa and one on the lower Nile. There are also possibilities in Manchuria, Argentina, Antarctica, Australia, and Spain, as well as one in Mississippi. We've tentatively ruled out those in the southern hemisphere because the link indicates that its TEF has a single-point galactic reference. That almost has to be Polaris."

"If you have Polaris as a reference, you should have a fix on latitude," Adam noted.

Teal pointed a small thumb at the holographic screen behind him. "That's what we're looking at now," he said.

"Three fixed dimensions," Adam mused. "But the fourth was soft. Sounds like anywhen in a stable where. Almost like a closed loop."

The rotation stopped, and figures scrolled across the display. Teal glanced at his console, touched pads there, and the display changed to a sequence of shifting overlays. Doubled configurations danced behind him, dizzyingly, then stopped.

"That's it," he said. "The lower Nile site. Your TEF link card was programmed to take its holder to Upper Egypt. West bank of the Nile, between the towns of Giza and Dahshūr."

"The land of the Pharaohs," Adam muttered. "Memphis, Giza, Abu Sir, the Sphinx . . ."

"Pyramids," Mandy added. "Equilateral pyramids."

"But we don't know when," Teal repeated. "A TEF can be anywhen."

"So can we," Adam reminded him. "I can go there and look."

"For what?" Zeem Sixten asked bluntly. "Someone or something that you can't identify, sometime within a span of millennia? I suggest it is we who must conduct this search."

Teal Fordeen gazed up at the two pre-Arthurians, thoughtfully. After a moment he said, "Zeem is right. It is our kind of puzzle. Besides, anyone who could and would alter an entire history—anyone who has access to TEF technology and has used it as the Deltas have—is quite capable of defending himself against inquisitive indigenees. Even timers. A T1 auto-emergence in his vicinity is bound to be noted."

"And a closed-loop emergence wouldn't be?"

"We have our defenses, too," Teal said. "If we know what we're up against."

Adam gazed at the little Whisper, thoughtfully. You *do* know what you're up against, don't you, he thought. What aren't you telling us? "You know more than you've said," he suggested. "You have an idea who it might be out there, don't you?"

Teal lowered his eyes again, apologetically. "We've told you everything we're sure about, Adam."

Mandy was studying the virtual field. "How about a harmless emergence?" Mandy suggested. "If the Delta control is attuned to T2 reentry at a stationary location, it shouldn't matter when one emerges. He'd see it. But what if it were an ordinary event? Something that might not be seen as a threat?"

Adam glanced down at her. "Like what?"

"Like tourists visiting the pyramids," she said. "Like the kind of excursion that Anywhen, Inc., might arrange. Maybe a group of travel agency clients who just want to see how those monuments were built. Lucas and Maude have had dozens of customers, and nobody has bothered any of them."

"You could get the word out, you and the Hawthorns?"

"To observe the building of an Egyptian pyramid? Of course, we could. Get the grapevine going—Maude and her telephone, a little networking . . . we might even throw in the quarries of Tura for a package tour. But which pyramid? They were built at different times."

Teal Fordeen studied his console. "The second one. The one that looks tallest. It really isn't, but it's on higher ground."

" 'Cheops was first the hereafter to call,' " Adam recited thoughtfully. " 'Then Khafre the Great, overshadowing all . . .' It's that one, then. The TEF link's focus was on the Pyramid of Khafre, the tomb of Khafre."

"Khaf-fer," Zeem Sixten growled. "Right out of two-seven-oh mission archives. Appropriate, isn't it?"

"That is mere speculation, Zeem," Teal cautioned. "We don't know that for sure."

"Don't know *what* for sure?" Amanda asked. But there was no answer. The Whispers had said all they were going to say.

Mount Vernon, Illinois
Autumn, 1996

At a public rest stop on a hillside embankment above the interstate, Eddie Ridge eased "Baby" to a stop and shut her down.

"I need an hour's sleep," he told Jack Higgins. "Don't wander off. When the hour's up I'm rolling."

He climbed down from the big Kenworth tractor and walked around it several times, stretching his legs and admiring his machine. It carried 1996 plates now, as did every other vehicle he had seen since leaving Kansas, and he thought again of those weird minutes he had spent at Lenexa, switching to them.

The roads around the truck stop had been deserted when he pulled in, the service station an island of light among dark, sleeping streets. He had parked in a side lot, facing the exit drive, and changed Baby's plates. While he was doing this the frontiersman, Jack Higgins, had appeared at his side, freshly bathed and dressed now in faded Wranglers, a plaid shirt that bulged at the shoulders and biceps, Redwing work boots, and a Coors gimme cap.

But for the slim long rifle in his hand and the powder horn, possibles pouch, knife, and tomahawk he wore, Higgins might have been just another burly freight handler on his way to work. Eddie had stashed him in Baby's sleeper and activated the little sparkling credit card, just as Lucas Hawthorn had taught him. Then he had climbed into the cab, fired up the diesel, and waited, watching idly as a gleaming new silver-streak Corvette appeared from somewhere, pulled into the station's lit lot, and disappeared toward the fuel bays on the opposite side.

Vaguely he had wondered what a car like that, still carrying its dealer tag, was doing at a place like this at this hour of the night.

Then the slow-heavy-fast-flash thing happened—time transference, they called it—and suddenly the only lights in the vicinity were the amber overheads of the nearby interstate and a scattering of dim streetlights further out. Every light in the station had gone dark. Warm, summer breeze had become cool breeze with the feel of fall. Overhead had been cloudy skies, but now there wasn't a cloud in sight—just the suffusing glow of a full moon.

Baby's big headlights showed a bizarre path: The concrete paving stopped short at a clean-cut edge seventy feet short of the feeder road curb—seventy feet of untrammeled weeds where there should have been a lit drive. Eddie selected a gear, and big wheels rolled. They bumped across the eight-inch drop at the edge of pavement, rumbled over the intervening space, took the curb in stride, and swung left toward the interstate.

In his rearview, Eddie saw the silver-stripe skimming around the dark building, its headlights sweeping the darkness.

The sports car hesitated at the edge of pavement, then bounded forward, bounced across the weed strip, and found the road. As Baby rolled under the interstate and swung left on the feeder ramp, the 'Vette was right behind her.

From the crest of the overpass Eddie looked left and blinked. Where they had just come from, just up the cross-road, there was no truck station now. Nothing but a moonlit vacant lot flattened in its center where great weight had crushed the undergrowth.

"Spooky," he muttered.

The black KW rolled high and handsome across Missouri with a quick stop at an off-road dive where Eddie bought bar-beque and beans while Jack Higgins persuaded some hotshots on Harleys to rethink their options and maybe even start going to church.

Now with splendid autumn all around and a long sun behind them, Eddie gave Baby a final perusal and climbed into the sleeper to rest his eyes for an hour while Higgins wandered around, gawking at the panorama of a bustling interstate highway. Eddie made sure the Kentuckian's armaments were stowed safely in the truck, then he curled up for his nap.

He awoke a half hour later to the sound of someone banging on his door panel. Autumn sunset painted the sky above the hills in shades of rose and violet. Up on the crest of the embankment Jack Higgins stood, facing out across the valley ahead, watching the lights of civilization come on in the distance. Eddie yawned and crawled over the driver's seat. The rest area was nearly deserted at this time of evening, though the highway below was a pair of wide rivers of traffic, flowing each way.

Nosed in just ahead of the Kenworth was a silver-streak Corvette with dealer plates. Eddie opened his door and looked down into tired, desperate eyes under a mop of unkempt hair. The young man's necktie was loosened and crooked, and his suit looked as though he had slept in it. He was hardly more than a kid—a confused, rumpled Boy Scout with a two-day growth of stubble on his cheeks.

"Man, am I glad I found you!" he blurted. "You *are* the same one from Lenexa, aren't you? Maybe you can tell me what the livin' hell happened back there, 'cause I been lost ever since!"

Southwest Kansas
May 25, 1952

"It seems so small," Tombo said quietly, pausing at a street corner to look this way and that along empty, sand-dusted brick streets lit only by little pools of glow from the incandescent lamps on wooden poles at each intersection and by the brilliant starlight filtering through the branches of stubby elm trees. "I guess this is really how it was, when I was a kid. Seventeen or eighteen . . . high school. Over forty years ago! I had forgotten how it was then. Or maybe I never really saw it back then. It seems like everything should be bigger. I remember it, but not as such a *little* town. I guess memories get pretty distorted over the years."

"It's a lot like the place in Iowa where I grew up," Jill Hammond said. "That was just a little town, too. Not so dusty, though. The trees were different there, and I think the houses were bigger."

"Yeah, I thought these were bigger, too." He stood slumped, listening to the dry song of the ever-present wind. A ghostly tumbleweed rolled languidly down the street, past where they stood, and somewhere in the distance a dog barked. All around them, the little town slept behind dark windows.

"A little island in an endless sea of wheat fields," Tombo said. "We used to live . . . I guess *they do* live . . . right down that street, a few blocks. Dad and Mom and Lucas . . . and me." He indicated a side street leading southward. But Jill noticed that he was looking to the west, along another street. In the distance there, car headlights were visible, just turning at an intersection several blocks away. It was the only moving vehicle in sight.

"Her house was . . . is . . . over there?" Jill asked.

He nodded. "About a mile." Tombo lowered his head,

shaking it angrily. "That was a long time ago, Jill. I don't want to think about it now. What time is it?"

"I don't know. My watch is still set like it was. It's after midnight, though. Maybe two o'clock?"

"We can't do anything for hours yet! Why did they put us down at this time of night? What did Lucas think he was doing?"

"Maybe he thought he was doing you a favor," Jill suggested. "Maybe he thought you'd want a little time, to look around."

"Well, I don't! I want to get this done and get out of here. Back to where . . . to when I belong."

Disinterestedly he watched the approaching headlights coming along the street from the west. It was still the only car in sight, meandering slowly along the old WPA brick street, weaving slightly as it approached. On impulse, Tombo took Jill's hand and stepped back off the walk, into the shadows of a spindly hedge.

"What's the matter?" she whispered, crouching close beside him. "Is it someone? . . ."

"Shh!" He gripped her hand. There was something about the approaching car . . .

It slowed, weaving uncertainly. Over the sound of its engine they could hear tinny music from its radio: ". . . *sends a letter of good-bye . . . it's no secret . . . you'll feel better . . . if you cry . . .*" Old sounds from a bygone time. Yet now, in this when, it was then, and Johnny Ray was the latest sensation on pop radio.

And over the music were slurred, drunken young voices: "Tombo, for Christ's sake, watch where you're going!"

"Shut up, Harold, you pissant! Let Tombo drive! Help me keep this old fart off the floor. Jesus, I think he's dead! Is he dead?"

"He's just asleep, dammit. That's him snoring."

"Tombo, he's your problem! Just get me home!"

"Me, too! Hell, I got school in the morning."

"You're both a couple of frickin' deserters! What the hell do you mean, my problem? What am I supposed to do with an old man?"

"You're driving. You take him home. But let me off first!"

"Me, too!"

In the intersection, the car—a gray '49 Hudson—swerved uncertainly, then turned right and meandered away, up the street. Dim streetlight shone briefly on some of the faces inside.

"My God," Tombo Hawthorn whispered. "It's the Bullet. My old car. That . . . that was me. Oh, God, Jilly! That was *me*!"

The Blue Goose was open all night. At a back booth, over pungent black coffee, Jill rested her chin on crossed arms and waited for Tombo to say something. He was visibly shaken, pale and trembling. When he tried to sip his coffee his hands shook so that some of it spilled.

Finally he raised tormented eyes. "It hurts, Jilly," he murmured. "To actually *see* yourself . . . so young, so long ago. It feels like . . . like a piece of you has been torn out and you can't ever get it back. And Harold and Corky! They were both there, just like they always were. But I know they're dead now. I even went to Corky's funeral, a few years ago."

Jill placed a soft hand on his trembling fingers. "The old man with them. Was that? . . ."

"Ed Limmer." He nodded. "We'd just found him, out in a wheat field. God, we were so scared! We were so drunk we could hardly see straight, but scared, too. We'd emptied a bottle of sloe gin. Damn! Stupid kids! But we found him, and I took him home with me. He was old! Ninety-eight, he claimed. Of course, by then he was living backward. I guess he's only fifty-two or fifty-three now . . . in our time."

"And that's how it all started? This time-travel thing?"

"For us it did. Especially for Lucas. He was just a baby then . . . or I guess it's *now*, isn't it? This really *is* 1952. Ed Limmer started the Limmer Trust. He invested in futures! Of course, he knew what they would do. He'd already been there. He named Lucas as his coexecutor. I guess Lucas was the youngest person he knew."

He paused, tried the coffee again, and this time he was less shaky. Jill understood. Just talking about it eased the reaction to that initial shock.

"He named you, too," she said.

He nodded. "I found out later, when I was twenty-five, that I was a beneficiary, too. For finding him, I guess. Ed Limmer isn't one to forget. But it was Lucas he wanted. Him and the Whispers. That's why Lucas and Maude are in the time-travel business. The Whispers needed an accelerator base in our time for their migration. Their house is Waystop I to the Whispers."

"They could have sent somebody else to this time," Jill noted. "Someone who wouldn't be hurt by being here. It didn't have to be you they sent."

"Yes, it did," he said, his voice strained. "I insisted. I *made* them choose me!"

"Why?"

"I've hurt too much and too long, Jilly. When the boys were in that wreck . . . when my sons died . . . I never managed to turn loose. I couldn't accept it. And then Betty . . ." He looked away, quickly, then turned his eyes upward, as though trying to hide the tears that pooled there. For long moments they sat in silence, then Tombo sniffed and wiped his eyes impatiently.

"Every morning when I wake up, I wish I hadn't awakened," he said. "I live without living, Jilly, but that's no way to live, and lately I've realized that. Maybe it's because of you, I don't know. I think about you more all the time, you know. But how can I really say hello when I haven't ever managed to really say good-bye?"

There were tears in her own eyes then, and they spilled over, little runnels down her cheeks, but she made no effort to wipe them away. "Tombo," she whispered. "Oh, Tombo, you . . . you damned old . . ." She shook her head, then gazed at him. "Then that's why we're so early," she suggested. "Your brother and the Whispers, they've given you the chance to put yourself—that part of yourself here in the past—behind you."

"And I guess this is why they let you tag along," he said. "It wouldn't do much good if I couldn't talk to somebody about it, would it?"

"Then again, maybe it's just because we know our way around this town. You do, anyway."

It was four-fifteen A.M. by the lobby clock at the Elspeth Hotel, and there was nobody at the desk. But there was comfortable furniture in the vacant lobby. Tombo stretched out on a couch, and Jill curled up in a big chair beside it.

"This thing you're supposed to do here," she asked, stifling a yawn, "what's it about?"

Tombo stretched and shifted, turning onto his side. "L-383 has lost its link with the Whispers' headquarters out there in the future," he said sleepily. "But Teal Fordeen thinks they can get a message through the way the first closed loop did, before it was lost. This time—and especially this place—are full of anachronisms. It has something to do with Arthur—the one who caused the time storm in 2050. Somewhere around here is where King Arthur started . . . or will start. Lucas and Maude's house is where he bounced.

"Teal thinks there are . . . preexisting anachronisms here, already in place when Arthur comes along. Like links between some of the fallout on this side of Arthur's mess and some on the other side. It really gets confusing. It has to do with alternate strands of probability that weave back together . . . downstream. I have to find an anachronism here in 1952. Anna Constantine. I know where she lives, and I've met her. I used to cut the grass at that house, when it belonged to Faye Jones."

"Faye Jones? I knew her. She was one of my first patients at Paxton. She used to teach music, didn't she?"

"Piano," he said. "And she took in boarders. Anna Constantine was one of them back then . . . back about now."

"I guess I don't know her. But I remember Faye Jones. A sweet old lady. And I remember when she died, about 1975. I heard some trust fund bought her house."

"The Limmer Foundation." Tombo yawned. "Yes, I know. Anna Constantine became the trustee. That was how Mrs. Jones wanted it. I guess Anna was like a daughter to her. Curtis has been in Anna's house. In our time. He was on some Chamber of Commerce committee with her son, Mike. He said the old lady had a Russian bearskin hanging on the living room wall."

"Constantine—that could be a Russian name, couldn't it?"

"I guess so. Anyway, I'm supposed to find Anna Constantine and give her this package from the Whispers. I don't know what happens then, but maybe she does."

"Tombo, this place—this little town out in the middle of nowhere—it's just a town. But Limmer was here, and you and Lucas. The time thing keeps coming back here. Why here? What makes it so special? Is it all because of that Arthur business in the future?"

"Partly," he mumbled. "But more than that, I guess. It's all tied up in the whole time-whatzit history, though. There's a . . . an anomaly under this place, deep down. A singularity, they call it. There'll be a . . . well, a global occurrence somewhere around here, a few years from now . . . from our time. Some kind of big bang. Physical or temporal, or both. Then later, King Arthur's Camelot will be here, and maybe the anachronisms already here will get past the new ones that event creates. Or cancel out enough of them for a probability strand—an anchor line to the future. God! It takes more math than I have, just to see the outlines. But that's all future. None of it has happened yet . . ."

Jill waited for him to continue, but there wasn't any more. His breathing became slow and steady. After a few moments he snored softly. His mop of silvery hair was a dim halo in the night-lit lobby. Jill touched a lock of it with gentle fingers. A sad smile tugged at her cheeks. For the first time in a very long time, she thought, here and now in this long-gone time that was so bittersweet in his memories, Thomas Bowman Hawthorn slept deeply. She wondered what kind of dreams he would have.

On a bright high plains morning, the twenty-sixth day of May, 1952, Tombo knocked at the door of Faye Jones's house. The pretty young woman who answered was Anna Constantine. Before he could speak, she smiled. In an accent noticeable but not heavy she said, "I know who you are. I've been waiting for you."

She led them into the living room, and Faye Jones came from the kitchen. "Thomas," she said. "My, but you did turn out just fine, didn't you!"

Jill stared at her. "You *know* him?"

Faye's smile became a grin. "Of course, I do, dear. I see him all the time. Of course, that's now, and you've both come from later. But I'd know your gentleman anywhere . . . or anywhen."

Tombo frowned. "Do you mean you're a—"

"A time traveler? Oh, no. But Anna is, you know, and she tells me all about it. But do sit down, please! I have coffee, and there's fresh cinnamon bread in the oven. We should celebrate or something."

"We should?"

"Of course! This is a red-letter day!" She looked at the banjo clock on the wall. "Right about now, I expect Mr. Limmer is waking up at your house. I mean your parents' house. And tomorrow he'll go to the bank and start the Limmer Trust with soybean futures. Then he'll come here to live. In my house! Everything is starting now, just as it did a long time from now. In both directions, of course. In a way, now is when time begins!"

Anna Constantine shook her head. "I wish you wouldn't get so excited, Faye," she cautioned. "We can't tell anybody about any of this, you know."

"Of course not. But Thomas and his lady friend aren't anybody. They're just visiting."

"Did you bring a message for me?" Anna asked.

"Just this." From his pocket, Tombo pulled a paper cylinder that might have been a roll of quarters. It might have been, but it wasn't. "They're CWs," he said.

He handed them to Anna. She crossed to an ornate cabinet and opened a little teakwood music box. Tiny chimes rang a few notes from Rimsky-Korsakov's *Scheherazade*. Anna placed the roll of wafers into the box and closed it. "It's done," she said.

"It is?" Jill blinked. "What is?"

"The message. It has been sent."

"I was just a little girl when my mother found that box," Faye Jones mused. "It was in Camelot, when King Arthur was away on his mountain campaign. My mother helped clean the castle. Nobody knew what that roll of discs was, but she put it away, in the old ITR display room with the Deep Hole artifacts. I guess it *was* found again, later. Otherwise how would the Whispers have known to send it?"

Tombo's mouth sagged open, then he closed it. *Known to send it?* Teal Fordeen's message was only a blind attempt to contact the far future. Or was it? Teal's intricate probability equations danced in his head. Feeling dizzy, he turned away to look out the sun-bright window. Along the street outside, children were passing on their way to school.

I wasn't in school today, he remembered. I did my finals early, so I could take care of Lucas while the folks were gone to Amarillo. But I was too sick from sloe gin to get out of bed. Ed Limmer took care of both of us. And B.J. Connors came by and chewed me out for sheer stupidity.

Others had gone to school, though. Up the block now, little kids were crossing the street on their way to the grade school. Older children passed on the sidewalk out front, heading for the high school. White bucks and blue jeans paraded past. Crew cuts and ponytails and faces alight with addle-essence. Poodle skirts and saddle oxfords, penny loafers and bobby socks and windbreakers with pictures on them. Cotton shirts, cashmere sweaters, and *Blue Tango* playing on a radio somewhere.

He caught his breath, staring intently. Then abruptly, he turned away.

Jill hurried to his side and looked out the window. "Oh," she murmured. Outside, a covey of young girls was passing. One of them—a small, quick creature with plaid skirt and a bouncing ponytail—wore school colors. Cheerleader colors and a too-big letter sweater. When the girl turned slightly, Jill glimpsed bright, blue eyes in a pretty face. "Is that her?" Jill whispered. "Is that . . . Betty?"

He only nodded. In his eyes was an ache so deep that it seemed to fill the room.

The other two women exchanged glances. "A memory?" Anna asked softly, catching Jill's eye.

"A very dear memory." Jill nodded.

Tombo had composed himself a bit by then. "I needed to see her, like that," he said. "I needed to see her once more, the way she was. And she is now, in this time."

"This time is all time," Anna said sympathetically. "Always remember that, Tombo. What was still is, in its own time. You've seen that now. As I see it, with my Alek."

Tombo gazed at her bleakly, trying not to look out the window again. "But I'm not here with her anymore."

"Yes, you are," said Anya Karasova Breskin who was called Anna Constantine. "For all the time that is her time, you fill her life. You always will, forever." She glanced at Jill, then up at Tombo again. "What needs filling is your own life—the rest of it."

Beside Thomas Hawthorn, Jill squeezed his hand softly. "Do you want to go home now, Tombo?"

"Home," he said. "Yeah, I think so. Let's go home. You and me, okay? Home, where we belong."

∞

Relative brevity is a comparative term. It refers to Time2 events as perceived from asynchronic Time1. It does not mean that all your uncles were short.

—AMANDA SANTEE

∞

XVI

The Rogue Loop

Giza, Lower Egypt
TEF T1 Coordinate: Minus 4,419.081 Years
(Ca. 2421 B.C.)

Nearly three hundred persons comprised the procession of Harsiesis Khafre, the living god and pharaoh of the Upper and Lower Kingdoms, from the barge docks below Saqqara across the causeway to the site of the Pyramid of Khafre. Pharaoh's court retinue and personal guard, coming down from Memphis, numbered more than eighty, and were met at Giza by four consorts of the finest Theban spearmen.

Bronze helms and shields flashed in the sun as the true descendant of the falcon sun-god Horus was carried through the sprawling workmen's village on the river's morning bank and up petal-strewn paths to the causeway above the valley temple of Osiriesis Khufu Mer, gateway to the mighty Horizon of Khufu. Following behind were the litters of kin, nobles, and priests and the barrows of scribes, surrounded by men-at-arms of the Behdetite consort. Slaves and menials by the score followed in the path of the procession, while vendors, traders, crafters, and opportunists crowded its flanks in unruly mobs.

It was the first time in three seasons that Pharaoh Khafre had come down from Memphis to personally inspect the progress on the great monument that would be his private gateway to eternity when Osiris welcomed him into his house. The event marked the ceremonial sealing of the tomb. From this day onward, for all eternity, no person would enter the pyramid except Khafre himself, in his immortal death-incarnation as

Osiriesis Khafre, and those who attended him. After today, none who entered the pyramid would ever leave.

Though not as large as the massive pyramid of his predecessor Khufu, Khafre's pyramid stood on higher ground and already its peak—its horizon—stood above that of Khufu's tomb.

Past huts and fields the procession wound, among a score of shrines, veiled temples, and mastabas, to the very foot of the grand causeway where huge pillars rose to form Khafre's valley temple, overlooking the floodplain of the Nile. Between the pillars stood twenty-three statues of himself, and over it all crouched the mighty Sphinx, great silent sentinel attesting to the king's majesty and might.

At the portal the procession halted and the god-king arose from his litter to stand with Ahmhotep, the architect, on a carpet of garlands beneath the cloudless sky. Just across the wadi, groups of scholars and scribes worked at their craft, separate and apart from one another and from the spectacle before them. The eyes of Khafre roved across them, approving their presence, then turned to the mighty silhouette of his monument.

Two-thirds of the way up each of the pyramid's four sides, scaffolds hung on ropes above a dizzying sequence of wooden stages mounted on cedar poles. Each stage was supported by the one below and, in its turn, supported the one above. It was along these stages that the red granite slabs were carried for the final encasement of the great structure.

According to the copious accounting of Ahmhotep's scribes, more than seven thousand men had so far given their lives for the construction of the pyramid, and three thousand still were employed in its completion. Slaves harvested from Nubia, Syria, and even Ethiopia, the men had sweated, suffered, bled, and died for the glory of the god-king, and barely a handful would survive to see the final product of their labors. Northward, beyond the workmen's huts and slave encampments, great flocks of vultures wheeled above the refuse heaps and the heaped remains of pyramid-builders, stacked for the daily burning.

Harsiesis Khafre looked upon his tomb on this day and was pleased. The sealing of the tomb could proceed. The god-king returned to his litter, and the procession proceeded—across the causeway to the east face of the pyramid. There the priests and their acolytes began a series of rituals that would be repeated four times more—once for each face of the stone infinity and once for the monument itself.

Carrying a smoking, copper-sheathed torch in each hand, and accompanied by a cadre of tall-hatted priests, Khafre himself strode the length of the east base, stopping now and then to touch the burning torches to the stone.

On the high, facing bank of the wadi, one of the observer groups crowded together, two dozen hooded figures speaking in low voices. Keeping a wary lookout around them, two or three raised cameras and snapped pictures of the ceremony.

"What's that little fart doin' now?" one asked.

"He's naming it," another explained patiently. "The pyramid will have five names, just like Pharaoh himself. Each face of it will have a name, pronounced aloud by the king and 'baptized' by ritual fire. That eastern face he'll name for himself—Khafre. The other faces will be named for his favorite mortal relatives, and the base—or the whole thing, depending on how you look at it—will have one of the names of the god Horus.

"Just like Pharaoh. His personal name is Khafre, but his first name—Harsiesis—means 'Horus incarnate.'"

The robed observers muttered among themselves, some scribbling surreptitious notes on pads of paper. "I wish I could get a stress analysis on some of those timber joints up there," one of them said, and pointed.

"I wish I could show those catwalks to that OSHA inspector from Topeka," another said, chuckling. "He'd probably have a damn stroke."

"We can't get any nearer than this," the tour guide—a graduate volunteer from the University of Kansas—cautioned. "Remember the rules you all agreed to: look but don't touch, and don't get involved. This is history here."

"Yeah, no anachronisms allowed. We know. Hey, have you seen my— Where the hell did he go?"

"Who?"

"The guy who was standin' beside me just now. The tall guy. Where is he?"

"Dunno. He was here just a minute ago."

In his transference to the interior of the pyramid, Adam ranged back several days, focusing his mind on the open portal itself, watching for any sign of movement there. Reasoning told him that any covert entry into the tomb would most likely be here, just before the ceremonial public sealing of the main entry on the north face. At any time earlier, the entry and its corridors would have been full of soldiers and slave gangs. Later entry would require extreme precision, because the pyramid would be opened only once more—seventy days after Khafre's death, when his wrapped and spice-cured body was placed there to dwell eternally with Anubis, god of the dead.

Positioning himself spatially in the shadows of a low ante-room port, Adam let his temporal senses flow along a narrowing vector of time, his eyes adjusting to the flutter of days and nights passing beyond the main portal—daylight flooding the massive passage, torchlight flickering in darkness, a high-speed review of unrolling events.

Streams of workmen were blurs against the unchanging texture of flickering stone. Then as the vector narrowed and perception slowed, he could distinguish individual figures of people passing. The passage he was in sleeved itself in granite as he watched, and in the final instants workmen and guards shot surprised glances toward the shadows where he lurked. Torches approached, and he altered vector slightly. They searched briefly, but the timer was always behind them, never quite when they looked. Then they were gone, and for long moments of scan the portal and shaft were empty as sunlight stabbed at one wall, crept to the other, and faded to evening hue.

It was then that he saw the intruder. Only a flicker of motion, scurrying past him, then after a few seconds repeating itself in reverse—but it was enough. In the dark hours before morning of the day the tomb was dedicated, someone had entered it, traversed the rising shaft into the darkness within, then returned and crept out in a moment of guttering torches and sleepy, in-attentive guards.

Adam had gambled that, if someone with T1 capability were penetrating the pyramid in this opportune moment, that someone would be too busy to scan for photogravitational wake. The gamble had paid off. The intruder had been unaware of his presence here, despite even the extended period of anomaly necessary for a multiday surveillance in slow-light mode.

By the tiny glow of a battery-operated penlight, in normal duration, Adam went searching. It was dawn before he found what he was looking for. Deep in the pyramid, at the top of the sloping ramp, a nearly thirty-foot-square pillared vault with a ten-foot ceiling opened off a low, obscured hatch from the King's Chamber. The hatch was a trap. Fluted stone flooring just beyond it, precariously balanced on a drift of loose sand, supported tall clay pots whose closed tops sealed a trough through solid limestone. The trough was filled with loose sand.

Khafre and his architect had made certain that none who entered the true burial chamber for his final entombment would ever come out to tell what they had seen. The weight of sandaled feet on the paving stone would break the clay pots, loosing the sand in the trough. The sand in turn would release the final granite block—a massive rectangle of solid stone, which would slide into place of its own weight, at once closing and hiding the hatch to the burial chamber.

It was a fiendishly clever trap, and in a future time it had done its job. The vault had never been found.

Clinging to the hatch wall, avoiding the fluted stone, Adam crept into the vault and shone his penlight around its interior. Everything that Harsiesis Khafre would require in his immor-tality as Osiriesis Khafre had been provided for him. The vault was a treasure house of the finest commodities that Fourth Dynasty Egypt could offer.

And he found something that had never been part of Egypt in any time—in a recess between pillars in the ceiling of the vault was a fully functional slave TEF, its power source apparently the faces of the pyramid itself, their cut stone serving as solar panels for a gravitemporal inertia mass.

Directly beneath the TEF was a single thin sheet of milled steel, twenty inches on a side, obscured by sand. Simple, but effective. A pocket TEF package within the giant pyramid, to be expanded upon by its user at his leisure.

Nearby, thrust deep into a niche in the stones, he found a second TEF cone, unmounted and wrapped in sheepskin. Whoever was setting up this system obviously believed in redundancy. He had stashed a spare.

Adam didn't touch the mounted TEF. But he took the spare and hid it inside his flowing robe. Then he stood for a moment on the steel plate beneath the mounted one, letting his dimensional senses memorize the taste of where he was. Carefully, then, he exited the vault and retraced his steps down the long, sloped corridor to the main portal. Outside, the desert landscape was bright with dawn.

Guards at the entrance blinked, startled by a momentary perception of slowness, then darkness that exploded into brilliant light, a perception only, gone before it could be realized. A trick of the eye. Two or three of them peered into the gloom of the stone tunnel, but there was no one there.

Among the observers on the wadi bank, as the Pharaoh of All Egypt proceeded with the personalizing of his tomb, Adam turned toward the horizon of high dunes to the west. Only a timer might have sensed what hovered there, just above the sands—invisible yet palpable, a constantly shifting anomaly that was not quite discernible to the eye, not even as much as the little trace-mists of fine sand disturbed there by the desert wind.

The perception was not of the spatial senses, but in the mind itself—a shifting of time, as though immediate past and immediate future resonated in slow sequence, a swaying, elliptical pattern of then and now. What he sensed out there on the high dunes was not in any particular location at any precise moment, but it was there all the same . . . waiting.

A loop. A closed temporal loop, idling in a vicinity, maintaining itself as a temporal resonance, waiting to link itself to the planted slave TEF inside the Pyramid of Khafre. Slightly smaller in spatial parameters than L-383, more compact and somehow different in its resonance, it was nonetheless the same phenomenon, and for a moment he was tempted to enter it.

For a timer, it required no more than an act of will to move himself physically and temporally into such a phenomenon and blend his own resonance with its pitch.

Finely tuned instincts told him, though, that this temporal event—this dancing anachronism hovering above the ancient desert—was very different from L-383 in its purposes and its defenses. The very resonance of it suggested danger. There were traps here, traps far more deadly than the one he had just seen in the Pyramid of Khafre.

And, too, he had made a promise to Teal Fordeen. He would search these early eras but would take no action of his own. He would share his findings with L-383. Desert wind muffling his voice, he muttered, "Well, Teal, I know when and where your nemesis can be found. The nest of the Deltas. And I have an idea what we're up against. Something tells me you already know the rest of it, though. I think you know who it is."

Peaks of Otter, Virginia
September 7, 1996
11:28 P.M.

Jessica stifled a yawn as her headlights brightened the reflectors ahead. Lookout Point coming up, she thought. Half an hour home. Two rows of reflectors—white on the right, amber on the left. The white ones were permanent, a graceful arc of diminishing displays bordering the fluorescent shoulder stripe of the highway where it curved around the mountainside. The amber markers and their companion traffic cones were commands, forcing traffic to the right as the open lanes narrowed around a section under construction.

Her little Volkswagen bug hummed peacefully as she eased

to the right lane, then into the long curve ahead. Traffic was light at this hour, out here in the hills. There wasn't a car in sight behind her, and only a dim glow ahead—someone coming the other way, around the shoulder of the mountain. The reflectors dimmed as she passed them, ticking by on the right as skinny shadows against the far silhouettes of the peaks across the valley.

She was tired, but she felt good. She felt, in fact, victorious. Nine candidates, they told her, and she was the one who made the grade.

This is where it all begins, she thought. The years of study, the years of clerical function in DMP, learning the practical aspects of research and investigation—this is where it all comes together.

Staff investigator! Her own cases, her own little sub-department, her own decisions and accountability. It was what she had worked for, what she had dreamed of. Jessica Tinsley, Investigator, Department of Missing Persons.

Now, with God's help, she might really do some good.

The caseload would be staggering, of course. People disappeared all the time, for all kinds of reasons. Some disappeared by choice, some simply as social dropouts. But there were those others among them—children who didn't come home from school and hadn't been heard from since, young people with everything to look forward to, but suddenly they were gone . . . missing children, missing mothers, missing friends of somebody who cared enough to report the disappearance.

I can do some good, she told herself. Sometimes there are patterns, if somebody can make the time to look for them. Sometimes the truly missing can be found.

Along the way, some might have wondered if it was Jessica's own experience—the mother who went to the store and never came home—that drove her. But those who decided such things knew about that. She knew it, herself. And they had simply promoted her on her merit.

It starts here, she told herself. Monday morning I begin.

The approaching headlights swung into view ahead, wavering slightly, and Jessica frowned. Idiot! she thought. Driving like that on a highway like this!

Curious, she focused on the car, wanting to see at least the make and color of it as it passed in the eastbound lane. All she could see at the moment were headlights—the low, racy headlights of a sports car, speeding eastward just beyond the median.

Then suddenly those lights bounced wildly, down and up, and were directly in her eyes as the other vehicle left its lane, bounded across the median and into her single lane, scattering traffic cones and flashers as it came.

Jessica gripped the bug's wheel, eased right and tried to slide past—but there was no room. In an instant the white reflectors loomed over her hood, a guardrail snapped, and the world fell away as the little bug left the road. It seemed to fly, then crashed nose down on hard, unyielding embankment. Down it went, first skidding, then flipping over to roll and tumble down the dark slope, into the trees.

Somewhere in the distance, in the little town below, a steeple clock struck one bell. It was eleven-thirty.

Peaks of Otter, Virginia
September 7, 1996
11:29 P.M.

Jessica Tinsley's Volkswagen hummed cheerfully as she eased to the right westbound lane, directed there by amber flashers and traffic cones that warned of highway construction in the left lane.

Traffic was light at this hour, out here in the hills. The only headlights she could see were in her rearview mirror—a truck and a car, some distance back, going the same way she was going. A glow ahead indicated maybe another car coming around the mountain eastbound, over in the uphill section of the divided highway.

Half an hour home from here, she thought. Half an hour to her snug little house down there in the valley. If I were there now, I'd be able to look up here and see me passing. She chuckled, feeling good—good about herself, about her new job, about life in general. Staff investigator for the Department of Missing Persons.

And I'll be a good one, she assured herself. With God's help and a little luck, I'll be the best they ever saw.

Thinking about her new job, she barely noticed the other vehicles on the road as the bug hummed along the long, curving stretch around the mountain. The eastbound car appeared, ahead and above, some kind of sports job, judging by its headlights. It was moving fast—too fast for a road like this. And its beams swayed in the night.

Idiot! Jessica thought, then caught her breath as sudden glare flooded her rearview mirror. The truck she had seen behind her was right on her tail, bearing down like a leviathan. Big horns blared and it occurred to her that the truck might have no brakes. Hauling hard at the wheel, she swerved right, sideswiping the guardrail as the big diesel thundered past. Her heart racing, she hit her brakes and slowed to a stop, gaping at the scene ahead. Even as the truck had passed her, the sports car across the highway had swerved, bounded across the median and directly into the single westbound lane. The diesel—a tall, black-and-chrome tractor with no trailer, hit high beams and blared its horn, not even slowing. Beyond it the sports car swerved toward the median again, skidded sideways a dozen yards, smashing through barricades and flasher standards, then spun its driving wheels and plunged back into the median. With a crash of rending metal it plowed into a parked grader.

Jessica sat in breathless shock for an instant that seemed like hours. Then there were people at her window—a young, disheveled man with a flashlight and a larger, shadowy figure at her window.

"Be ye sound, missy?" the big one asked. "Not hurt, I pray?"

"I—I think I'm all right," she managed. She struggled with a jammed door, then got out. Big, gentle hands steadied her on her feet. Just ahead, in the median, a twisted Ferrari lay against the swayed wheels of a road grader. She turned, but there was no sign of the truck that had passed her, that had probably saved her life by forcing her off the road. Maybe the trucker hadn't even seen what happened behind him.

Then she saw it, just pulling in to an island of lights a half mile ahead—a convenience center beside the highway.

"I'm all right," she said. "But that car over there—my God, he must have been drunk! We'd better—"

"No," the young man with the flashlight touched her arm, restraining her. "We're supposed to leave him alone. He'll live. What we've got to do is get your car off this road. There's a turnoff just ahead, a gas station where we can leave it. Then you're supposed to come with us."

Jessica backed away from him, warily. He seemed harmless enough. They both did, but one never knew. She glanced at their car—a mud-splattered racer, all sleek lines and engine space. Silver-streak, she thought. A Corvette. Or almost a Corvette. Its whole distinctive profile seemed slightly modified. Customized, she thought.

"I'm sorry," she said, "but I don't think I'm *supposed* to do anything of the kind. I don't even know you."

"Higgins, missy." The big one pulled off his gimme cap and bowed slightly, a courtesy like something out of the past. For the first time Jessica noticed that he had a long rifle in his hand—five feet of steel and sleek hardwood that he carried like a toothpick—and a powder horn at his side. "Jack Higgins, late of Butler's Rangers. An' that's Dewey."

"I didn't mean you have to get in my car or anything." Dewey grinned, and but for the darkness she would have sworn he blushed. "It's just—well, when we get your car someplace safe, would you just sort of, like, stand there with us for a minute? Beside my car? They said they'd take care of the rest of it."

She stared at him. "They? Who's *they*? And where do you think we're going?"

He shrugged, seeming confused and a little desperate. "Kansas, I hope," he said.

∞

If it looks like a duck, and walks like a duck, and quacks like a duck, then it's a duck.

—CURTIS WELLES, inventor

∞

XVII
How Time Flies
Altitude 420

Never had *Sparrow* flown as she flew now. Curtis Welles chirped and giggled with uncontrollable glee each time the dancing ultralight crested a thermal, and laughed aloud as the slightest nudge of the joystick sent her into powerful, climbing swoops and spirals. Beside him in the open frame beneath the great, cleaving rotors, Beejum clung to his Stetson and whispered, "Lord luv a duck!"

"You're a genius!" Curtis repeated to the bushman. "Hallelujah, just feel that control!"

The new rotors, eccentrically aligned and each acting separately as an airfoil, had made all the difference. *Sparrow*'s spidery support frame, devised from two racing-bike frames modified and joined by braces, hung now beneath a big, whirling boomerang. Into the tiny space between the open frames were crowded a wide-eyed Australian aborigine, an aging tinkerer in a bright red golfer's cap, and a lawnmower engine with two fuel tanks. The load was nowhere near *Sparrow*'s abundant lift, but the little craft's stowage space was packed. Beejum even carried his bulging tucker bag on his lap, because there simply was no place else to put it.

Sparrow wasn't designed for comfort, and certainly not for looks, but she was aerodynamically superb. She took to the air like sharks to bait, like a babe to the breast, like lawyers to politics.

"Like a duck to water," Curtis beamed as his idling rotors

227

found yet another thermal and soared upward, reaching an altitude of nearly seven hundred feet before he hastily sideslipped and eased her back down below five hundred. He circled a tight perimeter over the Hawthorn place, feeling frustrated. The area below was a patchwork quilt of manicured little acreages with houses on them—houses like the Hawthorn place down there, with a black diesel truck and a silver-stripe Corvette parked in front, along with Tombo's old Mickey Mouse van and Lucas's Explorer.

Though this was a county away from Wichita, urbanism had sprawled. There were people everywhere. This was a populated area, in the traffic range of tower radar at three controlled airports and two military bases. The free air was far less free in central Kansas than out in the high plains to the west.

As an ultralight, *Sparrow* was considered a toy and restricted to five hundred feet. Violations of the rule wouldn't help him if he decided to get her certified as an aircraft by the FAA.

Yet *Sparrow* flew so prettily that Curtis yearned to test her. Gone was the inherent instability of Curtis's original design— the fragile balance that had translated every shift of weight into sideslip. The boomerang rotors had eliminated all that. What Curtis's gear innovations had done for efficiency, Beejum's rotors did for aerodynamic stability. She rode the air now with competent, spirited grace, and Curtis ached to put her through her paces.

"I want to take her out to Progress," he suggested to Beejum. "Why not come along, if you can?"

"I can go where I bloody well want to, mate," Beejum assured him cheerfully. "I'm on walkabout. Let's go see yer outback."

"We'll give this bird a real test." Curtis leaned the ultralight into a slick left bank. "We'll just let 'em know we're going, and fill the tanks . . ."

His mouth dropped open. Just ahead, above Lucas and Maude Hawthorn's little acreage, a monstrous thing that might have been a black cloud—if any cloud had ever had such a shape and if black were not black but every other color in the spectrum— materialized in thin air. Wide as a city block and tall as a transmitter tower, it seemed to resonate there, directly above the house—a huge, eye-confusing saucer of almost-substance with little flickers dancing through it like lightning.

Beejum stared at the thing in wonder. Curtis grabbed his CB mike and thumbed the switch. "Sparrow One to Anywhen!" he shouted. "You got a damn UFO right on top of you! It's—"

Lightning danced and a cone of slow darkness emerged from the base of the cloud, descending toward the house below. Curtis slammed his throttle down and dipped *Sparrow*'s nose. The boomalight took wind in its wings and arrowed under the saucer rim, buzzing like a crazed wasp. In an instant it reached the descending cone of slow darkness, and a blindingly bright light flared all around it.

"Yer gone barmy, ye coot?" Beejum gurgled, wrestling with his straps as *Sparrow* shot abruptly skyward in hazed, smoky sunlight. Curtis's go-to-hell hat flipped from his head, ticked at the tail rotor, and disappeared from view. Curtis fought his controls as a diving aircraft—a little open-cockpit blue biplane with a machine gun at its nose loomed directly in front of them.

The biplane went one way and *Sparrow* another, barely missing each other. Curtis had a glimpse of amazed eyes behind wide goggles as the biplane's pilot gaped at them.

"Lord luv a duck!" Beejum commented.

Curtis eased his throttle and banked right. His altimeter read 620 feet, but a glance downward told him it was wrong. *Sparrow* was at two thousand feet above the smoky terrain below—a terrain of unfamiliar patterns. There were hedgerows and trenches, little scurrying processions of horse-drawn wagons, field artillery, and clusters of uniformed men running here and there. And over it all hung a pall of smoke and dust, punctuated by the flashes and smoke clouds of exploding shells.

A thousand feet below *Sparrow*, the blue biplane had righted itself and was maneuvering into a climb. Curtis now saw its insignia—dark crosses on both upper wings. But from somewhere two more little airplanes appeared, green machines with bull's-eye targets on their wide, fabric wings, and the sound of chattering gunfire drifted upward. The blue biplane banked, rolled, and looped, but it was a lost cause. As the pair of greens swept past, it burst into flames.

There were more craft in the sky now, a dozen or more of them, darting and circling. Their weaving, lethal dance jarred Curtis's memories of old movies and college history courses. "By the Lord Henry," he muttered. "A dogfight! The Western Front . . . I'd swear that's the Marne down there, and Château-Thierry. Just like the summer of 1914!"

The roar of open-pipe piston engines below *Sparrow* increased suddenly, punctuated by the more distant cacophony of the battle on the ground below. "Do we mean to bloody glide this thing?" Beejum complained.

And Curtis realized why the level of noise from below had increased. It was because of the sudden silence of the Briggs & Stratton engine behind him. *Sparrow* dipped lazily, gliding on freewheeling rotors, swaying like a falling leaf on a still autumn day. Her only sound was the chuff, chuff, chuff of eccentric boomerang blades cutting through the air. On the altimeter, digits ticked off busily, lower and lower.

Like a swaying, dancing leaf, *Sparrow* headed for the ground. The little ultralight had run out of gas.

Waystop I

From the TEF chamber, Lucas heard Curtis's crackling call on the radio in the same moment that Maude glanced through a darkening skylight and saw the cloud. They met at the control booth just as the photogravitational spectrometer there came alive and the little bell rang, signaling a transtemporal event. But whatever transference had occurred was not in the transfer chamber. Instead, it was outside, directly above the house.

With a muttered curse, Lucas spun the TEF focus to wide open and hit the generator switch. It was a trick Amanda had shown them. Without focus, the TEF radiated a field of photo-gravitational reversal that fed back and back upon itself, a humming resonance just inside the extreme ranges of gravity and light through which no force could pass because there was nothing there long enough to pass through. *Aphasia*, Mandy called it—a condition in which the temporal dimension of the TEF's immediate surroundings became self-anachronistic, a field of eccentric T1. With the field in effect, Waystop I wasn't doing any business, but neither was any business being done to it.

"What the hell happened?" Lucas wondered.

"There's something right over us," Maude said. "Like a big, shifting cloud. Curtis and Beejum flew right in under it and disappeared."

Lucas climbed the ladder to the generator port, threw it open, and gazed upward. Dimly he saw an angry darkness there, just overhead, and flickers like brilliant lightning dancing across the intervening space—flickers that dispersed without quite reaching the roof.

"By God," he muttered. "It's a . . . it's like L-383. A closed loop!"

"Well, make it go away!"

"I'll make it go away, all right," Lucas muttered. "Bring me Bud's old whale gun, hon."

Tombo had appeared from the sunporch. He peered up through the trap. "You want to harpoon a time loop?"

"Dammit, yes! The harpoon line is steel cable! Maybe I can short-circuit that thing's skin!"

"Worth a try, I guess." Maude shrugged and went to get the old harpoon gun hanging over the fireplace. By the time she returned, with Jack Higgins behind her carrying a heavy roll of what looked like clothesline cable, there was a crowd gathered below Lucas's trap.

Tombo loaded the gun and handed it up. The harpoon was a five-foot spear with a clip ring for its cable. The propellant charge resembled an eight-gauge shotgun shell.

"Secure the line to the TEF chamber's flooring," Lucas ordered. Tombo hurried to comply. When it was done, Lucas raised the gun. "Stand clear!" he shouted.

Darkness was spreading downward again from the monstrosity overhead, another cone of photogravitational transference. With an angry growl, Lucas pointed the harpoon gun straight up and set it off.

And all hell broke loose.

L-270

It was the boredom of waiting—waiting without knowing firsthand that his plans were proceeding—that finally drove Kaffer to reconnoiter the immediate pre–Deep Hole era. For a time he scanned what he could from his blind refuge inside the Pyramid of Khafre. There were traces of reversal wake in the vicinity—several separate photogravitational events starting in 1998. But the readouts showed no threat. They were just tourists—time junkets activated by that nest of indigenees the Whispers had recruited for Waystop I.

The sheer audacity of it galled Kaffer. The Whispers weren't even supposed to be here, in pre-Arthurian times. This realm was *his*! But not only had they slipped in, they had initiated primitives in their science and their methods, and turned them loose to use the TEF for their own purposes.

He knew exactly where and when the nest was. It was no secret. Even Delta Three had known of Anywhen, Inc., and had dutifully reported it. Kaffer had done nothing about Waystop I, because it meant nothing to him, but the trace wakes he found now—so close to his own base coordinates on the lower Nile at the time of Pharaoh Khafre—were irritating, if harmless. His own realm—the basis of his dream of infinity—was infested by protomorphs!

The scans reassured him, though, and he altered the vectors of L-270. It was time to have a look outside and get a progress report.

Part of it he learned almost instantly, scanning the city of Cairo. There was illumination there, and a lot of it. But it was only the archaic illumination of volatile fuels and electric arcs. Nowhere was there a trace of inertial energy lighting. Kaffer felt easier, knowing that. Had the Frank device surfaced in this period, certainly there would be some in Cairo who had it.

Kaffer felt a touch of elation. Without the Frank gravity-light device, Deep Hole would be confined to the fixed dimensions. All that raw force—it would be an implosion the like of which this planet had never seen. And in its wake would be one certainty: T1 would never be discovered. Time-travel technology would never be more than a myth, and only he, Kaffer, would ever have the power to move at will through four dimensions.

All around him, virtual screens unblocked by stone scrolled the reality of a world on the brink of destruction—a world at the portal of infinity.

Observation and verification, he reminded himself. Leave no observation unverified. Just for this moment, he missed Delta Three. The reports of Delta Three had often been sketchy, but never distorted.

But Delta Three was gone. A touch of a stud gave him a progressive current-duration scan of the earth's surface, corrected to 180 minutes. He activated the Delta blips.

The first to show was Delta Four, a blip in the vicinity of Beijing. Then Delta One's forehead implant registered, as the scan reversed its 180-minute interval and displayed the eastern United States. He was at his retreat again, in the Appalachians. Now one of the wealthiest and most powerful men in the United States, thanks to Kaffer, Carter Vaughn spent a lot of time in his mountain sanctuary. Kaffer knew what he did there, but it made no difference. Let the beast have his sadistic pleasures, he still belonged to Kaffer. And of the two Deltas, he was nearest at this moment to the rising singularity that would be Deep Hole.

With a sneer, Kaffer fingered the recall tab on the keyboard of L-270's TEF, then turned to the steel slab encased below the cone. There was no waiting. At his end of the signal, Delta One had some portion of 180 minutes to prepare himself for transport. At Kaffer's end, the transport was instantaneous.

A slowing darkness, a flicker of brilliance, and Carter Vaughn stood before him, angry but undefiant. Kaffer's summons allowed no resistance.

"Report, Delta One," Kaffer commanded, frowning at the odd, awkward stance of the man. Something was not as it had been.

"The Frank device is buried," Vaughn said. "As you ordered. Its files are sealed, and all rights to it are in my hands."

"As of when?" Kaffer prodded. "Have you verified recently?"

"As of now! Nothing has changed since my last report. How could anything change? The Frank device and all its principles belong to me . . . by airtight legal contract in my vault in New York. Now, can I get back to my business?"

"Your business?" Kaffer's voice was thin and taunting. "Which is it this time, Carter? A female or a child? And what new means have you found to enjoy it?"

Vaughn stared into the shadows, trying—as he always did— to see the face of his master. "Do you really want to know? Should I describe it for you, Kaffer . . . the exquisite sensations of the flesh? The screams? The delicious little trickles of blood over heaving soft skin? Shall I?"

"No," Kaffer snapped. "It is disgusting. You are disgusting, Carter. Shall I send you again to collect brains for me? Would you enjoy that? It has been a while . . . in your duration. Not since the Lipscomb infant, I believe."

"It's boring," Vaughn sneered. "Death—inflicting death—is not a pleasure, Kaffer. The pleasure is in the prolonging of life, once death is inevitable. It is in how they writhe and scream and beg. It is in what they will promise and what they will do, just to delay the pain."

"Enough!" Kaffer snapped. "Insane primitive! Do not taunt me." He touched a control, and Vaughn screamed and went to his knees, his hands clawing at his head. Kaffer released the control. "That is just a reminder, Delta One, of who is in charge here."

Vaughn groveled on the steel slab, stifling sobs, then looked up. "Yes, Kaffer." He stood, lurching awkwardly on his bent, crippled leg. "You—you said Lipscomb? I don't remember a Lipscomb."

"Of course, you do! An unborn infant . . . a latent timer. You collected its brain for me." Kaffer scowled, touching keys. Beyond Delta One a virtual screen scrolled, then stopped. There was no Lipscomb recorded there.

"But I had the infant's brain!" Kaffer snarled. "Specimen date December 31, 1959. I sent you from 1996 to collect it!" Kaffer's eyes widened in the shadows—eyes far larger than those of any human of Vaughn's time. "That crippled leg of yours, when did that happen?"

"In 1996," Vaughn said. "That night, when I wrecked the Ferrari. They never could put the bones all back straight. But you know all about that . . . don't you?"

For a long moment, Kaffer was silent. Then with a shriek of fury he arose from his console, out of the shadows, and for the first time Carter Vaughn saw his face—a tiny, almost childlike face beneath a totally hairless dome of a head. But in the eyes of that face—eyes far larger than Vaughn had ever seen—there was nothing childlike. A rage burned there like flaming ice. "Those indigenees!" Kaffer hissed. "Those primitives! They have the audacity to interfere with *me*?"

The little creature glanced at Delta One, then turned and touched a stud on a console. The merest shimmer of reversal—a reality that slowed, darkened, and blazed with intense pure light—and Carter Vaughn was gone.

Kaffer would deal with this himself. He couldn't reach the Whispers' closed loop, L-383, but by all the powers in the universe he could eradicate their pet protomorphs! He would send them all to oblivion!

Four-dimensional vectors aligned, resonances harmonized, and L-270 disappeared from the night sky over Cairo to reappear in the sunny sky above Waystop I. Kaffer wasted no moments as the closed loop's apparent dimensions stabilized there. Keying reserve power into the matrix of photogravitational flow that sustained the loop, he focused L-270's big TEF downward and keyed it.

His virtual screens registered the incoming blip of a small

flying machine, and mass contact triggered cycle completion as it touched the gravitational cone. Alarms and null vector lights came on, as the screens registered a reaction wholly out of keeping with what had occurred. It was as though the TEF itself had taken feedback from some source.

Below, the house stood untouched, and a trap opened in its roof. People appeared there, doing things. With a curse his ancient ancestors might have admired, Kaffer readjusted his focus and keyed again.

Near Montmirail, France
August 1914

Like a falling leaf, supported by free-spinning rotors, *Sparrow* settled gently to earth in a field of wildflowers. She had barely come to rest when a whine of rushing air passed over and a biplane crashed thirty yards away, digging topsoil with a shattered prop as it nosed over.

"Blimey!" Beejum erupted, and scrambled out of the ultralight's frame. Curtis was right behind him. They ran to the crashed airplane. It had a pilot, but he would never fly again. He lay sprawled, half out of the single cockpit, dead of a broken neck.

"Lafayette Escadrille," Curtis said softly, looking at the dead man's emblazoned jacket. "American, probably. Flying for France."

"Poor bugger," Beejum pronounced, then stepped to the little airplane's fuel tank and removed the cover. "Plenty o' foo-juice 'ere," he reported.

While Curtis siphoned fuel from the biplane's tank, Beejum retrieved tools from his tucker bag and went to work on the plane. It didn't have any mufflers to remove, so he removed the machine gun from its upper cowl instead. "Could be a handy thing," he decided, packing it into *Sparrow*'s little frame.

Back at the biplane he searched the cockpit and found three cases of belt-clipped machine gun rounds. Curtis was just heading for *Sparrow* as Beejum shouldered these. "Mind fetchin' me tucker when ye've a moment, mate?" the aborigine asked. "Got me bloody 'ands full 'ere." He headed for *Sparrow*, thinking of a way to stow a few more items in the tiny, spidery frame. The answer was simple. While Curtis poured gasoline, Beejum discarded the ultralight's little pedestal seats and replaced them with shell boxes.

Curtis returned to the biplane, gazed for a silent moment at the dead pilot, then straightened and snapped a solemn salute. "Lafayette," he said, "we are here."

Picking up Beejum's tucker, he wondered how the aborigine managed to pack so much metal into one small bag. The thing rattled with the happy sounds of accumulated tools and weighed at least forty pounds. Curtis lugged it back to *Sparrow* and dropped it on the ground.

"What do you have in here?" he demanded. "A whole tool shop?"

The bag had flopped open, and Curtis knelt beside it, then stood, holding a small, heavy cone of some material that might have been glass, plastic, silver, or any combination thereof. "What the hell is this?" he asked.

"Nabbed it from the shed." Beejum shrugged. "Haven't used it just yet, so I don't know rightly what it is."

Taking the cone from Curtis, Beejum started to return it to his tucker bag, but Curtis grabbed it and thrust it inside his jacket.

"Give me that!" Curtis snapped. "That's one of Lucas's time things. What are you doing with it?"

Beejum shrugged and climbed aboard *Sparrow*. "All 'ands to make sail." He grinned, pointing upward. Overhead, one of Kaiser William's cross-emblazoned wasps was circling to dive on them, its cowling gun aligned to strafe. "Lively now, mate! There's gunships aloft."

With a glare at the bewhiskered ebony face grinning at him, Curtis braced his foot against *Sparrow*, tugged twice at the Briggs & Stratton's starter cord, and the engine came alive. Curtis wedged himself into the space available, hunkering on a shell box, and took the controls.

Sparrow bit air, shuddered, trundled a dozen feet over

weedy sod, and took off. Her rotors thrumming, she headed for the sky as the German fighter came in for the kill. Curtis and Beejum clung to titanium-alloy struts as the biplane's gun chattered and bullets sang around them like angry hornets.

"Holy shit!" Curtis chirped. His flailing hand hit the rotor engagement, and *Sparrow* dropped, in free fall. Beejum's Stetson disappeared into the rotors, and his tucker flap flew open. Wrenches, drill bits, and a ratchet screwdriver drifted upward. Through the open flap of Curtis's coat, the shiny cone flared in the sudden sunlight. Still activated and volatile from the stored resonance of the closed loop's attack, the sunlight and the sudden loss of gravity were all Lucas Hawthorn's spare TEF needed. It glowed, flickered, and flashed, a sequence too quick even to register on the senses.

Suddenly the biplane was gone. So was the wildflower field below, and so was France. Curtis reengaged his rotors, steadied the ultralight, and looked around at mountain peaks ringing a wide, rocky valley where great, dark beetles crawled in column formation.

"What the hell are those?" he muttered.

As if in answer, several of the beetles raised their snouts, and blue fire erupted from them. A dozen yards to the right of *Sparrow*, searing energies sizzled in exploding air. Then again, directly ahead. All around, it looked as though bright lightning bolts—long, straight lightning bolts that fried the air they sundered—were striking upward from below.

For lack of a better idea, Curtis put *Sparrow* into a tight roll, banked out of it, swapped ends in a screaming dive, and headed for the white-topped mountains rising in the western sky.

∞

The quadrilateral pyramid as a three-dimensional representation of infinity goes beyond symbology. Like conceptual infinity, the pyramid has eighteen surface components: four triangular faces; a rectangular base, which is the fifth side; five points, of which one is the apex or pinnacle; and eight linear corners. The faces of infinity are eternity, universality, reformation, and combination. The base is stasis, the pinnacle opportunity, the angles directionality, and the tripodal "corners" dynamic stability.

Each plane in a pyramid adjoins other planes, none of which are at right angles to it. Yet a line drawn on any plane of a pyramid, in any direction, without adjustment of the line's prime vectors, will precisely meet itself at its starting point as the same line. The course of its path to its beginning can be predicted as

$$>PL \left[\frac{v1 \ v2 \ v3}{5L^{18}} \right] = vvPLX<$$

Given X as a universal constant, and any pyramidal vector as a temporal sequence, the pyramid thus becomes a "map" of both past and future with eventuality as its grid.

—Albert Lipscomb, *Theories of Perpetuity*, 1997

∞

XVIII
Probability and Consequence
L-383

"Most primitive cultures," Teal Fordeen explained, "and certainly a majority of advanced, civilized pre-Arthurian cultures, consider humanity as a given: a reliable and constant parameter identifying the entire 'human race' and every individual within it. To be Homo sapiens is to be human, and individual departures from the accepted standards of humanity, whether in appearance or behavior, are perceived and dealt with as aberrations of choice or circumstance.

"In many cases the idea that some human-appearing creatures are in fact devoid of such fundamentally human qualities as voluntary ego suppression, familial empathy, and basic compassion is shunned as an 'inhuman' concept."

"Mercy for the wicked." Adam grinned ironically. "What kind of humans are you talking about?"

"Any kind." Teal shrugged. "We're all pretty much alike—those of us who are human. But there are some among us who aren't. It wasn't until the late twenty-sixth century though, that humanity accepted the realization that the definition of *human* needed some elaboration. Those who behave monstrously are monsters, not human beings. Concepts such as *crazy, possessed, psychopath, sociopath, criminally insane* were used for centuries to obscure the basic fact that a person without humanity is not human and cannot be treated as one."

"So much for Maniac Rights." Adam shook his head. "And so much for the ethics of law. Now will you tell me why you were so concerned about my penetration of Khafre's tomb? Was it because you feared retaliation if I was discovered?"

"Probably not you," Teal said. "But we are tampering actively with his plans, and he'll realize it soon enough. And we can expect violent retaliation—the response of a monster thwarted. He may not know who has interfered with him, but if he finds any trace of you, you are in extreme danger. Still, you made it there and back, and nothing has happened . . . yet."

"And you know who he is, don't you!"

To one side, Oel Six glanced around. "Teal . . ."

Teal raised a hand, nodding. "Yes, we know," he admitted. "And you should know, too, I think, since you have just qualified yourself as a primary target for him. His name is 1KHAF4—Kaffer. He was . . . will be . . . a member of the team of L-270, the first closed loop to penetrate the Arthurian Anachronism. It is what we've called the 'lost loop,' but I suppose it isn't lost anymore."

Adam whistled softly through his teeth. "He's one of *you*? A Whisper?"

"Not a Whisper, no," Teal said. "But he is of our time. A Pacifican, from a thousand years in your future."

"I wondered about that," Adam admitted. "About your Pacifican culture, I mean. I wondered if the genetics that bred you could possibly have weeded out all the criminals."

"Not really, I'm afraid." Teal lowered his large eyes apologetically. "Not the genetic process itself. The bad seed goes forward with the good. Pacifican culture applied rational ethics to the phenomenon of antipathy. As I said, we have realized that evil is not a human condition. The test is in behavior—the voluntarily chosen behavior patterns of mature individuals.

"You *are* right, Adam. There are very few criminals among us. We ourselves weed them out. But only when we know who they are."

"And this one, this Kaffer—what is he capable of doing?"

"Anything." Teal frowned. "Anything that suits him, I'm afraid."

Suddenly panels dimmed all around, and there were warning flashes at the consoles. A second later Toocie Toonine appeared from a virtual reality bay. "Alarm!" she called. "Something has happened at Waystop I. We've lost contact!"

Teal stood and turned, instantly the picture of authority despite his diminutive size and pallor of age. "C6 response!" he barked. "TEF vectors WS1! Activate!"

Adam glanced once around him at the weary Whispers in their dim-seeming, probability-thinned loop. How could these gentle creatures be a match for the kind of beast Teal described? He saw the circuits closing aboard L-383 and made his decision. "This isn't just your world, Teal," he muttered, unheard. "It's mine, too." With just a turn of his mind, he focused on Waystop I and was gone.

Waystop I

Lucas Hawthorn's old harpoon gun was an antique—a memento from a friend, unearthed in a catchall shop in Maine. But though it was old, it still worked. The eight-gauge propellant shell almost knocked Lucas off his ladder as it hurled six feet of tapered, fluted steel upward, into the looming nothingness of the closed loop above. Quarter-inch steel cable sang as it uncoiled itself to follow.

L-270's temporal resonance now was set at three seconds, its existence in time ranging back and forward by half of that at a wave frequency of sixty cycles per minute. Had it missed its one-in-three-second window, the harpoon would have found nothing to impale. But at the last instant, just as the line began to slacken, L-270 and its wound coincided.

The cone of slow darkness that had begun its descent winked out of existence, and a blaze of light flared on the underbelly of the cloud, radiating outward from the point of penetration.

Enormous energies—energies of pure gravity and pure light—raced up and down the grounded steel cable, myriad instantaneous anachronisms cancelling themselves out as they occurred. The cloud seemed to shudder, went from slow dark to blazing white, and faded around the edges—then was

snapped back into instant reality by the TEF-impervious resonance of the steel floor in the Hawthorn house, projected
through steel cable.

Within L-270, Kaffer screamed his fury, his dainty fingers
dancing on the main console.

The closed loop's existence depended upon motion—
uninterrupted motion in at least one of the four prime dimensions. Abruptly, because of the archaic weapon hurled at him
by the primitives just below, he had lost three of these. L-270
hung at the end of a steel cable, unable to move in any spatial
direction. Immense energies strained as the loop attempted to
stabilize itself in time, and Kaffer fought to keep it resonating.

He narrowed the band to a half-second wave, and nearly lost
his loop to inertia. Frantically he reversed the adjustment,
gradually lengthening the wave and decreasing its frequency.
He had to shake off the tethered barb in the loop's substance.

He adjusted, and adjusted again, cursing those below. Moments of duration crept by, then the hook wavered . . . and
wavered again. Kaffer increased his resonance further, altering
his vertical coordinate as he did so.

Little by little, L-270 rose, pulling itself free inch by inch
from the restraining harpoon.

Kaffer snarled like an animal and turned to another keyboard. The zen-guns were emplaced now, to fire from the loop
on laser direction. Only one pointed downward, but one was
enough. A zen-gun on full power, wide beam, could wipe out
everything in its cone of radiation out to one thousand yards.

With a hiss of pure venom, Kaffer aligned the belly gun on
the house below and triggered it.

Lucas was just regaining his hold on the trap ladder, wincing
from the bruises of the harpoon gun's recoil, when a tall, drab-
clothed figure appeared above him, on the roof. Adam still
wore the rough, gray robe of an ancient Egyptian desert scribe,
but now the robe was thrown back to reveal the dark denim
clothing and sturdy boots beneath it. And in his hand he held a
large ax.

Without hesitation, Adam braced himself and swung the ax.

Its blade severed the pulsing, flashing harpoon cable and sank into the frame of the roof trap, inches from Lucas's fingers.

The cable sang and parted, and the great, dazzling-dark cloud shape above it seemed to veer upward and aside as blue lightning flared from its belly—lightning that sheared off a front corner of the house, exploded Tombo Hawthorn's old van into tiny fragments, then carved a smoking, sizzling trail outward, across the front lawn and into the street beyond. An elm tree exploded, and half a dairy van screeched to a halt, its sheared-off rear suspension gouging little trails in the pavement. Flame billowed high from its ruptured fuel tank.

Above the Hawthorn house, the saucer raced upward at an impossible angle, then seemed to hesitate several hundred feet aloft. For a moment it hovered there, dark and sinister, then it winked out of sight.

Beyond the Hawthorns' front gate, a mushroom of smoky flame climbed skyward and there were sounds of chaos—tires squealing, horns honking, people shouting. The wail of a police siren carried over it all, and a plain, dark Chevrolet careened through the gate.

On the roof, Adam grabbed Lucas's shoulder and shoved him downward. "Get everybody out!" he shouted. "That thing may come back. Use your TEF and get the hell out of here!"

In the hallway below, Lucas whirled to those gathered there. He almost stumbled over Peedy Cue and KT-Pi. The little Whispers were nearly lost in the press of excited people. Lucas stared down at them. "What are you two doing here?"

"We were making a delivery," KT-Pi said. "We got caught in the chamber when you broke connections."

"I can't believe you *harpooned* a closed loop," Peedy chortled. "Only a primitive would think of a thing like that!"

"Yeah, a closed loop. I thought that's what it was." Lucas's frown was thunderous. "Look what it did to my house!"

KT-Pi winced and backed up, tiny and startled. "Peedy just said it was a closed loop. He didn't say it was *our* closed loop."

"Well, whoever it belongs to, it's still out there someplace. We're evacuating. You!" He pointed at the rumpled young man staring at the wreckage of what had been a comfortable living room. "You with the Corvette!" He turned, opened a drawer, extracted an envelope, and a Smith & Wesson revolver. He thrust the gun into his pocket and tossed the envelope to the youngster. It contained a bundle of hundred-dollar bills. "Thanks for your help," Lucas said. "Now take this and get out of here! Go home!"

Pragmatic as usual, Maude stepped between them. "It really was nice of you to help out," she told the mystified youngster. She handed him an Anywhen, Inc., T-shirt and business card. "Keep us in mind when there's time," she said.

To Eddie Ridge, Lucas said, "Take Miss Tinsley in your truck and get away from here, now! Take her home. Use the link card. It'll put you back to '96. Go!"

Ridge headed for the blown-out front wall of the house, but Jessica Tinsley balked. Standing on strong, good legs, hands on her hips, she glared at Lucas. "Out?" she demanded. "I just got here! I'm not going anywhere until somebody tells me what the living hell is going on!"

With a long stride, Jack Higgins stepped forward, swooped the girl up under one massive arm, and rumbled, "Come along, missy. Time to go home. We'll tell you all about it on the way."

Lucas snugged Maude close beside him and spread his arms like a man herding chickens. "Everybody else, into the TEF chamber!" he commanded. "Come on, move! Help me, Tombo!"

"Where to, hon?" Maude asked.

"Wherever it's set for," Lucas snapped. "I'll have to activate from the chamber."

Tombo caught Jill by the hand and led the way, the rest scampering behind him.

Through the blasted front wall, distant voices carried, high-pitched with excitement. "Look up there!" someone shouted. "What *is* that thing, a flying saucer? My God, it's coming!"

In the TEF chamber, Lucas glanced around wildly. There was no time to count noses, not if that *thing* was coming back. "Hang on!" he shouted, gripping the manual override beneath the TEF's bell tower.

Heavy footsteps pounded across the kitchen floor, and a bull voice demanded, "What in God's name is—"

Lucas hit the switch. Darkness and light, and the room they had been in was gone.

"—going on here?" Sheriff Clay Connors finished his question, then turned, glassy-eyed.

They were in a large, open, vaulted room, like an old-fashioned storage warehouse. Tall, closed wagon doors dominated two ends of the lamp-lit enclosure. Between them, a wide double row of sturdy timbers supported a high, open-framed roof. Between and behind the upright columns were storage stalls and closed bins, each labeled with the name of its tenant of lease. The area where they stood occupied at least four of these spaces, confinable by heavy bifold doors. A TEF tower dominated the enclosure, and its floor was sheet steel, brazed at the seams.

A sturdy, middle-aged man stood in the open portal, smiling at them as though they were expected. Behind him were a mustached man and a woman in a lace-front blouse and long skirt.

"Hello, Lucas," the first man said. "Hi, Maude . . . Tombo . . . Clay. And Peedy and Katie, too! Glad you all made it. Welcome to Project Leapfrog. This is Booster Waystop II. This building you're in is a storage warehouse—actually a contract annex for the state capitol—in Topeka, Kansas. The date is August 9, 1887." Wise, amused-seeming eyes went from one to another of them—eyes that had seen a great many wonders and still found delight in the unexpected.

He turned, indicating the man and woman behind him. "I'd like you all to meet Robert and Adelaide Armstrong. This is their building, and they've agreed to assist us with a TEF accelerator relay here. Adelaide's father left instructions for them, along with some interesting artifacts from the future."

His glance lit on Jill then, and he bowed slightly. "Hello, Miss Hammond," he said. "We haven't met, but they say nice things about you in future memoranda. My name is Limmer. Edwin Limmer."

Sangre de Cristo Mountains
Colorado, A.D. 2037

When *Sparrow* set down at the edge of a little, mountain town with high peaks all around, the first thing Curtis noticed was the guns. The place had the look of a ski resort, but there were howitzer emplacements on the slopes, and what the men who gathered around the ultralight carried were not skis. Everybody he saw had a gun, sometimes two or three. Most were scoped hunting rifles and lever-action 30-30s, but among them, too, were plenty of assault rifles, Uzis, a few big Browning machine guns, and even a few antique Thompson tommy guns with drum magazines.

Curtis and Beejum had been greeted as though they belonged here. They hadn't been detained, searched, or even questioned. But they had lost something, somehow. Curtis had been climbing out of *Sparrow* when something like fleeting shadows brushed by him, and when he looked inside his coat the iridescent cone there was gone. He decided he had lost it, but he had no idea where.

There were people all around him now, people who looked as though they were preparing for an invasion—which, he soon learned, they were.

Rocky Mountain Militia Captain Mike Correll explained it to him. King Arthur's Royce AATV brigades were advancing westward from their stronghold at Pueblo, seeking out the entrenched rebels who had defied the reign of Arthur Rex.

The royal artillery, Correll said, already occupied Colorado Springs and had laid siege to Cheyenne Mountain.

"Now their cavalry's at Canon City." The rebel leader frowned. "We got them stopped at Royal Gorge, but I don't know for how long. His Fuckin' Majesty's got every Royce Armored ATV in the world, I guess. Fuckin' beetles are murder, and they can go anywhere!"

"You don't say," Curtis mused, gawking at the armed men all around him. Nearby, Beejum was gleefully showing off the *Sparrow* to a knot of men with gimme caps and hunting rifles. "I saw all kinds of aircraft out there north," he suggested.

"Couple of big fields with planes everywhere. Including some military jets. Whose are those?"

"Ours, I guess, for all the fuckin' good they do us." Correll shook his head. "The old governments are gone, and the whole world may have gone to hell, but there's still an authority. PACT is still around, and it has teeth. Arthur found that out when he tried his fuckin' air strikes on Leavenworth and Omaha. Thought he had the sky all to himself, I guess. Those dirt farmers out there didn't have a thing to throw at him. But not a fuckin' one of his planes ever came back. PACT doesn't fool around."

Curtis squinted at the big, bearded man, puzzled. "PACT?"

"Protectorate Authority for Common Trust," Correll said bleakly. "Probably the last fuckin' vestige of a world order. PACT is the treaty keeper . . . all that's left of the military and diplomatic establishments of the past century. It administers the Edict of Encroachment, and its rules are mandates. No nuclear or biological weapons, and no air wars. Even Arthur can't defy PACT. Nobody can, so whatever the son of a bitch does, he'll do it on the ground."

"So chaos has been grounded," Curtis mused. "Everything is limited to terra firma?"

"Or pretty close to it." Correll turned. "Air war doesn't include low-level, small-ordnance support, like up to a thousand, fifteen hundred feet. Where that thing of yours flies." Behind them, dozens of men were clustered around *Sparrow*, and Curtis's eyes went wide. They were dismantling her. Piece by piece, the ultralight was being taken apart, and its parts were being carried off toward a row of long, low buildings that looked like machine shops.

"Stop that!" Curtis shrieked. "That's mine! Beejum, you heathen, get them away from there!"

In the crowd of busy men, a black head turned and white teeth flashed an encouraging grin. Beejum was helping them destroy the *Sparrow*! He was showing them how.

"Damn it!" Curtis rounded on the captain of the militia. "You have no right to tear up my machine! What do you think I am, a spy? An infiltrator?"

"Oh, we know who you are," Correll said casually. "As of now, you're a senior supply officer in the Rocky Mountain Federated Free Zone Militia. In fact, you're CAOP—our chief of airborne ordnance production. We'll need a couple of hundred of those *Sparrow*s, for starters. With machine guns, Gatlings, and zens mounted on them. King Arthur is going to wish he'd never seen these fuckin' mountains."

From *THE CAMELOT CHRONICLES*
(UEB Sector 914, MS files B8)

As with any conflict viewed in aftermath, some degree of distortion can be assumed in the documentation of King Arthur's mountain campaigns. Official accounts recovered at Camelot during the Period of Empocracy, for example, treat the entire phenomenon of Arthur's kingdom—from his initial takeover of the Institute for Temporal Research and the Panhandle Federated Free Zone to his ultimate domination of virtually the entire central plains region—as merely an interlude, mentioned in passing.

The fact is, though, that Arthur's expansions by conquest occupied a span of more than twelve years, from the initial consolidation of Camelot until the very Day of Immortality—the event of the Anachronism—and were still largely unresolved when Arthur disappeared.

Much has been recorded on the subject of the Flint Hills annexation, for instance, and about the Cimarron Siege, largely because these were ultimately successful campaigns. Those same records barely mention the disastrous northeast invasions, which were withdrawn following incidents at Omaha and Leavenworth in which PACT called up elements of the old SAC command to enforce its edicts.

In the same manner, little was officially recorded regarding the so-called Mountain Campaigns, which continued virtually for the entire reign of Arthur Rex, with no real resolution.

The investment of Denver as a duchy was a victory in name, but never in fact, since Arthur's emplacements there—

numbering, at one point, three full divisions of infantry as well as royal artillery and howitzer battalions and the much-admired Royal Armored Cavalry with its Royce AATVs—were never able to maintain more than a tenuous foothold in the frontal range of the Rockies.

At least five times during the dozen years of the Mountain Campaigns, major assaults were launched into the back ranges. On every occasion, the invasions were driven back by Revivalist militias counterattacking under a screen of armed ultralight aircraft—those low-level, rotary-wing fliers commonly (and often fondly) known as Sparrows.

∞

We have met the enemy and he is us.

—WALT KELLY, *Pogo*

∞

XIX

Leapfrog

Topeka, Kansas
August 11, 1881

"You *harpooned* a time loop!" Edwin Limmer shook his head in amazement. In an alcove off the main TEF chamber of Leapfrog Waystop, in T2 1881, they were gathered around a big oak table spread with maps, smudged papers, and stacks of multicolumn numerical printouts. Now Limmer gazed across the table at Lucas Hawthorn. "No wonder he backed off! When you tied his temporal shift to something that wouldn't shift with it, you eliminated a point in his matrix. He was afraid you'd do it again!"

"I did what?" Lucas blinked. "All I did was punch a little hole in his bubble. I doubt it even fazed him. It was just an impulse."

"Not to him, it wasn't." Limmer chuckled.

Perched on the edge of the table, Peedy Cue spread delicate hands, as though indicating a space or an object. "A temporal loop isn't a *thing*," he explained. "It doesn't really have mass or substance. It's a *condition*. A four-dimensional anomaly. In order to exist at all, a loop must be constantly in motion, in at least one dimension. The . . . the lost loop was spatially static when it hovered over your house. So it had to resonate back and forth in time. That means in T2 sequence, it only exists for an instant at a time. Your projectile must have grabbed it as it went by, and interrupted its resonance."

Sitting together on a draped Elizabethan davenport at one

side of the cozy alcove, Tombo and Jill glanced at each other. "What are they talking about?" Jill whispered.

"Temporal topology, I think," Tombo said. "Time people are like this when they get together."

Lounging against a wall behind them, Clay Connors shook his head. "Amen," he muttered.

"But it pulled loose," Lucas pointed out. "The harpoon snagged *something*, but it was slipping when Adam cut the line. It wouldn't have held."

"Maybe, maybe not." Limmer nodded. "Either way, it snagged the loop like a fishhook snags a thumb. It must have left a puncture."

"Puncture in what? As Peedy just said, a loop has no substance."

"Not substance, the way intrinsically solid matter has, but it does have a topology." Limmer hitched a leg over the corner of the table and laced his fingers, looking suddenly very scholarly. "Think of that loop as a homeomorphic whole—a simple closed curve. Even without substance, a time loop has a finite surface. It is a contained field of electronic flow, analogous to gravity. Geometrically, its surface is a collection of physical points. An infinite number of points, but each point is essential to the connectivity of the figure. No matter what shape it assumes, it still has those same points, in that same order.

"The harpoon violated the loop's surface. A point of continuity was lost. Stay with the topological analogy here: geometrically, a time loop is a simple, closed curve. Elimination of one point in a continuum like that doesn't disrupt the continuum. But loss of two points—any two surface points—disconnects the entire figure. If you had done it *again*—and he had to assume that you could—the curve would have lost its integrity. L-270 would have simply ceased to exist."

"I don't remember any geometry like that from high school math," Clay Connors muttered.

"It's in the Riemann theories." Limmer shrugged. "Geometry goes way past Pythagoras."

"Lipscomb's theory of constants," Peedy Cue corrected him. "Albert Lipscomb defined the dynamics of field surface variation."

"Right." Limmer nodded. "Point set theory. It depends upon the configuration of the field. L-383's surface has been penetrated many times, for example, but L-383 isn't like L-270. L-383 isn't a simple closed curve. It's a torus field—like a doughnut. The topology has different rules."

"The point is," Tombo said, "Lucas hurt him with that harpoon even if didn't know what he was doing." He paused, looking quizzically at Limmer. "You keep calling that thing 'he' and 'L-270.' I gather you know who that was, then, shooting at us?"

"It was us." Peedy Cue lowered his huge eyes, looking terribly ashamed.

"It was not!" KT-Pi objected. The little Whisper had been at the partially assembled controls in the far corner where Robert Armstrong was working with a test console. Now she scurried around the big table and faced Peedy, her tiny hands on her hips. "It was probably 1KHAF4, but he isn't *us*! He just happens to come from our era!"

"Peedy, it's all right," Limmer said softly. "Nobody blames a whole culture for its deviants." To the rest he explained, "The renegade's name is Kaffer. Actually, it's 1KHAF4. He's a Pacifican, like the Whispers. A historian by specialty. He was . . . will be . . . an observer with time loop L-270, the first mission to penetrate the Arthurian Anachronism. My guess is that there was a mutiny, and Kaffer has the phenomenon all to himself now."

Clay Connors scowled, groping for understanding. "You mean now I don't just have future people running loose in my jurisdiction, but *renegade* future people, too? My God, why me?"

"Actually," the literal-minded Peedy explained, "it's because King Arthur bounced in your county. More correctly, he *is bouncing* in your county. He did in 2050, and he will, clear back to the beginning of time. Always. It's his immortality. He bounced here, too, and at points eastward. About every two hundred miles."

"An interesting skip pattern," Limmer mused. "It's probably because of the random vectors of the Deep Hole temporal incident, which might not even happen that way if Kaffer can manipulate kinetic reversal technology so it won't. That's what he's trying to do, I take it. If Deep Hole doesn't produce a temporal event, then there'll be a big bang instead and most of the world won't survive it."

Connors's scowl deepened. He pursed his lips, scratched his head, and finally lowered his eyes in simple acceptance. "If you say so," he mumbled.

On the far side of the alcove, Maude Hawthorn sat in quiet conversation with Adelaide Armstrong. They hadn't seemed to be listening, but now Maude turned toward Limmer. "What I want to know," she said, "is what will this Kaffer person do next? He must be really upset now."

"Me, too." Adelaide looked worried. "He—he *attacked* Waystop I. What's to keep him from doing the same thing here?"

"You got any harpoon guns?" Lucas muttered ironically.

"What would it gain him?" Limmer shrugged. "Admittedly, I'm sure he knows about this accelerator station. But it's not a problem to him. An attack here would be sheer vindictiveness."

"Unless he had a reason," Peedy Cue said, looking embarrassed again. "Like this, maybe." From his back pouch he produced a small iridescent cone and held it up for everyone to see.

"What is that?" Limmer frowned. "Where did you get it?"

"It's a slave TEF from Kaffer's hiding place," KT-Pi said. "A reserve unit. Adam brought it to L-383, and *someone*—" She glanced accusingly at Peedy. "—someone got it mixed in with some materials being sent to Waystop I. Then it disappeared from Lucas's supply shed, and we had to track it all the way to 2037 to get it back. We were trying to get to L-383 when we got caught at Waystop I. Lucas depowered the TEF just as we shunted."

By the light from high windows and from the incandescent gas mantles in the wall sconces, they stared at the cone.

"I really do apologize," Peedy said contritely. "It was my error."

"*Kaffer's* TEF?" Ed Limmer breathed. "From L-270?"

"Teal and Oel Six tested it," KT-Pi said. "It's just a spare, from loop inventory. L-383 carries several, for use as slave links to the main TEF system or for establishing tangent bases ... like this one. I'm sure L-270 carried a few, as well."

"Then it was never activated?" Lucas sighed. "He won't be homing on it, then."

"It was inactive when it was tested on L-383," KT-Pi said. "But it has been powered since, of course. Otherwise it couldn't have gotten as far as 2037."

"Then it can be traced," Limmer advised. "If he misses it."

"Well, I want it out of here." Adelaide Armstrong stood and moved to the table. She didn't touch the cone, but she looked at it—the way a person doused with gasoline might look at a smoldering cigarette butt. "Can you ... ah, send it away?"

In the far corner of the alcove Robert Armstrong turned from his control console, looking haggard. "I wish we could," he said.

"The whole base system is down," KT-Pi explained. "L-383's probability curve has diminished to basic survival, and Leapfrog doesn't have a generator yet."

"So much for time travel," Ed Limmer mused. "There are only two working TEFs in this era, then. One of them is in Waystop 1—a hundred and seventeen years in the future, shut down, and nobody there to activate it.

"1KHAF4 has the other one."

Springfield, Missouri
Present Time

With all the ceiling fluorescents turned off, the big assembly floor was like a vast, dark cave. Dim daylight slipping through the roof baffles high above, and the little glows of frosted glass panes in doors leading to other parts of the plant, were barely enough to outline the dark shapes of assembly tables, belt conveyors, boxing and packaging stacks, and the dark silhouettes of people at their stations, waiting for the lights to come on and the conveyors to roll.

In the entire central assembly complex of Jessup Manufacturing Company, only one light shone—a bright island in a sea of shadows.

"We thought you'd like to see the very first one in action," Leon Jessup said, grinning as he indicated the little lamp shining alone in all this darkness. He bowed slightly, as though making a formal introduction. "Frank Inertial Reaction Energy Light model 1, style A1, unit number 0000001, meet your creator, Dr. David Frank. David, I present to you the illumination of the future: FIRElight."

David Frank removed his glasses, wiped them, replaced them on his nose, and bent for a closer look. The thing on the table looked like a big shining mushroom, or maybe an hourglass—a wasp-waisted double bulb of layered plastic and metal, its lower section ornamented with lacquered vinery, its upper section glowing steadily with a bright, white glare stronger than any two-hundred-watt incandescent bulb. Between its little flared pedestal of polished bronze and the silly-looking floral shade that stood over it like a silk umbrella, FIRElight was all one piece of hardware. It had no seams, no joints, no sleeves. Its only integral adornment was a Victorian-looking toggle set into the pedestal.

Frank walked entirely around the device, then took off his glasses and cleaned them again. His eyes were moist. *Here it is, Irene,* he thought. *This is what we invested all those years in. I wish you were here to see it. You could tell me if it's really as beautiful as I think it is.* To Leon Jessup, he said, "It's a lot smaller than I imagined."

"You think so?" Jessup grinned. "Pick it up."

Frank gripped the lamp by its middle, tried to lift it, and blinked. It felt as though it were glued to the tabletop. He tried again, harder, and managed to raise it maybe an inch before it thumped down again.

"Shipping weight of this unit is just over three pounds." Jessup chuckled. "But its weight in use is nearly forty. The difference is pure gravity, and if anybody wants to know how that can be, you'll have to explain it to them because I can't and neither can any of our engineers."

"It's really pretty simple," Frank started. "It's a matter of inverse ratios in constant flux, within a matrix continuum where light and gravity are two of the four poles—"

"Don't explain it to *me*." Jessup laughed. "Just let me crank these out as fast as I can, before the purchase orders drown us."

"Sorry," Frank said. "I just—"

"I don't understand a word of quantum physics, or anything about sustained free fall or declining velocities. But I do know how to market a breakthrough product." Jessup raised his hands and his voice. "Everybody set?" he called. Then, "Okay, let there be light!"

At his command, bright stars came alive all over the big room—myriad brilliances flooding the manufacturing hall with bright light that David Frank knew could not be measured in the classical manner of photon output, but only by its result: a rising crescendo of pure, white lumens.

There were FIRElights everywhere—on work surfaces, on shelves and ceiling sconces, on pedestals above the conveyors and all around the walls. There were hundreds of them, each drawing from its own tiny capacitors just the energy required to maintain a stable analog phenomenon within the solid-liquid chemistry of the "mushroom"—less electricity than it took to run a quartz-action wristwatch.

All around the big room, assemblers and handlers applauded, the roar of clapping punctuated with whistles and encouraging shouts.

"Dr. Frank," Jessup said again, slapping David on the back, "the light of the future! And by the way, Number One here belongs to you. Courtesy of Jessup Manufacturing and its employees."

David Frank gave up trying to clean his glasses. He couldn't see the lenses anyway, through the pooling moisture in his eyes. Look at this, Irene, he thought. Can you see it from heaven? Just look at what a beautiful sight this is!

Later, in Leon Jessup's private office, as they stood at the window to watch the trucks leaving with the first FIRElight orders, Jessup said, "We're going to have to expand here, in record time. Meanwhile we'll contract out a lot of our production, just to keep up with the mass market demand. I don't suppose you're going to tell me how you did it, are you?"

Frank glanced at him. "Did what?"

"You know what! Not only is there a clean, unencumbered patent on every one of at least nine original processes, but there's no record of any prior licensing of rights. Not anywhere. When word got out about our FIRElight, while we were tooling up, Vaughn Enterprises had a battalion of ACN lawyers in six separate courts, trying to slap injunctions on us. But they couldn't come up with even a memo of intent, much less any contractual agreement to base their cases on. What are you, a corporate magician?"

"No." David shrugged. "Just an inventor. I don't know anything about business."

L-270

Those events that shape subsequent history set the course of T2 eventuality, and in so doing they determine the vectors available within T1. It was automatic vector analysis, occurring as a function of L-270's temporal resonance pattern, that alerted Kaffer. The fabric of continuity he had so carefully woven, to alter the main course of future probability, abruptly began to unravel.

The pivotal principle of temporal engineering—kinetic reversal of gravity and light—emerged from oblivion suddenly and with fanfare. It emerged not in the tightly secured back rooms of government contract or in the furtive alleyways of military secrecy, but strutting across the one stage no curtain could conceal.

FIRElight was launched into the public consciousness by simultaneous exposure at the American Association of Homebuilders convention in Minneapolis, the International Association of Architects conference in Montreal, and as a featured new product in every Wal-Mart, Marshall Field's, and Lowe's center in three nations, and as a customer attraction device in McDonald's stores worldwide. It was even featured at Bloomingdale's.

Within months, *photogravitation* would become a household word. Within a year it would become an accepted staple of human knowledge. Within three to five years FIRElight would be the principal illumination source for most of the civilized world.

Like the wheel, the lever, the combustion engine, and the microchip, kinetic inversion would become the paradigm of its age, spreading like wildfire—or wildFIRE—in the humble shape of a simple, superefficient device for general illumination.

When Kaffer learned about the FIRElight, he went wild with rage. Like a deadly, flickering dark cloud, L-270 emerged from the Pyramid of Khafre and swept eastward from Giza on tight resonance, lashing out at everything in its path. The Whispers and their base loop, L-383, were beyond his reach. In four-dimensional resonance, two time loops cannot coincide. Just as L-270—the phenomenon itself—was immune to L-383, so L-383 was immune to L-270.

But nobody else was immune, and Kaffer vented his rage. Transference fields and zen-guns are not selective. Across Asia, whole villages and sections of cities disappeared, TEF-transferred to spatial coordinates where there was no planet to receive them, or to temporal coordinates so far in the past that even dinosaurs had not yet emerged. Japan's southern islands reeled from zen-bolts, and Kauai's north shore was devastated.

News channels pulsed confusion and panic, and meteorologists scrambled for clues to what was happening. Everything from tornadoes to electrical storms, from anomalous earthquakes to meteor strikes was blamed for the trail of disasters. But within hours of L-270's strike at Beijing, CNN and the rest had something they could understand. For months there had been concern about the nuclear missiles deployed around Mongolia. Now those missiles began to fly.

In some future time, historians would sort out what led to the nuclear holocaust in Asia, and some might even guess what finally triggered it. At the moment, though, all that could be reported was that atomic blasts had occurred in central Asia, and that the electromagnetic pulse of the first explosions had knocked out every surface and orbital surveillance that existed there.

It was the beginning of the Seven Days of Silence of the eastern hemisphere.

Here and there, though, there were some who understood.

No cartography was adequate to predict where L-270 would go, and no dimensional awareness could read the course of a rampaging anachronism. Nobody knew where or when Kaffer would emerge next. But Adam knew where he had been.

Once before, the timer had seen the interior of Kaffer's lair. But that was more than four millennia in the past, before Kaffer had actually occupied the second great pyramid.

Now he saw it as Kaffer had left it, and what he found there told him stories—stories that made him feel sick in the pit of his stomach.

Now he knew why Delta One had removed and collected the brains of his victims. Kaffer had been using the brains for research, trying to find the secret of autotemporal powers. In the King's Chamber of the pyramid were rows and stacks of labeled containers, most of them containing the embalmed brains of innocent people. Among them were Kaffer's dissecting tables, his vats, and an array of tools. Nearby stood the slave TEF on its tower, above a span of steel-covered floor.

These things had been left here when L-270 departed the pyramid. Therefore, it seemed, Kaffer intended to return.

His dark eyes as cold as winter storm, Adam began a systematic exploration of the pharaoh's tomb. In his mind were the words of Teal Fordeen—the philosophy of a culture that had learned to recognize its monsters for what they were, and had long since quit coddling them.

"Concepts such as *mentally ill* and *sociopath*," the Whisper had said, "only obscure the basic fact. A person without humanity is not a human being, and cannot be treated as one."

What Adam found now, in the lair of the renegade Pacifican 1KHAF4, was not the work of a human being. This was the lair of a monster.

And Kaffer could not be considered as "their" problem. Whenever he was from, whatever he was, Kaffer was everybody's problem.

"Infinity isn't yours, Kaffer," Adam muttered, his eyes judging dimensions and distances within the ancient stone monument. "Infinity is ours. And that makes it mine."

L-270 was only a few miles off Catalina, a dark, saucerlike silhouette occurring instant by instant over a 180-second span of real time, when the loop's probing sensors—sensors designed for a temporal vehicle capable of threading a path through maelstroms of anachronism—located an anomaly in the vectors ahead. There in the distance, seventy-four horizons to the east and more than a century upstream in time, resonant sounders perceived an echo. The echo was in inactive registry among L-270's own banks, but not where or when it should be. It was a reserve TEF cone, and it should have rested, inactive, within the stone of the Pyramid of Khafre in Egypt. Instead, it registered an active duration over an erratic range of coordinates covering nearly a century and a half in a durational span of no more than 150 hours. By its own equivalent duration it was "now" at Topeka, Kansas, in 1881.

Kaffer's wild rage became a cold intent. With the blip as a target, he went hunting.

The line between ambition and abomination is determined by the tolerance of one's neighbors.

—Sir Giles Baldwin

Death is nature's way of telling you to slow down.

—Erma Bombeck

∞

XX

In Tempus Pro Tempore
Ex Tempore

Topeka, Kansas
August 11, 1881

There was no warning, and no place to run. At velocities exceeding light speed, earth has no distances greater than a moment. When L-270 registered the runaway TEF's activation, it simultaneously pinpointed its location. By the touch of a stud Kaffer accepted the four-dimensional vectors, and a slowing, darkening shift of polarity occurred over Catalina. In the same instant, in a flash of brilliant light, L-270 ceased to be a furious presence hovering over what would be the home of the Pacificans and materialized as a rippling, spinning vortex saucer two hundred feet above the Armstrong Security Warehouse overlooking the Kaw River.

With zen capacitors already charged, Kaffer opened fire. The first bolt struck the building's southwest corner, shearing away a third of it down to the foundation. Roof joists swayed there for a moment, freed of the headers and beams that no longer existed, then collapsed, taking portions of two walls down with them.

Inside, debris rained down on the floor below, crushing the flimsy partitions of storage cubicles and everything that they contained. Timbers and masonry pelted the interior as the sagging, collapsing roof swung down to seal off the south two-thirds of the structure. And all along the shattered walls, at intervals of sixteen feet, broken gas lines hissed and whispered.

In the cozy alcove off the TEF chamber of Leapfrog Waystop, Robert Armstrong crawled out of the rubble slanting against a doorway arch and looked around dazedly. Blood pouring from a gash in his scalp blinded him momentarily, but he wiped it away from frightened eyes. Darkness, confusion, and disaster were all around him. People scurrying here and there were only shadows in the dusty, choking gloom. "Adelaide?" he shouted. "Where are you?"

Lucas Hawthorn untangled himself from a webwork of fallen plaster-wire and shoved through dangling tar paper, ignoring the cuts and scratches of exposed nail points as he fought past a tangle of suspended plaster fragments imbedded with broken pieces of lath. "Maude!" he called. "Maudey, are you all right?"

Her muffled voice came from the darkness of a plaster-tented recess by the stub of a collapsed interior wall. "I'm here, Lucas! Adelaide and KT-Pi are here, too. Lord, but this is a maze in here!"

A fallen table moved, shifting bits of timber and fallen plaster as it tilted upward. In the gloom, Sheriff Clay Connors erupted, "Who the hell is that? Dammit, get your foot out of my britches!"

"Sorry," Peedy Cue said, somewhere.

In the dusty darkness of the place, Tombo Hawthorn dragged himself free of the upended Elizabethan davenport, turned, and burrowed back the way he had come. When he emerged again, he had a dazed Jill Hammond with him.

Lucas started for the dark recess where Maude, Adelaide, and KT-Pi were trapped, then stopped short as a heavy timber thudded down directly in front of him. Strong hands grabbed his arm and shoulder and pulled him back as another piece of roofing fell. "We've got to make an opening here," Edwin Limmer said urgently. "This place is filling up with methane fumes."

The two men went to work on the fallen mass beside the cubicle entrance, and within moments others had joined them there, burrowing through rubble, heaving timbers aside, clearing a path. When the frame was partially clear they could see the big, open runway of the building's center, dusty light from shattered high windows filtering downward in hazy beams.

At that instant, a bolt of searing blue light flashed, and across the open corridor another section of roof disappeared. The thing hovering above had discharged its belly zen again.

"I'll kill that bastard!" Lucas growled. Stooping, he pushed through the hole in the doorway and looked up. There, through a rend in the roof, he could see the flickering, eye-confusing substance of the time loop. He tugged the Smith & Wesson Chief Special from his pants pocket and raised it. Abruptly, his arm was locked upright, and strong fingers were prying the gun from his hand, a big thumb blocking its hammer.

"Do you want to blow us all up?" Clay Connors roared. "Dammit, Lucas, this place is full of gas!"

With a shake of his head, Lucas turned and scurried back into the shattered alcove. "Tombo, give me a hand here! We've got women trapped under a section of wall!"

Jill was already at the dark opening, working alongside Robert Armstrong to clear away sheets of rubble. Tombo and Lucas joined them, while Clay Connors headed for the main entrance at the north end of the building, facing West Sixth Street. The lock bar on the door there was bent and jammed, but there wasn't much that the sheriff couldn't move when he set his mind to it.

Even inside the alcove, they heard the rending crunch of big doors being swung open, and distant-sounding voices of people outside, shouting. Beyond the shouts was the approaching clangor of bells on horse-drawn fire wagons.

With a heave, Robert Armstrong upended a huge slab of plastered wall, and other hands reached out to help him brace it. Now inside the dark cave there was movement, and KT-Pi emerged, blood smeared on her bald head, gasping for breath. Tombo picked her up like a child and handed her back to Jill, who looked her over carefully, then set her on her feet. The little Whisper swayed, but Peedy Cue was there, quick hands and small shoulders catching her before she could fall.

"Here," Peedy hissed, spotting a two-foot break in the outer wall. Without waiting for assent, he dragged KT-Pi to the hole, scurried into it backward, and pulled her after him. Beyond was open air.

At the rubble heap, Robert Armstrong and Lucas Hawthorn shouldered in, searching for their wives, uncaring of the splinters and nails that tore at them as they heaved shattered timbers aside. A five-foot section of buckled wall split as they shoved past it, and Tombo caught it in the middle, upended it, and flung it aside.

Another flat was raised, and they were there. In the gloom, Maude Hawthorn raised her head, found a handhold, and pulled herself upward, clinging to Adelaide Armstrong's hand. She got her balance, tugged on the hand, then gasped and looked downward. She was covered with blood.

Adelaide Armstrong wouldn't be going on temporal junkets, or managing an accelerator station for people from the future. She lay crumpled and still in the little space behind a desk, plaster and dust coating her limp form. She probably hadn't even felt the big glass shard that severed her throat.

For a frozen moment, nobody moved. Then Robert Armstrong seemed to fall apart. With a scream—"Adelaide!"—he half dived, half fell over the fallen desk to kneel there, bending over the still body of his wife. Maude staggered back, and Lucas caught her. Jill tried to scramble over the desk, and Tombo stopped her. "It's too late," he muttered. "You can't heal that."

Behind them at the littered alcove door, Clay Connors roared, "Get out of here! Everybody out! There's gaslights still burning in the back!"

Lucas swept Maude up in his arms and crashed through the half-opened alcove arch, heading for the main entry. Just beyond the rubble, Edwin Limmer appeared. "I'll take her," he said. "Bring the rest!"

Lucas saw them heading for the open door, then turned and dived back into the rubble.

Overhead, things were coming apart as more and more of the roof collapsed.

They were still there, in the gloom, gathered around the dark place where Robert Armstrong knelt, rocking back and forth over his dead wife, his sobs racking him. The air reeked of natural gas fumes, and it was hard to breathe.

"We've got to get everybody out of here," Lucas told Tombo. "This place is about to fall down around us."

"Then let's—" Tombo's reply was drowned in a rending, shrieking crack from overhead. In that instant a splintered beam, thirty-five feet above, parted from its stump and plummeted downward like a falling spear, directly into the exposed back of Robert Armstrong. Sharp as a sword, long and heavy as a small tree trunk, the timber bore the man down, impaling him, joining him with the woman beneath him in a bond of solid, thudding hickory.

Jill screamed, tried to rush to them, and almost fell as Tombo dragged her back, barely out of the path of huge clots of roofing that rained down behind the timber. In an instant, the desk, the timber, and the two people it joined were gone, buried in rubble.

Tombo had no more time to argue. Carrying Jill over his shoulder, he crawled out of the alcove and staggered across the open areaway. Lucas was right behind him. Just inside the open door they paused for a moment, stunned and not knowing what to do next. And at that instant, somewhere toward the back, volatile gas seeping through rubble found a still-lit mantle lamp. The explosion that followed went mostly upward, riding on waves of superheated air, but its concussion was enough to lift the people in the areaway and tumble them backward. Dazed and stunned, they struggled toward the open door. Behind them, the entire south half of Armstrong Security Warehouse was a roiling inferno.

The first fireball rose through the fragmented roof, climbing into the sky like a brilliant mushroom. It billowed around the fringes of the flickering black cloud hovering there, and the smoke that rose to join it almost obscured the blue flash of another zen-gun bolt striking downward.

As though satisfied, then, the great, flattened cloud shape seemed to slow and darken. The instantaneous flash of brilliance that followed might have been no more than another lightning strike, to those outside who might have noticed it at all. Billowing smoke so filled the sky that the cloud's abrupt disappearance was hardly noticeable.

Clay Connors herded them through the doorway and out into the crowded street, going ahead of them to clear a path by power of plain, authoritative presence.

In the street a derby-hatted man with a *Topeka Daily Capital* banner pinned to his coat had set up a box camera on a wooden tripod. As the survivors turned toward him he pulled a film slide from his magazine, tripped the camera's shutter, and photographed the scene.

Lucas looked around at the growing, curious crowds, spotted Ed Limmer and Maude across the street, then turned and looked upward. There was smoke up there, spreading a dark blanket across the sky. But there was nothing else.

"I hope they get that son of a bitch," he muttered. "I hope they find him and hang him 'til he rots!"

Richmond, Virginia
Present Time

Jessica Tinsley walked up wide marble steps, then turned to watch as a squadron of police automobiles paraded into the guarded "official business" driveway and alongside the main portico. Ranked officers guarded the east side of the portico, above the prisoner entrance, but they edged apart at Jessica's approach, letting her pass.

At the marble-crowned portico wall she stopped, looking down as police cars all along the line opened their doors.

Then the monster was there. Shackled hand and foot, surrounded by large, alert young men with guns, Carter Vaughn didn't appear larger than life in any way. He actually looked small, Jessica thought—almost *shrunken* in the midst of that stalwart phalanx whose task it was to bring him alive to the courtroom where his trial by law was about to begin.

Kidnapping, murder, rape, sexual abuse, abuse of children, violations of the Lindberg Act, the Montese Act, the Rayburn Act ... watching as marshals escorted the Beast of Black

Hollow from a guarded car, Jessica hugged her briefcase to her side, craving some sense of fulfillment from the documents it held. There should be more satisfaction in this, she thought. There should be a thrill of victory. She felt no such thrill, though. Only a sense of completion. Nothing that occurred in that courtroom or after would ever erase what Carter Vaughn had done, in that secluded mansion hidden back in a cove of the Cumberlands.

It had taken her all these years—since 1996—to put it together. As a staff investigator with DMP, she had been thorough and meticulous. Nothing less would have done, in bringing down one of the most powerful men in the United States. Most of it would never be known except to a few. Even the public trial with its massive media coverage would bring out only bits and pieces of the atrocities with which Carter Vaughn—sole owner of Vaughn Enterprises and ACN, and one of the world's richest and most successful men—had amused himself in private.

Nothing would bring back the children he had murdered, the young women he had mutilated and tortured to death. Nothing would ever erase the scenes of that final search of Black Hollow from the minds of those who had been there.

But now it was done. It was up to the lawyers now and the judicial system. They were already predicting that Carter Vaughn would never be punished—only put away, wherever they put the hopelessly insane. No sane man, his predictable defenders contended, could ever have done the things Carter Vaughn had done.

She could barely see him as he was hurried from the car to the security door beneath the portico. They were taking no chances with him—no chance that he might, somehow, miraculously escape from custody. More to the point, no chance that somebody with a sniper rifle might thwart the methodical workings of justice.

She did glimpse, though, the fresh dressing on his brow, covering the little incision where doctors from Menninger and Walter Reed had removed the translobal implant behind his forehead. Little had been reported about that, because so little was known about the device they extracted. A tiny electronic device of some kind, it had never been studied. It had literally disintegrated an hour and a half after its removal from Carter Vaughn's skull.

And even in that glimpse of him, she noticed the characteristic limp, the twisted leg of eyewitness account, that had begun the trail of evidence leading to Carter Vaughn—the leg injury he had sustained when his Ferrari hit a maintenance grader on a mountain highway in 1996.

The people around him now knew nothing of Delta One, nothing about the murder of unborn timers, nothing about the man's alliance with a monomaniacal creature from the distant future.

What they did know, though, was that a monster had been brought to bay. The Beast of Black Hollow would face justice, starting today.

Jessica turned away from the portico rail, knowing that she would have safe passage through the police lines and the crush of reporters and cameramen. Jack would see to that.

She turned and there he was, big and quiet and alert as usual, hovering just at the edge of her personal space, always ready to protect her. He no longer seemed awkward and out of place in modern attire, but still he seemed like a big oak tree among saplings as he eased the crowd back to let her pass. A man of another, rougher time, his gentleness was unfeigned.

Jack Higgins didn't have anything to prove to anybody. He was what he was, whenever he was.

"Where to from here, missy?" he asked as she stepped to his side.

"I don't know," she told him. "It's out of my hands, now. I guess we just take life a day at a time, like everybody else."

Giza, Egypt

L-270 vectored back to "present" T2 as it returned to its lair, just as Adam had expected it would. All across the desert, FIRElights winked on as lingering evening set in, and Adam

suspected that Kaffer would be driven to see that spectacle—
the visible stigma of his ultimate defeat—as he sought refuge
in his fortress tomb.

Now, above the lit sands, cool breezes stirred the night air,
and stars in vast array stood in a sky not quite like that which
the builders of the pyramids had seen, but different only in
small detail. The timer shifted from place to place with the
slightest nudges of mind—first to the ancient, vaulted interior
of the Pyramid of Khafre to inspect his preparations, then back
outside, to the shadows of Wadi Saddaq, to wait.

It had taken him months to prepare for this event—the final
homecoming of 1KHAF4. Months, and a myriad of decep-
tions in alternate reality paths. In one probability sequence, it
had involved an elaborate scheme to paint the three great
pyramids—Egypt's primary tourist attraction—with sealing
resins to protect against erosion. In the process, hundreds of
workmen had labored up and down the faces of Khafre, with
winch-hauled pulleys involving thousands of feet of steel
cable. In another, closely aligned, it remained a great mystery,
the disappearance of cable spools and stone anchors from the
quarries of Tura.

But the work was done now, and all Adam had to do
was wait.

The wait was not long. He had gauged the maniac mentality
with accuracy. In the clear night sky above the Pyramid of Khafre,
anomalies of light disturbed the placid stars, and a shifting, pul-
sating saucer of almost-substance appeared, standing just above
the apex.

One more barely perceptible shift, and L-270 would become
one with the pyramid—one and invisible, as it had been for
thousands of years.

But as the moments passed, the huge saucer remained where
it was, simply idling there in three-dimensional stasis, maintained in the fourth dimension by a languid 180-second resonance that made it appear and disappear rhythmically.

Kaffer has no reason to go into hiding again, Adam realized.
He knows L-383 was deteriorating, and aside from the
Whisper loop, what is there in this world that might hurt him?

A dread seeped into the timer's thoughts. What if the renegade Pacifican decides to abandon his infinity scheme and
simply rule by force? He knows he has lost on the first front,
but what would stop him on the second? Images flooded his
human mind, images of all the atrocities committed in the
interests of 1KHAF4, images of L-270 standing above the
Hawthorns' house, unleashing the power of zen weapons,
images of a trail of devastation through Asia and of a half-
collapsed, burning warehouse in nineteenth-century Topeka.

Kaffer could not be tolerated anymore—not in this time or
any time. "Go on, you insane little bastard," Adam muttered in
the shadows of the dark wadi. "There's your hole, just beneath
you. Slip into it."

Still L-270 stood, dark and pensive, flickering above the Pyramid of Khafre like a cloud of death on a pedestal of eternity.

"Then somebody will have to make you move," Adam
decided.

L-383+3.1.6

"We can't do this!" Zeem Sixten protested, as busy Whispers
fed vectors to their TEF system—vectors that required override of numerous implanted constants because they had never
been tried before. "We can't go where we already are! It's
against every principle of eventuality."

"Then it's time for some new principles," Adam said.
"We're not going where you are, only *when* you are. All you
have to do is avoid yourself, and you won't feel a thing."

"Barbaric!" Zeem sniffed, shrugging his compliance as Teal
Fordeen raised a hairless brow in his direction. In this set of
probabilities, three years had passed since the reinstatement of
inertial reaction energy sources into the matrix of world history. The Whisper leader was his old self again, ageless and
energetic—just like his time loop.

"We're on station here to observe the Deep Hole phenomenon," Toocie Toonine explained to the protomorph timer

who—as usual—had simply dropped in unannounced and changed most of L-383's plans.

"I know." He smiled down at the little Whisper. "That made it easy to find you. And don't worry—" His smile became a grin as an ironic thought struck him. "—there's plenty of time to save mankind and get back before all hell breaks loose. You have all the time in the world."

Teal Fordeen closed his big eyes and shook his head, looking pained. "We can't come back here, Adam," he said. "It would be an irreconcilable paradox, because we'll already be here by then."

"Then watch the Deep Hole fireworks from somewhere else." The timer shrugged. "If you're already here, you'll get a double view, won't you?"

Teal turned from the tall man. "Vectors?" he demanded.

"Vectors confirmed," Oel Six advised.

"Then activate," Teal said. "Wide trajectory around present locus."

"And for mercy's sake, hold course to Egypt." Toocie grinned. "Let's don't veer through Kansas on this transit."

Pyramid of Khafre

"It's impossible!" Kaffer stormed, to no one but himself. "It can't be. L-383 is still on locus. And it's dying!"

Still, there was no disputing the evidence of L-270's scans. The loop was no longer alone in this place and time. Virtual realities swam with the truth of it. Right out there, not a hundred yards away, another, far larger closed loop shimmered from instant to instant, matching his own resonance. A torus loop, exactly like L-383, but not frayed and thin in its reality as L-383 had become. This was a whole, strong loop, a vortex of temporal probabilities in full control of its environment.

Acting on primitive impulse, Kaffer charged, aimed, and triggered the battery of zen-weapons he had incorporated into L-270's rim. Bolts of astonishing blue—pure electron force— shot out, lashed at the strange loop, and disappeared into its vortex. For an instant its entire surface flared with blue swirls of brilliance as it absorbed the charges into its own capacitors. His impulsive strike had done no more than make the challenger stronger.

He couldn't hurt the thing with bolts or with transposures. Such powers were its very element, just as they were L-270's. Neither, of course, could it wound him with anything less than a physical projectile, and no closed loop carried such arcane technology.

But then it shifted, rising slightly and edging toward him as its resonance came into tighter and tighter atunement with his own, and he knew what it intended.

L-270 was a simple, closed curve in topological terms—a rolling ball of temporal continuity feeding back upon itself at all points. The other loop, though, was a torus. Its structure was that of a recurring tube. It couldn't penetrate L-270, but it could enclose him—capture and blend with his form as a doughnut might enclose a marble.

Wild with panic and fury, Kaffer took the only course left to him.

Somewhere below, in the night shadows of Wadi Saddaq, a solitary man crouched, watching the pyrotechnics in the desert sky. As L-270 darkened, glowed slightly, and sank from sight, Adam smiled in serene satisfaction. "Gotcha!" he whispered.

L-383X

"Gone?" Teal Fordeen blinked large eyes. "You mean, no longer existent? How can that be? L-270 is encased within the pyramid, but it isn't gone. It's just hiding there, where we can't reach it."

"No," Adam repeated. "It's gone. There is no L-270. It dissolved the moment it materialized in the Pyramid of Khafre. You see, the environment in the King's Chamber isn't as Kaffer left it. There are steel cables in there now, two of them, running down from the air shafts to steel and stone anchors in the floor. When L-270 materialized there, it simply shorted out.

There isn't any temporal phenomenon there anymore. All that's inside that pyramid now is the hardware L-270 carried and a burned-out TEF system. And, of course, Kaffer himself. L-270 died of terminal topology. Its surface was interrupted at two points, simultaneously."

Zeem Sixten goggled at the tall timer, his big eyes wide with incredulity. "That's right!" he chirped. "A simple closed curve—point set theory! The Riemann and Lipscomb studies! But you—you're only a primitive, Adam. How do you know about such things?"

"I listen a lot." Adam glanced at Teal Fordeen. "Besides, a man with a harpoon showed me how it works."

L-383X—as Zeem had labeled it to distinguish it from the "other" L-383, which at this moment was sharing the same temporal space a hemisphere away—swung now on a lazy 180-second axis directly above the ancient pyramid of the Pharaoh Khafre. Virtual screens displayed every detail of the surroundings in minute, four-dimensional detail.

Teal paced the area among screens thoughtfully, little hands clasped behind his back. Finally he turned to Adam. "Without his TEF, 1KHAF4 is trapped inside that pyramid," he said. "He can't get out . . . and we can't go in after him, because that space is not in our matrix. No one in ordinary T2 has ever entered or left there, since it was sealed."

"So?" Adam shrugged. "Without his toys, he can't do any damage inside a pyramid."

"But we want him," Teal said. "I suppose we must ask you to go in one more time, Adam. Go in and bring Kaffer out. No one else can do it, but you."

Adam gazed down at the Whisper leader, then shook his head. "No," he said.

"What do you mean, *no*?" Zeem Sixten erupted. "It isn't such a big favor to ask, is it? Just go in there and bring Kaffer out. We'll handle things from that point."

"I said no," Adam repeated. His gaze met Teal's and held it. "Do you remember what you told me, about codes of human conduct and how your culture has reidentified psychopathic behavior as not human?"

"I remember." Teal nodded. "I said that a person who behaves inhumanly cannot be considered as human."

"And that applies to Kaffer?"

"Of course, it does."

"Then whatever you want him for, it isn't as a human being."

"We want to send him downstream to Sundome," Toocie explained. "His behavior here, in the past, is an aberration of some kind. Our people will want to explore why it happened— why 1KHAF4 is the way he is."

"Explore, how?"

"By studying his brain, of course!" Zeem snapped. "They will want to extract his brain and dissect it. With the resources they have—"

"Now *that* is ironic." Adam grinned. He turned away, then glanced back. "No, I won't get him for you. I'm sorry, but to me *that* is inhuman. Or at least inhumane. You'll just have to leave him where he is."

"You can't just—just go away and forget him." Toocie stared at the timer. "Can you?"

"It's all I can do." Adam smiled at her, gently. "As Zeem is always telling me, I am, after all, only a primitive. I have some old-fashioned concepts of right and wrong, and they apply to criminals as well as to real people.

"Leave Kaffer where he is. It's the only humane thing to do. Leave him in that pile of rock that he himself chose, and let him starve to death."

He approached a virtual screen, stepped into it, and was gone.

∞

From *The Tolafsson Definitions*:

Perpetuity "Keep on keeping on," kept on forever.
Eternity "Forever" in its Sunday clothes.
Infinity Eternity eight ways from Sunday.
Serenity Wisdom not cluttered by obscure words like perpetuity, eternity, and infinity.

∞

XXI

Chronoclysm

Western Kansas High Plains
March 21, 2003

Throughout the day a strong north wind had whined across the plains—wind that had ice in its teeth and that brought gray clouds to block the warming sun. The wind abated a little with evening, but the sullen, dry snowfall that came with darkness only made it more miserable.

Typical plains weather this time of year, Spangler told himself—winter outraged by a tantalizing touch of pleasant spring, roaring back in to raise hell one more time before it accepted that its time was over. The frigid bite of it seemed to seep right through the warmest clothing, leaving a man's body numb and his mind gloomy. Just like the big drill site around him that was his home for the duration of the project.

Cold and dark, Spangler thought gloomily. Dark and cold. Hell of a way to make a living.

Hard little flakes rattled against his parka hood as he logged his meters for the third time in this shift. By this time tomorrow there might be drifts six feet deep around the rig, but only if it warms a little. Too cold to really snow right now. Too cold for too long, and always the wind to make it colder. Nearest thing to a windbreak between Deep Hole and the North Pole, he thought, is a chain-link perimeter fence.

He snugged his drawstring another notch and punched in a Save to Main on his memopad. Somewhere above, in the snowy gloom, the blowout horn wound down to silence. The warnings had been sounding every hour or so since before dusk, as anomalous readings came from the shaft. He had tried to imagine what was happening down in that hole, that could cause drilling mud to congeal, casing to melt, and three-comb diamond bits to stutter like jackhammers.

He had tried, but his best scenarios were only conjecture. Nobody knew for sure what was going on down there, fourteen miles beneath the earth's surface. All they knew—any of them—was that they weren't dealing with relative gravities anymore. The force they were closing on was pure, raw gravity, and its effects on the drilling rig were increasing by the hour.

Upstairs in the doghouse, their digitals were going wild. It was hot and heavy down in the hole, and they needed continuous data confirmation from the field meters. All shifts were on alert now, as the phenomena of Deep Hole kept mounting.

The blowout warnings had become meaningless. They occurred because every sensing device on the drill site was programmed to set off alarms upon the occurrence of certain unusual readings in the hole. Spangler wondered whether any of those special circumstances hadn't occurred yet. But drilling had not ceased. The strange readings might mean a lot of things, but the nearest to a certainty was that PDH was closing in on what it sought. The drill's target was defined as a *gravitational anomaly*. Somewhere down there, beneath the surface, something was moving. And that something was contrary to every accepted theory of gravitation, to every known model of how Planet Earth was formed and what held it together.

It was why they were all here. The mission of Deep Hole was to find and identify whatever it was down there that was wreaking periodic havoc on mass and velocity calculations here on the surface.

Despite the cold and the darkness, the site was aswarm with activity. People hurried here and there—loggers and roughnecks mingling with geologists, tectonists, and stratum cartographers, oil-field veterans rubbing elbows with, and sometimes literally colliding with, Ph.D.s, USGS personnel, and a dozen other kinds of alphabet people. Just in the past hour, three copters had landed at the HQ pad.

In his career as a petroleum engineer, Spangler had met his share of theoretical physicists, stratigraphers, crustal tectonics wizards, and doctors of mathematics. But not until the past few days, when the downward-creeping drill of Deep Hole began to take on a life of its own, had he encountered them by the drove.

Overhead, in the murk, horns blared again, and frantic signals flashed like little stuttering beacons in the dark snow mist. It was the fifth time tonight that the blowout warnings had gone off. Spangler had experienced blowout warnings before, on ordinary holes, but one such warning had always been enough to shut down the bore until the hole was secured. This, though, was no ordinary hole. This was geodetic-tectonic exploration on a grand scale, a drilling project into regions where no man had ever gone before—straight down, fourteen miles and descending.

He headed across the apron toward the bank of thump recorders near the main lift, playing his flashlight ahead of him. With the drill-site lighting muffled by snowfall, a man could break a leg out here in the darkness.

No expense had been spared in equipping this project with state-of-the-art hardware, down to and including the strings of electric lights that illuminated the area. But still, a well site at night was a well site at night, and the low, heavy cloud cover, the increasing flurries of hard snow carried on gusting winds, muffled the light. It was cold out here, and it was dark.

Near the thump meters someone jostled him and he stepped aside. The glow of flashlights caught big blue eyes under the fleece-lined hood of an oversize parka. "Excuse me," she said, and hurried on.

"'Sall right," Spangler muttered. Going away, Dr. Delilah Creighton resembled an animated doll in her too-big parka and floppy boots. Spangler squelched a grin that threatened to crack his frozen cheeks. Even drillers' garb failed to hide the delicious sway of her hips, the lithe, feminine grace of her every movement. "Deli," he muttered. "That woman would look good even if she wore a packing crate."

He read the seismometers and fed their data into his electronic clipboard, then Saved to Main. "That'll give them something else to worry about in the doghouse," he muttered. The readings made no sense at all. It was as though the very consistency of matter was changing down there, minute by minute. Then he headed for the flow meters, threading his way among standing members, spools, cable-feeds, and section studs by the fitful light of his flashlight.

It was so gloomy under the towering apron of the platform, high overhead, that every step was perilous. "Damn, but it's dark out," he griped. He edged around a stack of spools, barely noticing the flicker of reality shift that occurred at that instant—an abrupt, general shifting of the scene around him. Like a flash of light too quick for the eye to register, it seemed nothing more than an instant of giddiness, passing as quickly as it had come.

Spangler blinked and looked around, an odd feeling of déjà vu lingering with him. As though he had been here and done this—this time—already. But not quite as it was now.

Somehow, he had the impression that it had been dark.

"Damn cold must be getting to me," he mused, glancing around at the brightly lit drill site. Like daylight. It was always like daylight, even in the dead of night. Even in weather like this. Everywhere were the bright little glows of myriad FIRElights—those ubiquitous little globes on their mushroom pedestals, that just in recent years had once and for all banished the darkness of earth.

Just from where he stood, he could see thousands of them, ranks and rows of them everywhere that anyone on PDH might need light.

Only one problem with FIRElights, he thought. They make light enough for anybody, but a man could sit on one all day and never warm his ass. Inertial Reaction Energy, they called the process. Direct production of illumination from mass, without mechanical or electrical interventions. Kinetic inversion. The perfect waterwheel: gravity to free fall to lumens of power with no steps between. A triple play and let there be light.

Kind of like the evolution of Deep Hole itself, he thought ironically. Tunguska to Kropek to a hole in Siberia, and let there be exploration.

Deep Hole was a colossus among well sites—the largest drilling rig ever constructed, drilling the deepest hole ever attempted, and all because there was something down there that drove gravitometers crazy and sometimes caused wrecks and collapsed transit towers and made birds fall out of the sky.

Something that moved now and then, and made things above it so heavy that a person could hardly walk.

Horns shrilled and warning lights flashed all around, and Spangler noticed abruptly how heavy he himself felt— dragged down, as though the frozen earth was sucking at his feet, as though he had a great weight upon his shoulders. Almost at his feet, pavement groaned and cracked, opening a jagged rift that ran for several yards. Up on the high platform, the big drilling engines slowed, sounding sluggish and strained.

All around him, people were moving slowly, painfully, plodding along in slow motion.

He made his way toward the seismometer bank, again feeling that faint tug of déjà vu. As he approached the meter bank, someone bumped him. He staggered, working to keep his balance as a strained, pale face in a fleece-lined parka turned toward him. "Excuse me," she said. She turned away, then stopped as warning blared anew and the great engines overhead ground to a squealing, rasping halt. "There's something wrong—" she started, then everything around them darkened, slowed toward stasis, and exploded in a tremendous flash of all-devouring light. In that last instant Spangler lost his balance. He fell forward, taking the girl down with him, and heard the whine of massive things flying through the air just above them—things unseen that, like themselves, seemed caught up in a maelstrom of pure, blinding light, moving in no known direction at speeds beyond imagining.

He clung to the girl, and she to him, because there was nothing else, anywhere, to cling to.

Dimly, through the spinning thoughts of a mind beyond

dimensions, Spangler realized what had happened. Deep Hole! The hellhole had reached its target. What was down there had been found, and now it wasn't down there anymore. Now it was everywhere—and everywhere was here!

Unbelievable power—the full fury of light—spun them, carried them with it, and they clung blindly. It filled their senses with sound that was at once the roar of eternity and the sweetest of music, with textures and tastes and aromas not of this world but of all worlds, the flavors of a universe complete. From light into darkness they whirled, all in a lingering instant. They saw a huge, red sun standing over a barren ball of rock. They saw mists rising from a quagmire that reeked of unchecked vegetation. They heard winds carving stone, saw ice fields come and go, felt the primeval pulse of life beginning. Creatures and times, ages and epochs paraded around them, spiraling through the maelstrom in majestic pageantry—life and death repeated and repeated and repeated again, and with each cycle a rising, yearning hunger to be more, to be better, to be quicker and stronger and smarter . . . and to understand—to *know*!

1901

A blade of grass tickled Spangler's nose. He opened his eyes, fought back the dizziness that swirled around him, and breathed deeply. The air was warm and dry, with a hint of smoke. He raised his head, and a meadowlark burst from cover and took to the sky.

Grass. As far as he could see, in any direction, an undulating sea of gray-green grass swept out and away, an unbroken carpet spread over long, low hills where only solitary yucca stalks and an occasional clump of sage stood sentinel.

Carefully, he untangled himself from the tumbled, parka-clad figure beside him and sat up. With gentle fingers he lifted back her hood and touched her throat, feeling the steady pulse there. As he sat upright she opened her eyes and gazed around in a confusion that lasted for only a moment. Then she looked at him. "You saw it, too, didn't you," she said.

He nodded, stood, and removed his own parka. There was no need for it now. It was full summer. And there was no need for discussion of what they had seen. There were not even words to describe it, but somehow they both understood what it was. They had seen time—naked, unlabeled, and unqualified time—and the images they held were what their minds could grasp of it.

Deli sat up, still looking at him with blue eyes as wise as the ages. "Do you have a first name, Spangler?" she asked.

"Woodrow," he said. "It's Woodrow."

She thought about it. "I'll just call you Spangler," she decided. She pulled off her oversize boots, revealing canvas shoes beneath. Then she removed her gloves and coat and stood beside him in floppy T-shirt and denims, shaking out her sun-gold hair.

Standing, they could see the source of the smoke—a creeping, antique train crossing a steel-girder bridge a mile or so away. Elm trees and willows lined a snaking, sandy-bed stream there, and to the west was a mirage-shrouded haze that might have been a settlement.

"We're still here," Spangler said. "Still where we were, but certainly not *when* we were."

"I thought Nick Tolafsson was a lunatic," she mused. "But he was right. *Relative* doesn't mean *not real*. So where do we go from here, Spangler?"

"Over there." He pointed southward, toward the railroad bridge. "Then we'll see."

The train was gone, but in the evening another came down the track, eastbound, and stopped for water at the Cimarron tanks.

It was June 8, or maybe June 9, depending upon whose opinion was asked. But whichever it was, the year was 1901, and the people riding the cars—many of them in open boxcars with tarps for accommodation—were people in search of a dream. They were from Denver and Pueblo, from Raton and Hugoton and Progress, and they were bound for Texas.

A bunch of Pennsylvanians had drilled a hole down there and found petroleum oil. Spindletop Field was the Field of Dreams, with money to be made for those who could work.

Spangler glanced at Deli Creighton and grinned. "The only way we're ever going to get back to when we were," he said, "is to live a long, long time. Do you think you might spend some of that time with a pretty fair driller?"

Chronology

Extracted from: *The Gates of Time Temporal Concordance*

TIME2 EVENTS	TIME1 EVENTS
2400 B.C. Burial of Pharaoh Khafre	1KHAF4 plants L-270 slave TEF in Pyramid of Khafre
1887 Leapfrog Booster Waystop activated from Waystop I	
1899 Earliest known timer, Anya Karasova	
1908 Tunguska event in Siberia	
1909	Disappearance of Rasputin Trove from St. Petersburg, Russia
1940–72 Time of the timers, origin of unknown number of individuals naturally adept at four-dimensional autotransference	
1947 Flying saucer reports in U.S.	L-270 emerges in pre-Arthurian time

1949–54 Deep Hole project anachronisms concealed by U.S. military, along with UFO evidence

Kaffer obtains anomaly data, deduces origin of Whisper technology

1951

Anchor loop L-316 bridges anachronism following Lost Loop final message

1952 Edwin Limmer enters mainstream T2; Limmer Trust, Limmer Foundation

1953

L-316 sacrifices itself to establish transanachronism T1 conduit; no reported survivors

1991 Second fuel war solidifies multinationalism

1993 Emergence of sector economies, realignments of political power

L-383 primary Whisper presence in pre-Arthurian time

1996 Dr. David Frank invents gravity light

1998 Booster Waystop I; Anywhen, Inc.

First Whisper encounters with temporal adepts, or timers

1999 Gravitational anomaly in Kansas; Siberian deep-drill findings lead to geodetic-tectonic exploration: Project Deep Hole

Ghost sightings of L-316 members

WHIS future history attacked by Kaffer

2001 Asian Concords collapse in Sino-Arab-Slavic disputes

2001–3 Asian wars; Seven Days of Silence

Merlin Base established by Whispers

2002 (est.) Timers' Concurrence of Privacy

2003 Deep Hole incident.

Subsequent global tectonic shifts strengthen earlier theories suggesting a gravitic singularity in earth's core; breakdown of most orbital comweb systems

2003–04 Verification of the Asian Abyss

2004 Global Paper Panics, power realignments. In U.S.: border mandates, regional wars; Protectorate Authority for Common Trust emerges as steward/custodian

2005 PACT enforces Edict of Encroachment

2009 Fundamentalists mobilize; deunification of states

2010–13 NSF/ISF maps tectonic shifts, first substantial evidence of relationship between Tunguska event and Deep Hole incident; gravitic singularity theories gain in acceptance

2012 Federated Free Zones; first Revivalist uprisings

2020 Institute for Temporal Research (ITR) established in Panhandle FFZ by John Jacob Royce, pursuing Ikebata-Tolafsson bitemporal theories; research into

laws and analogs
governing the
photogravitic spectrum

2029 Arthur's takeover of
ITR

2037–38 Arthur Rex
consolidates Camelot,
begins campaign against
Revivalists; temporal
effect focalizer (TEF)
perfected

2050 Arthur's Anachronism   Birth of Edwin Limmer in
reverse T2

2080–2210 Rational
Nationalism debates;
Cutter's "All for One"
address; Rise of the
Empocracies; PACT
reverts powers to Council
of Commonwealths

2388–2410 Science of
genetics achieves major
breakthroughs in Seattle
World Symposiums

2410 Transpolar rift

2450–2600 Era of origin of
Pacifica and the Pacificans

2744 Universal Experience
Bank of Pacifica sponsors
World History
Investigative Society
(WHIS); first T1 conduit
tested

2910 Whisper expedition
extends conduit upstream
through T2; discovery of
the Arthurian Anachronism

2910–81 Efforts to penetrate
  the time storm at 2050;
  closed-loop tests begin

2999 Activation of L-270,
  the lost loop

3004 Final L-270 report by
  random eventuality curve:
  dimensional access gates
  and bridges in early
  temporal latitudes

3005 anchor loop L-316
  extends conduit past
  Arthur's Infinity

3006 Plan to create boosters
  for upstream migration;
  theory of alternate
  temporal planes
  developed; 1TL-0014
  (Teal Fordeen) first
  volunteer for loop L-383

3006–? Whisper migrations

3008– Whisper tangent
  colony seeks origins of
  Pacifica; emerging
  theories on the Destiny
  Factor, vortex continuum,
  alternate eventuality, and
  corollaries of infinity
  suggest existence of
  Paradox Gate phenomena

Dan Parkinson is the author of *The Whispers* and *Faces of Infinity* (Books One and Two of *The Gates of Time*) and the *Timecop* novels (*Viper's Spawn*, *The Scavenger*, and *Blood Ties*), as well as many westerns and a number of successful TSR fantasy novels.

TIMECOP
Viper's Spawn
by Dan Parkinson

There are rumors that the Nazis have successfully unlocked the secrets of time travel, and it's up to the Time Enforcement Commission's top cop to discover the truth. Jack Logan is one of the best, although he does things in his own unorthodox way. His investigation throws him into the paths of killers, thieves, pirates, and zealots in an all-out contest—with the future as the prize.

Based on the television series *Timecop*, created by Mark Verheiden, and on characters created by Mike Richardson and Mark Verheiden, who brought us the *Timecop* movie, TIMECOP: *Viper's Spawn* delves into the further adventures of Jack Logan and the TEC team. Every change in time has a ripple effect, and it's up to the TEC agents to prevent the present from being altered in any way—even if it means they never make it back to their own time.

Look for all three
action-adventure *Timecop* novels
by Dan Parkinson:

- *Viper's Spawn*
- *The Scavenger*
  One man has a chilling plan for global murder!
- *Blood Ties*
  Logan returns from a routine mission to find his world altered.

Published by Del Rey Books.
Available wherever books are sold.